LOCO-MOTIVE

JACK KOHL

The Pauktaug Press
Pauktaug, New York

Copyright © 2016 by Jack Kohl

ISBN: 978-0-69275-244-9

Cover design/cover photo: Al Jarnow
Interior design: Gary A. Rosenberg • www.thebookcouple.com
Cover model: Kelsey Fiona Maguire

Printed in the United States of America

Contents

CHAPTER I

SIGNING UP

This is a book that concerns itself with running. However, it is not a history meant to join that niche of mildly saccharine and vaguely inspirational works that celebrate the sport for its physical and mental benefits—nor is this a work meant to counter that idiom in any direct way. And I have no specific physical or mental detriments to cite that I would attribute to the ongoing running phenomenon. But I do write a study with a warning—a warning that running, in a very peculiar, albeit rare way, can number your days, can shave and dangerously qualify your time on this planet, especially if you are very, very, good at it.

And I do not write a disguised tale of traditional moral warning. I do not warn anyone away from the vanities that initially drew me to running. This book is, instead, a warning, that if I were to come under the crosshairs of the dangers invoked by this warning—and I do not, for I am not the right kind of runner (I am not fast enough)—I am not certain that I would want to remove myself from the risks and dangers that I endeavor to expose with this narrative. With that last statement of cross-purposes left standing, I will say, again, that this is not only a work that may warn some away from running quite definitely, but especially warn away those who may excel at the sport (an admittedly rare effect for any book on any highly regarded form of exercise, but, alas, the effect that this unusual narrative may bring about).

But, to begin with, let me dismiss via review some of the traditional fears and warnings that surround the sport of running.

Those who do not run or exercise are apt to warn the runner of all the things that can happen to one while running. People cite car fumes to me. "Isn't that bad for your knees?" many have asked—including a number of souls (with good knees) living in corpulent frames that can hardly be raised from out of chairs. People cite wet leaves (in autumn), ice and snow (in winter), gravel and sand (at all times) and dogs (at all times). Running in the dark strikes the non-runner with horror for any number of obvious reasons. Running in the too-early morning is not safe because of its own concerns, others say. Running in midday is bad because of sun and cars. Running on a treadmill might be all right, they think, but how can anyone bear to run in place for so long? These doomsayers would have one sit and protect at all costs, even unto rot, the fleshy shell that protects the ostensibly all-powerful and all-important and all-sacred brain at the center of Man.

But save for the fact that in their list of the dangers of running the doomsayers cross off virtually every known form of training, I have often heard it said that a race "looks like such a nice, safe, generally secure and good place to run and enjoy one's self." There everything is taken care of—there are usually medics present, even doctors on hand. There are little bathrooms spaced at intervals along the course. Water and treats abound. Police are present to guard the closed roads from cars and other traffic. One does not run alone at a race. One is generally there with hundreds of others, if not thousands, and there are usually innumerable bystanders along the course to act as general witnesses and watching eyes.

But I have learned that it is in this very environment where a runner, especially a very good runner, is most vulnerable—mortally vulnerable. He is vulnerable to the wildest, most secret hope from his fellow man. And since this hope, I have found, seems engendered by the vigor, by the sunlighted strength and honesty created by running itself, it seems probable that the bearer of such wildest and most secret hope is likely to be a runner himself. This hope— What is it? This hope is not competitive. It is, rather, shockingly objective. Thus it is hard to detect. But it is there, and it can prove to threaten the very lives of those who show potential to run faster than any who have run before.

If this hope, this thing, you have to fear if you are perhaps a great runner, is not a vindictiveness from another close-trailing envious competitor, if I tell you it is not jealousy, if I tell you it is not another close trailing runner's wish to harm you (you, the good, the first-place runner), so that he (the second place runner) can win, then you might well ask what is this thing you have to fear.

One must fear the hope, the moiling, deep hope of the trailing other (that hope that simmers on the mind's brow of Man for always, and ever waits to bead its first run of sweat), that hope that the trailing other has for himself, but which is always just past his ability to realize—that hope, then, perhaps being transferred to another, perhaps to you, if you are faster than he. One must fear the hope that the trailing runner has for you, you the great runner. The will of that deep secret hope gets passed onto the unsuspecting—and the unsuspecting, he becomes part of a relay race to which he has no idea he has registered and entered. The unsuspecting begins to run for two, and from that particular, trailing, second runner comes the deep hope of Man—thus a piggyback burden of immensity yet untold is carried by the leader in certain, singular, races. The second runner, the trailer, the hoper, places all in this hope—like a parent stopping his own ascent and passing it onto his child. There is death and danger with this grand hope—so forget your slips and falls and soreness. They are as nothing, I assure you, to the other injuries that running can bring.

Yet I started to run with much simpler hopes. I started running out of vanity, or, rather, to preserve it. But I have learned to feel less self-conscious about this original, somewhat shallow, motivation—not so much because of the observations, experiences and peculiar grist that running has yielded me as I moved farther and farther away from my initial starting point and into a safe, reliable, forgetful and confident thinness, but because I learned that vanity, a kind of vanity as to how one is perceived as a runner, motivates not only all runners in a way, but motivates all runners throughout their careers.

The fast runner becomes so vain, in a generally secret and singular way, that he becomes proud of how brief the view is that he gives of himself to others—to slower runners and to spectators. In this is even a touch of the origins of simple, primal, vanity, as well, for some of the oldest of modern burlesque styles—dancing with large plumes, feathers, discreet stripping that really never allows a full view of the subject—run on this very same principle. And, as well, the fast runner becomes vain of how many can see him over the briefest span of time—and how little he can show each witness. He sees only himself at last, as speed becomes the full concern and the other faces blur. He creates a mirror for his refined vanity in his mind in which only he can see himself. And this kind of refined vanity of the runner begins to apply to the very ground, to places—for they are his last audiences—and his appearances indeed become as measured, as brief, as calculated, even for the mute and unsentient audience (the Earth), as that of the most artful of old-time burlesque masters.

He runs so fast after a time—this vain runner, now of the future and its yet unseen records of speed—passes between place to place (so that they do not seem to retain their distances), that he seems to trim the fat of the Earth that holds him—and thus even his last contacts, the crowds and the very ground, his last witnesses, lose weight and gain this mystic vanity, as well. Does the Earth itself run faster for this, when one of its sons vanishes via speed and is not reabsorbed into the soil, leaving her lighter—though with a loss of a child? The Earth he treads then becomes seemingly as thin as he; he travels it so fast, so quickly. The course he runs becomes as thin as finish line tape. Again, he sees only himself at last, as speed becomes the full concern, and the very Earth and matter waste away into nothing; they become so thin. But no one has run that fast yet. Yet records fall each day. Will Man not approach such physical law-breaking speeds one day, however?

Vain, fast, modern runners often wear sports sunglasses that make them look like privacy-hungry movie stars. There is a vanity indeed in the fast runner, but it is not so simple, so commonly vain, as one may think.

But, again, I started my running career with simple vanity in mind. When I was in my late twenties, and living in a small suburb of Atlanta, Georgia, a shocking thing happened to me. I passed by a mirror one day. I had no intention of looking into the mirror; it was only from an oblique, peripheral glance that I first saw the shocking thing it displayed—that I was turning into someone stout. *Stout* is a kind word. If I cringe a bit and close my eyes, I can bring myself to say the word that first occurred to me when I looked sideways into the reflecting glass. The word was *pudgy*. I was growing pudgy. I had always thought of myself as slender overall, and rather chiseled looking about the face and neck. But suddenly—or suddenly I could see—there had been a radical softening of the mediating places between my features.

How did this happen? I had always been rather athletic, I thought—if not in a literal sense as in my high school soccer days, which I extended through community leagues till age twenty, then at least in appearance and in rather reliable, stable, potential.

And that reliable, stable, potential seemed to last almost for a decade. During that time I can say rather truthfully that I was a serious walker. Not a day went by that I failed to tread about for at least five or six miles after each college school day was over and, later on, after a work day when I became a new part of the journalistic workforce.

I maintained this routine until I took my job in Atlanta about two years ago, in 2000, when I was twenty-nine. There I worked at a magazine for a large airline. And it was there, I suppose, that the coffee cart began to present itself as a prospect I looked forward to too much. Some runners, after a time, can predict how far they have run just by checking their watches for time; others can tell how long they have been out by knowing the distance of the course they select. Still others can sense both measures by their senses alone. I became adept, I fear, at sensing the coffee cart's position in the office as I sat at my desk and affected to work. Little clicks and rustles told me just how far away it was, and just about how long human variance would influence its arrival time before my cubicle. I became shockingly accurate.

And then there was the heat. Despite nightly resolutions, during drives home in the knife-sharp air conditioning of the car, to start evening walks, and despite the renewal of such resolutions when I was in the equally cold-whetted temperatures of my apartment, my habit of extended walking never seemed to get started in Georgia. I was born—and lived all my years up to and through college—in northern Illinois. And the soft, dull, weighted heat of the South was something by which my constitution was truly shocked. There remains today a quaint allowance of complaint granted to those who shift from a home in the South to the North, or for those who shift from a home in the North to the South. But my complaints deserve to be characterized on a level far beyond those of an attempt to maintain a remembrance of a romantic though true polarity between these two lovingly recalled as contentious regions. Since it is easy for me to draw a sweat even in winter back in my old home state—if I so much as take the stairs with a little extra force my brow begins to bleed a bit of the sea— it can be imagined how all the connecting areas to my torso complained and let forth a little watery protest if I even so much as made a trek from my car to the lobby of work when in Georgia (that lobby hardly twenty yards from my average parking place).

These considerations, the heat and the coffee cart, and the fact that my vanity had dropped low during my year in Georgia—as I could not seem to interest even one of the dozens of stunning Belles who seemed to seep verily forth in bright colors, tan skin, perfume, and smiles from the many offices in the building in which I worked—all contributed to an insidious, slow plot by Nature to give me day by day more and more the appearance and spirit of an apathetic, stocky gnome. And all this happened rather quickly— probably within the first four months of my time in Georgia. Thus, just after Christmastime and all its parties, I had looked in the mirror with that unintentional but telling obliquity I mention above and saw the shocking start of my transformation. But I fear that first sight was still not enough to shock me into reform. The heat that drove me away from exercise, the coffee cart that fed my chair-bound girth, the Belles who looked the other way because of that expansion, I think—all these things, perhaps, were no match for the more insidious (because it was kind and warm) influence that was about to direct me.

The crowning coup-de-grace factor to the expansion of my expansion project arrived quite suddenly one night. I lived in a suburb of Atlanta, about fifty minutes to the north in a depressed but beautiful little town that received the shadows of the distant Appalachians. In my first months in Georgia, still new to Atlanta —and still thin and confident enough, I suppose, to at least interest a few fellow office girls to go for drinks after work—I kept myself mainly in the city, save for my commute time and a quick, late, and immediate dash to bed in my little apartment on the second floor of the town's Main Street.

I have a great affection for America and its rural past, thus it might come as a surprise if I say that I hardly knew anything of the town I slept in for nearly four months. My move from my place in Chicago had been quick and easy. I had had few things in my self-styled Spartan Illinois apartment—for my parents had agreed to move and store most of my lifetime's collection of things to the garage of their Arizona condominium when they moved there after I finished graduate school. And because my little Georgia apartment was already arranged for by my company in Atlanta (the editor of the magazine owned the building in which I was to live), I had little to force me to explore my new surroundings. Under normal circumstances, I think I would have begun to explore the town's details, inroads to nature, history, and every other aspect of local character almost immediately had it not been for a certain and sudden social desperation that overtook me almost immediately upon my move to Georgia. I lingered in the city after work so long each night, and raced to it so quickly each morning, in the hope of running into the blonde who worked as a receptionist in the doctor's office on the first floor, or in the hope of running into the brunette who worked across the hall in the other suite, or in the hope of simply walking very slowly about town with some other fellows from work until nearly eleven or twelve each night, after taking slow and full dinners in restaurants where I was amazed still further by the Belles who waited tables. I succeeded in securing a single date apiece from two of the waitresses I encountered during this time period. But after the first dates my only further contact with these girls was a brief two- or three-call series apiece, entirely one-sided in each case—both girls assuring me that I should leave my name and number and a brief message after the tone.

I wish I could say that it was with my usual, lean, intrepid spirit that I started to explore the little Georgia town where my apartment rested atop a vacated hardware store. But I drove home from work one night in January with a rich, moist, rounded loneliness that compelled a search for some diversion in my little bedroom community. Thus it was that I found the warm, steamy, haunted though still living and kind place that filled my heart with its bold sadness of ready welcome—but also the place that would expand my sides to their widest reaches.

It was around six-thirty when I parked my car and flung my things in mildly disgusted routine into my apartment, and then went back down onto the Main Street for almost the first time in all of my months in Georgia. After I looked into the melancholy emptiness of the abandoned hardware store, I slowly made my way north along Main to a building on the west side of the street. In front of this structure were many cars, and from the roof of this seemingly popular building, slowly wafting like remnant wisps of clouds from the rear, came a constant supply of steam. And soon, when I was in close range of this inviting fog, I could smell that it was laden with the living ghosts of food juices. My lonely self drew closer to the building, and at the same time the worst instincts of my ever-widening frame grew quite excited. I stood before the front glass of this very large place, and it was evident that its interior had hardly yielded to the pressure from any nearby restaurant chain that now sprawled on some stretch of an exhausted farmer's field. Rather, this place was vital—but not a vitality that seemed to guarantee immortality. It was in its vital old age.

I looked closely through the glass to see dozens upon dozens of tables. Half of these tables were filled with pairs (or pairs of pairs) of senior citizens. Walkers, wheel chairs, and many heads of blue and silver hair radiated through the dark window. There was a handful of families there, as well, crowding into corner booths or forced to take possession of unwanted center aisle tables that were right in the way of the heaviest traffic. But as for any representatives (that is, without children) of the age group between eighteen and sixty-five, I was hard pressed to find even a single example.

What happened next I can only relate in its degree of emotional magnitude to, I think, one other experience in my life. When I was taking my master's at the University of Illinois, a girlfriend I had at the time had to suddenly leave campus and go home for a family funeral one Saturday night. With my plans altered for the evening, I took one of my long, uncharted walks through the hazy spring darkness and marched toward the inviting murmur of a small crowd and the seductive glow of the lights from one of the small ball fields of the college—intriguingly afire at an especially late hour and when nothing was on the master schedule for the sports teams. Soon I approached the little sunken valley where this small practice field could be found, and there I saw something endearing and powerful for all its surprise and incongruity—and powerfully attractive in its self-contentment, since it drew no crowd of casual spectators. There was none of the hoped-for casual horde of bright and approachable girls that any pick-up game in its waning hours might hope to attract. Instead, there was a powerful, self-reliant earnestness to this game played in remembrance of a far away homeland—once introduced to that homeland by visitors who were themselves far from home. And perhaps, as well, because of this pattern, this game will be as a universal flower from Earth on a future Mars colony. And somehow the Martians, too, they will carry this flower on their expeditions and feel it Martian. And there was something moving in the sight of this twice-removed foreign game then before me, but it was observed with a trace bit of condescension on my part, which makes the scene rather poignant in my memory.

Before me on that ball field was a game of cricket in progress. And all about the field, both in play and on the sidelines, were groups of East Indian men—mainly graduate students, I think, from the adjacent science building. I watched from behind the fence for a long time, and then I gathered the nerve to walk down the slope in the grass to the sidelines where a line of players had just left the field and was sitting down. On my introducing myself and receiving a welcome, I was then offered, after asking, a long stream of explanation as to the rules and workings of the game continuing before me—this explanation so earnest, so piquantly and poignantly hospitable, that I find it rather moving even now to recall.

I had the very same feeling of the piquantly and poignantly hospitable come over me, and a similar sense of gentle, condescending remove on my part as I was standing in front of the glass of the mysteriously popular and vital place that could be found right in the center of a depressed little Georgia downtown, and when a warm, corpulent hand came to rest on my shoulder and made me wheel about.

There behind me stood a bald, somewhat shy of elderly man of average height but stupendous belly. There stood his wife, as well. While he saved his most spectacular expansion in an incredible concentration about his middle, his wife was more easily described as just plain rotund all around.

"You got to get in line on the inside!" laughed the large man.

"He wants to feel his appetite a bit longer!" added the large woman.

It was then that I took one more quick look at the window and could see for the first time the faded stenciled letters in the smoky glass: *R, R, & Y Cafeteria.*

"A cafeteria!" I suddenly and involuntarily said with a smile.

"Sure!" added the man. "By yourself? You should eat with us."

"But it's a cafeteria. You mean I can go in? When I think of the word *cafeteria* I think of places for institutions—schools and industry."

"Where you from?" asked the man as he and his wife led me in the door. I volunteered Chicago but tried to add that I was living in town and working in Atlanta. I could not add the latter part before I was talked over.

"You're out to eat, aren't you? This is a cafeteria. Anyone can eat here. I always told my wife that they don't have these everywhere. Now she has the proof."

"Now I have the proof!" echoed the wife as she took a moist tray from a steaming stack after we reached the end of a long, dark paneled hallway.

Whether it was because of the call of food (and food's steam called me keenly then) or because I was in a new place without a new friend or Southern Belle to show for it, or because my parents had only two years before suddenly and to me unaccountably packed up all of our belongings and sold our house in Chicago and moved all the way to a retirement community in Arizona, I cannot say, but I felt an easy willingness to acquiesce to the call and almost parental control of my two new friends.

Thus began a new pattern for me. Rather than fear missed chances with my peers in Atlanta each night, I began to fear missing any chance of having dinner with my adoptive companions back at the cafeteria. And on nights when Fred and Rita, my original rotund benefactors, were not there, I simply relied on the regulars to whom they had introduced me. On that first night I met a conglomeration of regulars, mainly old men who had earned themselves a special, dark, recessed, almost reserved corner of their own in the dining room. From Fred and Rita, and my large group of nostalgic, corpulent, recollectors of better hunting and fishing days, I learned the ways of the cafeteria—how one tipped the women who carried the trays from the register to one's table of choice, and how one could eschew once and for all his Northern fears that a refill of a soft drink would cost him dearly. I learned that it cost me nothing in my new locale. In fact, if I count the cafeteria and its warm, welcome but insidious effects upon my mid-section, upon my weight altogether, as the coup-de-grace in the process of my physical decline, then I should count the beverage policy, especially as this included the substance known as *sweet tea,* as the coup-de-grace atop the coup-de-grace.

When I first tried sweet tea, it came to me entirely by accident. I had, in fact, only asked for tea from the woman who carried my tray, when she asked me what I wanted to drink. Of course this meant, by my Northern intentions, a cup of hot tea. Instead I was delivered an enticing glass of amber liquid filled with ice and covered with cold condensation. Not wishing to bother with any correction of my order, I accepted what she brought.

After Fred and Rita had introduced to me my new company—I became accustomed to referring to them collectively as *the boys,* after Fred's and Rita's and everyone's style—I took a packet or two of sugar from the middle of the enormous round table we shared in the dark corner.

"Whew! You sure must like it sweet!" laughed one of the boys.

"I'm just going to put the two packets in—maybe one," I smiled back.

"Try it first, Rex," said Rita from across the table, and then with polite discretion she affected to turn back to watching the little wall-mounted television that absorbed all of the boys, including Fred—save for two fellows, including the first one to see me take the sugar, who waited with eagerness for a reaction as I put the glass of iced tea to my lips.

I confess I consciously gave the old fellows a little of the reaction they were hoping for. But my shock at the taste was not entirely for show. This *sweet tea* was beyond sweet. It might be called *pure sweetness with a touch of tea color.* The substance was like electricity in a liquid form. It gave me a sudden, shocking boost that I had only counted on from vigorous exercise in the past.

I was proud of myself—despite the reality of the tea's power—for giving the boys an exaggerated reaction. This little gift of histrionics seemed to please them a great deal.

"What did you ask for?" asked my main tea inquisitor.

"Just tea," I said, as I took a swig of plain water to kill some of the sweet shock.

"Well, you see, you got to ask for unsweet tea if that's what you want. They'll bring you what you have now if you just ask for tea and don't say anything else."

"How do you order hot tea?"

"By saying you want hot tea. Anyway, why would you want that?"

"You're right," I smiled. "I don't know."

"Do you like sports, Rex?" asked my tea instructor. I volunteered that I did, though I hardly ever paid attention to such things on television. I still, though then quite erroneously, considered myself one of the fellows who thought it ludicrous to watch others play and be paid for what one should be doing themselves. What exercise or sport I then thought I took on my own I cannot say, however.

For the rest of that first evening and then for months on end I had dinner nearly every night with the boys and Fred and Rita. And nearly every night I conceded an hour or two of sports watching on television after dinner as payment of my silent, social debt to my new, generous companions. There was part of me that could never give back what they gave and be quite as generous as they, and whether or not they knew my lingering with the television was something of an affectation I cannot say. It was only just before I ate that I was most lonely, but during the eating itself—and during the now notorious sweet tea drinking (which started to become my custom to such an extent that I measured my consumption by pitchers)—I was consumed by what I must confess was nothing but the tragic concentration of a young man bidding farewell to even a shadowy remembrance of slenderness.

But I learned to affect as much interest as possible in the sports programs and sports news that Rita and Fred and the boys enjoyed so much until the cafeteria closed each night at 9:30. The channel that was favored in the corner of this cafeteria was from an unusual cable package that included some stations I had never seen before and have never seen since. The boys favored *Sports 143*, which featured after 6:00 PM and until 9:00 in the morning many little ambitious stories on small but still convincingly important events held throughout the United States. There was always some minor league team—even, at times, a little league team—that had some remarkable record that was worth seeing through to its end. And the stories were free of the now hackneyed background music that attempts to attribute pseudo-agrarian virtue-myth and importance to the games of these out-of-nowhere miracle teams. The channel simply gave time to events that would have been ignored by all other mediums. Fred, Rita, the boys and I watched all sorts of unusual things—we watched bike racing quite often, trans-saltwater swimming competitions, and any number of picturesque little road races for runners held in towns all over the United States. The boys took particular pleasure in shouting, "I never heard of that place! Have you?" when each new road race was given a little half-hour, and sometimes, though rarely, a full hour feature.

One night, just before closing—as I was extending my diet into the area of fried okra and collard greens—we all sat rather intrigued by a half hour story from a place called Pauktaug, New York, which is on Long Island. I would only remember the exact name of the village later on. Though the story had limited footage of the actual race itself—for it was pursued after the race took place and created a stir—it featured interviews with townspeople and racecourse volunteers. Piece by piece the story was given that two residents of Pauktaug, in this very first running of this town's 10K race, had not only won the event (taking first and second place), but had by all unofficial accounts broken the 10K world record not by seconds, not even by a minute, but by two minutes. Because the race was new, and had yet to receive official course certification and had only an unofficial, local man manning the clock, none of what happened could be certified. But notwithstanding this, no fewer than four people timing the race on the sidelines for the local running club came up with nearly the exact same results. The new race had drawn only a few hundred participants, and even fewer witnesses to the sidelines of the attractive little village's streets—as the weather had been fraught with heavy rain and some distant bolts of early spring lightning. But still, the spectators and the few witnesses that were monitoring the entire race told nearly the same story—the 10K world record (and this was measuring it on an extremely hilly, extremely challenging course provided by Long Island's north shore) had been broken. The rumored unofficial timings had the winner crossing the finish line minutes under the world record, and the second place runner was behind him by no more than five to ten seconds.

If one can put aside the astounding fact that a man crossed the finish line of such a course in such a time, and then put aside, as well, the fact that on the very same date at the very same race another man also came in so close to that record in the second place spot (such that his second place would be accounted a miraculous world record had it not been for the first place finisher), then can one put aside the fact that both men were from the same village on Long Island (the host town of the race), and that they both worked in businesses that were but doors apart from one another?

Rita and Fred—and some of the boys and one of the cafeteria workers—shouted that they could not when that much was asked by the television reporter during the Pauktaug 10K story.

The end of the feature gave attention to the doubters. Because of the proliferation of races in the last years—such that nearly every town, village, hamlet, city, county, and every other kind of demarcated geographical zone had its little race or even marathon —it had also become the suspicion that such races are merely concocted by town and civic officials who wish to boost visiting interest in their communities. Thus the numbers in the crowds and how long they spend in town mean much more than the numbers of the runners and how long they spend on the closed course.

After the above was suggested, one of the boys stoutly asserted, "Bet those times were faked."

But the reporter saved his most interesting information for last. Still in town when the camera crew arrived was the sole, established elite runner who had taken part in the inaugural running of the race. He good-naturedly stated that he had run the first half of the new and difficult course in the company of the now controversial winners, and that unless there had been one of the most fantastic, complex cases of course-cutting in the history of road racing, what he had seen in Pauktaug—where he completed his third place finish in a time not far off from his personal best—could only be described as one of the most remarkable feats of human physical advancement in the history of Man's glued journey on this stubborn, gripping sphere. He went on to say that what he had seen—or what he had been told he could have seen had he held with the leaders through the last three miles of the race—would give him pause as a professional were it not for the fact that he held an equal interest in the potentialities of Man as he held for his own vocational future. He did have to confess, however, that he was, indeed, worried if the competitive field and standard had changed so much and so suddenly. But he could not believe that such a feat was consistently repeatable (if it had happened at all).

It was felt that this elite runner, who was from North Africa (Morocco), may have been alluding, albeit very obliquely, to the possibility that some kind of performance-enhancing drug of a new, extreme, and shocking potency had been unveiled at this Long Island race. The two record-breakers were examined by a doctor after the event—especially as the first place finisher had some vague physical complaints about his chest and head not long after crossing the finish line. And both men voluntarily allowed themselves to be screened for drugs as the rumor of their incredible but uncertifiable record-breaking times made a minor sensation via small notice in the general news and in running periodicals, and in the running community throughout the world. Nothing unusual was found in their blood, however.

One further vote of doubt was cast in general by many when it was pointed out that both men not only lived in this Pauktaug Village and worked in the same building, but that both were members of the same running club and held high positions in the workings of that small local organization—a group that was elemental in getting the first Pauktaug 10K Race realized. How these coincidences could have in any way aided their performance in the race—or even, in the long run, helped them to organize a massive, sophisticated, course-cutting hoax so as to promote themselves, the new race, and the Village of Pauktaug—was never ventured.

Both the runners were offended to learn that there were intimations of foul play at the first running of the new 10K. Of course, they said, they were pleased to have shocked themselves and everyone else with times that they had only secret hopes (secret even from one another) of achieving. And, of course, they were pleased to bring attention to the town and great interest to the next year's running of the race. But, no, they said, there was nothing amiss in their running of the race. They only wished they could easily explain why it was that it took so long for both to discover in themselves this shocking ability. Both men declined to state whether they would be running any more races in the near future—so as to prove officially their capabilities. This reluctance only brought further scorn from those who were sure that there had been something amiss in the reports of the performances of the first and second place finishers of the first Pauktaug 10K Race.

I recall the night we all watched that program in the cafeteria with special fondness—not only because the show seemed to absorb my new friends and foster family to such an extent, but because they all gave me a little round of applause when they discovered that I had finished two entire pitchers of sweet tea all by myself. That was a new record for me.

By the time early June arrived in Georgia I found the heat to be incredible, and even my walks from my apartment to the cafeteria in the waning long light of the solstice season seemed a challenge. And it was on a Friday evening in that month when we were all finishing off large pieces of pie, and I supplementing my slice with large streams of sweet tea and then cups of coffee, when another program about running came on. As we were all sitting back and letting the formidable weight of the considerable dinner churn within, I suddenly exclaimed, just from my sheer admiration of a shot of vanguard runners ascending a hill at the start of the televised race, that I was going to take up running myself—maybe even run a race sometime soon. I used to run a bit in high school and early college, even though I was mainly an avid walker, I said. There was a long silence from the half of the group that heard me. Then my original tea inquisitor turned the sound of the television down and asked me to repeat myself. Everyone listened as I reported my intentions and my little running history a second time.

Then there was a great laugh, and I could tell then that I had suddenly and quite unintentionally given them my greatest social gift yet—nullifying all my efforts of lingering with them after dinner for nearly half of a year, thinking all that time that my secret condescension and lingering had been the best gift of all and a mark of true generosity of spirit.

"Run?" laughed Fred. "Run a race anytime soon? Why don't we all run a race tomorrow!" Everyone laughed again and then turned back to the television.

"What?" I demanded with a panicky, unattractive desperation.

"Don't listen to them. You don't look so bad. You look good, Rex," Rita assured me.

On the way out of the cafeteria that night, I tried to get a look at myself in the dark, Coke-colored glass of the windows. But I could see little then because I did not wish to pause long enough to let anyone know I was studying myself. When I reached the abandoned hardware store, I had my first intimation that the silhouette I could see in the glass looked rather foreign to me. But since my facial features and details were unclear in that last reflection, I was still able to defer any complete sense of identification with a new image. It was when I was readying for bed in my apartment, however, when I stood before the mirror in my bathroom, ready to praise the full and clear view of myself that I could catch in the bathroom mirror during a session of tooth-brushing, that I could see the extent of my new form for the first time.

When I had caught an oblique glimpse of myself in January and discovered that my body had taken its first leap in a new, sideways, and feature-blurring direction, the intensity was still of such a moderate level that it could be dismissed as but the seasonal or metabolic variableness of a young person during a holiday period of eating and winter inactivity—the type of weight gain that is but part of moderate, ever-present flux, which also belongs to periods of return to appropriate weight, and even to stretches of time in which one is under their average weight. What I saw in the mirror the first time in January had been nothing that could really be said to ruin my average if it did not remain for too long.

This second view was altogether different. Though I have never been seriously injured or ill in my life, I can report the following reaction from mornings when I have woken up to some new minor malady or slight injury—a small moment of eagerness, of quick, fleeting, but undeniable fascination with the sickness. Though there is a true fear, even a fraction of horror, upon looking down to the arm, say, when in childhood, after having felt it first warm and then burn and itch ferociously overnight, and then find in the morning light that one is in the midst of a case of severe poison ivy, there is also a moment of irrefragable curiosity, giving credence to the notion that there is indeed a part of the self above the self, a bit of Reason, even in a child, that can look at the inflamed arm as if it is a foreign specimen brought spectacularly close for one's examination. Yet that specimen is attached to him, so that his eyes need not be alone in the study of its peculiarities— he can feel and sense something that is and yet is not a part of him. I grant that my primary concern was the passing of my sick time when I had such an indisposition—and I doubt that those who are afflicted with more serious concerns have much inclination toward such speculative fascinations. But nevertheless, I have felt this absorption when granted transient contact with sundry childhood rashes, cuts and bruises from bicycle accidents, from many cases of the aforementioned poison ivy, and even from a late and serious case of chicken pocks that struck me when I was twenty-two years old.

When I stood before the mirror in my Georgia apartment, I experienced some of that same fascination again. Here were new details of nature, a new phenomenon for me to study, yet these details were attached to me, appended to that very form to which my Reason always had the most immediate access. Yet with this surge of newest fascination also came nearly that dread that must come when one has a view of those sorts of ailments that generally prove to be inescapable. There before me then on the mirror was no minor softening of my facial features, no minor curve or paunch of the stomach. There in the mirror was a person concealed. As I removed my shirt for the night, and forced myself to stand in profile before the white, critical light of the bathroom and the mirror, I discovered features that were more than the augmentation of a familiar frame. There were rolls that created an entirely new topography, such that one had to part these new waves, these bodily memories of my sweet tea habit and of hours of sedate, warm labor in the cafeteria. And there were myriad little waves, little ripples, fractions of waves yet to come—deposits of fat in the style that I associated only with women, and extremely obese, revoltingly feminine and rosy looking sedentary men. Again, my fascination for malady was there, but the fascination had its shortest existence thus far in my life.

But how to characterize my horror? It was not related directly to my health, I should say. Rather, it was fueled by an intense wave of wounded vanity. Hoping that I do not sound too repulsive when I say so, I must report that I generally counted myself—not only by self-estimation but by a sense of latent ranking one feels they hold with the opposite sex—among those with nothing to regret about his basic handsomeness. Standing before the mirror I felt a panicky rage at myself—as if I had set myself to committing a sort of fractional suicide without ever intending to do so. Thus my anger was at myself, and not really in any way for my adoptive guardians of the cafeteria—who, though they offered no encouragement that I avoid their example or seek out company of my own age in that bleak, blue, but sure-to-pass period, meant no real harm in feeling comforted by the social and physical surrender of an agent young person into their midst. Well, there is something sinister about that kind of behavior ultimately, but it is rather passive, I must confess, and I was only caught by it by allowing myself to be placed in its crosshairs—and staying in those sights day after day and hour after hour. I did feel a momentary wave of anger for my cafeteria company, but I let it go—and rather thank them now for giving me the sharp, perhaps momentarily unkind, but effective spur to reform that I was about to undertake.

I took a shower and went to bed—too stuffed to take up any immediate action. I slept off my last bout of marathon eating and woke to a new day of brisk and quiet work in the city that was carried along with the silent happiness of a sure and secret resolution. When the day drew to a close, my renewed, confident, remove already seemed to have an effect on some of the fellows in the office, for they were sure suddenly that they needed me along that night on their planned tour of town to look at waitresses.

I declined their kind offer and drove home with fixed intent. I changed out of my work clothes and donned a tee shirt, shorts, and tennis shoes—the first two items made entirely of cotton. I had studied a small map of the town in a local telephone directory over my lunch hour, and I was able to determine that a water tower (that should come into view if I were to proceed north along Main Street for some time) was about two and a half miles away. A five-mile run for a first try did not seem like too much to ask of my twenty-nine-year-old self. With great excitement I jogged down the stairwell of my apartment, and I even hailed another resident—I saying hello in the affected spirit of a long veteran of regular exercise.

As I stood before the empty hardware store in the bright but fading light, I took one last look at my widened self in the glass of the old shop. Then, without stretching or ceremony I simply began to jog, then to run, north. I passed the cafeteria and then the frontier of Main Street and the downtown within a few minutes. My pride and elation were great. My legs and arms did not feel at that point that they had ever been away from running, and the pleasure I felt in saying hey to fellow pedestrians, and in passing cars that needed to slow down for traffic lights, was gargantuan—and all this filled me with that sort of true glee and joy that makes one tear a bit at the eyes.

Soon I was on the outer edges of the business parts of town, and the flat terrain suddenly seemed less accommodating. I would learn later that this ground that looked level was actually somewhat graded. And to my great surprise, as I approached a driveway in a part of town through which I had never passed before, I could see Fred and Rita leaving the front door of what must have been their house, they heading for their car and for their trip to the cafeteria. I could see Fred nudge Rita as I approached at a heightened speed.

"Fred! Rita! I'll be late tonight. But I'll be there later!" I called to them.

They both waved. And then I saw Rita elbow and chastise Fred—though I could not make out the words—so as to say as much to him as: "Look what your insensitive words drove him to. See, I told you that you hurt his feelings."

Fred gave a gruff wave of dismissal, and I looked back one more time to see them struggling with their wide shapes to get into their car.

I continued on, nearly breathless and spent from my performance of speed before Fred and Rita. But when I was out of sight of their house, I slowed a bit and caught some of my breath back. It was then that I became aware of another discomfort. I realized that I bounced—quite considerably—with each step that I took. It was as if I had discovered that there was an outer tubing of flesh or material enveloping my chest and stomach area. I felt like a landed sea elephant or walrus. I had been latently aware of this disturbing bouncing when driving. A sudden bump or a crossing of a train track made me feel like there were two landings my body would make—first the inner trunk or core, then an exterior layer that fell in the same direction.

But because I am a fellow who is pretty reliable in holding to his resolutions, I decided that now that I was in the midst of the vigorous exercise of reform, I would refrain from disdaining each of these hideous torso bounces as I ran—and take pleasure in the fact that I would have such an evident barometer by which to measure the reemergence of my accustomed shape.

I was contemplating this when I noticed that I was having trouble catching my breath once more. And this puzzled me, the new runner, who did not realize how rare is truly level ground. I was climbing a mild grade at this point in my run—feeling that I must be almost in sight of the water tower (in reality I was hardly three-quarters of the way into my first mile)—and I gave one more little push to myself and increased the pace along the length of a fence that lined an elementary school playground. Some sort of late afternoon, early evening intramural program was going on inside the school yard, and young children looked in wonder upon me as I attempted to hold my pace during the first half of the length of the fence. Then they saw me halt to a desperate jog at the midway point, then falter to a walk that gave little immediate relief when I was but a few yards farther.

When I was out of view of the playground, I halted on the school's front steps and sat down. Little pools of salty water formed on the ground. After several minutes my breath returned to a comfortable rhythm, and it was then that I saw the other runner. He was approaching from the direction in which I had been headed. He had on a red pair of true running shorts, but nothing else save his shoes—and he moved along like a lean knife through the evening air. He passed me and had no chance to acknowledge me as a fellow runner, for all he could see in me was an unaccountably soaked fellow in wet cotton shorts and shirt—resting as if at the end of the day from setting up water sprinklers.

I resolved that I had gone far enough in the outward direction for my first day. (It would be quite some time before I actually reached the water tower with any sort of ease or competency during a run.) I picked myself up and jogged past the schoolyard again, but I was forced to walk the rest of the residential way that preceded my return to the little downtown. And then, though unsure that anyone would see me, I still forced myself to run all of the business length of town, all of the way to the front of my building, until I touched the window of the hardware store.

In the glass I looked at my reflection in the twilight and the glow of the streetlamp. It was difficult to distinguish the sight of me from someone, say, who had just climbed out from a fall into a pool or a river or the surf. I dripped to such an extent that the place where I then stood was marked with a dark circle, even after only a full minute of study had passed before the window. I pulled off my tee shirt—and this took a great effort—and then took pleasure in wringing it in my hand until it was twisted to dryness in some spots.

Just as I was shaking out my shirt from its twisted wet knot and preparing to go upstairs, a pickup truck slowed to a crawl as it passed my spot and three young girls jeered and whistled in mock admiration. Though it was hardly flattering, I will confess that this was a bit more concerting to me, now that I had completed my first step to reform, than any number of pleasantries from my cafeteria companions.

I began my ascent to my apartment, and I realized then how much I had taken out of myself from this run. Soreness was not yet a consideration—I had not even thought about that issue yet— and I pulled off my other wet clothes and took off my shoes when I was back into my apartment. My socks were as wet as if I had been running in the rain, or had been working at a car wash, or had been wading in the surf on a clamming expedition.

But I would be able to return to my cafeteria companions with a sense of proper distance restored between age groups. Though I had only just started my reformation, I already felt that I no longer needed to identify with anything about my dinner companions save their warmth and openness to a lonely stranger.

My shower was quick and brisk. I even experimented with slowly cooling the water down a bit near the end, for my arms and hands were afire from the run, and they were red from their own blood, like a rare London Broil—and not red from any burning of the sun.

When I stepped out of the shower and dried a bit, I realized that I had not taken anything yet to drink. Thus, however primitive it sounds, after brushing my teeth—so as to give the water a sharp, clean-tasting edge—I leaned forth into the bathroom sink and drank wildly from the faucet till I almost felt slightly sick to my stomach.

Though my air conditioner was on in the apartment, and though I felt its effect considerably augmented by comparison with the shower after I left the sealed bathroom, it came as quite a surprise to me that it was not as easy as usual to dress for dinner. I found that the slightest effort—especially that of leaning over to put on my socks and pants—caused me to perspire again. I paused and sat at my desk for a moment, on its hard, cold, inviting metal chair. But sitting there for a time let me discover, or be reminded, that I am a perspirer of such magnitude that even sitting still for nearly ten minutes after a run and after a shower was not enough to stop my cycle of sweating.

After causing an even further outburst of salty streaks from my damp hair during the labor of putting on a shirt for dinner, I sat as still as possible for another three minutes and then could contain myself no longer. I proceeded out into the beautiful Georgia night, an impenetrable wall now set up within me, even from just that one run—a wall between me and any past griefs. Only past joys seemed accessible, and melancholy was turned away by some unknown but trusted guard of elation.

Though my perspiration continued, it finally seemed to slow a bit, and I resolved to head straight for the cafeteria even if I was not yet fully dried. But the night air struck with its heavy, warm pall, and I began to fully bead with sweat as I made my way up the block. The sun was fierce and red in the west, yet the coolness of the dining room was gratifying, and I was dry enough after making my way through the line, register, and to my accustomed corner to be able to sit in my seat without much of a wince from the feeling of a wet shirt making contact with the vinyl back of my chair.

There was another race on television—something from a small town in New Hampshire—but I was too proud of my own first run to feel the need to identify with any other runners. I hardly watched the show. And it was clear that this program made the general assembly of the back corner, especially Fred and Rita, somewhat self-conscious on my account. Rita seemed to have admonished and scolded all—what with their polite awkwardness toward me—that I had been unduly pushed into an extreme exercise plan because of their remarks of the day before.

That night my enthusiasm and self-contentment moved me to avoid a second piece of pie, but I could not resist the sweet tea—even though the novice that I was knew that the caffeine and subsequent dehydration would only make me even more thirsty in the long run. But so long as I was with my friends into that lateness of the evening, and this followed me into my last months in Georgia, I kept to my sweet tea guzzling—rather sure that I could burn the sugar if I kept to my running. And my table of adoptive guardians relaxed at the sight of this concession, and suddenly a low murmur of commentary about the night's television reports on esoteric New England road racing cropped up, with the cautious spirit at first as of prairie dogs checking the outsides of their burrows before emerging.

I felt a bit stiff on getting out of my chair and taking my leave of everyone that evening, but I did not let anyone know about my mild soreness. It felt very good to be sore, and I knew that I could not make them understand this. My adoptive guardians would only have offered cautions had I intimated that there was any reaction at all in my body from a first run.

I went back to my apartment and relished the idea of lying down for an early bedtime for the first instance in a very long time. I changed for bed quickly, had a last glass of water, and then fell asleep with speed—but my sleep was attended by strange dreams, dreams in which I found myself walking and working in strange houses, offices, and fields. And each time I began to perform any of the tasks assigned me in these places, my initial willingness to perform my duties was checked by unfamiliar soreness.

I awoke from one of the more extreme versions of these dreams and found myself terribly thirsty. Though I felt very tired, and probably quite able to allow myself to go right back to sleep if I gave myself but a minute, I resolved to rise and get myself a glass of water. Without thinking, and without thinking that I should do otherwise, I rose with speed to my feet, throwing off the covers despite my sleepiness, since I felt a surge of pride at remembrance of my first run. At some point in between my initial start from bed and my landing on the floor, a feeling struck me—a comprehensive sense of bodily distress became shockingly evident. I was not merely sore in my legs—which were sore indeed, and in every component part of them (even unto the arches of my feet, as if they had been suddenly used and flexed as if for the very first time)—but I was sore in nearly every major area of my body. I was shocked to find that my arms were so taxed. I recalled that they had, indeed, been hard to hold up after a point in the run, and that nothing felt better than to allow them to dangle lifelessly at my side. But, of course, it is nearly impossible to run in this position for any period of time, and one is forced to raise the arms again out of necessity.

I also felt general soreness in various parts of my torso, which I found quite gratifying despite its intensity. I would not call soreness pain. I often wonder if some runners are referring to soreness when they allude to certain types of pain. But even from the very start of my new running career, I associated soreness with the signs of bodily transformation, metamorphosis—as the confirmation of torn muscle fibers repairing and reorganizing themselves into denser, more powerful forms. Soreness is the *is* of the metaphor of running and exercise. If one can say this is that—a fat body is this thin and powerful body, too, waiting to appear—again, the *is* is the soreness. The exercise, the running, create this alchemical verb that is best harvested on the morning after a severe workout.

I walked slowly—waddled, rather—to my kitchen and had my drink. But upon taking several glasses of water, I hardly felt sleepy at all, and in hobbling around my living room I took notice that my answering machine flashed an inviting *1* on its screen—perhaps my fortunes with the Southern Belles had changed with only one run, I laughed in my mind.

But the message—it had come in earlier, during dinner—was from my mother and father in Arizona. Even though they asked that I call as soon as I got the message, I thought it best to wait until morning to return the call. Their sense of urgency only lasts during regular business and early evening hours, and nothing is more sacred to them, I fear, than regular sleep. But they mentioned something about a job I should investigate—and this position was something for which they already had secured an absolute connection for me, if I wanted it. I was used to hearing about such job ideas from them, but rarely job prospects for which they said they could almost assure me of an offer. Still, it was not until I heard them mention Long Island and its north shore that something in my mind registered. There was something that connected my family to Long Island, but I could not in my wakeful fatigue recall what it was. And there was something else that registered in me when the message went on to say that the name of the job's town was Pauktaug. I had heard the name before—quite recently, but I did not take the time to search my recollection too deeply. Something else took hold of me as I lay in bed once more and slowly surrendered my soreness to sleep. That something else was my vague notion of Long Island's place on the cold, Atlantic coast. Despite socially climbing, speculatively and intellectually vacuous parents and immediate relatives, those that loved heat and ease and cocktail parties and pool service, nothing could shake the grip that I had had since childhood upon the idea of New England. And Long Island swam just beneath that enfabled first shore, and I wondered as I lay in bed, what it would be like to run on the hilly north shore of that island, to be able to look across from its sandy, wooded, precipitous cliffs and across the looming, tale-concealing Sound, to the green foothills of New England, where Puritans and Indians once clashed, to the placental hardwood mysteries and woods and equally forbidding and ominous tombstones—and under all this, Long Island still nursed and suckled, a fry unwilling to let go of this shadow-casting father and river-lactating mother of North America. I plotted long runs in my mind along these vistas and these childhood imaginings, and despite new soreness that revealed itself even as I turned a bit in bed for the last time that night, I was soon asleep, and not a cell of me did dream again while it rested—dream what it might run as it rested, and as it recovered and reformed itself for the course that lay enshrouded but undoubtedly ahead.

CHAPTER 2

CHECKING IN

When I woke the next morning, something that must have followed me throughout my first run, but which had only just started to catch me in the cafeteria and during my fitful night's sleep, then had complete possession of me. Perhaps gravity had chased me on that first run, and since I had lain down to sleep for quite awhile, it had fully caught up with me and permeated my frame. My soreness was complete. I could hardly rise from bed. It was as if some great set of imponderably strong elastic cords held me to my mattress. No matter which of my four limbs I tried to raise, I felt a great cord (as if gravity itself—augmented, transformed, into an injectable serum) possessed all parts of me. I felt the same resistance to movement even from my head and neck. As well, my torso, the very trunk of my body, seemed attached to cords—as if gravity held that part down, as well, lest it discover some means of escape and locomotion on its own.

But still this soreness felt good. I remembered my parents' message as I readied for work, and I looked forward to the prospect of calling them from my office later in the morning, when I could be sure that the time difference between the East and Arizona would not have me calling them too early.

I could hardly walk about my apartment. Showering and dressing were so difficult that the extremity of the situation made me laugh with the joy that often comes with a sudden change of prospects or events. Once I had made it to my car—which was accomplished by a gait so comical and awkward that I was glad that no one saw me—I took greater pleasure during my long hour's commute than I had ever before. I took great pleasure in sitting completely still for a time—though turning my neck so as to check around me for turns and for other traffic, and extending my calves and legs into different positions for the sake of manipulating the gas and brake pedals, were laughably extreme and sensitive affairs. But I would not say painful. There was something salubrious and constructive in this sensation. I would not have traded it away for a morning of no reaction to my first run, not for anything.

When I arrived at work, I could not escape the seeming inevitability of running into the stunning blonde receptionist who worked on the first floor of my building. For months I had tried to engineer a casual interception of this girl as she traveled from her car to the lobby and to her work. Not once had I been successful. She was nearly always at her seat behind a glass door when I went to the elevator—but on several occasions I had pulled into the lot only to see her just entering the building. And there had been a case when I lingered outside of the building one lunch time to wait for her to come out, listening for her distinctive high heeled shoes as a warning that I should set myself in motion—as if I were a person merely on his way out, our meeting then only a coincidence. But when she did come out, I accidentally let her pass, for my head had been down, looking at a pebble I shuffled about on the ground below the bench on which I waited, and I did not hear her tell-tale heel clicks. Instead I looked up by accident to see a beautiful woman running away from the building in running attire and shoes. I did not have the courage to call out to her and stop her then.

On pulling into the lot that morning, this girl was not on my mind. I strained to collect my things for work from the passenger seat, and when I managed to lift myself, to climb out of the car with a colossal effort and a truly involuntary but secretly proud groan, I found that the person getting out of the car next to me was the pined-after blonde receptionist. To my astonishment her generally regal and aloof face—or what I had imagined would be an impenetrable and inaccessible expression—was quite ready to hail a stranger. She called out a hey with the fatally endearing, honey-rich sound of Georgia, and we began to walk toward the building's lobby together.

Knowing that I had seen her run, I immediately rejected the idea of making small talk based on that incipient commonality. But just at the moment I feared she would notice my awkward stride, she asked me if I had hurt myself.

I foolishly volunteered that it was from running. But I did not say that it was from a first run.

"Yeah, that happens with a lot of hardcore runners." I could hardly imagine that anyone, from looking at me, could yet think me a "hardcore runner," but I gladly accepted her possible assumption.

"Yeah, you have to be careful about that kind of thing," she said, and then she continued this admonitory tack. She proceeded to describe a knee injury that she had sustained some years back in her own running. When she finished this description, we were at her door. Her grave tone ended there, and then she beamed again with an almost voluble citrus glow.

With a cowardly conclusion, I offered only a paltry leave-taking, but to my shock and pathetic anticipation she suddenly called to me before going into her workplace as I waited for the elevator.

"Hey, let me give you this," she said. And as she approached me she reached into her little purse and pulled out a business card. I could not comprehend my good fortune, and I did not even look at the card as she handed it to me.

I smiled for a time as she continued: "Here, why don't you take this? Call me here at the office, and I can schedule you for an appointment to see the doctor if your limp doesn't go away in a day or two."

"Thank you," I smiled outwardly—and I inwardly reproached myself more than she could possibly know.

"Sure, you're welcome. See you later."

(I offer this and the other little stories of my failures with women in Georgia so that what happens later in my narrative is not taken as casual boasting. What I have related thus far of my general romantic experiences and prospects is the most common scenario, I must confess.)

I spent the first half of my morning working at my desk in perfect stillness. Nothing made me stir until I heard the creak of the coffee cart making its first rounds of the office. Though my senses were still called by this, my new pride allowed me to resist the cart with ease as it came to my desk.

During this break in the morning, I called my mother and father in Arizona in place of eating pastry and drinking several cups of coffee. My mother was in, but my father was out playing golf under a merciless, blazing, dry sunshine. Sometimes, though rarely, they complained about the heat, but as they reported contentment usually—even boasted several times within the course of a call about their new way of life, new friends, and their condominium's perfections—I rarely suggested to them that they try anything else for retirement. They described their new position as if it was that upon which their whole lives had been driving, and when I was struck during one telephone conversation by this realization, I doubled my efforts to resist mocking anything about their lifestyles. As I asked less and less about their lives, and as I do not play golf—and as that is what into which they both seemed to be removing themselves entirely—our strained telephone conversations were usually brief summaries from me of what I was doing for the magazine. My mother always asked for clippings of the articles on which I said I was working, and I religiously mailed them off to my parents until my mother called the magazine one day and asked for several subscriptions.

Part of her enthusiasm for my work on the airline magazine was because my father had secured me the job. He had worked in the Chicago offices of the airline for most of his working lifetime, and the magazine job was the first thing that he could offer me from that world that caught my interest. I do not believe that he had scanned very long, looking for something that I would like particularly—so much as he had jumped at the chance to provide a reliable name to his superiors for the position I now held in Atlanta. It was simply a little coup for him, I fear, and hardly an effort to find his journalizing son a better place in the business in which he was then struggling in Chicago. My first jobs after graduate school in Illinois had all been at small newspapers—most of the time I was not doing any writing at all. Though my interest had always been real, daily newspaper work, I was discouraged by the tasks I was assigned at the smaller though significant and paying papers at which I could find work. And on top of this disappointment, something about those jobs embarrassed my rather superficial parents, and so it pleased them, and me, when for the first time in my life I was willing to take work that my father had found for me in the airline's vast empire, just when he was about to retire.

Thus when my mother began to relate to me the substance of the message she had only alluded to on the answering machine the night before, I was almost shocked. After she asked me her obligatory question as to whether I had met any nice girls—yet this time she asked as if she hoped I had *not* met anyone that would tie me to my new place—she reported that *she,* and not my father, was now taking a turn at finding me new and better work. She recalled my longtime passion to work at a real paper, where I might earn perhaps just enough to make a living, but also feel an active part of a real American community, a real locality with character. It was hard for me to believe that even if she had come across something like that for me, she would recommend it to me or even let me know about it. There were, of course, papers that had tempted me all around the country when I saw little notices for openings that might suit me, but even I had grown slightly cautious after my post-graduate school experiences back home, and slightly more cautious as I grew fat and comfortable in Atlanta, with nothing but the hope of finding some beautiful but indifferent girl to marry driving me on—with the latent desire to take up golf also perhaps lurking in my decaying bones.

I knew there was some little, presently inscrutable, but soon-to-be revealed advantage to be gained by my mother in whatever this new job would offer. My parents loved the idea of my place and position in Atlanta, so I knew—though I did not yet know what it was precisely—that there was some sense of vanity or primitive though shallow sense of obligation motivating my mother's campaign. And as my father was not there when I called, I was fairly sure that this was an interest that only concerned my mother. In fact, I suspected that I would have his support if I declined her offer, for he was not even at home to press the idea. His disappointment that the comfortable spot he had recently won for me might already be considered for abandonment was registered in his almost palpable, angry absence. I felt that his irritation would devolve almost entirely on me for whatever decision would be made, for it was evident that as my mother had already made up her mind to offer this new scheme, it would, in a sense, become entirely my decision whether I left the airline or not.

My mother told me that one of the airline magazine subscriptions she had ordered was that for a great-grandmother of mine—one that I had never met. Yet I could recall three or four times in my youth that my mother had flown to Long Island to visit her paternal, long-widowed grandmother. This woman, in her early nineties, now found that my mother was more or less her last viable familial connection, and I suspected at first that my mother was beginning to receive latent pressure from her grandmother for an invitation for her to move down to Arizona—or to make some large caretaker's gesture to her in her twilight. Though she was entering her tenth decade, my great-grandmother was still remarkably strong and independent. She could not drive, but otherwise she was fully capable of living on her own in her native village of Pauktaug, Long Island. (When my mother reminded me of the name of her grandmother's town, I still knew I had recently heard or read of it for other reasons, but I still could not think of how I knew the name.)

As I have observed above, my parents lived their lives almost entirely with the goal in sight that they had just realized—moving into the heat and ease, and thinking of themselves as deserving and justly-rewarded seniors. Thus I quite sincerely believe that my great-grandmother's latent search for an invitation—if there even was one (my mother's vanity may have exaggerated her own sense that everyone wanted to be where my father and she were)—terrified my mother. And I also believe that even the slightest chance that my mother might be thought indifferent toward a family member, even by an almost unknown and generally unheard-from stranger, was also terrifying to her. Then there was another consideration that I was able to piece together of which I am sure my mother was thinking. My great-grandmother was independent to such an extent that it seemed likely that her ultimate demise would be at home, and that nursing care or nursing home expenses seemed an unlikely prospect, at least at the moment. I am sure my mother—though she is not, as this may make her sound, entirely a covetous, chilling, collector (but she is almost that, I fear)—worried where my great-grandmother's savings would go upon her death. She had been left with considerable money upon her husband's demise, and she was also rumored to live rather simply, so surely this money would survive, in part, even her passing. And finally, my mother had learned—and this only added to the last fear—that a young neighboring couple had been looking after my great-grandmother. My great-grandmother praised these two, especially the young man, and I am sure that even the slight mention of an imagined competitor for a possibly imagined family fortune made my mother worry until she had convinced herself that it was just plain foolish, and not even morally right, to simply, passively yield prospective wealth out of a false attempt to appear indifferent to inheritance. (And, indeed, any indifference on this count would be but a display from my mother!)

In the midst of these worries—my mother knowing, or at least confident, that she could not invite her grandmother to live in Arizona, also knowing that she herself could not move to Long Island to keep her grandmother company, yet fearing (again for a combination of acquisitive and clannish reasons) that someone outside of the family would do the keeping in place of her—in the midst of these terrors that haunted my mother's days of golf and monitoring her blood pressure assiduously, came a chatty call from my great-grandmother, asking if I were still on the hunt for work at a real, small-town paper.

Pauktaug not only had a viable, nearly thriving local paper, *The Pauktaug Press*, but it had as part of its paper that most rare of incarnations (at least rare in that it can also keep itself afloat): a literary magazine that came as part of the weekly paper. The paper itself was a conflation of local reporting and local intellectual speculation—a sort of grand, truly unique combination of a Perry White's *Daily Planet* and Ralph Waldo Emerson's *The Dial*. How was such a thing accomplished? It seemed that the paper was more a thriving newspaper than anything else for so long, that having become an institution, no one, even in this utilitarian age, much noticed when the paper augmented its aims each week with literary supplements. But this augmentation happened only in 1996, and though the paper still thrived as a regular newspaper, it was said that this literary expansion only came in that year with a new, young editor-in-chief, one Lawrence Hare, who it was suspected would ultimately move onto bigger things, and then the paper's eccentric inserts would simply disappear. But at the time that I spoke with my mother on that morning in 2001, the literary portions of the paper were still said to make reliable appearances with nearly every edition.

This same Lawrence Hare, a fellow in his early thirties (he was about thirty-three, I think) with a wife of the same age, was the same man that my great-grandmother boasted of to my mother—and caused great consternation to my mother concerning his suspected diversion of our family fortune. (My mother should have suspected that my great-grandmother was a woman who boasted of whomever had accomplished something worthwhile to whomever she was talking to at the moment—thus this Mr. Hare could have been as threatened by what my great-grandmother said of my mother, or of me, for that matter, every time he paid her a visit with the possible designs my mother was sure he had, designs on an old lady's alteration of her will.)

But it was also this Mr. Hare that read some of my articles— one on the phenomenon of the Southern Cafeteria, and another on the grand liquid itself, sweet tea, and another on air travel—after my great-grandmother had boasted that I was a regular writer in the very magazine that her granddaughter in Arizona had arranged to have sent to her. And it was this Mr. Hare who said he had long been considering the creation of an assistant editor's position at *The Pauktaug Press*, and he told my great-grandmother that if this sweet-tea-musing kin of hers wanted such a place on his paper, it would be his for the asking.

My mother did confess that my great-grandmother mentioned this fact rather casually at first, but after my mother asked for further details—the gritty details of business—my great-grandmother had called again some weeks later to report the salary and benefits of the possible job. It shocked my parents that the offer from *The Pauktaug Press* was actually a bit better than what I enjoyed from the airline in Georgia. It shocked me, as well. Thus under the guise of directing her son further and further along on his chosen path of passion, and under the peculiar guide of hoping that most would suspect that her choice was truly motivated by the lesser of two greedy evils—that being the hope that I would move on to this new position because of the better pay—my mother hoped I would go to this new job, just so that I was close enough to my great-grandmother's vicinity to keep the old woman from contemplating any redaction to her legacy. In some sad and latent way, I really do believe that this was my mother's line of reasoning. She knew that no one she knew would believe that I was on a mission of kindness to my great-grandmother, but she hoped my great-grandmother believed it. It was enough if she could let her friends know that *The Pauktaug Press* gave me a little more money and dental benefits—which latter perquisite, incredibly, the airline magazine did not provide.

In a bland soliloquy of anger I told my mother how obvious she was, and that her apparent process of self-deliberation and planning was apparent to me after only a moment's suspicion and subsequent thinking during a pause in our conversation—this while she surveyed the pill count in one of her medication bottles and mused aloud that it was time for a refill.

She told me that I did not have to decide anything right away, that only after I looked at a few copies of *The Pauktaug Press,* which were on their way from Long Island as we spoke, did she hope that I would conclude anything. I did not say a word in response to the idea of the imminent mailings. But I did launch into a peculiar announcement that struck me by surprise, and it only upset my mother and made her a little weepy. I said that though we all knew that the job I had in Atlanta was only a sort of family coup (and that we all knew that it was related to my journalistic and literary concerns only by luck, considering the airline-limited connections of my father), I had come to be pleased that I could please my father and myself at the same time. It gave me some gratification at last to work at something that was close enough to my desires so as to keep me out of sadness and shame and in the dawn of hope at all times—and at the same time by coincidence give my father endless pleasure to say that his son worked for his company. I was glad that I could do that for him. I would not be glad to have to take that little gift from him, take my own good spirits away, and move onto a nearly evil little plot so as to please my mother.

Once more, my mother cried at this, but recovered herself and seemed to be at the emotional start of the argument again by pointlessly reiterating, "The copies of Mr. Hare's paper are in the mail. They may be in your box already when you get home today."

When my mother began to cycle in this manner, I would end a call, and that is what I did in this case. I told her I had to go to lunch—that it was lunchtime in the East (it was not, really, but I knew she could not think that fast)—and that I had someone waiting for me.

She irritated me one last time by asking, "Is it a girl?" Of course she hoped in this case that I was not developing anything to hold me in Atlanta.

Feeling a bit sick and irritated by all of this, and doubtlessly a bit irritated, as well, because I had forgone my usual allowance of pastry and coffee, I got up from this call to walk it off. I had forgotten my soreness entirely, so it was with shock when I followed through in my leap to my feet and felt the jolts of the previous day's run still developing in all parts of my body.

One of my coworkers passed me as I was making my way to the water cooler, and he asked me what had happened, considering I still looked angry in my face, I think, and looked debilitated physically all around.

For some reason I quipped back in a cavalier way, "I was in a fight," and much to my surprise, amusement, and sense that I should disabuse him of this at some future point, I could see that he took me quite seriously, and he raised his eyebrows apologetically and exhaled silently from puffed cheeks as he scooted off in silence.

I worked in removed, respected and feared quiet for the rest of the day—worked on a little piece that was slated to appear in the late summer issue of the magazine. Though my mother's proposition floated through my mind with distaste every few minutes, I also caught myself wondering how I would go about breaching my intentions of leaving my present position if I were to go indeed to New York. But I quickly put this out of my head. I did not know why I should even think or wonder of such a thing, I told myself.

At the end of the day I drove home—having declined an invitation from the boys in the office, and from some in the adjoining suites, to go on a dinner raid (perhaps the intimation I had made to one fellow that I had true bellicose blood and the injuries to prove it made them think that we could be more successful with the ladies of Atlanta). And despite my continuing soreness, my single-minded purpose and enthusiasm found me searching my drawers at home for a clean tee shirt and my second and only other pair of shorts. This second pair of shorts were almost dressy, and hardly appropriate for running—so I decided to make them a reserve in my then small arsenal of sporting clothes and found instead my only pair of sweatpants. They were of heavy, gray cotton, and hardly appropriate for a very warm spring day in the South, but they seemed better to me than the dress shorts. For a moment I even considered using my shorts from the day before, but comfort for myself and common decency for those that I might pass for only an instant ruled that I should leave my first running shorts in the swamp-like mire and darkness of the hamper.

Again, without stretching of any sort, and without having recovered from my last run to any real extent—and probably having failed to hydrate myself properly, as well—I stepped out to the street with the sometimes dangerous but still winning fuel of indefatigable early motivation and the good spirits of self-reform in progress.

Somehow, despite what I should probably characterize as a sort of pain in different places in both of my legs, I ran and intermittently jogged all the way to the water tower that I had appointed as halfway point during my day of map consultation and route creation. Because I reached this goal, the difficulty of my run back was ameliorated by a great sense of joy and goodwill toward almost all matter and objects upon which my eyes and feet landed. And then it began to rain when I was about a mile from town, and my cotton tee shirt and heavy cotton sweatpants became altogether saturated with a rich, odorous, perfume of Southern spring rain. When I was so wet that I knew that not only was every area of outer clothing darkened and wetted by rain, but that even my underwear and socks were permeated in every place that my own perspiration had missed, I also began to notice that despite my tight retying of the string that held up my sweatpants, nothing could be done to keep them in place around my waist. The rain insisted that this garment should make its ways to my knees, and so in a sincere fit of joy and laughter—which doubled my efforts and breathing requirements as an aerobic novice—I was obliged to run with one arm attached to the side of my pants at all times. My arms, taking turns, became a sort of living pair of suspenders: one arm free to dangle and sway like a part of an incompletely buttoned farm boy's overalls. The awkwardness that this situation enforced on my running style was not unwelcome to my arms—even though this new task was fatiguing, too, after awhile—for I discovered on this second run, and this just before it started to rain, that it was very difficult to hold my arms up after a time. This fascinated the new runner in me, for the arms, though obviously indispensable for balance, seemed so free of load-bearing duties during running that I hardly suspected that they would crave rest after use by an unconditioned runner.

But I made it home with my joy undiminished by any of the pain, soreness, windedness, and general fatigue that permeated my entire form when I was again standing before the night-opaque glass of the abandoned hardware store. I was sure that I looked leaner to myself already in the reflection.

The rain had kept me cool, and thus I had less trouble with perspiration after my quick shower than I had had on the first night of running, and soon I was at my place in the cafeteria.

As I sat watching television with my adoptive family, I tried again to recall why the town on Long Island my mother had mentioned seemed so familiar to me. But, as had happened already in those early stages of my running career, my joy in the new process gave me great energy to dismiss almost anything that I might fruitlessly dwell upon in my mind.

I endured questions from my companions as to whether I had run in the rain or not—"You mean you ran in the rain?"—questions to which I had already become somewhat inured because of my companions' equal and fatiguing astonishment from the previous day concerning my profuse perspiration, profuse even long after a shower and a run. "You mean that's your sweat? You mean it isn't raining out?"

Save for the questions about the rain on that second night of running, Fred and Rita and the rest of the cafeteria group already seemed adjusted and indifferent to my new pursuit—especially as it did not interfere with my appearance for dinner. And save for my resistance to limitless helpings of pie (they did indeed fight me on that, saying that I would need more energy if I was going to run so much), they took pleasure in noting that I maintained my sweet tea habit in full force.

After dessert that evening I felt an overwhelming desire for sleep. Thus, in addition to restoring the appetite into a healthy form (in which food is craved because true effort has been put forth; and yet gluttony is immediately reduced somehow, as well), I found that running had restored my true appetite for sleep—for this fatigue was not the tiredness that accompanies a generally demoralized and languorous lifestyle.

But I did not fail to check my mailbox before going back to my apartment, and there, as my mother suggested it might be, was a large manila mailing envelope with a Long Island, New York cancellation across its stamps. The cancellation was a little picture of Long Island itself, in addition to the traditional horizontal, wavy bars of black ink.

In the large, stuffed envelope I found three copies of *The Pauktaug Press* and a little letter. It read:

Dear Rex, I am sorry that we have never met. I had always hoped that your mother might bring you along on one of her trips, but that never happened. But I feel I have met you in a way. Not only has your mother supplied me with a subscription to your present magazine work, but she gave me, during one of her visits, some of your articles and pieces from your younger days, and I always felt that you and I had a little connection through my reading. And I think I may know you better from these than if I had met you in the company of your mother. My good, young friend, Mr. Lawrence Hare, Editor-In-Chief of *The Pauktaug Press* and also my neighbor, chanced upon one of your articles when he and his kind wife, Lisa, were checking in on me one evening. As I had always had a feeling that he and you might be very much alike and sympathetic, I told him what I knew of your history, and I gathered together my little collection of your work. He asked if he could borrow my clippings of your writing, and I gladly gave them over to him—feeling I had introduced, somehow, two possibly like minds. Mr. Hare does not get the response I think he deserves for the changes he has made to the local paper, and I thought he might like to see that there are others who labor with a similar vision of the world (if I may venture my belief that you both share a common strain). I have also developed a certain hope that I might do something for you one day—as again, I feel that I never could have come to know you so well if it had not been that I had come to know you in this distant yet revealing way. I hope you do not take exception to any reflections that this may seem to cast upon your mother from me. I appreciate her visits and continued contact and do not think she means any harm. But, again, I appreciate her visits mostly for the accident of finding this sympathetic voice of mind and kin in a place that I thought was leading not only to the final disintegration of my personal line but also to a disintegration of a line of thinking and sensibility. Thus I feel a pleasure in addressing you finally as a true great-grandson—or grandson, if I may simplify the connection. As I have a similar admiration for Mr. Hare and his work—and as his daily kindnesses have been such a blessing to me in these last years—he has also become a true grandson. Thus I feel that I may be uniting two lost brothers with this little effort of mine to have Mr. Hare know something of you through your work.

But never did I think that my plan would go beyond his reading of your work. By the time you have this in hand, I hope your mother will have told you the terms under which Mr. Hare would like you to consider coming to work for him as Assistant Editor at *The Pauktaug Press*.

Please take your time in considering this offer. I enclose

three recent issues of *The Pauktaug Press* and advise you that you can take your time in deciding. Please think about it, at least until the end of June, and then send Mr. Hare your thoughts. Take your time, as well, because he would like the position to start in September—which would mean that you would have until August or late-August to move here if you decide to join him.

But perhaps you are happy where you are. Please know that no matter what your decision, you have won a new friend in

Yours Most Sincerely,
Nancy Whisker

I read this note with fascination—and with even greater satis-faction. The latter feeling came because it was clear that this great-grandmother of mine was in no way unfamiliar with my mother's true nature. And it seemed of even greater interest to me that she could discern this yet still keep a connection with her, and even extend herself generously to a direct descendant of my mother—and not summarily dismiss my mother and any that follow directly in her line. And, of course, it was evident to me that there was no oblique or latent request for familial company and protection in this letter. I felt that the communication was sincere in the limits of its described affections and in the parameters of its offers. My mother was so excluded from this part of the exchange that I immediately felt a special privilege, not only in this most recent contact from my great-grandmother to my family, but also in all the other contacts my mother had ever had with her—for I felt, in a curious way, that all those other visits had left my mother an eas-ily fathomed stranger to my great-grandmother. And thus I felt for a happy, private, gratified second, that my great-grandmother had tolerated my obtuse and acquisitive mother for so many years in the hope that she might meet someone better in her line through my mother one day. I do not venture to say that my great-grand-mother was correct—I may end up, one day, the same panicky status seeker that my mother had become—but I was flattered that she had read my articles. And I could say, indeed, that one who had read them would know that though my mother is my mother, I am not my mother's son.

As comfort and the first touch of sleepiness began to overtake me, I turned next to the papers themselves. I decided to look carefully at one edition to start. My first feeling about the paper was that it not only fulfilled its role as a seemingly careful and complete reporter of local happenings in this village of Pauktaug, New York, but there was also a deeper layer, something riding below the obvious local paper's duty of covering things to which larger papers could not afford to give attention. There was something below these same local stories, most of them written by this Hare himself, I think—after I recognized a tone that ran through most of the columns (and the literary pieces in the supplement)—something that said by the most oblique intimation, or some angled terse concluding sentence, or some uncommon ordering of the unaltered facts, that there was order in all these random events of a smaller community. Some Universality, some timeless verity was written via the *Headlines, First Page, Police Beat, Editorials,* even in the tide charts, some hidden sentence bespeaking a magisterial reconciliation of opposites, some first ordering as if of some new astronomy to Men, ran backward and forward, up and down, in trackless inscrutable truth and credo across this humble little paper. Looking at this publication was like looking into a telescope or binoculars backwards—all was crushed and made clear and close together. Again, there seemed to be some one sentence, some hidden headline that ran about in different directions as one read ahead and backward, but I could not find it. Yet I suspected it was there.

I walked about my apartment for a little bit as my spirits rose with my reading—and as I tried to walk off some of my further compounded soreness and felt a need for several glasses of water. (In the morning I would find my newsprint fingerprints were on the walls and corners in many places where I had decided to lean while standing and reading, so as to alleviate one or the other sore leg.)

And when I felt sleepy again, I turned into bed one final time and began to examine the little literary addendum to the paper. Again, save for one or two exceptions, I suspected that the entire opus was produced by one, sole voice. In the regular paper there had been several features on Long Island's lobster fishery—discussing problems both with the crop and with the industry itself—and when I discovered the second part of a continuing essay on lobstering in the literary section, I suspected that I was merely going to find more of the plain reporting on the subject (though, again, plain with a transcendent compass attached). But in this continuing essay I discovered a dispensing of contemporary fishery trials and challenges, and a direct pitching into a to-me as yet untapped gristmill of facts that yielded to symbols, and of symbols that yielded to irrefragable constants of the world's few, great, undeniable abstractions. It was a strange essay at the same time, and I spent more time wondering what the regular reader must have made of it as my feeling of sleep came on harder and harder, and I pushed aside the papers from my covers and put them on my night stand.

Out of the pile of material fell one of my own articles—apparently a clipping that my great-grandmother had lent this Mr. Hare and that he had returned to her. It had a few passages underlined and a scrawled note or two by the marked lines. The article was from my piece on airline travel, and Hare had marked the following with dark pencil strokes: "The modern airliner is as a stationary room in the creative mind. One enters and leaves by the same doorway to find that though the room has seemingly remained in place, the exterior world has changed. And if one sleeps during their ride, this change is even more sudden and extreme. The airliner squeezes distances into nothing. I have slept on some of my rides and found certain great distances utterly compacted. I have entered the seemingly stationary room one minute and left it seemingly a minute later to find that hundreds of miles have been squeezed and lopped off from the Universe."

Soon I put all my reading away. But after I turned out my light I found that the envelope was still there, and as my eyes took to the moonlight and I could gradually start to see via its dusty blue beams, I studied the cancellation mark on the envelope. It was a clear, good strike of the cancellation, and not only was Long Island's outline clear, but the rest of the wavy cancellation lines looked like waves, suggestions of the bordering Long Island Sound and Atlantic Ocean, those waves crinkled and fraught with an inviting, unsettled malaise.

The more I looked at the little image of that massive, glacially-formed lane of Long Island, I found myself turning the envelope so that the image was up and down for me, so that I seemed to be viewing it as if my body were a line of latitude, and not in the common human position of consideration, like a line of longitude before a map. And in the dim light and in my fading wakefulness, Long Island started to suggest the image of a sort of monolith, a stone sculpture that vaguely sought to intimate an abstracted monument of a runner. At the top of this stone a great gaping mouth seemed to be at the top of a paused, breathless body—the mouth making gaping use of the water stop of the Continental Rivers. The barrier islands on the south shore of the island appeared like this runner's fatigued, airborne limbs (his arms)—his arms to dangle in brief, fleeting rest before the race was to resume. Long Island, I vaguely knew, had been formed and left behind by one of the latest great glaciers, and thus this island seemed a representative of the mobile, running Earth—its plates running, of its slowly jogging crusts. Long Island came with the glacier, or perhaps it ran there secretly from the ocean and underneath the ice, so as to cool itself in the race under the frozen bergs and sheets (like runners who dump ice and ice water under their caps on nearly Genesis-blazing days).

Even the road runner's course is never truly fixed. The plates, the crust, move. They move, too, seemingly in race with some driving, unforgiving but improving competitor. Thus man runs ultimately in place on the Earth, for it is as a giant treadmill—the jealous, speed-aspiring Earth, that rocky primitive runner, having this much over the stealthy, ever-honing and lithe footman, her son, Man.

And I slept deeply yet again.

CHAPTER 3

STRETCHING

As suggested in my great-grandmother's letter, I postponed responding to the circuitous offer and invitation of this Mr. Lawrence Hare. I mulled over the strange and inviting little papers and their attached literary supplements, even though in the recesses of my resolve I had already decided to accept the offer. Though I had come to feel that I could live with the satisfaction of my father in my present position—and, again, I came to be glad to give him that satisfaction—I decided to ignore as best I could any satisfaction that my mother would gain from my accepting this new position which would put me in proximity of her grandmother. But since I intended to use nearly the entire allotted time before an official decision had to be made (though I did send my grandmother a little postcard saying that I had received her mailing and that I was considering very seriously her message and would do so until just before the deadline was reached), I told my mother nothing of what I was thinking. And I took, instead, perverse pleasure in being evasive whenever she brought up the issue over the phone. She asked me questions about the sample newspapers I had been sent, but I was so vague and affectedly indifferent when speaking on that subject with her that she could hardly suspect that I had even looked at them. She often ended our weekly phone conversations in disgust, but my father, however, seemed encouraged by my seeming indifference—but I suspect he had suspicions as to my true intentions since my descriptions of my long-range Georgia plans and projects became more nebulous and indefinite. Soon I could hardly conceal the truth if he had asked me directly, for it was clear that I was not entertaining any new ideas for articles for the airline magazine. He remained quiet, however, and I appreciated his tacit stance. In a way, he may have appreciated my efforts in frustrating my mother's immediate desires to know my plans—and even if her wishes would be satisfied, he seemed to like that I not only kept her uninformed, almost misinformed, but I also indicated with this secretive conduct a desire to take on this new project for reasons other than my mother's. Whether or not my father really thought this way, I cannot say. But it did mean, if that is what he thought, that he credited my aspirations more than I had suspected, and that he would rather see my desires fulfilled, even if they only served him by undermining my mother's unattractive goals, than that I remain in a position that he had secured for me—secured for me for less disreputable reasons than my mother would ever conceive for chasing down a job prospect for me herself.

I let my Atlanta editor know that I would be leaving in late July, and I wrote a letter to my great-grandmother and enclosed a note of acceptance for Mr. Hare.

Through the increasingly hot and powerfully moist Southern spring I continued to run every day. I had so much enthusiasm that I ran no matter how I felt physically. Thus I probably committed every new-runner faux-pas (in a literal sense in many cases, too). There even came a day in early July, when I was in the midst of already clearing out my Georgia apartment, that my still keen novice enthusiasm sent me out on a long run—I was now past my five-mile limit already—one late afternoon on a Sunday (before my cafeteria preparation time) when I knew in all parts of my mind and body that I should really take a recovery day. But it still seemed logical to me that the more I might run, and the harder I would try to run on each of these outings, the more I should improve.

But when I was in a pretty little neighborhood of streets well past the old halfway point of the water tower and had just turned around for the start of my return trip back into town, something new and rather shocking happened to me. At first I felt a general, comprehensive aerobic fatigue on that run as I did on all my runs, but this fatigue passed more and more quickly, until it was that by the time of my second month of running, I could get past the urge to stop completely and get into a stage where I could cruise and breathe rather comfortably and shallowly. Perhaps what was happening was that my aerobic ability to resurrect myself was inherently out of proportion to my skill at reconditioning my muscles. Thus it might be said that my lungs and heart and mind had adapted more quickly to running than could the direct mechanism of my running—that is to say, my legs and general physical frame. So it was that as I entered a lovely, tree-lined street with whispering lawn sprinklers and enormous magnolia trees and attentive cats, my aerobic self carried my body beyond where it was able to go. At first it was a physical sensation that took hold of my legs and lower back that was not entirely unpleasant. In fact, my first reaction was like that which I have described well above in regard to my perverse fascination, even anticipation, at the first signs of a new and unknown malady taking over the body. Rather like a cramp that comes over the muscles of the calves at times, I almost allowed, almost passively encouraged this new sensation to advance so long as its curious new aspects seemed short of pain. But then the sensation began to feel like it dictated a less and less articulate strike of the ground with each step of my legs. It was not like the sensation one has when one lets a limb fall asleep. It was more as if I were letting my legs take something that they should not be taking—and that I was just discovering that the legs had a language that was more subtle than direct (by direct I mean as in quick reactionary calls of pain, as in the effect of touching something that is too hot, or as in the case of being cut or wounded). My legs, and my back, I think, were speaking a runner's language that I did not know, and I simply continued as they made quiet and polite warnings of imminent distress. Nor did the language of my legs and back, of my running mechanism, take on the vocabulary of direct reactionary pain when the crisis level was reached. No doubt the running mechanism could speak in those terms, but mercifully my affliction was not entirely something it wished to characterize in that way. My running mechanism did not wish to cry wolf quite yet, though undoubtedly I flirted at least with a fox, if not a small cougar. Though no doubt I skirted near an injury, and perhaps a serious one, what I experienced was a grave warning. Suddenly I did not stop because my aerobic will gave out or because my anaerobic level of fatigue was such that I felt it difficult to keep even my arms raised. I needed to stop, rather, because the slurring speech of my legs suddenly became incoherent, and then, as I approached a little corner yard where I was accustomed to make a turn onto another street, my legs, my entire running mechanism did not seem to be in touch with the ground. I had feeling in them, but I felt like I was sending increasingly numb and senseless appendages to the hardness of the blacktop. Perhaps the sensation was like the incipience of a hypothermia victim's lack of tactile sense. I cannot say for sure. But I can say that this half-numbness of my legs almost made me *more* aware of the hardness and texture of the road for a moment. Since the elaborate cushioning and adaptive network of all my many running systems' muscles seemed to be running at a quarter power at best, I felt for a moment I had a more honest impression of the road's true harshness. In a way, healthy legs hide this truth from us. Runners who complain that their legs complain of hard surfaces—or of any surfaces after a significant or major injury—do not realize, I think, that their legs are merely legs that could no longer tell noble lies. They are as soldiers or pilots who have lost their nerve, these legs. Feeling the road's true harshness with an increasingly numb pair of limbs, that harshness seemed expressed through the half or quarter remaining sentience of my legs—they not adapting to the subtle contours or unforgiving hard flatness. My ailing, failing legs seemed to take each step with too straight an impact, as if they were stilts or feeble jackhammers—but, alas, the asphalt would always win against them if they continued in affectation of the latter state. My legs ran in their final running moments of this run, like a senseless and stiffened LP player's arm and stylus—no longer able to ride with a slight warp of a disc, but only able to make one type of contact, doing damage to the surface, perhaps, but ultimately doing the most damage to itself.

When I was before the corner yard and house, I suddenly stopped—again, not from fatigue, but as if my legs were no longer present. I stood still effectively for a moment, and then I was able to stutter step to the lawn and sit down as my last gesture of possible motion. My legs and back had seized up, locked up, to such an extent that I could not move. Yet there was no pain. But I could not command them to move at all, such that I feared that I was having a sudden revelation of a critical and life-altering neurological problem. Yet there was great calm about me, as well. And my first thoughts were of whom I might call. I do not say that I could not walk, at least at that moment, from some unwillingness to bear the pain of my affliction. I simply could not walk or stand for a time even if I had wanted to. Again, there was no pain. And that fact, doubled with the condition that my legs were as removed from me as if they were nothing but large hairs dangling down from my torso, left me calmly considering certain extremes.

I thought someone might see me sitting on this corner lawn.

Occasional cars, pedestrians, children on bicycles, dogs, were not uncommon on my route. But for a ten-minute interval, a strange, motionless picture was before me—both presented by myself in a shocking, mechanical way, and by the surroundings. Only the birds still seemed to command any motion. There was no wind.

Thus I truly began to contemplate crawling to the doorstep of the house behind me, thinking that I might ask anyone that might be there if they would call Fred and Rita for me—and if they could not be reached, then the cafeteria. Perhaps one of my companions of okra and sweet tea was at dinner early and could rescue me by car. Then I realized that any sensible citizen that I found inside that house would most likely ignore any of my elaborate rescue plans and call directly for an ambulance. Again, I thought for a moment that I had somehow run myself out of walking and even being able to stand—that a deep neurological trigger of defect had been pulled. Perhaps all that bouncing up and down was something that people in my family line could not take, and that I was simply the unfortunate one to discover it for the first time.

After quite an interval passed, I decided to see if I could roll over onto my stomach and crawl a bit. To my relief, when I assumed this position I found that I could move my legs enough to crawl. And then I felt some abatement of my frozen state—or some latent command from within, rather, that I could command myself again as a biped if I made a cautious and slow attempt at standing. Using a birdbath as a prop, I slowly ascended to my humanoid stance once more and tested my legs like an infant. I even muttered a few words out loud—as much in astonishment and relief as in yet another manner that resembled a self-testing baby.

Then I tried my first step. It was unsteady, but I found that as I walked more and more, and very slowly, that I seemed to be able to walk myself out of my brief paralysis. I resolved to walk the rest of the way home and to say nothing of my little incident to anyone—especially to my adoptive family at the cafeteria. I resolved then, too, that I should get a few books on running from the library or from a bookstore, so as to see how much running one should really be doing.

But not only was I pleased to be on my feet as a general human being once more—my fears of neurological disorders forgotten as quickly as they had surfaced, my malady self-diagnosed and relegated to some sort of muscular overload that demanded attention for the first time—I was even more pleased to suspect, and later, within a few days, to realize fully, that my new career as an avocational runner was not in jeopardy. Somehow I feel I passed a gauntlet with this little episode. It came—as other types of intimidations may come to the novice runner, as well—as a threat to my enthusiasm. It was a test of the sincerity of my enthusiasm. And somehow the physical joy that I earned from even a short career in running seemed worth chasing still—even if my common career as a biped was challenged for a stunning moment! Though I did not long entertain the idea that I was really paralyzed, while I thought of such things, there was perhaps a dangerous and perverse part of me that regretted more a loss of running because I might not be able to stand than I regretted a loss of walking or mere standing from not being able to stand.

Though I was cautious for a few days after this incident, a wonderful little milestone did meet me soon, however, as I came back into town after another run and paused to take stock of myself in the reflective opacity of the abandoned hardware store's window. Though only a little over two months had passed since I had started running, I looked into that window and knew that form of flesh and bones for its old self much more once again. My face was also once more its old angular self. My legs were showing the first signs of runner's muscle, and I took pleasure in shifting my weight from side to side and watching the definition in my thighs reveal and announce itself as I posed on the old pavement.

And just then, too, I thought of how I had ceased to notice at some point that my torso did not bounce any longer when I ran. I jumped up and down vigorously in place. Only my shirt moved now. Much to my relief, my chest was no longer developing into something like a woman's. It was now a young man's again. And my stomach, it was no longer developing into something of a middle-aged or old man's stomach. It was lean once more.

Somehow this moment before the glass of the old store made my lonely, humid, melancholy, rich, yet somehow umbilical, chrysalis- and future-pointing-time in Georgia seem parenthetical. Not only had I taken a detour from which I might be free with little consequence, but it was as if another body had taken the detour for me, and now my accustomed self was returned and ready for some primal return to the drawing, calling shores of a new Northern home. I even seemed on my way—as I looked one more time at the image in the glass via the light of the setting, red-burning sun reflecting from across the street in other darkened windows—to a leanness and readiness to life that I had never known, even when a child and youth in bracing Illinois. Some greater leanness was readying me for my journey to lie below the great native hen of New England, to be a nurtured egg lying in the nest of Long Island—to hatch there and leave about me then an Island of Shells.

I showered and readied for dinner. That night, sitting incongruous but welcome amongst my sedentary but actively warm friends, I announced my plans to depart Georgia by the month's end. There was much endearing complaint and remonstrance from my good and loyal company, but fortunately for them and for me, this was abated and left behind in its most forceful forms as soon as the majority decided to visit the line again for coffee and pie.

CHAPTER 4

WARMING UP

Not long after sending the note of acceptance to my great-grandmother, I received a short reply from her, saying that she looked forward to my arrival in late August and looked forward to meeting her great-grandson and, hopefully, a new friend. I had thought to reply to this in kind and to inquire about the apartment situation in the village of Pauktaug, but I found a little enclosure with a lease and a stunning photograph of an enormous apartment with her note. These last two items had been given to her, she said, by Mr. Hare, and she reported his eagerness to meet me as of September 3 at work, and that the pictured and documented apartment was mine, without need of deposit, and with astonishingly, almost movingly, low rent, if I wanted it and if I just signed the lease and sent it back to Mr. Hare. Mr. Hare, it seemed, was not only the owner and editor of *The Pauktaug Press* but he also was the owner of two fine, historical residence buildings right on the Main Street of Pauktaug—both these buildings on the same side of the street as the office of the newspaper which was ensconced between them. My great-grandmother lived in one of these buildings, and the Hares lived in the same one as she. My apartment was to be in the building just to the north—about forty yards away, and only about a ten yards from the front door of my future site of employment.

Though it puzzled me that there was no direct word from Mr. Hare, I decided to suspect that he had merely given to my great-grandmother the pleasure of an excuse for corresponding with me—and the happy task of offering me the grand apartment and the ease of forgetting entirely about where I was to live. She also sent a little postcard of the village taken from an airplane, and as the prospect overall was so pretty and perfectly mythological in American rural archetype, and so pretty in its little Main Street that led to the bay and the Sound, and from there all the way across the salty prospect to Connecticut, I had no qualms about the exterior location of the apartment itself.

I mailed back my immediate acceptance of the apartment and my confirmation that I would be driving up to New York in the last days of August—sending this all to my great-grandmother— and turned to one more quiet month in Georgia and at work. About a week after sending this last mailing, I received an immediate reply from my great-grandmother—one that was as surprising as the first in its lavish simplicity and generosity. The reply was another note of welcome, a copy of another issue of *The Pauktaug Press,* and a set of keys to my apartment at #283 Main Street. I sent a little postcard back to my great-grandmother from downtown Atlanta, and that was the end of our summer correspondence.

I continued to run with the same excitement that characterized the first weeks of my new hobby, but I took to running my five- to six-mile course every other day so as to give my legs and frame a little more time to recover between each outing. I began to peruse some books and magazines on the subject, and mid-August saw the first fruits of that new study result in my first purchase of a pair of true, formal, running shoes.

I left my job in the middle of the third week of August, hand-ing in as my final effort an article—more an essay, really—on "Four Good Runs in North Georgia." I do not think the magazine used this article or ever intends to.

During the last days of that third week of August, I packed up my things—only so much as I could fit into the car for the trip. As for the rest, I sent a few boxes to my new address on Long Island, a few boxes to my parents for storage in Arizona, and I gave away the few small bits of furniture I had bought for my little Georgia apartment. And then, on the night before my departure, I went to the cafeteria one last time for dinner—and to take leave of Fred and Rita, and my other aged, rotund, yet warm companions. They all wished me well and warned me not to become too thin, too hard on myself, and too much a Yankee. I could promise them complete compliance on the first two points, but as to the latter, I could not pledge to refrain from beholding with childhood zeal the ancient implications of that old vanguard corner of the continent—and those of its people and smells and leaves and soil that still breathed of *Mayflower* austerity and mystery and autumnal darknesses.

After my last swigs of sweet tea and coffee, I left my new address with Fred and Rita (and Rita left me their address, and her recipe or process for making sweet tea written on the back of her address paper), and I said goodbye to the cafeteria. And then I took one last run amidst the Spanish Moss and lawn sprinklers—they seeming still to offer something for which to remain, as if they saw a newcomer in my reestablished thinness and called out to that part of me that could always see something new and beckoning in a place I needed to leave. But I took leave of the water tower and the town, and the young high school people who shouted unaccountable and inscrutable things to me from out of their cars as I ran by, and then I went to bed.

I left myself two days to make the drive to Long Island, and I left the last day of August and the first days of September for settling in to my new apartment so that I could be ready for work on September 3. I decided to avoid the main route of 95 up to New York, and instead I took a slower, less direct course, along the west side of the Appalachians, but I made my way up to Maryland on that first day, and stayed in a little place not far from Antietam Battlefield.

On the second day of travel I left my hotel and then the battlefield at precisely the time of day, it seemed, that allowed me to later enter New York City during the evening commute home for millions of people. But my pleasure at seeing the New York skyline again—my parents had taken me there several times when my father had business for the airline—made the crawling pace seem bearable. However, there were moments, I thought, when one could have walked or run faster than have driven in that traffic. And because my mother had never taken me out to Long Island— even during the times she went out there from our New York City trips to squeeze in a quick call on her grandmother—the rest of my journey was not only absorbed by the great sense of fun and imminence that accompanies one's approach to a place that promises to hold the events for an unknown number of future years, but also by the fascination of the evident dissolution of complete urban development as one traveled east along the northern spine of Long Island. One was never presented with anything approximating a prospect of total wildness, or agricultural vastness, but there was a slowly unfolding touch of darkness, presented not only by the failing light of day but also by the thickening trees and the thickening spaces between the developed places.

When I left Route 25A and pulled onto the road that leads into downtown Pauktaug for the first time, the last shards of twilight were giving way, and I coasted down the Main Street toward the bay's edge along a course of preserved but now long disused trolley tracks. Though I could see where Main Street ended—it ran till it met the bay—I rather hoped that my locating of my apartment would be delayed for a moment longer, so that I could hold the spell of the story not yet started for an instant more, but my disappointment on that count was countered by my first sight of a shingle in front of a large old frame house (now business site) that boasted the offices of *The Pauktaug Press.* I looked immediately to my right then, before I reached the offices of the paper, and knew that the brick apartment building right at my side must be my great-grandmother's and the Hares' residence. Thus, when I approached an equally appealing apartment building, also of brick, and just to the north of *The Pauktaug Press* and its adjoining legal and medical offices that occupied the same site, I suspected that I was near #283 Main Street. And I was. I parked in the lot in the rear of my new home.

With the fading light I went around to the front of my building and found the stairs to my apartment. The door was at street level, in the center of the building's front, in between the entrances to two little antique stores that seemed to have a healthy hold on the ground floor business space. When I ascended to the second floor, I found that the apartment on the left—one that I suspected would have a grand, distant view of the water—had a little penciled name card tacked below its knocker, and it read *R. Shell.* I went into what was evidently my new apartment (the door was unlocked, and there was a second set of keys on the kitchen counter), and I was quite astounded by what I found. Not only could I see the length of Main Street to the bay out my north windows, but I could look directly down to Main and across to the harbor via my west windows—and out to the near, rolling hills and woods from the east side of my apartment. And the apartment itself was better than anything I could have longed for. It had rich, newly refinished hardwood floors, new appliances, and a sense of cleanness amidst the attractiveness of a long, long established structure. And there were even some basic furnishings that I had no trouble imagining as a permanent part of my collection—a serviceable table and chairs for the kitchen, some other basic chairs and a surprising but appealing old bench (like one from a park) in the living room, and a few more little tables in the two bedrooms.

I spent the next few hours leisurely carrying my carload of things into the apartment. When the hour was somewhere between ten and eleven I was done with my carting, and I sat on my little bench for a time and pondered what I should do next. Remarkably, though I had been driving since late morning, and then carrying my things up and down the stairs for several hours, I felt quite awake, even if I felt a little sore from all the sitting in the car and the later lifting of heavy boxes.

Had it been a little earlier in the evening, and had I been back in Georgia in my old routine, I think I would have wandered down to the cafeteria under such circumstances, even if I had already been there for dinner. But since this was not an option, I made myself busy in my wakefulness by going into my boxes and getting out a deep pot, a pitcher, some glasses, and a box of tea and a container of sugar. After my supply of sweet tea was made, I put it into the refrigerator to cool. And I also found that I had to make some ice when I looked into the freezer. Thus I could not drink and brood over my sweet tea at all for quite awhile.

It was at the moment when I finished pouring water into ice cube trays that I thought of going for my first run in New York. I changed for a run, pulling out my still usual cotton tee shirt and cotton shorts. And as I jogged down the stairs to Main Street, I had the foolish suspicion that the great perspiration that was common for me in Georgia would be greatly diminished in New York, not only because of the actual greater coolness in the North, but also because of my hopes for a new place's cathartic properties. One often feels—and I have discovered this feeling when I have gone to run in other new places—that somehow one will not have old burdens on speed follow into a new running terrain. At least this is true, I think, when one is still new to running.

I decided to go south on Main Street for a time to start. I passed *The Pauktaug Press* and its silent offices, then passed my great-grandmother's building, where I could see that the lights in many of the windows were still on.

I felt disappointed quite quickly to find that my first mile was the same rather breathless and sweat-drawing warm-up that it was anywhere else. But by the time I had run out of the business area and out to the little elementary school and its surrounding field and woods, the shallow, easier breathing that I had earned as part of many months of running came into play quite suddenly after I took a deep breath and sighed under the clear, cloudless light that gave my arms a beautiful case of moonburn. I ran back onto Main Street and realized that some of my early difficulty had been because Main Street runs entirely and slightly uphill so long as one moves away from the water (it is said to have been laid on the path of a pre-Columbian fishing stream and trail). Rather than lose all of my uphill gain, and rather than run over Main's length so soon again, I took my first turn into the steep western hills that overlook the harbor, the bay, and the Sound.

Up to that point in my running career, my reading on the subject had been rather slight, but I had not failed to notice that hills and hill training were a subject all its own in the literature. Though the town in Georgia I had been living in was not far from the transitional, inclining, Piedmont terrain, the area that I could practically reach with my early mileage grasp had hardly a hill in it. There were a few little spots where one could easily discern an incline, but I only discovered hills—better described as slight grades—in my Georgia town in areas that I thought were more or less flat until I ran them and found them to be somewhat pitched. And most of these pitches are imperceptible to the driver's eye. Again, not until I ran them—and even in some cases carried a little level with me to prove to myself that I was not simply burning out for unaccountable reasons—did I realize that the world is almost never flat. It rarely is, in most places, at least.

Thus when I hit my first real, glacially-carved hill of Long Island's north shore, I was shocked. Not only had I discovered that my sweat—since I am a true sweater—fell with an intensity equal to my Georgia runs, even though Long Island's early autumnal air was already intimating a hidden coolness, but I also found out how little the new ground allowed me to bypass or to forget the usual labors of a run. And this new challenge, the first of a series of almost roller-coaster-like hills that undulated through compact, inviting, dark residential and wooded streets, added a labor unlike any I had yet encountered in running. But despite this new challenge, I resolved—with that false energy that the new running scenery still seemed to provide—to climb the first, long hill with the same pace that I had just achieved on the elementary school's cool and grassy field.

I felt all right, though greatly taxed, as I wound up the long, nearly quarter-mile ascent of that first hill. In fact, I even felt strong and not in fear of being overly winded. But then something happened—though short of the shock of my brief paralysis back in Georgia in the spring—that quite unnerved me. I felt a sudden, and at first, I thought, controllable surge of nausea. I thought that I had been swallowing in a funny way perhaps, and that combined with my deep breathing had created a sort of purgative effect. So I gritted my teeth and breathed through them, and tried to regulate my entire mouth and throat and breathing with intense method for a moment, and I did not abate my pace. But then, only a few moments later, a rush of nausea, as attends the worse effects of sickness, sent me into a quick, full stop in the very center of the road, and just short of the summit of the hill. After a series of three or four very disconcerting retches, I somewhat recovered myself. Thinking that this was some sort of anomalous circumstance, I began to run again as soon as the first wave of post-nausea, post-vomiting relief came over me. But the relief I felt was gradual, and hardly the overwhelming and consummated sense of permanency that comes over one when they have finished vomiting during a real sickness, such as in a case of food poisoning. Thus I started running again with trepidation, unsure of what would happen if I resumed my same, intense pace. But I did so notwithstanding my fears, and within moments the feeling of nausea returned. Thus for the first time since my peculiar, transient, crippling episode in Georgia, I had to pause during a run for some time—though not as long as in the Georgia case. I walked for a bit and then resumed a slow jog, secure in the suspicion that there were aspects of conditioning that I had yet to begin to acquire. I followed the course of hills along a single road (and some of its tributaries, always working back to the original road after a short detour) past an increasingly appealing prospect of dark wooded areas and recessed houses. On my right for quite some time was the Pauktaug Rural Cemetery, which seemed to boast a peak along one of its little paths that promised a view of the Sound, but as I was still on a series of hills unlike any I had yet run in my athletic career, even such a new and promising vantage seemed something I could save for my next run. After I reached an area that was between two and three miles west of the town, I descended a steep hill, which was an enormous challenge in itself (for it was difficult to hold one's self back during the descent). This descent turned me around and took me to a beautiful road that appeared to run near the water's edge, and was level all the way back into Pauktaug. So it seemed not only an aesthetic discovery to me, but also a relief if it indeed bypassed the hills where I had just discovered my new limitations and their truly sickening consequences.

As I cruised east again toward the village, I encountered a sign that announced the village's outer limits and felt relieved on that account, so I began to examine the seemingly consistent way in which the winding, curved, but still level road had been developed for housing in the early centuries of New York's settlement. Along my left, on the water side of the road, and below me, at the water's level proper—so that the second story windows were often parallel with the level of my knees, was ancient house after ancient house, spaced an acre apart, at most. Their many gabled roofs and wrap-around porches and widow's watches peered and spied from behind equally ancient looking maples and oaks that yielded to views of the water.

It was when I turned away from another consideration of the houses on my left during my continually unfolding view of the road that led back to the village, that suddenly, though I could not say why, the course I was running looked very familiar to me. A series of small, steep roads to my right—intersecting most likely with the route that I had taken away from town—ran perpendicularly to the course I took back into the village, and each looked inviting and tree-covered and dark. But each was also extremely steep, and I was done with new hill climbing and exploration for the first day. But after I had passed about four of these little side streets, and was halfway—about fifty yards—to the next one, a sight that had not presented itself since my very first run back in April in Georgia came along. It may seem odd, but not since that first run in the South—when I saw a fellow blaze past me as I rested on the steps of the school building—had I seen another runner during one of my runs. In fact, I rather had come to believe—save for this other man whom I never saw again—that I might be the only person who ran in my Georgia town. There had been occasional pairs of middle-aged women out for fast exercise walks, but never had I seen another runner. I did see high school students on their track doing workouts, but never a single other person on the road.

But now, in New York, on my very first night, I was encountering another runner on a run. At first all I saw was a quick figure descend the precipitous hill with great bounding steps, as if this runner were rolling with the hill and not trying to hold back—and this figure made a quick turn in the darkness onto my route and in the same direction that I followed, and then vanished around a slight bend in the distance.

It had long been a latent desire of mine to encounter another runner under just such a circumstance. Though, again, I was feeling rather tired on this night, I could not resist the desire to test myself for the first time. At this point I should confess that having nearly four months of running behind me, I was beginning to feel that I must be a bit exceptional. I was religious in my regularity of runs, and after enough time had passed since my transient crippling incident, I went on increasingly longer runs, and runs that I thought were of increasing intensity—even though my times were remarkably similar for each outing. I felt that such discipline must be rare, and so—even without other information or examples against which to test it—I thought my new skill must be rather high. In other words, I thought I must be rather fast.

So, again, despite my fatigue and my discovery of my new limitations on hills, I began to press myself at this moment to see if I might breeze past this runner who had just come into my sights. I accelerated to a rather extreme pace, I felt, but not one that I felt I could not hold for a time—for to accomplish not only my test, but also a gesture of vanity, I would not only need to catch this person, but also to pass them with little evident effort, and to leave them behind until they were altogether out of sight.

When I approached the little curve behind which the figure had vanished, I continued with power, and with sureness that the other runner would be in sight and close if the road were straight again around this little bend. But even before I rounded this little curve, I noticed that my new pace not only reminded me of the feelings in my gut and mouth connected with my retching episode, but I was beginning to feel winded in an altogether new fashion. I was breathing deeply and with an unsatisfying intensity, and my deep breaths made the air have my mouth produce an almost ammonia-like bitterness with each dry gasp. And yet my mouth was moist, too, in the forbidding way that had preceded my last bout of nausea.

Yet I pressed on, carried at this point by my curiosity to see the other running figure appear when I rounded the bend. Rounding the little curve did bring a straight, long stretch of road into view, and it did bring the other runner into my sight, but the figure was only hazily visible in the far distance, already past the halfway point of this straight stretch before it rounded another little curve—this time a curve in another direction. I was not sure how this figure could seem to be even farther ahead of me than when I had first seen it, especially considering I had increased my pace to such an extent that I was again toying with a test of thresholds.

But I found it in me to increase my speed even a little more. And just after I did this, the figure passed under a street lamp, and I could see it well for the first time. Before it had passed under this light, a strange effect had seemed to aid the darkness in obscuring the details of this figure. From afar, the waist and upper legs and the upper back seemed to be eclipsed, part of the darkness, and so did the head. Thus I had a glimpse of what appeared to be only a runner's lower back and legs—somewhat shiny from sweat and glimpses of light from the distant, hidden houses. And the shoes also shone, but only from a single little reflector at the back of each heel, so that it looked like the feet, at a distance, were merely leaping straight up and down with each step, rather than striding forward. But when this figure came into the light of the street lamp, it became a definite, striking *she.*

The eclipsed portions of her body were clearly discernible, then. She was wearing form-fitting tights that covered her from perhaps just below her navel to just above her knee, and these were of a matte black color, matching the surrounding night. And she had an equally black top—or a severely truncated sports top for women, I should call it—tightly stretched around her shoulders and under her arms along her tense back, leaving her spine and upper waist exposed. And her brown hair was a deep, deep, shiny black in the night, like deep-smoked stained glass somehow given flexibility, like black pearl ground and liquefied and spun into fibers of cola. Though over the years I had rarely seen any woman with long hair run without pulling her hair back into a pony tail or holding it in place with a cap, this striking young woman let her straight, somewhat-below-shoulder-length hair, dangle loose and free. She seemed like a running, enlivened statue of the village's standard of mythological beauty, and it seemed I had landed in a secret civilization that had abandoned statuary for representative figures in the flesh—and they were somehow called to make the entire ground of their village a sprawling pedestal. And before me, fleeing in the darkness, was the representative goddess of fleetness, she of perfect long hair, form, and legs.

I continued to run across the lovely, tree-lined, and hauntingly familiar pedestal of this road, courting deeper breathlessness and enticing a second wave of nausea, just to see if I might catch this moving statue. She left the lamplight quickly and rounded another corner and vanished, and as I finished the straight road and was underneath the lamplight myself another bout of extreme nausea overtook me. Now I had no hill to blame, only pace. I feared in this case—since I was very near an interesting old house at this point which boasted several circa signs and a plaque about its heritage as a sea captain's home—that I would be heard in my dry convulsions. But, mercifully, I had no evident audience for my second introduction to my running threshold.

After the nausea passed—this was after twenty to thirty seconds of standing completely still—I began to jog very slowly, and soon I was at my accustomed pace once more. But I had given up that night on the intense pace with which I had hoped to overtake the runaway sculpture on its civic rounds of inspiration.

Thus it was with considerable surprise, when I rounded the next bend and found myself on another straightaway—where I found a *Welcome to the Incorporated Village of Pauktaug, Est. 1658* sign, large and wooden and well-painted on my right, followed by an old iron historic sign considerably in the distance, both of these found along an ancient fence that met the rolling north slope of the cemetery (I had run along the south boundary and entrance on my way out of town)—I saw the living statue with a perfect tan, kneeling about midway along the length of this straightaway. She was about midway, as well, between the two aforementioned signs. She was off of the road at this point, kneeling down to her shoes, and tying one set of laces with a somewhat vindictive speed.

I was not sure if she had been aware that I had been behind her, but considering the time of night and the isolation of her circumstances, I began to suspect that she had not known that anyone was behind her since she seemed totally at ease and off of her guard as she tied her laces. She kept her back to my distant approach, which made me nearly sure that she felt she was altogether alone. But then, again, even though I was new to Pauktaug—only there for a matter of hours—the village and its surroundings already seemed to me a sort of anachronistic bastion of safety, and perhaps it would take more than the approach of a strange fellow runner to put a lovely young woman on her guard along the quiet streets by the Sound. Only some catastrophic disaster seemed like it would be enough to unsettle this sprinting Venus from her graceful pause— and that disaster needed to be something much more than even a giant storm or other transient disturbance that would ultimately pass and leave the Earth still more or less as it had been before. It seemed that it would require something much more considerable to rattle this Venus from her postures.

She was sure she was alone. Thus, when I came within the ten- to fifteen-yard range of her, I purposely made contact with some gravel and kicked several large pebbles into motion so as to make a bit of noise. Her head moved from side to side, and she rose to check the darkness in front of her before she turned about to survey the area behind. And when she turned around, in the light of yet another lamppost, I saw her front and features quite clearly for the first time. No longer did her scant black clothes meld with the darkness. The full details of her front and full body were clear and earthly then. Her eyes were as dark as her hair, and she had dark brown lashes and brows that were also a complement to the stretched dark fibers of her running attire. And as these details of face were small, tight, little features (miniature coverings on their own account), they seemed to function in tandem with the tight black clothing that covered her chest and waist—that is to say, they seemed to hint at some key aspect of magnetic and crucial femininity. If her small and tight clothes covered her keystone claims to fair sex magnetism and luxuriance, then her dark eyes seemed to hug and tauntingly conceal, with an equal pretense, a womanly curve and devastation of heart. And her lashes and brows seemed like miniskirts to the mind—only pretending to conceal all the intense expectations and standards that such an accompanying body might demand. And this demand of the hourglass-shaped mind seemed to place its justifications in the body on which it rode and in which it resided, as a beautiful princess might refer her wildest whims to the power of her throne.

But this is not to say that I thought her a shallow beauty with this first sighting. I only mean to say that she possessed a command of presentation with her body, coupled with the fact that she was using it to full force during my first glimpse of her, that would seem to make the use of her mind almost a last resort in any common circumstance. Hers seemed almost like a speaking body, and I wonder what droves of small talk she could skip because of the voluble sway of her figure and the seemingly ever-bantering curves of her outermost and innermost physical forms.

As she turned to see what was behind her, she also rose, and in her rising suggested a thousand images I have seen of classical statuary. She summarized—as she rose and turned and wrung her sinews and skin about and twisted to face another direction—innumerable studies of discus and javelin throwers ascending to their full extensions of form, innumerable studies that depict the rising of figures struck down yet re-ascending, they sure even during their brief moment on the ground that their elasticity and indefatigable power could include that grounded time as part of their projections of grace.

As I came in range of voice, I noticed one last physical detail of her form that ranged across her entire body. She seemed to be acutely aware somehow of just how much vigorous and constant attention to physical perfection her body could bear without losing that ever-so-thin but necessary and flattering layer of soft baby fat that preserves a fatal feminine attractiveness on the woman athlete. She had a perfect layer of this womanly internal velvet all about her body, such that one felt if he were allowed to touch her with his finger on any part of her surface, the resistance and give would be uniform, firm, yet soft all about her perfect shape. And this applied, as well, to her face. Though her aquiline facial features were flawless and finely carved and distinct, neither was there too little flesh, too little softness beneath that surface. Thus a grace of impact seemed promised by her cheeks, her lips, even her forehead, if the premium of a kiss were granted.

And then I looked to her hair one last time, and in the closeness of the light of night and the light of the lamp, it looked a wild summary of her slight bodily coverings—a summary that said these black clothes could be shredded and eschewed if need be, not tossed aside entirely as if by some precipitous disrobing lover, but again, shredded with wild care like secret documents that needed greater concealment than even the substantive secrets they contained. Or perhaps the hair concealed something feminine behind itself, as well. But in the night light I could only imagine night air and darkness was hidden at the nape of her neck, and perhaps a latent bit of sweat and runner's dew where her collarbone rode in secret below the bounce of her brown hair (coal-black in the night).

And I noticed, too, just before I called out good evening to her, that a slight betrayal of her feminine softness was visible as she flexed herself around and up to face me. Then one could see a slight touch of over-development in her stomach, and as she twisted herself a bit and perhaps tightened involuntarily at the sudden approach of a stranger, her stomach muscles bristled in a soldierly pair of columns up to her first rib, but then vanished below the under-velvet beneath her skin when she was fully erect.

To my surprise when I hailed and passed her, she answered my call not so much with caution or surprise at the sudden sight of an unknown running male approaching her from behind, but with what seemed a sense of inconvenience. For all her fitness, blaring youth and conditioning, it seemed to fatigue her, more than any-thing else, to have to say hello when she did not expect to. Of course, I did not know this woman at all, but such seemed the case since she did not appear to be even slightly out of breath. Or per-haps it was caution after all, for when I thought to turn about and to pretend that I was not altogether sure of the way back into town, I saw only a last glimpse of her legs running up along one of the steep drives of the cemetery hill. Though I do not think I pre-sented that much alarm or threat to her, I do suspect that she took something of a shortcut via this turn so as not to catch up with and pass me. However, I would hardly think that passing through a cemetery of any kind would present much comfort to anyone that already felt ill at ease. But perhaps she had already taken stock of how spent I appeared as a runner at that point, and she was sure that I could never take after her on such a hill, and that the eerie darkness of the cemetery slope was worth the evasion it would surely provide.

Thus, after this remarkable moving statue vanished up the hill, I felt free to slacken my pace even more than I had done after my last fit of nausea, and then I allowed myself to pause altogether before the large, iron Town of Huntington historical sign. It read:

> *This through road, once a dead end access to the former center of Pauktaug's burial ground in the seventeenth-century, also passes the site of the "Sunken Cemetery." To the south the main cemetery remains. Just north of this marker the Pauktaug Cemetery grounds once extended well into the area that is now occupied by a part of Pauktaug Harbor. On the slope and beach below, remnant tombstones of sea-consumed graves can still be seen—standing as a reminder of the days when the shifting shorefront gave residents suspicions that no one buried in the "Sunken Cemtery" could bear to stay in their grave. Skeletal remains have emerged from the sand as late as 1962.*

After I read this, I looked up the slope to the present, large, and secure part of the cemetery—into which the Venus had vanished—and then I jogged over to the north side of the road and looked down onto the beach. There, indeed, where the sand yielded to the first traces of topsoil and root systems, in the dark shadows of ancient maples, sat two completely illegible but evidently funereal slabs of stone, resting upright against the little slope that climbed to the road on which I stood. And a little beyond them, closer to the water and scattered in several places along the beach, were several old, broken stones that were surrounded by neat, little wrought-iron fences to protect them from extreme high tides. There were dune grasses growing at their bases, and there was a mixture of topsoil in with the sand, which made their immersion in water seem like a rare occurrence. But, remarkably, on several of the stones, and even at the very tops of the monuments and their surrounding gates, were barnacles and traces of dried seaweed. In the midst of one old tombstone site—which, to my amazement, still bore some legible letters near its base and top—a pair of horseshoe crabs meandered about at the pace of a primitive yet effective jog. They floated, rather, over the ground, seemingly, much like the motion of hoop-skirted women from the nineteenth-century. I had never seen a horseshoe crab before.

I walked down a neat set of steps to the beach, and I rested on the sand for a moment and looked across the harbor and bay and across to the Sound and then to the quiet lights of the Connecticut cities. And looking out to the junction of the bay and harbor, I was sure I could see what appeared to be a long, flat, open fishing boat, piled with square traps of some sort. But it was hard to tell if the engine sound I tried to match to it was really the boat's or merely a car that motored by in closer but still unseen range— somewhere behind me, casting off untraceable acoustic shadows into the steep hills and dark night. But soon I started to feel rather cold, and when I rose up from my kneeling examination of the graves and the crabs, I felt rather stiff and spent. But I jogged back to the road—pausing only one moment more to listen to the enormous choirs of crickets (which creaked like a million digital watches whose beeps are feeble and warbled because of low batteries), and to listen to the scream of hundreds of little frogs that seemed to cheer as if for a foot race for their kind that I could not see in the darkness but was sure was there all the same. And soon I found myself, after a little jogging through a last stretch of dark, tree-lined street, at an intersection with Main Street once more. There I learned that the last street on which I had been running was called Sunken Cemetery Road. Rather than leap right onto Main and go directly home, and despite my fatigue, I decided to jog north along Main Street's western parallel road, Harbor Road, which also intersected with Cemetery Road. Thus I took one last look at Pauktaug Harbor again before retiring, and I was able to have a closer look at the little flat fishing boat I had seen before while I was at the southwest end of the harbor. Now the boat was well into the harbor and making its way not to one of the docks, but to a little buoy about fifty yards out from the shore. I slowly jogged to the end of the main dock and then back to land so as to watch this mooring process.

Again, piled on the boat were several box-shaped items that I took to be traps of some kind, though I could not say precisely what kind they were. As the man who had been driving the boat—which had a fairly large outboard controlled by a wheel about a yard or two forward of the stern—moved from behind the little wheelhouse, I could see that he seemed to be dressed in a rather unusual way. In fact, he seemed to be dressed rather like a runner. I had expected some kind of rubber-based overalls to come into view as I made my examination, but instead I saw a man wearing a white tee shirt. And this shirt was not made of cotton, I could tell—despite the distance and the darkness—since it had a slight shine as do many of the shirts that are designed for running or sports, made in such a way that they do not retain water or sweat as much as cotton. And his shorts had the distinctive cut of shorts used in running. They were blue and also had the synthetic shine of the shirt. And, again, their shape made it sure that they were designed for running, as they were cut rather short and had the distinctive little notches or splayed seams at the sides of the leg. His shoes, too, were certainly not the boots or work shoes of a common seaman; they—more than any other item on him—were meant for running. And they had distinctive little reflectors at the heels that shone quite distinctly when he faced away from town and let the light of the closing restaurants illuminate them.

A small, multicolored and extremely active but silent dog, rather like a boarder collie, if not one in fact, jetted about the open spaces in the boat, and seemed eager to complete some imminent phase of the journey that appeared to be waiting just in range of the buoy. The boat itself obscured my view of what excited the dog, so I paused near the dock's end and hid in the shadows of the gazebo and benches there so that I might watch for a moment longer.

After the man wrestled with some ropes and lines, I saw both beings—the biped and the quadruped—seemingly leap into the water on the far side of the boat. But there was no splash, and soon I saw them both round to the near side of the boat in a little dinghy, the dog in the foremost part of the tiny bow, the dog looking eager and laughing, and appearing rather statuesque in his own way that night—for he resembled those iconic goddesses that often lead the prow of old wooden vessels.

The man seemed to be paddling toward a large mooring float that was attached by an aluminum gangplank to the very dock where I stood, so I jogged off the dock while the man's back was still toward me (since he was rowing). The dog let out one assertive but friendly bark when I came into view from out of the dock's gazebo, and I do not know if the man turned to see me.

Soon I ran along a little side street that connected Harbor Road to Main Street, and my apartment came into view. I went upstairs into my lonely but happy new spot, feeling rather elated by my taxing, purgative, but still somehow seemingly healthy first run on Long Island. I took a shower and then readied for bed. And after I drank a great quantity of water, I allowed myself a glass of sweet tea—since I was rather sure that my vigorous day would outweigh any wakeful qualities that one glass of sweet tea might inject into my mind and body.

I had discovered that there was a new, fine, single bed in the north bedroom, and I made that with the sheets I had and found them a good fit. I pushed the bed to the side of the window, where one could look down to the short one-way street that accessed the east parallel road to Main. But I looked out to the left and to Main Street, and out beyond to the water.

As I sat on my bed and sipped at my sweet tea, I thought about my soaked running clothes that lay in a twisted heap in my hamper. Though I had long pledged to keep to a certain rough looking, masculine style for my running clothes, I had then my first serious doubts about my trusted old gray tee shirts and sets of shorts—they all made of cotton. Somehow, combined with the images in all the books and magazines I had been reading of late, the sight, albeit brief, of possibly two more runners that night dressed in the appropriate apparel of the modern runner made me feel sort of foolish for sticking to my old habits. I had long felt that the often tight, often shiny, often sparse look of running apparel had a certain androgynous, if not effeminate, quality to it, and I had also felt that giving in to the implication that running had its own set of necessary equipment compromised the basic initial principle that running was a sport that required virtually no equipment whatsoever. There were even people who ran—even in the paved Western world—barefoot, though I felt *that* gesture to be as much an affectation of unnecessary simplicity as I had thought the use of technically specific running clothes was over-precious and rather offensive, as well.

But somehow, seeing the statuesque woman runner, and then the fisherman—he also, it seemed, a runner, in strange transit— made me feel that even this new, cooler place on the globe would prove that certain universals apply (that it was most likely easier to run in apparel that did not retain every drop of sweat, as did cotton). But as my second wave of perspiration cooled—the post-shower wave—I thought no more of this, and thought that perhaps the imminent autumn and winter would make me dismiss this new consideration. I took a last swig of my tea, put the glass on the windowsill, brushed my teeth, and then climbed into bed in the early, early hours of the dark morning.

As I lay looking out the window and allowing a welcome sleep to creep over my entire self, a rapid and suddenly manifest flash of white at Main Street's north end made me sit up and look with care despite my fatigue.

I could not say for sure—though I watched the figure run the full course of Main till he passed out of my sight—but the figure looked like the same man I had seen getting off of the fishing boat with his dog about forty-five minutes before. I could only confirm that the man had a similar shape and white top and blue shorts. It was hard to see anything too clearly because of the darkness of the sky and the mottling effects from the lights of the different store-fronts, which obscured the details of the man from my plain sight. But I could say this—he advanced south along Main, which I had already determined was slightly uphill, at an incredible runner's pace. He proceeded at a pace that would have been a sprint for me, I think, had I been near him, yet his body looked taxed by nothing more than a cruising ease. There was no dog with him. So it was hard to say if it was the same man on that account.

But what was strange, again, was the impression of speed he gave. I have observed above that he seemed to cruise along at what would be a sprint for an average athlete. Yet when he came very close to my building, and I could see clearly the objects that passed in his line of sight—so that I could imagine what the passing appearance of those objects must have looked like to his eye (only from having used and studied such objects myself for gauging rate of speed: parking meters, parked cars, regularly distanced cracks in the sidewalk)—I had a sense that there was something almost preternatural about his speed. Somehow, not only did he seem to pass with an unnatural rate once he was in range of objects that would give my night-confused eyes a clear sense of his pace, but I had a brief moment, again from imagining what the passing world must have looked like to him, when I was sure the objects in his own view must be almost blurred together, almost fused. But his pace seemed within the possible. It was remarkable, at the miraculous edge of human potential, I thought.

I rose and looked out my living room window to see if I could see him proceeding south along Main Street. But he had vanished altogether by the time I reached there. I resolved that it merely had been a runner, one with magnificent form, sprinting at the end of a run, and that he had vanished into a doorway of an apartment very close to mine, perhaps. I even listened at my own door for sounds in the hallway. But there was nothing.

I went to bed again and slept soundly for a time. Then came a rather fitful interval of half-dreaming, half-waking. I dreamed that I was running (my first such dream), and that I was terribly thirsty, but that I refused to stop at various water sources when the opportunities arose. Somehow, though I had never yet concentrated on this aspect of running very much in my then short career, I was concerned, preoccupied, even a little obsessed (though I had no fear that I could not accomplish my goal) with the notion of shaving a specific amount of time from off my run on a certain course. In the dream, men and women on the course would approach me with offerings of water that they were sure I needed, and which I was sure more and more that I would need so as to sustain my health and pace. But they backed off, with the same confident spirit with which I evaded them.

But then in the dream I felt that I would become ill, as I had on my run that very night in reality, if I sustained my pace with the same intensity for too long. I thought suddenly that what I needed was one, just one drink of water. But when I looked about at what the water stop personnel were offering me—and strangely, they were running beside me with their cups, they not in any way straining to keep up, yet it was still I who was thought of as the runner with a point to prove somehow for mankind—in the water cups was sea water and in some cases soil and sand. I decided to break away from the pack of water pursuers with no potable water, but within seconds of sustaining my new pace, my pace of escape, I awoke and found myself almost nauseous and indeed thirsty to a great degree.

I found the glass of sweet tea still sitting on my sill, and I finished off the now iceless, watery, but still cold mixture, and that seemed enough to allow me to crawl back into bed with comfort. I looked at my clock, and it read that the hour was just short of four in the morning. As I allowed sleep to happily return, and my dream about to become one of those dreams that is lost forever if it is not consciously reviewed with immediacy, through the window I saw the same running figure come into view again that I had seen quite some time—even hours—before. He ran through the close area of reference once more with the same astonishing pace—the parking meters and quiet cars a sort of blurred mixture almost in his sight, I was sure. And then he continued to race north and down the gradual slope of Main Street toward the bay. Soon he vanished around the corner from where he had originally appeared.

The greater lateness or earliness of the hour gave a sense of supernatural overtone to this view I had of the runner, and as I leaned toward the window to look down the street one last time, my glass fell from the sill and rolled under my bed without breaking. I must have been only half awake even then, for I did nothing about the glass, and when I looked about me seemingly a second later, the full sunlight of seven-thirty in the morning gleamed in my room. My first thought was of my continued thirst, and then I thought of my belabored running dreams, and then what I thought must be the dream's extension into what I had thought was a period of wakefulness—the times of the two sightings of the astonishing runner of the night.

But when I looked under my bed, there was the empty glass that had held the sweet tea, lying clean and clear and empty next to one of the legs of the bed—lying there with all the clarity, abandon, and civil incongruity that accompanies a paper cup that is thrown aside by a road runner who has just visited a water stop in a race.

CHAPTER 5

ACROSS THE STARTING LINE

I continued my unpacking at a leisurely pace on my second morning in Pauktaug, and during the late morning I went out for my first trip to the grocery store and to call the phone company so as to have my line connected. After returning home I fiddled about a bit more, had my lunch, and then thought that it was time for me to go about announcing my presence. Though it was Friday, and my starting date was Monday, September 3, I felt obliged to at least let my great-grandmother know I was there. And because of the increasing signs of the largesse and generosity of the rather mysterious Mr. Lawrence Hare, I felt compelled to seek him out, as well, before my starting day at work—so as to thank him not only for the job at *The Pauktaug Press* but for making so many arrangements for me as to my living circumstances. I was still quite flabbergasted by the quality of the apartment he had more or less left to me with all the arrangements made. I reasoned that even if he was accustomed to business transactions on such a level, such that any premature or excessive expression of gratitude from me for such a gesture would seem unnecessary to him, I simply had to tell him how out of the ordinary such a thing was for me, and that such a gesture gave a fairy-tale ease to my first hours in New York. He had made things easier and more comfortable for me than my own father had ever been able to do in similar circumstances.

I did think it curious, however, that for all the obvious trouble that had been taken to make my arrival a rather easy one, there was no obvious and final personal touch left behind. There was no note—save for the effort taken to put my name onto the makeshift card above my front door's knocker (and that appeared to be in the hand of a young woman)—and no other sign that I was even supposed to be where I was.

There was a hospital-like cleanness to the apartment, despite the building's age. The renovations and the apartment's fresh paint and refinished hardwood floors were so extreme in their perfection that there was something, at times, a little alien to the scene. The interior was not of such a radical modern style—save in the precision and antiseptic perfection of its rendering—that it did not match the stylistic impression of the Long Island village and old hardwood trees that I could see out of my windows. But, again, there was something alien in its perfection. It looked as if someone who had all the requisite skills for the workmanship I was examining had done the work all on his own for his own sake, so that he would never have to live in sight of some lazy, careless moment from the past. Or, at least, it seemed that the work had been overseen by someone who had all the skills that each separate worker had possessed in order to complete the task of remodeling the apartment—and that he had imbued them with the same sense of standard or urgency or necessity that he felt himself, yet did so somehow without offending, irritating or alienating them. But as I could tell that all the work was truly brand new and that no one had lived in the remodeled apartment before me, I could not imagine what had driven this level of labor.

Anyone who has done the kind of carpentry, electrical, or

painting work I describe will suspect the kind of situation to which I refer. No matter where I looked, I could not find evidence of modern carelessness. There was an eternal sense of workmanship. I could not find a wall socket that was slightly crooked in its placement, not a single bit of evident carelessness in the carpentry, not a run in the paint (anywhere), and not a single trace of the labor it had taken to clean up after the jobs.

And the eternal sense of workmanship had been accomplished with modern materials. Only poor and careless living would bring discredit to the almost Hellenistic or Roman care that had been taken to prepare this apartment. Stone had not been used, but the rooms had the same classical sense of permanence and investment that stone from antiquity would imply. And, again, only my carelessness could topple this figurative stonework—such that any carelessness that would cause undue wear on such work would be akin to a vandal sacking.

I continued to explore the apartment in the early afternoon when it suddenly occurred to me what the atmosphere of the apartment suggested. It had the perfection and cleanness that one imagined was proposed by the idea of aesthetically experimental and pleasing hospitals. It was like an ultimate birthing- or maternity-room might be in the future—somehow clean and necessarily metallic in places, yet also dominated by wood and natural light and vistas of a welcoming Earth.

This strange feeling that my apartment had somehow been given a supreme effort of extra preparation disturbed me a bit. Of course I was pleased that my apartment was so finished, perfect, and attractive, but something about the fact that an almost unnatural standard of perfection had been achieved made me feel ill at ease. It is curious that finding an example of workmanship that most would only praise would bother me, but it did. Who would say that the work that went into their new apartment—and a new apartment, I should observe again, that I was allowed to have at less than the average rent than what is usually charged for less than average efficiencies—was too good? I would not. But I would say that there was some reason other than mere pride in workmanship that had produced this perfect apartment for me. I have no objection to largesse and generosity, but when it comes in too great a form when it is not needed, and when it comes in the form of a monument to some effort or cause to which I am not privy—yet I the inheritor of the monument—I may say that I feel naturally on my guard. The apartment seemed suddenly to bode of expectations for me of which I was not aware. And it seemed as if I were being given some special place of comfort for some mysterious effort I was supposed to ultimately make yet could not yet suspect.

But I put these thoughts aside for a time, and ventured out onto Main Street, where I marveled at the busyness of the village—especially in comparison with the little Georgia town I had just left. Young mothers with baby joggers abounded, and there was a crowd even at my building's front door, where people thronged to look into the two antique stores that occupied the ground floor.

After a brief unquiet interval of further exploration, I plucked up my courage for an introduction, and went toward the enormous, old, subdivided house that held, among other offices, the offices of *The Pauktaug Press*. The house still maintained a front yard and hedges despite its having long been converted for office space. In fact, I remarked to myself that those who worked on the lower floor of #281 Main Street probably found the environment, or at least the outside approach to their working environment, far more traditional in a rural American domestic sense than the apartments or small newer houses they may have occupied outside of the village. There was a pleasant backwardness in this, and yet there must have been something disappointing in such a thing, as well, for some.

I rather felt that I should knock at the front door when I reached it, even though it was clear the original front hall, parlor, stairway, and upper hall had all been relegated to a common area for free passage from one business to another. On the ground floor was a dental practice that took up the entire area, so I followed a sign in the vestibule that directed me to both the offices of *The Pauktaug Press* and *Charles Pocket, Esq. Attorney at Law*. I took a deep breath and then jogged up the stairs that followed the north wall of the house. On the second floor, unlike the ground floor which had been reconfigured (save for the preservation of the parlor, common area), a long hallway that ran perpendicular to the course of the stairs had been retained, and thus I concluded that the two second story business offices were merely the conjoining of contiguous former bedrooms on their respective sides of the hall. On my right, as I went down this hall, and on the street side of the house, the first door I came to was that of this Charles Pocket, Esq. His door was like the rest of the remodeled house's interior—a clean, modern, expensive replacement for its historical predecessor, but hardly a disappointment because it was not an original. In fact, the workmanship in this door outweighed anything that probably originally stood in its place—especially considering the doorway was probably only a bedroom or closet door at one time. It was even more imposing than the true front doorway to the entire house. This law office door was of a great, heavy, deeply stained wood, and elaborately carved into the face of the door, from the knob's height down, was a study of a richly attired Victorian young woman in an enormous hoop skirt. Above this image was a moderate sized window of visually tasteful and attractive smoke-gray stained glass—but gaudy and somehow tactless in the degree to which it finally made the entire door an extreme example of something foolishly expensive and excessively customized. Set into the panes were the scales of justice.

The lights were on in the office, and the front window blinds appeared to be up and letting the competing light of vibrant Main

Street give the interior lamp bulbs a feeble aspect. Discreetly slowing down as I passed this doorway, I could make out, through the smoky glass, a secretary at the front desk opening letters.

I moved farther on then, until I reached the office of *The Pauktaug Press,* but though it was a Friday and in the middle of the early afternoon, the door was locked and its lights were out. The door for this office was a sturdy, dark, and heavy one, but nothing like the affair for Charles Pocket, Esq. It had a window of clear glass with simple black lettering that read, *THE PAUKTAUG PRESS.* And below that was written, *THOMAS CRABBE, EDITOR.* I did not know anything of this Mr. Crabbe, but before I could think very long on this little surprise, I noticed a small, well-policed bulletin board just to the right of the door and just before the edge of a south-facing window, with a clear view of the side of the apartment building that was, I believe, my great-grandmother's and the mysterious Mr. Hare's.

Only two notices were on the board. On the top was a printed bill. It announced the Second Annual (Spring, 2002) Pauktaug 10K. It gave a little map of the course, several boasts from small local sponsors, and a general boast that the course had been officially certified for the first time. It further reported where entry forms could be found, and I noted these places, as I thought it was time that I tried a race. 10-kilometers sounded like a good distance, and I imagined that I might do rather well in the race—especially as I could train on the actual course, and also because my new enthusiasm for the sport was sure to carry me to an extremely high level by the springtime. I must confess that there was a truly silly, small, but also sincere idea deep within me that thought that I could even train to win such a race.

The second notice was handwritten. It read, *The Pauktaug Press, not issued the last week of August and the first week of January. Please leave all deliveries with offices of Charles Pocket.* With the strange pleasure that one receives from having an inevitability deferred, I started out of the old house with the sense of a social and business duty faced for the day, without the price of having to face any social and business duty.

But while my social courage was still up, I decided to face the less imposing though still somehow awkward obligation of meeting my great-grandmother for the first time. I do not know why it did not occur to me then that I might still run into this Mr. Hare in his apartment building, since he lived in the same building as my great-grandmother, but something gave me an unspoken confidence that this would not happen. Perhaps I was sure that he vacationed away from Pauktaug during the two weeks a year that the paper suspended publication. Hare's precision as to the September 3 starting date for my position had a clear motivation in my mind then, and I wondered how busy things might be when the paper started up on Monday in order to squeeze out an edition by the end of the working week.

I left the old house and jogged back into the bright light of Main Street and prepared myself for a different kind of introduction and different kind of extension of gratitude. The original gratitude I had felt for the position offered me by Hare, and for the apartment he had arranged for me, had been tempered by what I felt to be something odd in the extremity of his efforts in terms of the apartment. Somehow I felt free to be less grateful and personal because my unseen employer and housing benefactor had been overly generous and personal in a way that was strangely and obliquely offensive to me since it put me ill at ease. I can say, however, that his absence from the business that week and possibly from town made me less suspicious. At least there was no personal welcome from Hare and his wife to match the strange perfections of my new apartment and the ease of all my other arrangements.

Now I took a deep breath and prepared myself for the awkwardness of meeting someone with whom I had only corresponded, someone who knew my mother's true nature rather intimately I suspected (and this rather embarrassed me), someone who seemed to extrapolate a great deal of what I wished people to know and think of me from my writing (yet this also made me feel slightly embarrassed and shy, as well), and someone who was reputedly so elderly that I could not help but feel that awkwardness that attends the young when they need visit a relative stranger or distant relative in a hospital.

When I entered the lobby of #279 Main Street, my great-grandmother's apartment building, it was clear that the building was of a comparable age and pedigree to my own apartment's, but in the lobby of this building was a memorial to the former and original purpose of the structure. This building had been turned into residences only in the early part of the twentieth-century. But from the mid-nineteenth-century and into the early years of the twentieth—up until 1921—the building was part of the *Pauktaug Stay Works*. A plaque to this effect gave a little history of the company around which the Village of Pauktaug rose to security in the mid- to late-nineteenth-century and then fell into its fate as a New York City bedroom community in the early twentieth-century. And above this plaque was another plaque, a sort of shingle really—reputedly in the same place it had been since 1844—bearing an image of a young woman dressed in an enormous hoop skirt. This image was remarkably like the one on the office door of Charles Pocket, Attorney at Law. The hoop-skirted-woman was evidently a logo of the *Pauktaug Stay Works*, and the attorney, Pocket—as had other people in the village—had appropriated the image as a general Pauktaugian symbol, both freed from yet still somewhat attached to its original commercial associations.

Unlike my own building, there were no street level retail businesses in #279 Main. But there was, near the front of the lobby, a small office that touted *Crabbe Lobsters, Inc.* on its door. Of course its logo had a little crab in its crest, the crab piloting a small boat and fishing for a lobster crawling below the waterline. But the

Pauktaug Hoop-Skirted Woman could be seen here, as well—in this case, the *Crabbe Lobsters, Inc.* logo was depicted as a sort of large design in the woman's skirt. But overall, the door for *Crabbe Lobsters, Inc.* was more humble than Mr. Pocket's, Attorney at Law. There was one large apartment toward the back and possibly some service and storage space, but right next to the original Pauktaug Stays Girl sign was a very modern elevator, giving indication that this apartment building had been remodeled more than just the one time after its conversion from a stays/whalebone products factory in the 1920s.

I went up to the second floor, to my great-grandmother's suite in the building. I knocked hard and waited for the appropriate imagined interval of elderly transit to take place. There was no response.

Thus I had another foolishly gratifying reprieve from an inevitable duty. I attended then to the business of my telephone line, and I spent the rest of the day quietly alone—finishing the night with a run and with the purchase of the previous week's edition of *The Pauktaug Press*.

After returning to my apartment for a final time that night, I took my paper and my tea and sat on my bed and intermittently looked out the window to an evening fog. I located Hare's continuing series on lobsters and lobstering, and I recall underlining the following passage as unusual and strangely interesting to me.

"Many lobsters are said to forage from trap bait—and are caught again and again until they are of legal size and are kept. I wait to see the lobster that will evolve out of this, for the lobster that within its own lifetime becomes too big, too strong for this cycle and lives out a hermit's, a rogue's dignity. This lobster was not a content individual, to wait as part of a possibly adapting and self-protecting evolutionary chain—it stands, instead, as a proud and independent dead end. And in that singularity might be an immortality—a species that is a species via a single instance, as an individual. Thus if it relies on its acquired characteristics to achieve this grand, lonely singularity—and not some instinct, some bit of lobster mind, to avoid the trap—then is not this new lobster's body *thinking*, perhaps?"

Then I found myself very tired, but still a little thirsty. I foolishly took to my sweet tea reserve and downed a full glass as I also turned down the cover and sheets of my bed. I was tired enough that all the tea seemed to have no effect on me at first. I fell into a deep sleep in which I seemed to have no dreams. Then my sleep became fitful, and I looked up into a wakefulness and out the window to find the fog magnificently deepened. And to my astonishment—and also with a little chill from the strange coincidence—I saw what appeared to be the same runner I had seen the night before, careening up Main Street. He was in the center of the street, as there was so little traffic at that hour. Thus, since he was farther from objects that would have given me as direct an idea of his speed as I had had the previous night, and since the fog obscured the very ground upon which he paced, I could only look to his form itself and determine whether he seemed to suggest the same nearly supernatural pacing that he had the night before. And he did—and then I saw a dog appear behind him, the dog merrily giving all to pursue the runner with whom he seemed to be in company.

The runner and dog passed out of sight, and I curled back into my bed. I tried to dismiss the image as simply that of a man finishing his run, or a selected stretch of it, with a fierce pace on Main Street—that he probably let go of his intense rate just after he left my view. But even the length of Main that I saw him traverse was farther than the length over which one could support normally such an intense pace. It was not a sprint, but rather his form suggested a cruising technique—as if he had been holding something like the pace I had seen for a very long time.

I woke again perhaps an hour later. Still feeling thirsty, I took a few glasses of water and then some more sweet tea, and I positioned myself in my brief wakefulness to look out the window once more. With a sudden rush of forethought, I went into my kitchen and put my sweet tea glass into a peculiar position in the sink, and I also moved a few other items into odd places. I had never needed a future reference to check whether I had dreamed certain things in the night—such things were usually clear for me—but I did this anyway, half out of fun, and half because I really did wish to be absolutely sure I was not simply dreaming some latent, third person aspiration of my own in which I was a supernaturally speed-gifted human being.

My wakefulness, to my amazement, did indeed catch the return of the mysterious runner. He was going a bit slower on his return, and there was no sign of the dog. But there was still a speed to the runner that seemed just above the natural. I do not mean to say that he was unnatural in the usual sense—that his appearance of speed suggested some occult workings or biomechanical assistance. No, I merely wish to observe that his appearance was supernatural in the purest sense. The eye accepted what it saw as possible. But the mind knew that it had never seen an instance of such a possible display ever before. Or perhaps it was the other way around—the mind in the eye's place, that is. Again, there was a nagging feeling that this was a display of merely the supernatural in the purest sense—a display of something just above the commonly natural (something a part of the natural, of common destiny, but just not seen yet, until now). I felt programmed to accept what I saw though it astonished me.

But this night of sitting in my strange, lonely grandstand before this peculiar solitary track or road event was not yet over. I think I slept again, and then with the first light of day I awoke and watched the dawn spread over the village and the Sound. I went into the kitchen to get some juice, and I smiled to see my intact dream-test arrangement still in the sink.

I was taking my juice when I looked back down to Main Street from my front window. I could see a delivery truck and several cars parked in front of the little diner across the way.

And this diner would give me a view of several people at this only half-lonely hour of the day. Thus it was they that made the next scene have a new remarkableness and more readily confirmable reality to it—more than anything I had seen thus far from out of my windows. Two men with newspapers under their arms came out from the diner in company of the man who was the driver of the delivery truck, and they were talking intently on some subject to which each thought of something further to add before they could bring themselves to part. And then one of the men pointed up the street, to the south. I craned my neck to see what I might of what they all began to point and wave and laugh at in friendly mildness. Then the sight came into view. It was a runner, and seemingly an entirely different man than the one I had seen for two nights then, and he passed the three onlookers on Main with a friendly hail, a brief slackening of pace so as to say just a word or two, and then a quick restoration of a pace that had its own but somehow seemingly equal supernatural speed to it—a speed, a pace held by an evidently veteran long-distance runner, and the naked human eye could tell that there was something new in the power of this man, as there had been in the man I had seen in the darkness. If this second runner had passed by on a track, an indifferent eye might have said that they just saw a sprinter go by in the midst of recovering from a recent burst. But what I had seen, I knew, was yet another man holding to a pace over a long course, and at a rate that was of an intensity that seemed to be above what was known to be the human limit, and doing so with a disturbing ease.

Perhaps it was only evident to the eye if one were really looking for it, for the three onlookers, though they did wave and guffaw at the man (as some always do in good humor to suggest that a runner is crazy for being out at such an hour and killing himself with unnecessary exercise) did not seem too disturbed by what they saw. But after he passed, I know I saw one of the men look behind himself once more, and then the other two did as well, as one will do when he checks to see something that he is not sure he really saw.

I closed my window, confident then that I was not seeing things. And then I took my breakfast slowly, for I had an intimation about that Saturday, that it would be much like my Friday, my first full day in Pauktaug. I tried calling my great-grandmother several times that day. There was still no answer. And I saw no one go either in or out of the building that held *The Pauktaug Press*. Yet my Saturday night was different. I took my usual night run, then drove into Huntington Village some fifteen minutes to the west to see what girls there were to see. But I was hardly as brave as I had been in Atlanta at times, and I drove home feeling foolish and unscholarly about my preparations for my imminent work. I went to bed and slept the whole night through and did not wake up a single time.

CHAPTER 6

WITH THE PACK

I spent my Sunday continuing to set up my apartment and in making a few trips out in the car to buy things that I would need for housekeeping. In the light of late afternoon, I went for my fourth run, my first day run on Long Island. I was amazed by the leisure crowds on Main Street—by the volume of baby strollers and walkers and runners. And in the streets about the village was an astonishing array of perfectly equipped bicycle riders, each seemingly outdoing the next with the gaudiness of the color scheme for his shorts and jersey. But it was when I slowly took to climbing the hill that ran to the present entrance of the Pauktaug Rural Cemetery that a sight of true volume astonished me. I had never yet—even with the advent of my running career—been to a foot race, not even to watch one in Atlanta. And I thought it was a race that was moving in my direction when a horde of runners met me as they descended the massive hill near town that I myself was climbing with an intensely conservative pace so as not to have another bout of nausea. They all moved toward me with great speed.

I concluded that the group must be a sort of running club—

many of them had matching shirts with the Pauktaug name and the logo of the Pauktaug Girl emblazoned on the shirt's front (the same image I had seen by then in any number of places, including in statue form in the center of the narrow park along the edge of the bay). I could have asked the runners who they were, for my passing elicited a number of hails, hellos and waves, but I let them all pass in order to prove, I thought, my equal firmness—in regards to my own pace and course—as a runner.

In the late afternoon I slept for a time—thinking it my last opportunity for indolence and napping for a long while, perhaps— and then I forced myself to forgo eating dinner out for once. I had some supplies for eating and cooking by this time, and I reluctantly went through this process and tried to feel proud of myself for this exercise in self-discipline.

I went through the regular news items of the paper once more and began to have a notion that nothing too serious generally happened in Pauktaug in the way of crime or disturbance. There were articles about the schools and their budgets, the defense of a building slated for demolition on Main Street (some said it was historic; others said it was too new for such a distinction), and articles about the dismissal of the last building inspector. There were also pieces about the upcoming high school sports seasons, several columns on fishing, and several items on the harbor, bay, Sound, and environmental concerns being handled under the aegis of New York State. There were in connection with these last pieces and notices several articles about the lobster trade—but these articles seemed totally independent of the essay in the literary magazine I had read earlier. The lobster articles in the paper dealt with issues of low catches, low lobster sizes, and the possible connections of both of these concerns with water contamination from either (or both) the Connecticut or Long Island sides of the Sound.

Finally, I put the paper down for the night and had one last glass from my first pitcher of sweet tea. Then I felt compelled to take one more stroll of freedom along Main Street on my last day before work would presumably begin. I walked the length of Main and satisfied myself that no lights were on in my great-grandmother's apartment (I was beginning to be concerned about that), and then I selfishly remembered that I could not recall where the flyer (near *The Pauktaug Press'* doorway) had said that the Pauktaug 10K race forms could be found. I half-heartedly, and with a feeling that I must look a little suspicious—but there was hardly a soul about by that time (it was around ten, I think)—tried the front door of the old-house-turned-office-building. To my amazement, the door gave way and the lobby presented a lighted and open prospect that seemed to be maintained with the trust of the occupants and the town itself—almost as if it were a little public commons or forum. I jogged up the stairs so as to have a quick look at the bulletin board, and that is when, on my fourth evening on Long Island, on the night of my third full day in Pauktaug, that I noticed that the lights of *The Pauktaug Press* were on. I had no desire of announcing myself at that hour, and I felt foolish for not suspecting that such a thing might happen on this night, so I slowed to a silent walk and took a quick look at the bulletin board—just to give some legitimacy to my presence should someone be watching me, though I could not imagine that anyone could really see me in that hall. Why I had thought that my interactions in Pauktaug would remain confined to midnight and early morning sightings of two seemingly unreal male runners, and to a fleeting single vision of the fleshed banshee beauty of something like the Pauktaug Girl in modern running form, I cannot say.

I took a quick look at the poster as I heard the door open on the ground floor, and then going through only the motions of looking at the poster I found that I did not even read the announcement carefully enough so as to recall the locations it gave. And as I turned about and put myself into a silent quickstep, something just short of a jog, I found myself moving right toward a man who had apparently just finished the stairs and had stopped right at the start of the second floor hall—had stopped because he caught sight of me. I had heard no footfalls on the stairs—which made me think the person who had entered below was on his way to the first floor office—and somehow he seemed to have reached the second floor without the due time of passage that one's brain unwittingly calculates for any unseen figure's approach. He was not out of breath, and he was in perfect command of himself, as if he had been standing there resting all the time, which I knew he had not.

"Rex Shell?" he asked right away, with an affectation of caution, mixed in with a sure but moderated friendliness.

"Yes. Mr. Hare?" I asked back, still feeling a little like I should not have been where I was at that hour.

"Please, call me Lawrence. I'm glad you made it all right. We stopped by your apartment—my wife and I (and I did by myself a couple of times, too) in the middle of last week—but there wasn't anyone there. I didn't know if there was anyone home yet, so I didn't leave a note."

I did not see why anything had stopped him from leaving a note, but of course I did not mention this. I spoke right up.

"I've been in and out, getting things in order. But how can I really say that anything needed to be put in order?" I decided to test things right away about the apartment. "What can I say? What can anyone say about such an apartment? It is so perfect! And the way it is already set up, that's perfect, too."

And then I risked adding, "It's almost too perfect," with a laugh to make the phrase seem like I meant it as banter, but I was eager to see his response.

He did not really pick up on any latent malaise I wished to broadcast. That made me feel a bit better, and so did the sincere, perfunctory dismissal of the issue of the apartment and its preparations.

"Well, I'm glad it's okay," he said. "To be honest, my wife and I own both of the buildings on both sides of this building, so it was easy for us to hold it for whoever might take this job when a couple of the apartments became vacant some time ago. I had wanted to remodel some of them anyway, but I certainly was glad to make it nice for you. If it turns out to be too close to work for your tastes, just let us know, and we won't hold you to that place. It's just there if it makes things easier for you."

"Gosh, no! I don't want to move. Not at all. Again, it's perfect. Too perfect. I mean it."

He picked up on, or finally decided to acknowledge my second characterization of the apartment as *too perfect.*

"Well, again, I did want to offer you something nice for being willing to come all the way up here. But if it makes you feel self-conscious, know that plans were in the works already to do something to fix that apartment, and another one on the floor above, no matter what." This put me at greater ease still.

"And any true perfections or other touches," he added, without giving any undue, alarming weight to the word *perfections,* "you can credit to my wife, Lisa. She put a lot into that apartment herself. It gives her a lot of pleasure to do that kind of thing."

This put me *completely* at ease about the apartment. Now I seemed to have two peer friends with parental generosity in my new village, and not a mysterious sole employer who offered me an abode that seemed out of keeping with the expectations for the assistant editorship of a small paper. I felt free of any final, silly suspicions that my apartment was part of my compensation for joining some sort of small, shady front of organized crime—Mr. Hare in that case thought to be the prime agent, my great-grandmother perhaps the Queen Mother of it all. Perhaps having such foolish fears were more attributable to the fact that I did not think that anyone could possibly wish to hire me and offer me such a comfortable situation based upon the mere merits of my writing samples. But I dismissed once and for all my latent, growing fears that my great-grandmother's letters had been in a sort of code that the Pauktaug faction thought I knew to decipher, but which I did not recognize at all.

"Rex—I may call you *Rex*?" I nodded and shrugged an *of course* to this. He smiled as he continued: "We're not going to do any work tonight, but do you want to come into the old office for a bit, look around, and see where you'll be?"

After the usual questions about my trip up to New York and my first few days in Pauktaug, Lawrence Hare opened the door of the lighted and unlocked office rooms—he apparently had been in there for some time before my arrival, and had only just stepped out for a little when I chanced to enter the building.

Of course, I surveyed this man for any suggestion, though I knew the odds were against it, that he might be one of the two mysterious runners I had seen out my window thus far during my seemingly half-sleeping reveries. But this man did not suggest a runner to me. Though he appeared extremely fit, he did not have that almost distressed, thin frame that many very advanced and serious runners acquire after years of unremitting training. He was fully covered in long pants and a long-sleeved shirt, but it was clear that he did not conceal any common corpulence of torso that one might expect from a desk-ridden man of his age. He was hardened and conditioned by some sort of routine that did not hold him to one specific physical task, yet he seemed lean and even all over his upper frame despite the un-runner-like strength of his full person. (I should also remark that I had not yet learned that it is difficult to identify many runners whom one has seen run until one sees them running again. They are often quite disguised, other-wise—as when they are standing still, and in their common clothes. But I have learned to identify individuals from a distance when they are running, when no other factor would allow for iden-tification at such distance.)

Hare had gone straight to his office to retrieve a few things while I was taking in the little gallery (maps, local scenes, historic photographs) that adorned the main office room. He returned to find me looking at yet another image of the Pauktaug Girl—similar to the statue of her that I had discovered that afternoon in the park along the bay.

"Is this a rare poster?" I asked him, as he took some papers from a bin on one of the desks in the main room and prepared to go back into his office.

"Yes, it is. I don't know how rare it was in its day. But today there are only two of those that I know of. Mr. Crabbe bought that one, and the other is right across the hall, in fact, in Charles Pocket's office."

I knew the name Charles Pocket, Esq. But I did not know the name of Crabbe. I asked about this as Lawrence Hare invited me to join him in his office and to take a chair.

Lawrence Hare seated himself behind his desk and put a few papers in their places. As he prepared to speak, I could see him clearly for the first time in the bright lamplight of his office. What seemed especially remarkable to me was that his eyes—and hence, his mind and spirit—expressed sincere fatigue (but, I should remark, with all that he showed no sign of irritation or shortness with me). Yet what made this remarkable was that his body seemed to stand in direct opposition to this fatigue of the mind. One might be a bit jaded after intellectual work, say, and—and more from boredom of the mind than sincere tiredness—only feel able to take refuge then in some sort of hard physical labor or exercise. But rarely in this life have I seen anyone that expressed a true, spent look with his eyes, and thus his mind and spirit; who looked yet as if his body, however, stood as a separate entity—almost ready to take over since the mind was spent. He looked completely hale and fit for his body size, in complete and direct opposition to the fatigue his soul seemed to express. It was peculiar looking—this entire effect.

To add a comparison—I have felt instances when the body may be totally worn out (as was often the case for me by then on the morning after a run), but that if I lay perfectly still and allowed myself to forget my soreness and fatigue, I could find my mind still rested and sharp. But, again, I had never seen the sight—virtually in any human being—that Lawrence Hare presented. His body seemed all the stronger for his mind's lack of vigilance. I could only imagine what kind of powerful impression Lawrence Hare would make if he was well-rested entirely. And I wondered if his body would yield to his rested mind—since it seemed to do so well without its leader. I even wondered if his mind was not tired after having served his body, perhaps, in some way. Thus his body might be left of an evening, a sort of overseer that could outdrive its worker in its own work itself by day, and be left alone with nothing with which to divert itself save more work when the feeble employee, the mind, had given up for the night.

"Mr. Crabbe was the owner and editor of *The Pauktaug Press* from right after World War II—when he took over from his father—until his own death in 1996. He left the paper to his daughter and me. His daughter, Lisa, is my wife."

"So I guess you two met—you and your wife—after you started working here?"

"No, I knew Lisa ever since high school—and knew of her even before then. In high school I started to work in Mr. Crabbe's lobstering business. And then after college, I wasn't sure what my next step was, so I came back home to Pauktaug and went right back to work on the lobster boats. Mr. Crabbe somehow took a liking to some remarks I made after I came home from being out on the water one day, and he offered me a job working at the paper. I was already going out with Lisa then, so he was already pretty familiar with me anyway."

"But you studied journalism in college?"

"Oh, no," laughed Hare. "I was a physics major—and not a very good one either. At least my school didn't think so. But I passed and got by."

I remarked silently to myself that his eyes and mind appeared even more fatigued than earlier, and he surprised me by saying something that I was just able to make out as I myself also started to say something.

He said: "You know, I can really use you here now—"

I started to say at the same time: "Forgive me for changing the subject just for a second—"

Then there was a polite silence between us both, and we both insisted that the other proceed. My new employer won out, and I continued.

"Again, sorry to change the subject for just a second, but I've been trying to contact my great-grandmother since I arrived, and I haven't been able to."

"Oh, Nancy is in Manhattan—at her city home. I thought this kind of thing might happen. I warned her that you were coming this weekend, but she seemed convinced that September did not start until next weekend. I let it go because she's been getting a little more and more mixed up these days."

I liked that he did not pause before saying that she was mixed up—by which, of course, he meant that she had grown feeble of mind. I did not want the Hares to think that I was in any way hoping to gain ground on the intimacy of their kind and generous role as volunteer caretakers of my great-grandmother. And I was glad that he did not seem to think he should be delicate with me about my great-grandmother's condition—and did not discreetly, silently allude to any trouble she might be having, as if he were passing off a burden to me that he could only pass off for sure and certain if he kept the knock in the engine only to a whispered euphemism on his part. No, he reported things as they were, as if he were still accustomed to his role of guardian (or better said, friend) of my great-grandmother, sure that his role would continue, and sure that my appearance did not necessarily grant me any special privileges or access to her just because of my blood kinship.

"It's okay," I interrupted. "I was just concerned that she didn't answer her door or her phone this weekend. I thought she would be here when I got here."

"Well, again, she thinks she will be. I'm sure her letters to you were lucid and even striking. But somehow she forgets a lot after she leaves her desk and goes about her business. But she is still a powerful reader, writer, talker, and thinker. Just expect her to get a little mixed up when she suddenly wants to go out and see the town or the city. She's still surprisingly fit, amazingly agile. She took the train into the city herself. And she's ninety-two! She'll be back here by tomorrow."

I suddenly felt that I should thank Hare somehow on behalf of my family. He nodded to this, but it left an awkward gap between us for a moment, and I was sorry I did it. But Hare broke in again.

"I'm really glad you're here. I really don't think I can do this much longer—even with help from someone like yourself. After I read some of your recent pieces for your magazine, I thought you might be our man. I'm looking for someone to help me share the general tasks of the writing of the paper. *The Pauktaug Press* has always been more or less a one-man affair, even though I have several others in the office handling a fair share of the columns. But in 1990 or so, about two years after I joined the paper, Mr. Crabbe let me introduce the magazine, or the magazine-like element of the paper, and with his help that gained a foothold. So then there was even more work, and when he passed away the hiring of more help was the first change I made. But I've always protected the magazine—left it as much a one-man affair as the paper used to be. But I still think I'm penning a majority of the items in the regular paper. Anyway, I've been looking for someone who might finally help me with the magazine, too, someone who seems to have a similar voice that I won't have to guide or mould. And such a person would be rare."

In a moment of modesty, so as to defuse any imminent praise, I mentioned Hare's series on lobsters and lobstering, and said that I not only admired the essays, but that I admired someone willing to offer such material to the general public and willing to maintain at his own risk a forum in which to publish such material.

"Well, we do pretty well, I suppose. Thank you," he replied with a little modest embarrassment. But I noticed that his *we* could be none other than the imperial *we,* and I wondered at his use of this style of self-reference. One can use the imperial *we* if it is acknowledged and discredited with a passing smile. No such glimmer came over his face when he said it. But I should remark on the general appearance of Lawrence Hare's face. It showed no constant state of arrogance or undue confidence. Rather, beaming from a set of balanced, well-chiseled but not too aquiline features, appeared to be a rather cheerful, constant, benignly complacent, yet somehow also resigned spirit. This resignation, again, I thought might be only the fatigue that seemed to come from his mind but not his body. I could not yet say for sure, having only seen him for a few minutes. Yet there was a cheerfulness in him that seems to come only after a certain aspect of life has been given up and accepted for gone. It was as if I were meeting someone who had just reached the full state of recovery after one of life's strongest cycles of disillusion, recovery, and reconstruction had been passed through. He seemed cheerful because whatever may have been worrying him for some time on an epic scale was no longer a concern. He was cheerfully focused on something new that gave him a disquieting peace to someone like myself—someone like myself who had only known so much loss as the loss of a few bad teeth thus far in life.

Hare continued: "But, Rex, I think I knew I could give over at least part of our small little magazine—it's really a little insert, I should say—to you when I read your recent pieces that your great-grandmother showed me. You think you'd like to do some writing for the magazine as well as the paper?"

"Sure," I replied enthusiastically.

"Good. In the morning I'll delegate columns on the paper to you—and it will seem like a lot, but I think you'll have no trouble with this town—and some other tasks, and then we'll discuss what you and I might squeeze out for the magazine in the coming months. But the paper itself—this issue—goes out on Saturday morning."

Just then the phone on his desk rang, and Hare picked it up and explained to his wife, Lisa, that he was with me in the main office of the paper. Hare laughed and hung up the phone, and then he said, in a humorously peculiar way, that he could take the call in the other room, and that though I should remain where I was and relax, I could still follow him with my eyes and see what he meant about taking the call in the other room. It turned out that the Hares' apartment, in the building just next door to the south, though one floor above the level of *The Pauktaug Press,* could easily communicate window to window with the paper's office window just below it. Hare opened one of the south windows of the office and had a discreet conversation with his wife after looking back to me so as to laugh and see that I saw how close his home was to his work.

Any conversation like the one they had could hardly be discreet in content, even if it is was in volume, so I could make out that Hare, when asked, reported my safe arrival and my satisfaction with the apartment. Then Hare asked his wife to call my great-grandmother for me in Manhattan and say that I was in Pauktaug already, and that I would be there at work, most likely, when she got back into town. Then I heard a rather unusual answer, I think, to a rather usual question. Though it did not seem I could have heard correctly, it seemed that Hare said "no later than four, four-thirty" when his wife asked when he would return for the night.

During the Hares' exchange, I rose from my seat and ambled about his little office. On his north wall he had a rather extensive gallery of framed articles, pictures, and prints. One rather small one caught my attention, at first because it shared the apex of the gallery's arrangement with yet another image of the Pauktaug Girl—this latest incarnation of the Pauktaug Girl nothing unusual in the way of rendering, save for the fact that it was a clipping of an image from an old, old edition of *The Pauktaug Press,* from a time when the Pauktaug Girl seemed to have had a place on the front page as a part of the masthead of the paper. The newsprint was yellowed and brittle, but it was neatly and expensively mounted—apparently put there by Hare, for the mounting work looked recent.

But the image next to the Pauktaug Girl, sharing her place at the height of the display of many frames, was different than everything else on the wall. Not only was it evidently framed in the most expensive and secure manner, with very careful and professional mounting and means of protection and preservation for the peculiar type of artwork or memorabilia that was inside, but it seemed to be something of value in a collector's sense—though somehow I did not think that Hare had a collector's instinct. There was nothing else of its kind on the wall. There was just this sole example of what seemed to be an animation cell from an early, but highly stylized and high-budgeted cartoon. There was a little card at the bottom attesting to the authenticity and date of the cell, and an artist's signature. The signature was a ragged scrawl, as that of an old man's, and I could not make out his name. But the cell was dated July, 1941, making the old man surely rather an old man if this item had indeed been framed recently and had it been a work of the fellow whose signature appeared below the cell.

But the signed card did not say what the image was. The card was a rather formal looking affair, so it seemed to presume that the viewer should know what the image was without question.

The picture—and despite its small size one could make out a great deal of striking detail and bold coloring—was that of a strong-jawed man attired in a sort of art-deco-styled attempt at predicting clothing for what I took to be a future or alien setting. He was pictured in what looked to be a kind of laboratory, and the rather sophisticated image seemed in the midst of a tracking or panning shot—the man looking away from a table, one that seemed appropriate for a kind of science lab of imaginative purposes, and he looking toward an enormous window that overlooked a vast city that seemed pitched more on the edge of space than on the edge of the night sky. The man seemed anxious, as if in this panning shot he was marking the limits of his time.

My eye then caught a glimpse of a modern photograph of two people posed on what appeared to be one of the local beaches, when Hare returned to the office and to me.

"Taking a look around?" he smiled.

Then I committed a terrible blunder. Next to the girl in the photograph—the girl lean and taut and tan in the picture, she on the verge of explosive fitness, and wearing a two piece bathing suit—was a corpulent, dowdy, pale young man, in a terribly unflattering attire of swimming trunks. The sun made him squint and look distressed. But there was an easy familiarity about the two, and I thought that they might be cousins or siblings of Hare.

My blunder was this. I asked Hare, while pointing to the girl in the picture, "Who—is—*this*?" with such an emphasis on my evident physical interest in the girl that my belief she could only be posed with the pictured man if he were her relative seemed to come through, as well.

I did not think I risked much with this. And on the supposed terms that I risked my statement I made no error. But his response made my soul sink.

"This," he began as he tapped the image of the girl in the bathing suit, "is my wife, Lisa." Then he tapped the other image: "And this is me."

He could tell I did not know what to say. But he was all courtesy to me that evening, and he leaped in with a dismissal that put the moment at ease but did not erase any of my sense of terrible blunder.

"This is me several years ago, the way I used to look. Don't worry about it. I have people who have known me all my life walk right by me like strangers after I was well into losing weight toward the middle and end of last year."

I could not help but look at the picture again. It was indeed Hare's face if one looked closely a second time. But what really captured my attention during my second look at the picture was that the fatigue I now saw in his eyes was not as fully present in the picture—or if it was, it was hardly detectable in his paunchy expression. His body was the distressed being then, and his was not a fat of some brief, indolent period of inactivity and overeating, but a long-honed fat that was sown in childhood, and worked on well through adolescence and early manhood.

Then to try to make me feel more at ease still, and as a belated acknowledgement of the currency I had invoked of men's admirations and common dependencies and cravings, he generously added, while tapping the girl's image once more, "And Lisa really is something to see. She looks just as good or better now. She really does. You'll meet her."

There was something endearingly humane in the way he offered these last phrases. It was not only an exchange of the currency I describe above, and even an allowing of his wife to be moderately considered in this way in a controlled manner, but it seemed to indicate, as well, that he did not defend or consider his wife as his. Her beauty was hers, and he did not thank me as if I praised something of his. Though I did not take it that he would be lazy about defending his proper territory if there was a true threat of a breach or a bawdy conversational impropriety, there was something of an admirable confidence in him, an intimation that nominal defensive postures were not something that he had time for or the will to affect when they were not necessary. I took from all this that there must be an appealing soundness and confidence in this Lisa Hare, as well.

Then as my own gesture of breaking the awkwardness I felt for myself, I asked about the other image, the animation cell that hung just to the right of the little picture of the Pauktaug Girl.

"My wife gave that to me as a wedding present. We had been to an exposition in New York, and she had seen me looking at it. I didn't know that she bought it for me that day."

I could tell that he assumed I knew what the picture was. Not wishing to commit any more foolish blunders—even if this one had only to do with a cartoon that I could not really place—I was slow and deliberate in the only thing I could think that was safe to ask about the little image.

"So this is a favorite story of yours?" I asked, hoping he would let a little clue slip for me.

"No, not the whole story, really. Just that little part of it, at the beginning."

That is all he said about the picture, and I was glad that he did not ask me anything about the story itself at that point, for I certainly still had absolutely no idea what presumably familiar story the image suggested. But he seemed glad that I said nothing more about that picture, as if he did not care to discuss it further—as if it were somehow more personal to him than even the picture of his wife and him on the beach. Perhaps because he associated the animation cell with the time of his wedding he did not wish to betray the image's real meaning to him by discussing the picture's common associations for the general public. I could not say.

"Do you feel tired?" Hare suddenly blurted out, a bit louder than we both expected, and we both laughed at this.

"Well, no. I actually slept very deeply last night. I didn't wake once, and after yesterday, I really didn't have much housekeeping work to do. I feel pretty rested."

Hare continued, as if he were sounding me out not only for a single instance, but in general: "I guess what I mean is, Are you awake now? Do you feel too tired to do something right now, tonight?"

"No. What do you have in mind?" I asked, thinking that he was suggesting some late night trip to a diner or bar for something to drink.

"Can you swim?" he asked to my surprise.

"Yes, but I'll confess that I don't really feel up to a swim, even though I feel pretty awake."

"No, that's not what I mean. I'm in charge of the lobstering business that my father-in-law left to my wife. I have to go to check some traps and a few other things tonight. We employ several full crews in our business, but I've had to go out myself lately to keep certain things in order. Feel like having a brief tour of the harbor, bay, and then Long Island Sound?"

This idea intrigued me very much, and I said that I would like to go.

"Now we might not get back for awhile, but I can think of no better way to really see this place than to have an idea of the way people used to see it for the first time over a century ago—from the water. Before the automobile, I think about just as many people came into Pauktaug via steamship or sail as they did by the Long Island Railroad—coming in from all over: Connecticut, New York City, and from other places on Long Island and beyond."

Hare closed up the office, and we walked out onto the magnificent quiet of Main Street at eleven o'clock of a Sunday night. My new employer asked me—as we cut left onto Hale Street and made our way to Harbor Road—if I had any ideas yet for the magazine.

"Yes, actually. I've already been intrigued by Pauktaug's unique —at least it seems somewhat unique—industrial past. I thought I might start with some studies of the place as it has appeared to me as a newcomer, and then work backward and backward until one reaches the time when Pauktaug was at its height for something unique and truly local, and then address the draw it had for new-comers back then when its identity was definite and clear. But per-haps this has all been gone over to death—school children being tortured by projects about local history and such. Perhaps such an essay, if there isn't enough material will just turn into something like that—as, again, when children are tortured, or betrayed really, with displays of candle-dipping and horseshoeing so that they can presumably have a grasp of eighteenth-century American Revolu-tionary thought. It really is absurd."

"Well, it has been addressed—Pauktaug history, I mean," Hare interjected. "I had just the kind of thing you are talking about in first through fourth grade. In fact the elementary school here was once one of the stay factory buildings until it was sold to the dis-trict and converted to a school during the WPA period. They had their use, those historical demonstrations, in school. But I know what you mean, and that is just what the magazine is for, is here for, as a counter. And, again, I think you're just the man, from what I've read, to address it correctly—the local history—so that it isn't just left behind for children and done in a childish way to boot. That's good. I challenge you to tackle that. And keep to the angles, the unique bents, you follow in your writing."

"I've been somewhat intrigued by that Stays Girl on the sign. The Pauktaug Girl," I said.

"You mean Lara?"

"Is that her name? The girl on the sign?"

"Yes, that's her name. I'm not altogether sure where the name comes from. But there is a story there, too, I'm sure, a part for your essay."

We came to the frontier of the harbor, and I noticed for the first time that there were flatbed trucks piled high with what Hare identified as lobster traps parked in the lot—many of these trucks with the *Crabbe Lobster* insignia painted onto the doors of the cabs.

Hare led us down an aluminum walkway to a large mooring float that had many dinghies tethered and knocking against it with the rhythm of the shifting tide. The moon was obscured by a deep cloud cover that seemed to be descending so as to form another Pauktaug night of fog, but what was lost in visible crystalline brilliance was made up for by throngs of brittle crickets singing back in the grass—and in the distance, along the shoreline to the south, near the houses that cropped up by the Sunken Cemetery, legions of frogs screamed without restraint, sounding rather like school picnic hordes on roller coasters, or crowds of good-willed bystanders who cheer and caterwaul near the finish line of a race.

We tenuously climbed into the dinghy and fitted ourselves into it like we were trying on a sort of giant shoe. Hare took to the front and rowed with his back to the prow.

Soon we were alongside a long flatboat with a large outboard. As I took a place in the middle of this empty boat, I settled in and watched Hare start the engine and take his place by the tiny open-aired wheelhouse toward the stern. The distant sound of the crickets and frogs vanished as the harsh cough of the engine began. Hare stood as he piloted us speedily north and out of the harbor and out toward the bay. Though he still did not definitely suggest the figure I had seen on that first night—that man attired in running clothes and assisted by the presence of a spry, agile dog as first mate, and that man somehow looking leaner and taller, more a lithe runner, from a distance—I could not dismiss the possibility that Hare might still be that man, especially as he stood behind the wheel and seemed in my view to move bipedally forward without moving his legs.

Somehow, when we were out in the bay, and the engine fumes and the smell of old lobster rinds were entirely blown away before they could reach the nose, and when nothing but a constant stream of salubrious salty light fog went into the nostrils, this combined with a sweet breeze of incipient autumn from both shores, the sound of the engine did not seem so cacophonous. I thought I might test for myself Hare's possible pedestrian identity more directly.

"I've been running for some time now," I shouted. This elicited no response from Hare.

"What are you looking for? Are we near the first traps?" I had to ask, since I knew Hare had heard my first question, but seemed suddenly intent on the water's surface in the near distance on both sides of our immediate front.

"No," he shouted back. He eased the engine considerably, and the liquid warble of the boat lazily but smoothly cutting through water became the most prevalent sound. "There haven't been seals or harbor porpoises in this water during my lifetime. But some people have been reporting seal sightings again in this area. I'm hoping to see one. I'm sorry. What did you ask me before?"

"I was saying that I've been running, not for too long yet, but I feel that I can safely say that it is a permanent interest of mine now. I was thinking of addressing through some essays or pieces the process of learning to be a runner. Or I thought I might journalize a newcomer's time in Pauktaug as a runner. I think I might try something like that for the magazine instead of the history idea to start. What do you think?"

Hare gave no answer or reaction. I could not tell for sure if he was truly transfixed by his watch for seals, or whether he let that ostensible concentration allow him to escape having to dismiss out loud an idea he had no interest in encouraging. Either way, I let this silence steer me in my mind back to the idea of the Pauktaug

Girl and the old modest boom days of Pauktaug Village. And this silence steered me away, too, somehow from any last suspicions that Hare was the boating runner I felt I had seen—and the fact that Hare made no allusion to a dog.

Thus, as we slowed even more, and the engine was hardly an offense at all but merely an annoyance (a tiny, just tolerable, and therefore intolerable chortle unto an otherwise silent landscape), I followed the running line of conversation, not as part of a literary suggestion, or as a way to expose any secret pursuit or interest of my new employer, but as a way to render my most recent and exciting personal experiences into conversational grist.

Hare smiled in acknowledgement of what I said, and in such a way that he seemed to say that he was listening but could not respond because of the trapping area's imminent appearance. He seemed to encourage me with slight, kindly nods of his head, as he peered through the blackness and the light salty fog. I pitched away into a narrative about my former paunchiness and my discovery of the remarkable panacea of running. Strangely, my talkative enthusiasm, or perhaps mere nervousness at having to hold a one-way conversation in the middle of the night with a stranger on the open rolls of the impenetrable black greenness of the Long Island Sound, made me forget that there might have been some sort of aerobic exercise source to Harc's weight loss since the photograph of him in his roundness had been taken. I forgot all about that possibility, and became for a few long minutes, a sort of incessant, preachy runner. I preached my sudden weight loss and my ability to run longer and longer distances—but more than anything else, I preached that running had given me access to a supply of grist that I had never before suspected. Rather it had proven so many common, seemingly already sounded depths of grist to be but unscratched surfaces, boundless new deeps of analogy and metaphor. One felt a keenness, an awareness after one reached a certain base of running that was almost threatening to old perceptions.

I barreled on in this manner for awhile, and in my latter material I seemed to have some sort of reaction from Hare for the first time. He seemed to grimace, and he looked a bit tried as I reported my more abstract reapings from running. But then I suspected that he was not reacting to this at all, perhaps, for suddenly he turned off the engine and let the boat drift to the west side of a large rocky outcropping that stood, he later reported, more or less precisely at the edge of Pauktaug Bay and the start of Long Island Sound proper. There had even been a small, unmanned lighthouse on this little island at one time, but it had been lost to a storm well before the lifetimes of Hare and myself.

I suddenly thought to ask Hare how he hoped to accomplish much at all in such darkness. And then I recalled, as well, that we had not had any kind of search lighting or running lights in use during our trip out to the Sound.

"Do you usually do night work under such complete darkness? I mean, we didn't even have so much as a lamp going to let anyone see us coming."

Hare laughed, and he tethered the boat to a large piece of driftwood that was jammed into a crevice of the tiny shoreline of the little rocky island. As he motioned for me to jump onto the rocks with him, he said, "Well, I didn't mean to scare you. I didn't want anyone to see the boat tonight. You see, we're just going to sit here for a bit and look to the east from here for a little while, in the silence and darkness—for a reason."

I followed him to a little flat crest on the rocks where there was evidence of an ancient foundation. Then he explained the rest.

"A large majority of our traps are spread as far as the eye can see from here. I've had some reports that someone, another trapper—from the Connecticut side—is helping himself to some free lobsters. This is the hour when he has been seen. And if you have it in you, I'd like to invest maybe just a half hour in waiting to see if he shows up. I'd like to challenge him myself."

With his last words, Hare held up a large, powerful, searchlight that he had carried out of the boat with him. I had been preoccupied with keeping my own footing on the slippery, seaweed- and mussel-covered rock, and I had not seen that he had carried anything with him.

I said that I did not mind keeping a brief lookout for a time, and in fact, now that I knew his purpose, I found the little mission quite interesting. As we sat for a time in silence and stared north and east out into the clearing blackness and the fading gray fog, a little bit of the moon began to break through, and I could gradually begin to make out quite a few of the floats that bobbed at the surface and marked the presence at Sound's and bay's bottom of a lobster trap.

Hare became quite talkative as we conducted our little vigil on the lighthouse ruin. He reported that during the earlier half of the week of his vacation his wife had convinced him to take a little trip up into New England. "But then she had to come back by Wednesday for work. She had a lot of appointments, and she is still trying to build a base. She didn't want to lose any old customers or miss the new ones."

"What does she do?"

"She's a personal trainer—general fitness, nutrition, aerobics and yoga classes, things like that."

He seemed to suppress a slight smile when he said what she did, and seemed, as well, to glide quickly into the little list of qualifications, not so much for elucidation, but for the slightest, almost imperceptible but somehow palpable reason that the title of her position seemed slightly funny or embarrassing to him. His attempt to cover this seemed so discreet and so almost totally successful and subtle, that it was more to his credit, I thought, than if he had concealed his real feelings altogether with a completely deceptive and unexpressive face and voice.

As he continued to talk at an only slightly lowered conversational volume, I then noticed something else in his speech and manner that struck me as creditable. His voice, manner, and dialect, were somehow cultivated just short of the very edge of affectation—without striking one that he was making any considerable effort to conceal some original, unattractive, local accent, or making a show of his education.

He further explained that though his most consuming work kept him in *The Pauktaug Press* office from sunup to sunset and beyond, it was a rare day that he did not have to log several night hours in the lobstering offices or to have to attend to a problem at the docks or out on the water itself. This seemed evidently true from his own appearance, for despite the fact that one was just leaving behind a long and presumably fair weather summer, there was not the slightest trace of tanning or redness to his skin. Though, again, he looked fit beyond question, and his skin presented a hale look, there was not a trace of sun exposure, and his dark brown hair seemed free of even a touch of summer sun bleaching.

Yet somehow, his radiant haleness, and his total freedom from complaint—which did not strike one as an act of suppression in the least—did not leave one feeling shock or pity for the hours he kept. Not only would any offer of solace to him for his circumstances have seemed like offering pity to one who had found some sort of universal panacea, but I must confess that his evident health and good spirits did not allow me to think then of the unusual length of the schedules he cited for himself. They seemed so normal, strong, and salubrious upon hearing him speak, and seeing him then in the evident course of carrying out one of those days, that I only felt pity for my common fatigues and my lack of energies.

"It's usually me that is too anxious to keep going with things to take a vacation, but my wife somehow wanted to cut this last trip short, again because of her work—she just started at a gym that is new to her. And I'm glad that she made us come back. Not only has it been good to get a head start on this week's paper, but I really would like to resolve this theft problem out here. We're beginning to register a definite sign of loss because of stealing. And, again, if what I have been told is true, it is one person that is responsible for all of—"

Hare stopped himself suddenly and raised his hand, first before his own mouth then into the space between the both of us. I looked intently out onto the water and listened, and for a time all I could hear was the lapping of the Long Island Sound's gentle, almost inconsiderable surf against the ruin of the old lighthouse rocks.

After a time I turned to him, smiled, and whispered, "What?" But he quickly rose to a bowed posture, gestured for me to follow, and then we both scurried up to the apex of the rocks. We hid our bodies along the west slope of the ruin, but allowed our heads to creep up over the impromptu breastworks of the little rocky island, so that we could still look out to the east prospect we had been studying since we first sat down on the island.

Soon I could pull out of the lapping rhythm of the little waves a pattern of an aggressive artificial sound, and just as soon I could discern that this was the sound of a motor boat—not unlike the one, it sounded to me, that Hare and I had just ridden from out of Pauktaug Harbor. And like our boat, this little vessel had no lighting whatsoever—neither lighting by which its pilot saw his way through the salt fog and appealing nocturnal gloom of the Sound, nor lighting by which others were supposed to mark his position and avoid collision.

The sound grew louder, and after a full minute, my nervous system really impelled itself into excitement when I could tell that I heard a bit of the rolling of the fast boat's wake cutting and bouncing on the rather flat water. Then I really started when I could hear some sort of large shift on this boat, as that of a container or other object being moved or tossed out of the way and crashing against the boat's inner side so as to make room for movement.

The engine began to slow up, and Hare cautioned me to stay down with another silent motion of his hand between us. I fixed my stare onto the water, and to my amazement, less than twenty yards away, a lobstering boat of similar dimensions to Hare's coasted into sight and cut off its engine as it came in range of the floating buoy that marked the closest trap site.

A fascinated, incredulous, but not malignant smile came over Hare's face as we studied the actions of what appeared to be a lanky, balding, weathered, and haggard looking man in perhaps his late thirties. Though it might not be uncommon to see someone working with speed and efficiency at a task to which they are long accustomed by vocation and great skill, and to be accelerated even beyond this speed and efficiency if the task at hand has some felonious twist added to it, there did seem to be some somehow perceptible over-earnestness, over-zealousness, some maniacal right-eousness in his celerity and forceful application to his tasks.

Hare's smile grew more intense—and he displayed a look of now affable disbelief that marked the passing of some former, dis-missive disbelief (as, perhaps, when one of the *Crabbe Lobster* employees first told him of this problem)—as the man on the boat efficiently and skillfully fought the dying bobbing motions of his boat as he hauled one of Hare's lobster traps to the surface.

"Wait just a second," Hare whispered to me, even though I had made no motion, speech, or proposal that we do anything. "I want to see what he does when he pulls the trap up. I can get an idea of what kind of fellow he is as a thief if I see what he takes. If he's leaving the undersized ones behind, then he's probably a fellow member of the lobster fishery with some kind of grudge that I don't know about yet. If he is taking everything, then he is just a crazy thief. But then, again, if he is looking into the traps for some other reason—though I can't think of what it might be—then I want to see for myself what he might be doing. It is possible, if he doesn't take anything, and just toys with the trap for a little while—takes the bait out or appears to be cutting the wire—that he might be some kind of animal rights person, or some kind of radical environmentalist. But not one of our people—our employees in the company, I mean—has reported anything wrong with the traps or the bait. There's just been a big drop in the yield lately—just as if someone else is taking lobsters out of our traps before we're getting to them."

From what we watched next, there seemed to be perhaps many tangled shreds from many different incensed motivations in what the man on the unknown boat did. He pulled up the trap with experienced but hasty and almost disdainful vigor. Hare whispered that he himself, from where we lay concealed on the rocks, could make out two lobsters in the trap. When the peculiar, limp, gangly lobsterman had finished pulling both of the animals from the trap, Hare commented that only the first of the two looked like it passed the legal size minimum for harvesting. The other was clearly too small, he suspected, even from the distance from which we were spying.

"I've held too many lobsters in my hands, and seen too many in the hands of others, not to know an undersized lobster when I see one."

Then we watched as the man stored the lobsters on board and proceeded to throw the trap back into the water. "Well, now we know that he isn't turning them loose. This is no animal rights guy," muttered Hare.

Then we watched as the trap thief finished his labor over that particular buoy. He did not re-bait the trap, nor did he, however, cut or damage the trap in any way—giving Hare the last bit of evidence he felt he needed so as to know that this man was only a thief and nothing more.

"What are you going to do?" I whispered.

Hare took a quick look at his watch and noted the time. "This guy must be pretty consistent. This is the only hour of night I've yet to be out here myself looking for him (the hour I was *told* to look), and here he is. Well—" he said to himself and broke off. Then he took a deep breath and rose to his feet. Lawrence Hare carefully made his way to the east base of the little lighthouse ruin of rocks. The man on the water, who busied himself with something on the floor of his boat, had his back to us as Hare rose. The lobster thief's boat had drifted closer to the island in the minutes since he had hauled the trap to the surface, and now the boat was getting near enough to the little shore so that he would soon have to turn his back to check where he was. This he suddenly did, and it was then that Hare turned on his blinding searchlight.

"Hello!" called out Hare with a loud, stern, but still not unfriendly voice. The man on the boat rose to his full height. He squinted angrily with a sincere surprise in the light. And he looked on all sides of himself, too, to see if he were surrounded by more than one presence.

"I can't see you at all. Turn that off," he yelled back.

"All right," Hare laughed. And he turned off the light. "Now you put those lobsters back in the trap you just took them from."

"Why?" sneered the man, and he boldly turned his back again and proceeded to fiddle once more with something on the floor of his boat.

"Because those are my traps."

The man in the boat rose again and faced Hare. "These are your traps? You're from the Long Island side of the Sound?"

"Yes. The traps are clearly marked. This has been my company's grounds for decades."

The man in the boat was not easy to see in detail after Hare turned off the searchlight, but I could almost detect the assumption of an offensive posture and expression when he spoke next.

His voice had escalated to a threatening, incensed, hollered rasp, at a rate far beyond that necessitated by Hare's challenges thus far.

"Yeah, you're right! The traps *are* clearly marked. And that is why everyone from my side, the Connecticut side, and every little guy on your side, should help himself from your traps. Not only have the big operations like yours fished these waters to death—until there is hardly anything left in them—but all of big business on Long Island and New York has polluted this water to death, as well. The runoff from your streets and fertilizers and pesticides has ruined the lobster here!"

Then Hare answered the man with a logical challenge that had not yet occurred to me. "Well, if we've overfished the water, then why are you compounding the problem by taking undersized animals? I don't understand what you're doing right now."

The man turned back to the floor of his boat and showed his back once more. "You haven't left anything else. I take whatever I can find to make a living," he shouted with an anger that meant his face must have been red, though I could not see by the darkness to prove this.

To my intense pleasure, this kind of righteous, working-class dismissal did not satisfy Hare in any way.

"Well, no. You can't take whatever you want. That's not—"

The man, who was mainly a silhouette now as the fog closed over the moon once more, stood up suddenly and whirled around. His arm was leveled at Hare, and even in the dim, light, salty fog, it was clear that he held a handgun.

"Sure I can!" he raged. "I can do whatever it takes to survive. You can't ruin the Earth and its resources, and then accuse me of destroying the last bits of it while I just try to survive."

Hare did not move. But he did have possession of himself. In fact he seemed to be looking at the boat very closely now—as if he were trying to fuse its details to his memory so that he could recall them later.

"Well, go ahead then. You know which buoys are ours. They're all around here. Help yourself."

The balding man moved toward his wheel. "Thanks! But it's a little late for your disgusting generosity!" Then he lowered the gun and started his engine once more. Soon the boat vanished to the northeast at a swift pace. It motored away until we could hear it no longer.

As the engine faded, I rose and carefully walked along the slippery rocks to where Hare had stood firm all that time.

"You didn't catch the registration number on the side of that boat, did you?" he asked with incredible self-possession.

"No, I didn't. Hey, are you all right?"

"Sure. I'm fine. You cold from lying on those rocks all that time?"

"I'm okay. But you're the one that just had some crazy man pointing a gun at you."

"Yeah, some of these guys are real zealots. It could have been a flare gun, though. I wasn't really sure. But I didn't really think he was going to shoot me."

Hare paused for a moment and then looked straight at me.

"Well, I really should apologize for your sake, Rex. I hardly thought your first night out here would be like this. I thought at best that we might catch a glimpse in the distance of this guy. But I'm sorry the situation had you out here hugging the cold, wet rocks, taking cover from a gunman."

"Except for the fact that I felt agitated for you," I answered, "for anyone who could have been standing where you were, I'm afraid to confess, and this isn't from some perverse love of fear or danger, that I could not have had a more interesting evening. What I mean to say is, I enjoyed myself. But I wouldn't want to go through it again."

"No, no. I think I understand you well. Don't worry." He refrained from smiling when he assured me of this, and his assurance was so free of condescension or suspicion that it was quite inspiring of my goodwill toward Hare. Though I did not know what I had proved, he seemed reassured that I had somehow confirmed something in person that I perhaps promised or intimated in my writings—and that I had perhaps somehow confirmed his decision in extending to me the Assistant Editor's position at the paper.

We got into Hare's boat, and I found my spirits remained high though I had grown tired, even though I was anxious when the motor started, for it seemed to announce our presence by its volume to just about anyone who might be within five miles of our position. Although I knew he was no longer searching for trap thieves or seals with his piercing, fixed gaze onto the south prospect of the approaching lights and land of town, Hare's mind had fixed on something else as he stood in relative silence—choosing not to fight out a conversation over the chewing, gnashing grind of the motor. However, he seemed like he would have remained contentedly fixed on his thoughts even if we had been able to freely converse without the noise of an engine. And then I felt I recognized what characterized Hare's look and appearance at that moment, if not the substance of what stoked his inner, low-burning but steady wakefulness. It was just that—that he was totally wakeful. And I do not think that he was made wakeful or vigilant with that nervous energy that generally follows some exciting encounter or event. He simply was unjaded and without fatigue. And then I knew that he was one of those rare people who requires very, very little sleep. It was clear to me that he was one of those men who steals by with three or four hours of sleep each night or day—and that he had long learned to tolerate the needs of everyone else. And he was right in applying that tolerance to me, for I was fading with speed even as we lapped across the liquid corduroy of the seemingly equal sleepiness of the Sound. Hare was quite simply wide awake, and I could tell that he was focused on whatever private task it was that he had fixed for the very deepest hours of night.

It was some time after midnight when Hare and I tethered the lobster boat to its place in the harbor and then paddled our way to the float and the ramp that led to shore.

"So, what does one do about that sort of thing?"

"The lobster robber?" Hare smiled. "I don't know really. I'm going to have to ask a few people when morning comes what they think I should do. To be quite honest, I've never directly encountered this sort of thing before, even in all my years in this business. I've heard of it before, though. But I've never heard of any of the culprits being quite so adamant or obvious."

His last line gave me comfort. It seemed to confirm that Hare acknowledged that the affair out on the lighthouse ruin was not something to dismiss lightly. It made him seem comfortably human despite the fact the he appeared with all the freshness of eye and face and form of nine-in-the-morning sensibilities—though he was, perhaps, from his own hints, in the seventeenth or eighteenth hour of his day. And it was nearly two in the morning when we parted in front of my building.

"I'll see you at nine, Rex. Sorry to keep you up so late on the night before your first day. And sorry that you had to see that out there. I should have known better."

"No, I wanted to go. Again, I really enjoyed it, if I am honest about it." This pleased Hare. Then I added: "I mean, what boy hasn't dreamed of watching mad pirates at work on the sea?"

Hare liked this, too, and as he walked south the short distance to his apartment I called out to him, "What are you up to now? You're not staying up now, are you?"

"No, not for long. I have to take my dog out first. Lisa is good about taking him out, but his schedule was a little thrown off tonight, so I want to give him another little stretch."

"I'd like to meet him."

"Good. I'll introduce you to him tomorrow. Let me get going to him now—and I remember now that I still have something *else* to do, too. Goodnight, Mr. Shell."

"Goodnight, Mr. Hare."

I went up to my apartment and readied for bed. I set my clock for seven, so that I could try to get a run in before work. That was the last task I could muster out of myself before going straight into deep sleep. I did not even have the energy to review the night's events for a few moments before losing consciousness.

But perhaps something about the night was enough to bring me forth from even that true, profound sleep. I sat up and realized that I felt very thirsty. The clock read just a bit before five in the morning, and though I was well into the exclusive hours of orange juice, I thought I would finish off the dregs of my first pitcher of New York sweet tea.

With a lot of ice, I was able to fill the glass with the remnants of the first supply, and just as I was walking about my kitchen and looking aimlessly about the ceiling as I swallowed my first deep swig, it came to mind clearly for the first time that Hare had said he had a dog. This set me to my foolish speculations about the seemingly mythical super runners I had seen from out of my window in the hours of deep darkness in my first nights in Pauktaug.

I smiled at myself as I finished off the last of my tea, and then I climbed back into bed again, covetous of the nearly two hours I had left before rising time. But it was when I was on the edge of sleep once more—thinking of the crazed, thieving lobsterman of Connecticut, slowly rising and falling as he stood on his little deck on the foggy Sound, and thinking of the ethereally but somehow at the same time humanly approachable and sensible Lawrence Hare, he facing the scene on the water from the lighthouse rocks— that I chanced to open my eyes one last time on the sight of Main Street.

And just as my mind had settled that it had seen the last bits of September's morning darkness—and that the next time I would look on that same scene the street would be full of light—and as I took the last slow blinks before my eyes closed for those last hours of sleep, I was nearly sure that in between one of those blinks, I saw a runner pass from one end of my limited view (perhaps twenty yards' width) to the other. He moved with the same preternatural speed via means of natural human locomotion as the first sighted male runner I had seen during my night watches. But I could make out hardly any detail. From the north end of my little Main Street view—seen via the window from bed—to the south end he moved with that now increasingly familiar, uncanny, but not nonsensical speed that characterized him. Then I slept fitfully, half feeling in my mind a light narrative dream that I cannot recall, and half feeling the roll of the boat with my body's memory of the recent trip on the Long Island Sound—feeling a motion that suggested that the Earth did not merely turn on its axis in the night as I slept, but rocked back and forth in some sort of stride, making my body feel like the sole of a shoe, pressing to the ground and then rising again with fluid, rolling movements, as if guided by a giant's stride on some unseen but imperturbable track that describes laps around the anchoring ball field that is the ancient sun. And when my alarm clock rang I looked again to see the light of day crawling along and up and down Main Street. But the runner was, of course, gone—he had more than a lead of minutes on the sun, and the light of the star looked humble to me for the first time, coming in strong and reliable, but undeniably crossing the line long after the finishing tape had been cut some hours before by the sharp and scissoring kick of a driven man in motion.

CHAPTER 7

SPEEDING UP

When I woke up officially to Monday, September 3 at seven, I really did not wish to head right off for a run, but I did not know if I would have the energy later in the day after experiencing my first full day of work. And as I was still fearful of letting anything that could be construed as a lazy gap into my planned schedule for my new running pursuit, I forced myself up and out unto the morning and the town. All the fog had blown off with the night wind, and there was a bright, blue, cloudless sky puffing a cold breeze that made the first part of the run seem very difficult. It was the first time I had ever had to fight to warm myself during a run. All my previous endeavors had been in the spring and summer heat of Georgia, and then just a few in the incipient autumn breeze of Pauktaug, but this particular morning blew cool unto the fringes of coldness, and it was then that my body's powerful tendency to sweat profusely under all conditions proved itself truly unstoppable.

It was well past eight when I returned to Main Street, and as I reached my apartment, an incredible sight came into view for me and let me know that some of the mysteries to which I had been privy were soon to have at least the potential of being answered.

With the same uncanny speed which I had seen from him once before—on Saturday morning, after dawn was well past—the second mysterious runner that I had sighted from my apartment windows came into view on the sidewalk. He was passing Hare's and my great-grandmother's apartment when I first saw him. And even though I could tell that he was fast beyond any runner that I had ever seen in person, it was clear—especially from this level point of view—that there was nothing unnatural or even uncommon in his form or method of locomotion. He passed several people who only took note of him as one would take note of anything that passes one on the sidewalk with greater speed than a fellow walker.

But what was of greater interest to me than even this additional sighting was the fact that this runner—who was a very tall, strong and lean looking man in his mid-thirties—slowed to a halt right in front of the building that housed *The Pauktaug Press.* He looked about to the street and the blooming day with a smile and a pause so as to catch his breath, and then he took the walkway and the steps into the building with speed and ease and vanished into the lobby. And then it was clear that there were stirrings in the front, second story office—the office of Charles Pocket, Esq. The lights went on in the front room, then in what I supposed was the main office, then a little back room that was in the southwest corner of the suite. I could detect nothing else after that, but I was intrigued to have final proof that I had not dreamed the sight of at least one of the odd-hour runners I had seen from my lonely apartment. Feeling sure that I could easily learn more about this situation, since I was due very shortly to be working in the office across the hall of the same building, I jogged back to my apartment and readied for work. After a quick shower and breakfast, I bided the last minutes before it was just past ten to nine, and then I walked to work for the very first time in Pauktaug.

When I entered the old house, there were already people filing in and out of the dental office on the ground floor, and I had a first glimpse not only of the light of human life in the building, but the light of day as it played in through the bay windows that fronted the landing of the stairs to the second floor and at the stairway's summit.

Before I passed by the office of Charles Pocket, Esq., I looked through the smoky gray glass and image of the Scales of Justice in Pocket's window, and inside I could glimpse a man almost fully dressed in business attire (save for a jacket) leaning over the large reception desk and shuffling through either mail or some kind of paper work with one hand. With his other arm he was engaged in towel-drying his hair, as if he had just completed a shower.

But all of this left my mind as I entered the already bright and busy offices of *The Pauktaug Press*. As soon as I entered, Lawrence Hare caught sight of me from his office and jogged over to welcome me. He apologized once more for the previous night's adventure, and I told him, again, that it was nothing for him to think twice about.

"My wife, Lisa—who is the real, true, and final owner of *Crabbe Lobsters*—bullied out of me what happened last night. And she can't believe I took you out there. Anyway, to make it up to you—But wait a minute. Forgive me, everybody."

Hare then introduced me to the three other members of *The Pauktaug Press* who were already at their desks—they then looking up in anticipation of meeting the new member of the office. To begin with, I was amazed that everyone was so punctual.

"Am I late?" I asked everyone.

"No," said the two men at the far desks. And then the fortyish woman at the near desk said no, as well. And then she added, "Lawrence starts us off and running at precisely the same time each day. No exceptions," she laughed. "You can leave when you think you are done, but we all have to start precisely at nine, even if we have insisted that we are no good in the morning."

This last phrase she addressed humorously to Hare, as if there really had been a discussion of taking on another schedule.

Hare merely laughed back at the woman (her name was Randy).

In addition to many general articles, Randy pounded out most of *The Pauktaug Press'* humble yet vigorous pretensions to sensationalism. With the plain, small-town columns forming the core and equator of the paper's output, Hare's extensive speculative essays in the editorial section opposite the miniature tabloid-like attempts of Randy formed a polarized sphere for the little newspaper, with fascinating tugs from the radically opposed poles. Yet this all seemed organized by agreement, as if Hare had intentionally set up his little planet in this way.

After I shook Randy's hand, the two men in the back rose to meet me. The man who had his desk in the southeast corner, Hank, was in his late fifties and affably indifferent to me. He was a retired teacher from the local school district, and he handled the sports columns and other random assignments on the paper. In fact, after greeting me, he excused himself and left the office, on his way to the high school to collect material for a piece on a complex of new ball fields that was to open that autumn.

Finally, there was Kee-Poh, a beamingly friendly young man in his late twenties who spoke faltering English, and yet pained his listeners in his indefatigable attempts to extend himself via those means. Of course, I immediately wondered how it was that he carried out his duties as a columnist, but it was something I learned not to ask about, for time after time, and always ahead of time, he turned in nearly perfect submissions as to style and mechanical concerns—and I was left to suspect, since I have yet to see him on his beat, that his style of spoken English forced his local sources into a style of succinct expression that often enabled him to achieve a clarity in his reporting.

Hare showed me to my office, which was more grand than

anything I had ever enjoyed before. It was parallel to Hare's. After I took a humorously proprietary place behind my large, antique, rolltop desk—which was quite splendid, and which Hare had said was his before Mr. Crabbe passed on—I turned around and listened to a little friendly briefing from Hare.

He would be able, now that I was there, to augment the editorial section to the almost literary-journal-style he envisioned for the paper. He was, that very week, he said, going to commence a series on the seals of Pauktaug Harbor, now that his series on the lobster was almost finished, and he was grateful to me that he could give more of his mind to that than he had ever been able to before.

(Passages from Hare's essays on Pauktaug's seals would prove to be as unique, at times, as some of the material from his series on lobsters. And, curiously, while he seemed to be fascinated by the return of seals to Pauktaug, he seemed, as well, to intimate a latent and peculiar fear at the prospect of the water's recovering quality—that recovery marking the return of the seals. But primarily Hare dwelled on the seal as an evolving animal—as an animal still adapting to life in the sea, having once been a land animal. And he seemed particularly fascinated by their breath-holding feats. From that fascination he segued to images of mermaids and to their equal transitional positions in the evolving Universe and to their equal feats of breath-holding. And then he transferred to mermaids of the land, to glamour girls and the ideas of breath-holding they, too, seemed to suggest to him: "Even the tight-skirted beautiful girl of the modern club, this land-bound mermaid, cigarette still in hand, seems to hold her breath with her gesture of smoking—seems to intimate that her bodily power need not breathe of this home, this planet, that has been offered her. And she struts away—her skirt and shoes making her as awkward as a mermaid in fins, in a way—but assured that her physical beauty can hold its breath and run on its own power while confidently waiting for a world that will better reflect her physical due.")

Hare delivered to me a pile of material that had to be gone over for Friday's trip to the press. But before he left me to my first morning of work, he appeared again at my door and said that his wife and he wanted to know if I would have dinner with them at their apartment at five-thirty that evening. Not only did Mrs. Hare want to meet and welcome me, but she wanted to apologize for my first experience of Pauktaug Harbor and the Sound, and to assure me that life-threatening trips on the high seas were in no way part of the expectations for the Assistant Editor of *The Pauktaug Press*. I said that I would be happy to accept the invitation.

Before he left to return to his part of the office for the morning, Hare added that the three of us—the two Hares and myself—could call on my great-grandmother, Nancy Whisker, before the evening was out.

"Or do you prefer to do that by yourself?" Hare asked pleasantly and without expecting one answer or another.

"No, that will be fine if we go together," I answered. "It will probably be easier for me that way. Quite honestly, I hardly know her at all."

I settled into a large mound of work that gave me great pleasure, for I was in the very environment that I had pined after for so long, and the prospect of pursuing series after series of speculative articles (after I knew the routines of my editorial duties proper), articles not entirely beholden to the exact science and laws of dry reporting, filled me with a burning sense of anticipation.

I had just put down—with amazement, I might add, at its correctness—one of Kee-Poh's articles about a town hall meeting, and had just taken up something of Randy's on Long Island north shore celebrity spottings (which had an error in its very first clause), when I realized I had nothing with which to write.

Feeling a bit foolish and embarrassed over this I thought first to ask Lawrence Hare for a pen, but I found his door closed when I went out into the main room. Randy noticed me right away, I with a look as if I were surveying the sights of the scene for the first time.

"Do you need something, Rex?"

"Actually—and I feel like a child who has come to the first day of school with everything but the absolutely essential item—I need a pen or a pencil."

"Oh, no shame in that! We should of looked to see that your desk had everything you will need."

Randy gave me a large box of office supplies—with more pens and pencils than I could use in five years—and I worked in happy solitude until nearly lunchtime.

Hank came back into the office near noon, and I suddenly thought to ask him who it was that I had seen running that morning just outside and then into the building.

"Where did he go after he came into the building?" shouted Hank with the remnants of being out of breath from his climb to the second floor.

"Right into the office next door, I think."

"You saw—" Hank began.

"Pocket," said another voice over Hank's from behind me. It was Lawrence Hare, standing at his own door with some papers in hand that were destined for me, I think. He had stood behind me as I asked my question, and had beaten Hank to the answer.

"Did the guy look like a fast runner?" asked Hank.

I laughed. "He sure did."

"That was Pocket all right! He may just be one of the fastest men, if not *the* fastest on Earth."

I smiled to acknowledge this hyperbole and to credit his admiration, but Hank would not accept this from me. "You think I'm kidding? And, oh, if you think he's fast, just wait till you see what may be coming out of—"

"Rex!" interjected Hare at this precise juncture, in a tone that affected to be self-absorbed, as if it had not been following the course of my exchange with Hank to a precisely calculated point of interruption.

"Rex, can I give you just a few more things, and then show you a few others if you have a minute?"

Hare and I went into my office, and Hank left the scene again for the afternoon. After Hare finished this first of many small orientation sessions that would unfold over the course of my first weeks in Pauktaug, I rose for lunch at twelve-thirty, at the invitation of Randy and Kee-Poh, who were going to go across the street to the little diner that I had already visited myself in my first days in the village. I heartily accepted, and when I looked back at Hare's closed door as the three of us were about to leave, Randy assured me that Lawrence Hare, while not antisocial, always worked through lunch, and hardly stirred from his office till near the closing hours of the working day.

Thus I crossed busy Main Street in the bright, clean, keenly scarce perfection of September's cool and sweet sunlight. Kee-Poh had his lunch with him—a thin broth of some type that looked like it would not be filling to a hamster who had any intentions of running on his wheel—but the waitress did not take exception to this, as if by previous agreement.

Randy and I ordered for our booth, however, and after the lunch appeared, and as Kee-Poh slowly worked on his broth, and scribbled shockingly lucid paragraphs onto a tablet whilst having nothing coherent to add to our conversation, Randy affectionately dismissed with feminine-masculine violence our third and indifferent wheel, and proceeded to assess my social prospects in Pauktaug.

She herself was long into marriage, so she indulged in the joy of an immediate shocking probe of my status.

"Married, been married, have a girlfriend, children?"

"No to all four categories."

"But interested? You're looking, I mean?"

"Sure," I smiled, "at least for your third category, for now."

"I have a sister in Shirley, on the south shore, that I think you would like. She might be just a year or two older than you, but you wouldn't know, and everyone says she's real attractive. It's just so hard to meet people these days."

"Well, I'd be glad to meet her. Where is this Shirley place? How far away is it?"

"It's a little over or under an hour from here, but you two could—"

Just at this moment, Kee-Poh looked up from his broth with a sudden gregariousness and a large smile, and he made the following surprising contribution.

"No good! Long distance relationships are bad news!"

"We're only talking about someone on the south shore," chided Randy with mock anger. "You just say that because you tried to have a relationship with someone on the other side of the planet that you met on a cruise."

Though I could never quite join in the banter-and-bicker-based relationships that characterize some offices, I tried to appreciate the kindnesses of my two new lunch partners for the day. When it seemed that the exchange about Kee-Poh's long distance relationship was about to die away, I thought I might raise the issue of Charles Pocket, Esq., the remarkable runner of just across the hall from *The Pauktaug Press*. However, the completion of Randy's and Kee-Poh's last exchange led to a long, melodramatic monologue from Kee-Poh concerning the woman from Madagascar he had pursued via telephone after meeting her for a day in the Caribbean during a vacation.

This tale continued until we returned to the strong light of the sun on Main Street, and I took conscious note of its gleam on the ancient trolley tracks, maintained by the town in memory of the line that used to run from the harbor to the Long Island Railroad. As I was looking at these old rails and trying to interrupt Randy—who was talking of her sister again—trying to interrupt her with an attempt once more at a question about Charles Pocket, I was suddenly shocked to hear Randy herself, without my prodding, invoke the name of a Pocket.

"Kee-Poh, what do you think about Dale for Rex?"

"Dale Pocket? No way!"

"Why not? You hoping for her for yourself?"

"Dale Pocket? No way!"

"I don't know why I even talk with you, Kee-Poh!" hissed Randy, and then the pair moved to the office's porch and up the stairs as a unit. When we reached the front office of *The Pauktaug Press,* Hare was waiting for me, and all my thoughts about this new little mystery faded as Hare saw me through a course of guidelines about the running of the paper. After I talked with him till about two, I worked the rest of the day in solitude. And when I looked out of my office again I was shocked to see that the clock read ten past five. Randy was there, and she said that she was just about to tell me that she was going to leave and turn the lights out. I asked where everyone else was. Everyone else was gone already, including Hare, who had left the office at four, she reported. And so I said my goodbyes to Randy and ran down Main Street to a small liquor store that was just south of the movie theater, where I bought two bottles of wine, and then I stopped in a bakery that was just across the street and bought a large box of cookies. The cookies were for myself, but then I felt I should err on the side of generosity, and I decided to take them along to the Hares. I had just enough time to run back to my apartment and to shower and shave, and I was back out onto the sidewalk just short of five-thirty, the back of my shirt and my hair looking rather like I had just been for a run since I had had little time to dry.

The Hare's door was plain, and no effigy of the Pauktaug Girl flashed her wooden but lively eyes from any panel in that entrance-way. After just a modest knock, Hare opened the door, and he welcomed me into a vast apartment with a loft-like floorplan. Hare was nattily dressed in a collarless shirt and slacks of all black—a set of expensive informal wear that matched his dark shining hair and complemented the almost black-and-white comic book angularity of his features. He was very warm in his greeting, and he thanked me for the cookies and the bottles of wine.

There was not a sign of dust or wear in the apartment. The few pieces of furniture in the enormous living room had been chosen with care and with a view to being parts of an intentionally spare scheme. Overall the apartment gave the impression of the intensity that had constructed and furnished my own apartment.

Just then a second party presented itself, and it was then that my day of Pauktaug night dreams confirmed by daylight sightings came closer to being utterly completed. At my feet was an extremely awake and interested border collie. He had a black and white color pattern, a large area around one eye and ear covered in a half mask of black, and a virtually equal area covered in a half mask of white. He was equally black and white on the rest of his body, as well. I kneeled down to meet this affable fellow: the same dog I had seen, I was sure, on my first night in Pauktaug, when I had seen what I was now sure was probably Hare, dressed in running attire, leaving one of the lobster boats with a medium-sized dog as company—and running later on in the company of a dog, as well. This was almost certainly that same dog, I thought.

"Who is this?" I asked Hare, as I rubbed the dog behind its ears. I had always loved dogs very much, but my parents would never think of having one. And I had never been home enough after living on my own to conscience having a dog. But I felt free and easy around nearly all of them.

"This is Reginald, Reginald Hare. He is pretty new to us, too. We got him only a few months ago from a shelter."

"Hello, Reginald. Hello. You know, Lawrence, I think now that I saw you earlier than at that first meeting we had on Sunday outside your office. Now that I see Reginald, I think I saw you and him on one of your boats late on Thursday night."

This did not create much of a reaction in Hare. He only added, "Probably. Reginald likes to go out on the boats when I don't plan to be out too long." He would have continued, I think—perhaps even addressing my sighting of Thursday night—but then a third and final party appeared.

"I'm sorry everybody. Hello. I've been trying to get Nancy on the phone—at her place just below." This was Hare's wife, and she was referring to my great-grandmother, Nancy Whisker. "I was getting worried, and I thought that something might have happened to her on her way back from the city. She did say that she was coming back today. But I just reached her at her Manhattan place. She said she fell this morning."

"She fell?" Hare repeated, with a gentle incredulousness that might have been taken for impatience had I felt that he would venture anything of that sort in front of me.

Mrs. Hare raised her eyebrows. "Yes, Lawrence, that's what I said. She fell." But then she looked to me. "But don't worry, it was just a little fall. And sometimes little accidents seem to jar Nancy back into a better state of awareness. She suddenly remembered that today was September 3, and that you would probably be here."

I nodded, and she smiled and laughed: "*You* being Rex Shell?"

"Yes, yes. I'm Rex. It's nice to meet you. I'm sorry I didn't say. And you must be—"

"Don't be sorry. *He* should have said something." Here she motioned to Lawrence Hare, who was sitting now on the floor with Reginald—and looking up at us from Reginald's point of view. This is not to say that he was affecting a boyish posture, as if in passive acknowledgement of his wife's censure of his manners. He merely seemed to have retreated to Reginald's place so as to interact with him—and to be out of the way until Mrs. Hare and I had finished our introductions on our own.

"Anyway, Rex, Nancy will be back here, downstairs, by tomorrow. But I'm so glad that you're here with us tonight. It is so good to meet you." Here she extended herself for a hug. Then she shook my hand and offered her first name: Lisa.

I smiled and offered my first name again.

Lisa Hare, née Lisa Crabbe—heiress to the modest *Crabbe Lobsters, Inc.* business, and daughter, as well, of the late Editor-In-Chief and owner of *The Pauktaug Press,* Thomas Crabbe (1920-1996)—was strikingly attractive, and not in a common way. I suspected that she was about Hare's age, and that the trace lines and dryness of that period could be seen about her eyes and at the corners of her mouth—but she presented an extremely maintained figure. She was just short of being too maintained, and one could make out the tone of her muscles in her arms as her limbs gently flexed in the task of ordinary walking, and in the shifting of one's weight while standing. But since I knew that she made her living in the field of exercise, this did not come as a surprise to me. What was surprising, and quite lovely, was the unique chromatic quality of her hair and the tone of her skin. She had long, straight, shining, chestnut hair, but it was one to two shades redder than any common chestnut coloring. Yet hers was not red hair. And via a mild tan, one could only just see a cloaked, altogether comprehensive pattern of freckles that underlay her entire skin's surface. But this was only apparent with furtive, close examination. From afar her skin presented a lightly tanned, solid appearance. But when one chanced to have a close view of that latently and pervasively freckled youngish skin, it looked to me like her surface suggested the dawn or dusk on a red planet like Mars, when its stars could only be suspected with the eye in the red glare of such a planet's dawn or gloaming.

To her credit, she wore a short, form-fitting dress that was just at the frontier of being loosely fitting. So while she never had cause to think that she did not have the pleasure of showing her hard-won figure, never did I once see her have to pull at her dress for modesty's or comfort's sake when she rose from or descended to a chair.

And she had a pair of eerily lighted blue eyes that looked very much like the solid color of glowing blue that is suggested by the cloud-mottled images of the Earth when photographed from space. These were borne, lodged, in a face of chiseled, sharp features—that would one day lend themselves to the impression that wives and husbands often come to resemble one another. But they were not of the hyper-drawn precision and angularity of her husband's.

"Well, we can come back out here and sit after dinner. I have dinner almost ready now, so why don't you fellows take your places at the table."

Hare, Reginald, and I moved into a spacious dining room that was on the north side of the apartment. With sincere human admiration for a beautiful form, I continued to watch Lisa as she made a few final trips between the kitchen that faced down onto Main Street and the dining room table where I seated myself—and one of the windows near the table was the spot from which Lisa had conversed with Hare, I was sure, window-to-window-style, when I was in the offices of *The Pauktaug Press* for the first time during the previous evening.

As Lisa Hare made her final round trip to the table and back, I noted that her beauty was as the kind of holding-tight, early- to mid-thirties, tweaked bodily allure that suddenly gives over all its wound-up power—if not all of its appearance—to the mother role, for there was something soft and unselfish in her very frame and appearance. It was then that I felt what Hare had said was altogether true—that it was to her I owed most of my thanks for the standard (or at least the finishing gestures) of my apartment, for it was also evident in their home, and somehow in the peculiar con-flation of physical self-vigilance and desire to serve that was encoded in Lisa Hare's very stride, and in every baby-powdered swish of her dress.

"Did you bring the wine and cookies, Rex?"

I confessed that I did, and she thanked me as she finally took her seat.

"Well, I hope you don't think that I'm going to let Lawrence take you on any more trips out onto the Sound when there is a chance for you to get shot. I still can't believe he took you out there to check the traps under those circumstances. And who would want to show a tired traveler those smelly old boats and traps dur-ing his first days in town?"

Hare just shrugged his shoulders at his wife's further censure, directed toward him through this rhetorical question to me. And then he just smiled as I had to repeat my insistence that not only did I never feel that I was in danger, but that the entire trip and the ostensible hazards were well worth the atmosphere they granted me.

"Lisa," I inserted at this point, "I must tell you that the only sensation that has outdone my sense of gratitude for the apartment you worked on and set up for me is the shock I felt on seeing how magnificent it is. I really can't believe it—not only how large and nice it is, but how much work has gone into it."

"Well, I'm glad you like it," smiled Lisa in a rich, kindly way that even eclipsed the prettiness that was otherwise the most formidable part of her face. "But don't give us too much credit. We had these two buildings in our possession for a long time. My father bought them a long time ago, and he did the main renovations years ago. Lawrence and I just started to go over a few of them again recently—two of them in your building, and then we had the two apartments in this building redone a few years ago. I just hope you're happy with us as landlords."

"I never thought I would be saying this in this way, but the rent you're asking is really unfair! I don't think I can pay you so little."

There was an awkward look between Lisa and Lawrence Hare. Hare held a pleasant but baleful look in Lisa Hare's way a bit longer, finished it with a probationary raising of his eyebrows, and then said, "Don't be silly, Rex. Again, you're the one doing me a favor. Believe me. You weren't even looking for another position when you agreed to take this one."

Lisa Hare suddenly leaped in, evidently having abandoned any silent challenge to her husband's largesse, and she said with a sincere sweetness: "Anyway, Rex, it was my pleasure to make it pretty for you. And if you ever find something you like better, don't think you are locked into that place for our sake."

I just sighed to express my disbelief and gratitude.

"Well, still," I finally continued, "the money you must have put into the renovation—I mean the labor costs!"

"Oh," said Lisa, as if she had found a point in which she could be happy in supporting her husband's unchallengeable generosity, "Lawrence did all of that work himself."

"What?" I gasped.

"Lawrence is quite amazing. When other people say they don't know when he sleeps, I can really confirm it. I'm his wife, and I don't know when he sleeps."

I was about to give another one of my futile, embarrassed debtor's sighs, when Lisa jumped up and remembered the wine.

She brought out three glasses, and then she filled mine. She then filled hers with ice water.

"Won't you join me?" I asked.

"Oh, I love it. But I'm giving a class later, at seven tonight. And this really dehydrates you, you know. But thank you so much for bringing it."

"Lawrence?" she asked, and she made a gesture with the open wine bottle toward his glass.

"No, thanks, Lisa. I'll have the water, too. But we'll make good use of that. Thanks, Rex."

Lisa shook her head and torso a little back and forth with her next statement, so as to give a little self-deprecating self-awareness to what would otherwise sound a little extreme or affected, not to mention mysterious in Lawrence Hare's case: "Well, we're both kind of in training!"

Certainly, from what she had just said, it seemed clear to me that Lisa Hare assumed I knew what it was for which her husband was in training. Perhaps she just meant his superhuman work schedule, but I suspected otherwise, that she meant something else and very specific.

As is often the case when there is a lapse in a conversation, I fall back on a rather feminine element in my repertoire—at least, I have heard this question put mainly by women under such circumstances. I asked how the young romantic pair had met and fallen in love.

Hare smiled, because he knew he had given me some of this information before. Lisa asked if indeed this was what that smile meant, so she said it would be fun for her to start again with the story.

"Lawrence and I are descended—as is your great-grandmother, I hope you know (so you are, too)—from some of the highest families in the stays business that used to make Pauktaug one of the strongest villages on the north shore of Long Island." To her credit, I must add that she offered the phrase, "some of the highest families," with a tone of mock-solemnity. But nevertheless, I later learned in my research that what she said was true.

"But it was lobster that brought Lawrence and I together, not whalebone, ultimately. My father—he was born in 1920—was one of the first to start lobstering in this town sometime after the war. And he eventually came to be editor and owner of *The Pauktaug*

Press. But it was the lobstering business he started in and started for himself."

At this point Lisa suddenly dropped the strand of narrative concerning her father. She would pick it up later, but at first I thought she had altogether let it go.

"Now I knew Lawrence since elementary school—even in kindergarten. But I never liked him. He was stout, even tubby, and a real cranky little guy. I even thought he was mean. But during summers and weekends in high school, Lawrence started to work for my father on the lobster boats. He started to look a little less out of shape from all the hard work he did out on the water, and I used to see that he could smile when I went to bring things to my father on the docks—or when I went to have lunch with my father in the office (which is still downstairs in this building) and Lawrence was there. But I think I really started to care for Lawrence because of something my father said. I could never find anyone my father liked, and as I started to be interested in Lawrence, my father said something very striking one evening when he and I went out together for a little ride in one of the boats just to check a set of the traps after a storm.

"He said that he wasn't looking forward to the fall—this was when Lawrence and I were about to go away to different schools for college for the first time (but Lawrence and I still weren't a pair at all at that time yet). He said he wasn't looking forward to the fall because he had come to look forward to his rides out onto the water because of what Lawrence might, or would, say most of the time. My father said that some of his high school workers—or workers of any age, for that matter—liked to say what they thought were backward things all of the time, but things that weren't funny or perceptive. Most of the time they were just crass or vulgar and obvious. But Lawrence used to say truly backward things, dissected things (*dissected,* that was my father's exact word) all of the time, unrehearsed yet somehow perfected and new. Lawrence came back from a day out on the water not with things assembled, but with the world apart—somehow gutted and examined like the very bait he put into the traps each day.

"But that isn't what caught me. Again, I had never met anyone that my father had liked for me. And then, on that same day, as my father was pulling into the harbor after we had checked the traps, he said that because he had had no son, and because I wasn't interested in the paper, he wished he had someone to whom he could give the paper who really had new, even if odd things, to say—even if it wasn't news and caused a little trouble for the newspaper.

"I had never known my father to like anyone that much. And I had never known that I would come to like anyone that much, too. And Lawrence was always handsome, but as we continued to see each other more and more when we came back from school and both were around my father on the boats and in the office, I knew that I couldn't resist this unusual, beautiful man. And then to my luck, he suddenly—rather than going the other way—suddenly got himself fully in shape over the last year or so, and now look at him!

"But we were married not long after college, Rex, and I never thought I could be so happy."

She seemed to realize that her story had the subjective intensity that could rarely interest a third party after a certain point, and to her credit, she suddenly broke into a smile and then a mock-condescending look once more, rather like the one she had used when connecting herself, and all of us, with the old main industry of stays in Pauktaug.

"Not that Mr. Lawrence Hare has never worried me! When I learned what kind of working hours he keeps, and what kind of hours he has been keeping the last few years—what with the paper, the lobstering, the renovations, and every other part of living—I've been hoping that he would take someone on with him at the paper. So, Rex, believe me, it really isn't you that should be doing any thanking. It really is me.

"The only thing that puzzles me," she continued, and here she looked with affectionate reproach at Lawrence Hare, "is why he finally and suddenly did hire someone, you, now. And you'll see this, Rex, for yourself, that despite the superhuman schedules and hours he keeps, he seems to be able to handle it. His hiring you surprised me now because I had almost come to accept his ability to bear the loads he puts on himself. And then he suddenly did what I had wished for after I had stopped wishing for it. I'm not going to probe for reasons too much, because I'm still glad that he did it—even if it does seem like he doesn't need to sleep.

"So, again, Rex, you can imagine that it was my pleasure to make your apartment as pretty as I could for you. I feel like you're here to save my husband, even if he doesn't think he needs saving."

"I'm glad to be here for all reasons," I said, which does not make too much sense to me now, but that is what I said. I had finished my glass of wine, and Lawrence Hare rose to fill it for me. I continued: "I hardly feel like I'm here to do any saving. In fact, everything has been so overwhelmingly comfortable—and I don't use that word lightly or casually—that I feel like I am the one that has been saved. I feel like I'm the helpless foundling who has been taken up by fairy godparents. Really, I mean it."

Hare just laughed as he gestured with the wine bottle toward my empty glass.

I gave an involuntary look of hesitation at the prospect of another glass of wine. Lisa, in her consummate feminine awareness leaped up: "Lawrence, you can sit back down with Rex. Rex, can I get you something else to drink?"

She moved over to Hare's seat and leaned her side against his shoulder as I vacillated about what I felt like drinking. I really craved a glass of my sweet tea—or at least something close to it— but I announced that a glass of water would be most welcome.

"But do you really feel like something else?" Somehow she knew that I had another drink in mind. While I lingered on this silly hesitation, Lisa Hare took the chance, while she was leaning in against her husband in a partially protective, possessive, connubial way, to suddenly let down some of her generic feminine etiquette as a general hostess—as she had when she intimated, via a look to her husband earlier, that there had been some words between herself and her husband about the extremely low rent I was going to be charged for my palatial apartment. She seemed, as in the former case, to slightly hint that there might be idealisms in her husband that might make him seem vulnerable to the world. This protective quality was forgivable somehow in Lisa Hare, for it only had a motherly overtone to it—and not that of a general territoriality or acquisitiveness.

"Lawrence tells me you might do some articles on the Pauktaug Girl."

"I'm thinking about it—at least I'd like to have a little series on the old stays industry that would end in an examination of her."

"I was just kind of surprised that Lawrence gave over the Pauktaug Girl to you. I always thought that the Pauktaug Girl was an interest of Lawrence's and that he was close to taking it up as a subject himself." She offered this challenge without it seeming offensive.

Hare made it unnecessary for me to answer: "Lisa, I was the one who encouraged him to take up that subject. Rex is doing that for me." This satisfied her altogether, and she did not even listen to the cryptic appendix he added to his statement.

"I'm ready to skip over that subject."

"Now, Rex, what would you really like to drink," she smiled in a kind, irrefusable way.

"Sweet iced tea," I said with a grimace and a shrink, as if in a confession that I knew would meet with reproach.

"Oh, I have some powder!" Before I could stop her from fetch-

ing this totally inadequate substitute (I should say, totally unqual-
ified imposter), Lisa left her husband's side and jogged into the
kitchen in good spirits.

Reginald jogged after Lisa to the kitchen. Lawrence Hare and
I discussed the paper and its Friday deadline for a few minutes, and
then Lisa and Reginald reappeared in the dining room. Lisa had a
large glass of instant iced tea all ready for me and she handed it
over as she took her seat and caught her breath.

"You may want to stir that a bit more. Now, where was I in my
own story of my own romance? Well, this will say a lot about my
ability to see to the true golden core of a person, of a man.

"Lawrence Hare used to be quite stout, quite chubby—well,
quite too big!" Here Lisa let out a warm, intimate laugh, and I
thought for a time that it must be that she was easily sensitive to
wine, but then I recalled that she had not taken any alcohol. For
some reason she could tell, I think, that her husband had quite
accepted me, in a reserved and inexplicable way, and she made me
aware of this for the first time by her ebullient laugh. At least that
is how I first perceived her growing acceptance of me.

"Actually, Lawrence Hare was a chubby little bunny! Did you
know?" Lisa laughed quite vigorously again and leaned forward to
catch herself against the table. "But I was able to fall in love with
him anyway. And, as you can see—and by no effort or encouragement from me—I was rewarded with another kind of inner
Lawrence Hare, the thin Lawrence that was under the chubby one.
But of course I know that the thin Lawrence Hare still isn't the
real one. The real Lawrence Hare I fell in love with is still the one
I fell in love with—the one that is still at the very center of him,
maybe that part that is the heart that is really in the mind."

With her last phrases Lisa Hare became as endearingly earnest
as one can be about an intimacy that is of no interest to anyone
save for the couple concerned. Fearing that she had tried my
patience, however, she decided that she should try Lawrence Hare's

just a bit more so that she could escape the serious tone into which she had lapsed. Thus with another lapse into laughter, but this time with a compliment for Lawrence embedded in the joke, she asked me, "But did you know? Just look at him. Did you know how different he was physically in the past?"

Hare, with a light laugh that was meant to imply to Lisa that we were already ahead of her joke, gently inserted, "He's already seen a picture."

"Well, I wish I had been in on the process of whipping him into shape. I'd feel a little more like he did it for me, then!"

Perhaps I looked somehow like I was thinking about the food from our dinner at that moment, for Lisa suddenly pushed her chair back from the table just a bit and smiled.

"So, what did you think?"

I started to answer and to say how much I enjoyed everything when Hare interrupted me and asked, "Rex, was that enough for you?"

I assured him that it was, and I felt I would be relieved if Lisa could not read me as well as when she had suspected that I really wanted something else to drink, for all I could think of at that moment was a steak or a hamburger. The dinner had been very light.

"Well, you guys don't have to lie if you don't like it. I'll give Lawrence credit, Rex, he'll try and eat all the things I make, and eat all that I give him, but then I know he is eating other things on his own, too. But with all the energy he burns, I forgive him."

Lisa and Lawrence got up to clear the table. "More iced tea?" I welcomed it, even though the powder did not touch my beloved sweet tea.

"But don't drink too much. I have coffee to go with those cookies you brought."

Lawrence Hare did most of the table clearing, and then he disappeared for a time into the kitchen to take over the task of readying the coffee. With her motherliness somehow altogether restored, Lisa sat at the table with me and began to take the conversation, in a lowered, quieted way, in a direction that I experienced many times before when such a tone was invoked. This direction was unsure to me at first, however.

"So, Rex, you look in pretty good shape. What do you do for exercise?"

I told her a little version of my decline and fall in Georgia and of my resurrection of the last few months. And then I told her with a little laugh about my love and dependence on sweet tea.

"Well, you should be careful. Not only will that—anything with caffeine in it, and alcohol—dehydrate you, but if you keep drinking iced tea with that much sugar in it all the time, you're going to find yourself a diabetic someday."

I thought for a moment that the tone I had heard was really, in fact, the overture to her professional, admonitory routines. But she left the health topic, or at least the diet topic, with her last comment.

"So you run! Good for you!" There is something so condescending in that phrase of praise, "Good for you," that I am sure that if those who mean it with sincerity actually knew what it sounded like to perverse and precise fellows of language like myself, they would never use it again

I kept smiling, and I mustered all my attentiveness, but I was actually beginning to grow tired and irritated with Lisa, which was not fair. But such was the case. Then it suddenly became clear that the tone I had had my suspicions about above was indeed the tone I had thought it was: a matchmaker's tone. My interest in the conversation returned.

Lawrence Hare came back into the room when this confirmation came. Lisa looked back over her shoulder as Lawrence approached the table with the tray of coffee and cookies. Lisa was sounding me out as a bachelor, and she was indeed the matchmaker.

"Lawrence, what do you think of Dale for Rex?"

Lawrence Hare put the tray down and began to distribute the cups and saucers. He said nothing.

"Lawrence! What do you think of Dale for Rex?"

"Yes, I heard you. I was just thinking." Hare sighed. "Yeah, I don't know!" he said after another moment's pause with a smile, a rolling of the eyes, and a shrug of the shoulders.

"He's just sighing because it's frustrating to have found already his perfect, gorgeous girl. There's no hunt left for him. He's jealous of you, and giving you a totally incorrect impression of Dale."

It intrigued me not only that two women in the same day had made romantic speculations as to my appropriateness for this Dale Pocket, but also I wondered for the first time—and it seemed likely—whether Dale Pocket was a relation of Charles Pocket. And then I began to wonder about the mysterious Charles Pocket once more.

A lot of answers were easy to come by when I simply said, "Hey, I'm always looking. Tell me about this Dale gal. Who is she?"

"Well she's Charles' sister, to begin with." Lisa said this like I should already know who Charles was. I was pretty sure who he was, but I had a right by all my circumstances and by any consideration to affect total ignorance.

Thus Lisa asked, "You mean Lawrence didn't introduce you to Charles? You are so strange sometimes, Lawrence. I don't know what to make of you. Anyway, Rex, Charles is the attorney with the office right across the hall from *The Pauktaug Press*. And he happens to be Pauktaug's fastest man, if not the world's fastest man, as it may yet be proved."

I would have asked Lisa more of what she meant by Pocket possibly being the world's fastest man were it not for a unique expression that illuminated Hare's face for an instant. I had seen it once before, for a moment, back in the office that day, when Hank the sports columnist had first mentioned the name of Charles

Pocket. The expression on Hare's face was of equal brevity then, and I failed to think about it after I saw it, so I had no theory as to why Hare had formed it. But now that Hare presented this same expression at the mention of Pocket once more—and particularly at the instant when Pocket was described as possibly being the world's fastest man—I not only took the chance to question and analyze it in my mind, but took a chance to peer more directly at Hare's face than I had during the first instance of the expression's appearance.

There was only one way I could identify and describe Hare's expression. It was one of pride—and not of self-pride. There was a deep, inscrutable, but still palpable—however fleeting, for it was gone with Lisa's next phrase—expression of pride in another, in another's accomplishment, as if that accomplishment or potential stood to prove something in which Hare deeply believed or that would achieve an aim in which he had a deep and mysterious investment. Thus there was a curious mixture of conceit and self-lessness in this moment on Hare's face—which was articulated by a long, deep, inhalation, and a squinting of the eyes, like a man on the edge of a great vindication, at least in regard to some secret challenge he had set to himself.

Hare's pride was somehow articulated as much—if not more—by his body language. His torso seemed to react, as did his legs (from the shifting he did in his chair), as if these parts of the body could have said something to me about the man's pride if I was not already so attuned, as generally all human beings are, to reading the most complex of silent gestures via the human face.

Proceeding right from her last line, Lisa continued: "And Charles has also been a kind of friend, big brother—mentor figure, I guess you could call it—to Lawrence, even though he's just two or three years older than Lawrence." Between the final words of Lisa's sentence before this last one, and the point in this last phrase where she referred to Charles Pocket's role as a mentor, lived Hare's expression of pride. It vanished instantly when she referred to *big brother* and to *mentor figure.*

Lisa then suggested that we get to the coffee before it cooled off too much, and then she looked at her watch and said that she had to get ready to go to her gym. Having forgotten to do so during the regular course of the dinner, I thought I should raise a little toast—even if with coffee—to my generous hosts on all fronts.

They accepted my gesture, but Lisa was a bit embarrassed.

"Oh, Rex, this wasn't anything tonight. We're going to have more formal welcomes and parties than this. This was just a little something to have after your first day at work."

Hare then assured Lisa that he would take care of the table and that he and I and Reginald could entertain ourselves while she readied herself for her class. This he did quite well and warmly. He had also been quite talkative during the dinner itself, even though his occasional silences seemed the most telling aspect of his behavior that night.

My new Editor-in-Chief and I were talking about one piece I had been going over toward the end of the day, when Lisa Hare reappeared again. She was dressed remarkably like the woman runner I had seen on my first night in Pauktaug—black yoga shorts and black top that left her midriff exposed—but it was clear that this was not the same girl, the same woman. With nearly all her latent freckles exposed, and her feminine but precise muscle tone ready to harden at any shift of her frame, one could tell that, though this was a woman's body of equally extreme conditioning as the one I had seen on that Thursday night, this body was meant to speak a different language. It was not tense or guarded—even though hers was a slightly more hardened, muscled form than even the athletic statue I had seen on my first Pauktaug run—and it did not seem vigilant or tight even when her abdominal muscles sprouted intermittent messages of mysterious feminine brail when she stretched back her arms to adjust her jacket.

"We're all going to do something this weekend. I'm going to start planning it," Lisa assured me as she gave me a hug and peck goodbye, her motherly and enthusiastically solicitous concern for my comfort and possible loneliness quite touchingly sincere and warm—this erasing any vestige of her two small demonstrations (intimations, rather) of material defensiveness, and also ameliorating (but only a little) the increased, sexualized shock of her appearance in this second outfit.

After Lisa was gone, I could not help but raise my eyebrows and smile at Hare so as to silently compliment his good fortune, and then I asked the obligatory question as to whether Lisa had a sister.

Hare just smiled and laughed quietly. Then we talked a bit more and finished our coffee, and it was during this time that I watched Hare slowly finish all the cookies that I had brought. After Hare cleaned off the table, something in his mind called him to look through the dining room window over to *The Pauktaug Press.*

"There are still some things I have to do over there before I go out onto the water this evening for a bit. Rex, do you want to go for a little walk with Reginald and me before I have to go back to the office?"

I pleasantly declined, for I was growing incredibly sleepy by this point. But Hare and Reginald and I walked down to the sidewalk together.

"Rex, I'll see you in the morning. Feel free to ease into all this. There's no hurry for you. I mean it. Go slowly at first."

"Thanks, Lawrence. I will. Goodnight, Reginald. Nice to meet you."

We parted ways, and then I heard Hare's voice one last time that night. "Come on, Reginald. Let's go up to the office for a minute and take care of a few things, and then we'll go for our play session."

I intended to rest for just a bit, and then to rise for a few hours and work on some things of my own as ideas for the paper. But when I opened my eyes the radio was already sounding the morning alarm. Before I left for my run, I had to put an extra effort into making my bed, for though my mind had slept soundly and I had no memory of fitful wakefulness or sleeplessness and no memory of dreams, my body, my legs particularly, had kicked the covers and sheets from my bed so thoroughly that I had to retrieve them from the knotted mass they had formed a full yard or two from my bed, in the corner of the room.

CHAPTER 8

THE PACK GROWS

My second day at work was different than my first in that I worked for long stretches completely undisturbed. Hare already seemed pleased with my work patterns and with what I had gone over for the Friday trip to the press. I did not see him even once after coming in for the morning. Kee-Poh was out in the field that day, and Randy and Hank had their lunches with them, so I took my lunch on Main Street in solitude. But later in the day, around a quarter to five, Hare suddenly appeared at my door.

I was just then sketching out my first editorial, putting forth a broad exposition as an unprejudiced newcomer to Pauktaug with no historical knowledge of the town—part of my projected series that would eventually end in an examination of Pauktaug's heyday as a stays town and with a look at her symbol, the Pauktaug Girl—when Hare wanted to tell me about a call he just had from his wife.

"Rex, I was just talking to Lisa on the phone. Your great-grandmother still wasn't back as of this afternoon, so Lisa called her again in the city. Lisa said she sounded fine—remarkably alert and awake—but that her ankle and foot are very swollen from her fall of yesterday. And your great-grandmother would like to wait out the swelling in the city—and get back here by the weekend or early next week. But she's clear of mind, and very upset that she missed your arrival because of her forgetfulness of last week."

"Does she injure herself a lot?" I asked.

"Actually, no," Hare answered. "She slips in and out of her forgetfulness, but this is the first real physical injury I've known her to suffer. So I think it must be fairly serious for her to want to rest in the city for so long. She doesn't usually stay there very long—just a few days, usually, just to check on her townhouse there. Again, Lisa said she sounded extremely alert, even shockingly young of mind, so I think the sprain or injury must be pretty severe to have knocked her into a state of such lucidity."

"Is she all alone in the city?" I inserted here.

"No, not at all. She has a full-time, live-in maid there. It's only out here, where she lives more rustically that she relies on Lisa and me to look in on her. But you and I can go in and check on her soon if it doesn't seem like she plans to return here by the end of the week or the weekend."

"Can I call her there?"

"Of course," Hare said as he handed me a slip of paper. "I was just about to give you the number when you thought of it. You can try right now, from here. I'll leave you to it."

Hare vanished for a time, and I closed my door and tried to make my call. But my attempts to reach my great-grandmother in the city were no more fruitful than my attempts to reach her by telephone at her Pauktaug apartment. So, almost thinking her a mythical, non-existent figure by this time—and one that the Hares seemed content to monitor and care for on their own anyway—I guiltily confess that I quickly forgot about my great-grandmother not long after I put down the telephone. And despite the lateness of the day, I was able to lose myself once more in my editorial sketch of a newcomer's first landing on the shores of Pauktaug.

I had left my door ajar after finishing my failed attempt to contact my great-grandmother, and my concentration on my work did not prevent me from hearing the departure of Hank and Randy, who left together to share an umbrella in a light and misting rain.

For a long while as I continued to scribble on a legal pad, I thought I heard the murmur of Lawrence Hare's voice in the main office—he on one of the telephones in that room. It was not till well past five, as the thin, vanguard drops of the misty rain were followed by large packs of downward racing showers, when I started to ready myself for my short walk home for the evening, that I could tell that there was more than one voice quietly murmuring in the office. I thought for a moment that the second voice might be Kee-Poh's—he having returned from his long day out on the town. But soon I could tell that the second voice was new to me. All I could detect about the voice was a confidence in it—a curt solidness that seemed sure of its assents and dissents as Hare fielded low murmurings of questions and descriptions.

So though I was not surprised to open the door and see other than Kee-Poh sitting with Hare, I was rather astonished to see the man I presumed to be Charles Pocket, Esq., sitting back in the chair that belonged to Randy's desk—his feet propped up on a spare chair that was usually kept for visitors by the front door.

Before I announced myself, I allowed myself to eavesdrop for another moment as I put my desk in order and gathered those things that I wished to take home with me to work on for the evening. From just a few tiny phrases and discernible words, I could tell that Hare was describing to the presumed Pocket the details of our encounter with the thieving lobsterman out on the Sound just two nights before.

And I could make out a few topics that were shared between the two as I prepared my arrival into the room with noisy shuffles in the back corner of my office. The topics I made out seemed to have to do with police involvement with the issue of the lobster theft, and something along the lines of Hare and this Pocket fellow taking photographs of the situation if a similar circumstance cropped up again before any official remedy was applied or took effect.

I turned out my light, and I walked into the room. Lawrence Hare rose from a chair.

"Rex, this is Charles Pocket. He's our nearest neighbor—just across the hall—in this building." Pocket rose from his chair, took a few steps forward, and shook hands with me.

I surprised myself when I suddenly said to Pocket: "I think I've seen you running—and running very fast—each morning down Main Street."

"Well," answered Pocket, with a friendly, impressed smile, as if I had proven more observant than he had expected, "you probably did. I do end a lot of my runs right here at work. We have a little shower room in our office across the way, so it's easy for me to start work right away at the end of a run here. Yes, it was probably me that you saw—unless you were seeing a fast runner around the time of midnight or so. In that case you saw Hare."

This was the first time that anyone had alluded to Hare's running. Now I was sure that I had my two mysterious runners identified. And I did. Yet Lawrence Hare gave no definite reaction to Pocket's last phrase. In fact, he merely bided the time of Pocket's talking, as if he were allowing a charge, almost a child of some kind, a bit of expected free time.

Pocket, in a fatherly, rather condescending way, had patted Hare on the shoulder when he had alluded to Hare's running. Again, Hare did nothing. I waited for Pocket to take his seat again—and then took one myself after Hare pushed one to me— and then I picked up the talk along the same course.

"I'm pretty sure that it was you that I saw, Mr. Pocket, in the morning." Here, of course, he quickly commanded that I call him

Charles. "But I have seen Lawrence running, as well, I think. I'm pretty sure of that, too. And it was indeed around the midnight to early morning time that you talk about for him."

I looked to Hare then, and he still appeared indifferent, almost not present, but his demeanor was not without a pleasant look to his neutrality.

"Well, as to my running, Rex," continued Pocket, "don't mention any frequent sightings to my wife. I'm not supposed to be running that much, really." He then gently tapped his chest—somewhat lower than where people gesture to indicate their heart. Thus it was unclear to me if he meant that his running was a threat to his heart, or his lungs, or some other organ in the torso—or perhaps the gesture was just an unusual invocation of a confidence meant for me.

Somehow Lawrence Hare must have felt that his silence was beginning to speak something after a time, or bringing an attention to itself that he did not intend. The content of what he broke in with surprised me, however (though he still deflected all such subject matter away from himself).

"You know, Rex, Charles here is the president of the Pauktaug Running Club. You've started to run yourself, you say. Maybe you'd be interested." This comment set Pocket into a mild excitement. Not only did he seem zealous about the topic of running in general, but he seemed to enjoy the recruitment duties of his position as president of the local club—as if he felt he fulfilled a sort of social task of goodwill, a sort of male, fatherly, counterpart to the social solicitude that I felt Lisa Hare had displayed the night before.

"That's right, Rex. We sure do have a club here. We have four organized group runs each week. If you think you can stay out for at least a little over an hour, we can pair you off with someone of your own level. We have all levels in the group. But why don't you start by coming to our monthly meeting. We're going to have part of this month's meeting at my house this Saturday night. Let me tell you how to get there. But wait. Hare can take you."

"Sure, Rex can just come with me," volunteered Hare. He had just then come away from the window where he had been watching the light rain let up and suddenly cease altogether.

"Lawrence is on the race committee in the club," Pocket volunteered. This surprised me even more about Hare. He had seemed so secretive about his running, that it surprised me that he would involve his running interests with any club, let alone a committee within the club to promote and organize races.

I did not react to this, and yet Hare seemed to have reached his mysterious limit as to running discussions for the day. He took advantage of the abatement in the rain to announce, "Rex, Charles—I'm going to head out now onto the water to check some things while there seems to be some dry air and clear sky out there. I'll see you both later. Oh, Rex, did you reach your great-grandmother?"

"No, I didn't. But I'll try again later."

"That's odd that she didn't answer. Lisa just talked to her at that number. But I'm sure she'll pick up eventually. All right, see you both later."

"But, Lawrence!" interjected Pocket as he craned his neck far to the left so as to catch Hare before he was entirely out of the door—Pocket looking rather like a disappointed father who was losing the full group he had planned to have at hand for some activity that was about to happen. "I thought we were going to watch this tape."

Hare paused in his tracks in the open door. He stopped with a governed intensity that almost suggested one who was running in place at a street corner and waiting for traffic to pass and a light to change—this though his body did not move.

"No. I really have to get out onto the water—even get started right now with what you and I were just talking about, Charles. Anyway, I've seen that stuff before."

"Only some of it—just a little of it actually. This is a much longer version. This is the one that they couldn't show on television because it was too long."

"No," Hare smiled, and then he looked over his shoulder and into the hall as if his invisible traffic light was about to change. His body, but not his eyes when he looked back in the room one last time, seemed to indicate that the light had just turned green.

"No, why don't you and Rex watch it together. Rex is doing his first piece—for next week's paper—on being new to the terrain of Pauktaug. He'll enjoy that tape. It will show him some parts of the village that he hasn't seen already, perhaps."

"All right," sighed Pocket. Then the door closed and Hare was gone. "What do you say, Rex, want to see a long tape of Pauktaug's last road race?"

"Actually, yes. I'd like to see it in fact for the very reasons that Lawrence just mentioned."

"Great, come on over to my office. I have a television and VCR in the reception room."

Pocket and I left the office of *The Pauktaug Press*. I turned out the light and locked the door when I left. I was not sure if I should have done that, and I muttered as much to Pocket as we moved down the hall.

"It doesn't matter. Hare has a key. He goes back and forth, in and out of there so much, he won't even remember who was out of there last. You know, he does so much in one day, works so hard, he's going to kill himself one day. He really is."

In the company of Charles Pocket, I passed through the doorway with the heaviest carving, the darkest and most weighty representation of the Pauktaug Girl, and entered the lavish, expensively clean and sparse office of Charles Pocket, Esq.

Pocket produced a chair for me and offered me something to drink. He said he was going to have a bottled water, and I agreed to join him in that. As he went about the process of getting the water, I was able to note that he was a rather tall man, who needed to take fewer strides than a man of average height in order to cover the same ground. He was several inches over six feet tall, but he was not what one would call lanky. He did not present the impression of well-proportioned strength that Hare did with his body, though Pocket's was most definitely the form of an extremely well-conditioned athlete for his age—that age I took to be either mid-thirties, or a well-disguised late-thirties.

Pocket's body resembled more of what one would expect from a runner's body. But though he was not as strong and muscular as Hare, Pocket was not of the thinness that one sees in some of the world's most skilled and ambitious distance runners. To compare him to Hare in one final way, his eyes did not have a look of incongruity with his body—that is to say, both his body and his eyes seemed on an equal plane. He looked rested and conditioned when one looked at his person, and more or less in equal sorts when one surveyed his inner resources via a look into his eyes.

Otherwise, one might note that he was a man with firm, well-defined features, attractively weathered in his skin, and with a full head of rusty brown hair and a full mustache of the same color.

Pocket and I sat for a time drinking our water and watching the fading daylight and the return of a light rain over Main Street. He told me that Hare had given him a fair idea of my story, but he asked me to give a little summary myself as he readied a large television and a VCR that were in the northeast corner of the room. As I told him a quick version of my recent autobiography I was able to confirm that his friendly responses and hospitality were somehow founded on a mild condescending confidence that had never failed him nor had been challenged. It was a condescension couched in just enough amicability to make it tolerable, thus one did not feel compelled to check the man or remove one's self with great haste from his company. And somehow one knew that he constantly relied on this same consistent dosage of self-confidence and latent, paternal didacticism—which translated then, at that moment, as affected interest in one's personal history. One felt that he was sure that his material prosperity was based on his unfailing application of this middling intelligence, but combined with a rational acceptance that chance or acts of God could tumble it down. Somehow this all breathed forth from him, even when this runner was at rest.

I was rather sure that my mother would like him and be glad that I had fallen into his company. I tried not to hold this against him for his sake, for though I was altogether sure that my mother might find reasons to like one who prospered even by questionable means so long as it came within the confines of the law, it was even harder to find affection for a man that I knew she would think was exemplary—for Pocket was one who not only believed in material and temporal things, but he had a slight, specious, set of foxhole moral checks that can make some materialists nearly repulsive to me.

I was thinking too intensely on this for a moment, for I suddenly heard Pocket repeating a question to me. After I answered and apologized, I registered what I must confess now: that for all that I could evidently perceive in Pocket, I did not find him unlikable. I felt that so long as I did not give him an impression that I would totally accept the hackneyed emptiness of his condescension, then he would have a fair knowledge of me, and therefore no misunderstandings could creep into any connection that might develop. Thus with the intention, as well, of never allowing him to believe that I did not know he only spoke of abstractions and spirit for trivial or practical purposes—spoke these things against that time (death) when no one's theory can seem utterly certain—I allowed Pocket and myself to proceed with an acquaintance and an incipient friendship, so long as it stayed in the realm of casual observations.

Just before the tape began, I asked Pocket what kind of law he practiced.

"I'm in real estate." He seemed transfixed by the tape at that moment. "I know Lawrence has seen most of this already, but I wish he was here to see the new parts."

Suddenly the first logo and picture came onto the screen, and I can easily say that the excitement and pride that were evident in Pocket's contained stillness were matched, if not exceeded, by the sensation that went through me on seeing that particular image and those that succeeded it within a few seconds—a sensation of sincere shock.

There before me were the familiar images of a small cable sports channel that I had not seen for a seemingly long time, though in fact it had only been days since I had last been in the cafeteria back in Georgia. I did not have much time to wonder at the coincidence of seeing these images again so soon, or time to tell Charles Pocket, for the sake of friendly small talk, that the taped channel had so many pleasant and recent associations for me, for suddenly I was not only looking at a program from a station to which I was accustomed, but a program that I had seen already during one of my dinners in the cafeteria. The program began with a pictorial and narrative survey of a ten-kilometer course in the northeast, a new course and a new race, and to my greatest astonishment yet on Long Island, it was clear that the rolling, dark hills and streets shown in the preamble of the program were the dark hills and streets of Pauktaug. Now all my puzzlement as to the familiarity of the village—so many vantages seeming somehow vaguely known to me as I ran the streets in the evenings and early mornings—was erased by this simple evidence that I had indeed seen Pauktaug before in intimate detail via television as I mulled over catfish and pieces of pecan pie.

I was about to speak up to Pocket about my familiarity with the program when more material suddenly appeared on the screen. Evidently, at Pocket's request, the cable station had mailed him the extended version of the program that had not made it to the broadcast. Because Hare and Pocket were difficult to find at the end of the race, the station had decided not to include the material that the camera crew and reporter had hunted down some days after the event. While Hare had slipped quietly away at the end of the race, even neglecting his duties as a Pauktaug Running Club member in disassembling the course, Pocket was taken to the emergency room of Huntington Hospital because he complained of mild dizziness, weakness, and even chest pain a few minutes after completing his nearly superhuman, but very unofficial, ten-kilometer course record.

"This is the material I wanted Lawrence to see," muttered Pocket as scenes of himself resting outside the hospital on a bench came onto the screen. "Neither of us has seen this yet. They went looking for Lawrence, but he wouldn't have anything to do with an interview."

"Why was that?"

"He felt that the furor over our times took away from our efforts to get this new race firmly established—especially as there was suspicion that we rigged it just for the sake of advertising next year's race. And, anyway, he said I was the only one who won."

"I think I can understand that," I said.

"But let me tell you, Rex, that race was not a publicity stunt. Hare and I just ran some kind of freakish time. I can't totally explain it. I don't know if I could ever repeat that achievement. I still don't really believe it myself."

Then Pocket shushed me, even though I was not saying a word. A look of pride came over his face, as he listened to himself being interviewed on the tape. This look of pride, it was nothing like the look I had seen on Hare's face more than once when the subject of Pocket's running had surfaced. This was a truly self-absorbed pride, a childlike pride, even though the shush he had hissed to me was as paternal and condescending as all his usual utterances, gestures, and expressions.

From this interview, and from things that Pocket told me himself after the tape was through, I learned a great deal of Pocket's general history, as well as his unusual and ultimately unique history as a runner and racer. I had been about right in my guess as to his age. He had been born in 1966. Thus he turned thirty-five during my first year in Pauktaug. But I soon found out, despite his relatively advanced age as far as athletes are concerned (but not necessarily distance runners), that his running career had been shockingly short—even though it had begun during his second year of high school, when he was in the tenth grade. But how could it be such a short running career if Pocket had started when he was fifteen years old, and here before me, then (twenty years later), I found him reviewing a tape of a running achievement that had occurred only months before? Curiously, his high school running career, which was extremely significant and weighted with the mute prescience that only hindsight could give it (a hindsight that I was far from applying to it yet), had been very short.

It seemed that one autumn, in 1981, Pocket had gone out for his track team on something of a lark—not realizing just how fast he really was. When the call went out for walk-ons to appear at the first track meetings and practices, Pocket made only an acceptable showing in the very short distances, the sprints. But when the longer runs were tried, the coach saw a very young man that not only was the fastest at those distances—a boy that could sustain what would be another student's average sprint, and could sustain that sprint for any amount of time—but a young man who showed no signs of being winded at the end of such runs. So it was that Pocket, after a few practices, broke, though unofficially (but officially enough for the coach by his own stopwatch) the world record for his age groups. And as the time of the first meet approached, the coach had long given up his worry about the competition and had Pocket semi-secretly working on solidifying the possibility that he could beat the standing world record, by an extreme margin, in the mile.

Of course this semi-secret was almost impossible to maintain, and as the final practices leading up to the first meet took place, Pocket spun around the Pauktaug High School track for a larger and larger audience—spun around that track like a long playing record to which some giant, unseen being suddenly gave extra pushes by placing its finger on the inner label of the disc and pressing the speed so that the very air about Pocket seemed of a higher pitch, and the dust and early fallen leaves flew outward as if by the centrifugal spirit of his laps.

And thus the community—even agents of *The Pauktaug Press* (Thomas Crabbe, Lisa Hare's father and then Editor-in-Chief of the paper; and Hank, who was then still a teacher at the high school but already a columnist for *The Pauktaug Press*)—waited for the day to come when Charles Pocket would give an official timing that could be published, and point to the shocking fact that the world's fastest man over an extended distance was a high school sophomore from the north shore of Long Island.

But then a greed set in—and as is always the case with sports of racing, this greed is based on how little one is left with rather than how much (of the commodity, time)—and two weeks before the first track meet, when the high school was opened to all the other schools in the district for an arts festival, the coach held a practice meet for his athletes during the lunch break for all the visiting students. The stands were filled with children from kindergarten level up to high school as each distance was run as a sort of little performance—replete with an explanation via a bullhorn from the pride-bursting coach. Though very few of the children in the stands were in any way aware of the impending expectations for the first real track meet that would be held some weeks later (including, surely, Lawrence Hare, then a pudgy, non-descript junior high school student, or Lisa Hare née Lisa Crabbe, both of whom then had only a passing awareness of one another but were both in the stands that day), the audience was fascinated when the mile was announced by the assistant coach. The head coach seemed to have lost interest in his role as emcee for the children, and now took the peculiar step of mounting a bicycle in one of the outside lanes after he lined up his four boys for the mile. The coach seemed to give particular attention to one boy, and after the assistant coach fired the starting gun, this same boy distanced himself from the others after only half a lap. The coach, with the bicycle, took the lane beside the lead boy (a stopwatch was taped to the handlebars), and as the other boys faded away, the coach began to visibly shout the ever-accelerating lead runner unto greater and greater speeds.

The sight of this miraculous runner in motion seemed to tell the eye it was being fooled somehow (for though the runner's form and gait, and even gestures indicating effort, were quite common, the background moving behind him let one know that an almost supernatural speed was being reached). He neared the start of his third lap. Soon it was clear that the coach on the bicycle was having trouble keeping up with the runner while shouting his admonitions, checking his watch, and checking to see that the crowds could also see this miracle unfolding—having trouble doing all this at the same time. But it should be observed that this coach was not an old man with little athletic skill. His cycling style was clean, conditioned, and practiced. It was just that he went from being the pacer to the paced quite suddenly—but the frustration of that discovery was far outweighed by the sight of his miler pulling out farther and farther, fulfilling the greed of little time more and more with each accelerating step.

The coach pulled the bicycle up before the first turn in the third lap, and pedaled back to the starting line so as to holler young Charles Pocket through the start of his last lap, and then a bit later into the finish line. But as Pocket finished that third lap and came into direct view of the stands and the shouting coach, the desire to press on, the desire to realize what Pocket knew the coach was expecting, the desire to realize what the crowd of all ages was beginning to suspect might occur despite a million years of negative proof that thwarts such constant instinctual hope, was not enough to drive him through a sudden violent constriction in his chest. It came suddenly as he was nearing the start of lap four and as he was approaching a pace he felt he had never before grazed. He had felt this constriction coming on during the last phase of the coach's ride with him, but he was able to contain it via a little lessening of the pace on the far side of the track. But as he rounded to the stands' side of the track once more, that driving hope of so many became as his own hope, and Pocket pushed himself into a pace he had never tried before, and that is when the full vice of the pain seized him.

Pocket was going so fast when the pain came that he almost fell, almost fell off of himself, he felt—as if his legs, his body, were independent of him, of his mind (for he felt no dizziness or light-headedness, or even windedness)—and when he crumbled to his knees on the grassy inside of the track, those that were standing nearby remarked that Pocket was in remarkable command of his breath. He did not seem to be out of wind at all, and yet he was just able to mutter under his controlled breath, and from behind a tightening band of intense pain in his chest, "Something in me won't let me do this."

The coach ran over to Pocket and shouted: "That was fantastic. You look good. What's wrong? Why did you stop?"

Pocket could only repeat his last phrase a few more times. He remained on his knees for several minutes, genuflecting under a clear, cool, autumn sky—afraid to move again, since the pain had vanished and he was terrified that moving his legs once more would bring back the feeling of an invisible vice squeezing against his ribs.

But after a brief interval, the coach and assistant coach raised Pocket to his feet. The crowd, somehow using the silent time while Pocket was on his knees to bury again their universal, mysterious, recognition of a long disproved but somehow still constant and viable and impossible expectation, applauded lightly as Pocket was led back to the school by his coaches and several teachers and teammates.

Pocket was taken to the hospital, and later to his family doctor—and from there, too, to a specialist—but all pronounced Pocket a completely healthy young man. But something in Pocket's mind would not allow his body to be such a complete winner that day, so it was Pocket's mind that won. No one would ever say that he seemed forever wounded afterwards—a man plagued by anxiety or any kind of mental disturbance. But Pocket's mind won out in this particular, singular kind of activity. The boy refused to run competitively ever again. He was always game to play light sports and to tussle outdoors in games of catch or basketball—so that, again, no one felt that he had been comprehensively wounded with an insurmountable fear. But he would not take to any kind of pure running, neither on the track nor on the road. He would not again let his body be tempted by himself or by others to any such speed and pain.

Thus Pocket's seemingly imminent and miraculous entrance onto a new stage for humanity was dismissed rather sadly and quickly by all who had pledged such interest in those last weeks before the first official meet, and after that season even the coach resigned from his track work to retire exclusively into a laconic passiveness of classroom health education. Since the track coaching was one of the implied duties of his high school position, this teacher was moved to one of the junior high schools the next year and was never heard to volunteer for coaching again.

And thus Pocket slipped quite quickly into the adult world of those who do not run, of those who lose memory of the feel of breaking out of the stride that carries one through the fastest of walks and into the inchoate stages of running. Nearly twenty years passed for Pocket—twenty years, a time in which Pocket walked through college, law school, the early years of his work as an attorney in the city, his marriage, the birth of his children, and the recent flourishing of his solo law practice in his home village of Pauktaug.

But then a year before the running of the *First Annual Pauktaug Ten-Kilometer Run,* Pocket found the gratitude of the Pauktaug Running Club to be so intense (because of his pledges as one of the first sponsors of the race, and because of his volunteered legal services for many aspects of the new race's launching committee), that he suddenly found himself, a non-runner, not only inducted into the club—hardly a member of which remembered or ever knew of Pocket's glancing blow with dashing fame and disaster in the past—but also nominated for president of the club when the end of the last president's term coincided with Pocket's volunteer efforts on behalf of Pauktaug Village's new race.

Pocket's interview and the continuing overview on the extended cable program went on to explain further. Not only did Charles Pocket accept the nomination and win the election for president of the Pauktaug Running Club, but he also began to run again—discretely and quietly at first by himself for about six months, and then he even attended a few of the group runs with the club. At the group runs he kept with the moderate runners and kept up many leisurely conversations about the business of the club and the new race—not wishing to reveal that he was rediscovering that much of his old skill of speed seemed still to be intact. And

Pocket carefully avoided the Tuesday track workout nights with the club so as to avoid extreme temptation.

But as the race drew nearer he found the business of the club and the race made extreme demands on his time, so when he ran in the last few months before the race, he ran by himself in the early mornings—save for when he had the company of his business neighbor, Lawrence Hare. But even his runs with Hare were confined to a few occasions.

And then came the race, and Pocket discovered not only his old speed intact but also the intimation that the malady that followed his miraculous track performance of so long ago might still be there, as well. But, again, nothing serious was ultimately found when doctors examined Pocket, and so even he dismissed his latest pains as merely a psychosomatic memory.

The augmented but unaired version of the program ended with a few, rough, home video camera long-shots of Pocket and Hare finishing the race, and then the credits (which I had seen before) rolled with panoramic aerial scenes of Pauktaug.

"I guess Hare was right," mused Pocket. "If this version of the show—or even more talk from him and me about this last race—was out there, then he and I would have an even harder time attracting a large elite field for the second race. And for the second running of the race we hope to have the course officially certified and to have the race timed in the most advanced and professional manner—probably by computer chip timing."

Pocket said his last phrase in one long, indifferent breath. I took a guess at what I should say next, and I was right.

"But I for one—and I am sure many others—can't wait to see you prove your time, or beat it, when everything is official. Surely the hope of that happening will bring even more attention to the race."

Pocket smiled. The childlike part of him had been flattered and pleased. That part of him at peace then, his paternal self was able to safely slide into place again: "That may be true," he laughed, "but not only am I not sure if I'm going to run competitively again, but I really do want to keep the bad press (the rumors that the race is nothing but a self-serving vehicle, and some think a hoax, too) out of the picture. But, again, despite what I just said on that tape, I'm not sure I want to challenge my health with this kind of thing. I'm not really sure—I'm really not—that the super-timings that Hare and I came up with at the race weren't really some kind of mistake or mix-up somehow. But, still, I don't know how so many things could have gone secretly wrong so as to give us the timings that we got. Yet in my training runs I never pushed much faster than the 10K record for my age group, so, still, even I think that something may have gone wrong with the whole thing at the race. Maybe the elite guy ran slower than he thinks—had a bad day—and the course is just short, giving Hare and me our times. I don't think that could be, but I still don't somehow believe in what happened anyhow. And I'm afraid to test it again—at least right now. People in the club are always after me to try the course again and get a good, clean timing. But I'm not going to think about that right now."

"Well, I believe you did it," I chimed in. "Why shouldn't it be possible?"

"That's exactly what Lawrence said," nodded Pocket as he smiled again and got up to stop and rewind the tape—and to stretch a bit, both conventionally, and in the manner of an athlete's routine. "I see why Hare liked you and picked you. You both think alike!" laughed Pocket.

I feigned to laugh, as well, at this rather meaningless, commonplace observation and joke, and I unwittingly gained an unsought bit of ground with Pocket from this little bit of forced affability.

"No, really," continued Pocket as he recovered from his affected laugh at his affected witticism, "I can see why Hare likes you, I think. I haven't read any of your stuff yet, but I bet you're just enough like Hare in writing style to please him, but also enough of a different kind of person in practical respects to help him clean the paper up."

After Lisa Hare, Pocket was the second person to imply that I came at the right time to help Lawrence Hare. But Hare's wife had never intimated that the quality of the paper needed changing. Pocket was implying this, and any circuitous praise he was offering me was not enough to quell a sense of involuntary irritation for Hare's sake.

"What's unclean in the paper?" I smiled. I knew he did not mean obscenities, but I really did not know what he meant otherwise. Thus I was curious to hear his answer.

"Well, he doesn't tell anyone, but from some of the conversations he has had with me, I don't think the paper is paying for itself right now. I really don't." And then Pocket offered a leap of intimacy that I found disturbing and undesirable to hear in many respects. "And, you know, no one reads those things of Hare's—those editorials that are more like rambling nineteenth-century philosophical essays than anything else."

I could not help but show my indignation at that point—not only for the allegiance I felt already for Hare because of his kindness, but also because of my very interest in those *philosophical essays.* And there was also something of that embarrassment that comes over a newcomer when one hears the first bit of confirmation that any new place is like any other—filled with the same petty, tiring whisperings, and unattractive assertions that pry into one's confidence (pry more than one would expect, or anyone else would expect for the seemingly confident newcomer), pry into the decision of having moved one's entire life a thousand miles because of the faith one might have in the sudden appearance of rambling essays in an increasingly specialized, certified, and materialistic world.

"Well, *I* read them," I said with enough flat neutrality so as not to throw away the sincerity of my belief (or to compromise the degree of my allegiance) with too much of a heated response too soon. For, after all, I realized that I had not been there, or hardly anywhere yet, long enough to form any kind of allegiances.

Though I could be convinced then, and rightly so, that Pocket knew nothing of my true intellectual or social interests, somehow the tone of what I said pleased Pocket even more than my last, forced, little laugh. I was unwittingly and successfully working, running, my way through a gauntlet that Pocket perhaps subconsciously administered to newcomers with regularity. To begin with, he must have thought that I did not take myself too seriously. Secondly, I had loyalties, and he understood that though I had not yet offered them to anyone exclusively, he approved of my caution.

Either this last gesture of mine impressed and embarrassed him, because it intimated I had a maturity that he wished he had displayed, or his next gesture was simply his process of expressing full approval of me. For Pocket rose and went behind his desk and proceeded to affect his most confident, paternal, and condescending tone yet. And this seemed to have a quality of probationary intimacy, I believe he thought—and this was, I think he believed as well, rather like my intimated hesitation to express full loyalties at such an early stage.

"So, Rex, you know that you and I are the only ones that have seen this tape. I have a copy at home of the broadcast that aired. Now that I've seen this one, I don't think I'm going to bring it home. I never told my wife about my problem—or perhaps my imagined problem—during that high school mock track meet from so long ago. It just never came up. And since I do like to run for myself now again—though lightly—and since I don't know if I might like to push myself in the future, I don't want to worry her. I'll show it to her later, after I've been running again for awhile— maybe for another year or so. She's a kind of hypochondriac for everyone but herself."

I did not care to be included in keeping any sort of petty family secrets, but I was suddenly put off the track of all thought when

I then saw a photograph on Pocket's desk of the woman I was sure I had seen during my first night run in Pauktaug.

"Dale," Charles Pocket suddenly said with a smile. With equal suddenness I emerged out of the imperious line of a million years of self-replication, consciousness of that line affording an immense temporal view into the primitive past, but at the same time devoid of all individual personality—such that one wondered why the urge to mate and to keep the human chain growing would be so strong if it sublimated the individuality of the very links that lived in their slivers of brief uniqueness.

"Are you seeing anyone, Rex?"

"No," I muttered.

"Good. I was already thinking you would be a good person to introduce to Dale." Pocket picked up the photograph and pointed to the young woman in black. "This is Dale—Dale Pocket, my sister."

"*That's* your sister," I involuntarily said, without the intent of lewd levity that is usually meant when men use italic emphasis when referring to a woman. My astonishment was that this woman should be related to anyone at all, somehow—and not that Charles Pocket in particular appeared to be of a stock that could not share in this woman's line.

"When were you born, Rex?"

"1971."

"Good, close enough. She'd be perfect for you. She'd hate me for this—would say that I don't think enough of what she does for a living. Maybe I don't. I can't remember the term for what she does. It's the same as Lisa's. What is that called?"

"Is she a personal trainer?"

"Yes, that's it. That's what it is called. Dale! That girl got out of college, could have done anything—instead she's been a personal trainer for the last ten years. There is a mind there. She proved it in school. But the more she gets in shape, the quieter, and I think more sullen—or unreachable, I think—she gets. But nothing bad has ever really happened to her. So except for the long line of men she's had pounding at her door for her to interview and reject, I can't figure out why she isn't all settled down by now. Maybe she's waiting for you."

This unusually candid and generous suggestion from what was usually the most protective party (a brother) of a beautiful woman filled me with a foolishly warm regard for my present companion.

"So, Rex, I was thinking, even before we started watching this tape, of asking if you might like to join my family for dinner on Thursday night. But let's make a double effort of it. If you're available on Thursday, I'll see if Miss Dale Pocket can't be persuaded to meet someone who strikes me for her. I know we just met, but I thought I'd counter her assertion that she likes to act on impulse in her selections with an impulsive selection of my own for her. But don't be surprised, or offended, if she tries to resist simply because she'll maintain that I'm not really capable of the same kind of impulsiveness and spontaneity that she thinks she has."

"No, I won't—won't be offended. I'll just be happy to meet her."

Pocket and I parted ways, and my day of revealed identities ended quietly. I tried calling my great-grandmother again, but this time I reached an answering machine or service, and I could not tell if it recorded my message properly for I never heard the traditional beep which was the signal to begin talking. But I was so immaturely interested in the prospect of meeting the statue, Miss Dale Pocket, that I confess that thoughts of my injured great-grandmother were scandalously far from my mind.

The week went quickly. Most of the time was spent in the happy rush of getting the paper ready for the weekend deadline. I saw little of Hare during the rest of that week. And, of course, I kept my appointment at the Pockets' for dinner—at their enormous colonial house some two miles or more west of the village on Sunken Cemetery Road. There I met the Pocket children who agitated the entire evening by pounding on a distant piano in the living room—even during dinner. There, as well, I met Mrs. Lynn Pocket, an attractive but peripheral figure whose only role was indeed a vague hypochondria on behalf of her husband, children, and guests. But I did not meet Miss Dale Pocket. I was stood up on my blind date, and I absorbed this blow with the good-nature that succeeds the outcomes of most long-shot hopes. The Pockets were profusely apologetic.

And I learned, too, that evening that Dale Pocket and Lawrence Hare had been connected romantically at one point—before Lawrence Hare had married Lisa Crabbe. Why the Pockets told me this bit of childish gossip—especially when they had hoped to connect me with Dale Pocket—I cannot say. This topic came up when the Pockets were speaking to me about Lawrence Hare—and how no man had changed so much in his appearance as had Hare when he suddenly decided to regularly chase Charles Pocket in his training for the first 10K to be held in Pauktaug Village. But nothing was said of the remarkable speed that Hare had shown in his second place finish in the race itself. Too much talk of Hare seemed to agitate Charles Pocket in a singular way, and the topic slipped away—even though it was Pocket who had brought up the subject of Hare.

I could only divert myself that evening in observing Charles Pocket. I helped to keep his little secret for him from his wife (his high school track experience)—even though I had caught more window glimpses of his Main Street training when I rose from bed each morning, and I had many questions about his running. But I could not help but notice that something else preyed upon him. For all his paternal confidence, he would look about his estate at times in a helpless, childlike way—as if some elemental, chastising force was imminently due for arrival, to remind Pocket of an inevitable task that lay ahead and exclusively on his shoulders.

CHAPTER 9

CROSS TRAINING

The next morning's run banished my disappointment of having been evidently dismissed as a blind date prospect by Dale Pocket. And my first Friday at work in Pauktaug held a quiet excitement for me. Though I had had experience writing for the airline magazine for some time, and had been in its office working against deadlines on more than one occasion, I was always detached from the final production of any given issue once my own piece or pieces had been submitted or revised. But even though I was not yet to the point of contributing an original article of my own to *The Pauktaug Press*, the excitement of the busyness in that small office as Hare, Randy, Kee-Poh, and myself (Hank was done with his sports labors) worked to make the most of each minute, and raced to make it to an unseen but somehow palpable tape of a temporal finish line held as if between the fingers of the printer's employees, was quite exciting. But I should qualify this last statement just a bit, for though Hare could not be said to have ever rested for even a moment from his writing and editorial duties that day, nor could it be said that he ever showed a sign of anxiousness during this period—never showed an indication that his labors, his efforts toward celerity in this intellectual and manual challenge, were motivated by any sort of fear that we would not finish on time.

I recall that on that first Friday I finished my editorial labors before Hare. It was nearly four o'clock, and the paper was due at the printers at six-thirty. Kee-Poh had just submitted the last of his columns to Hare, and Randy was already calling out her goodnights at the door, when I entered Hare's room myself and handed over my final material. Though I wanted to impress him as a fine worker, a reliable worker in every respect—and especially, in this business, in regards to timeliness and punctuality—I did not want to seem somehow competitive with him. I was aware that he delegated about half of the paper's major editorial work to me and the other half to himself, but I did not want to seem too cocky or important in having beaten him to the wire. But he seemed pleased and quietly confirmed when I appeared and not the slightest bit perturbed. He called to me as I made my way back to my little room, and he asked if I would like to accompany him with the finished work to the printers.

I accepted, and the tone that revealed his inscrutable satisfaction vanished into the mundane suspension that characterizes the vigilant scanning of a pressed proofreader. When it was nearly five, Hare appeared at my door. He asked me what I was working on.

"It's my first piece on Pauktaug History—of my little series that I hope to culminate in a description or essay on the Pauktaug Girl that haunts so many of the doors and walls in town."

I saw a glimmer of Hare's indescribable and secret satisfaction again, but I thought little on this then, for the invitation he had recently offered suddenly expanded.

"Rex, after we drop the paper off at the printer's, want to go over to the gym with me? I have to pick up Lisa there when she's done with one of her classes. And she and I thought you might like to look around the gym and then have dinner with us."

I assented heartily to this, and I told Hare that I had never been to a gym, a health club, before.

"You seem to enjoy your running, Rex. How come you've never been to a gym?" Hare asked me as we made our drive out of Pauktaug and west to Huntington Village to deliver the paper to the press.

"Oh, I don't know. I haven't really been running, running seriously, all that long. And as for the times that I've thought about gyms, I guess I always felt too self-conscious to have other people watching me while I'm exercising."

"Well, believe me," Hare answered in a very sure, sober tone, "no one ever really sees anything of anybody else at the gym. Nothing of importance has yet really been seen at the gym. Believe me, I've watched, and it's true."

I just smiled and laughed silently at this cryptic comment. But I did not have long to mull over this, for suddenly Hare had news for me.

"Rex, your great-grandmother tried to call you at home a few times today. You were at work, of course. But I was talking to Lisa on the phone earlier, and your great-grandmother called our place, too. Nancy said she would have tried you or me at work, but she didn't want to bother you—or me. Anyway, she's due back on Sunday morning. I have the details at home. She needs a ride from the train station. Something really did happen to her foot. I don't know what the story is with her injury. I really don't. But I'll have to pick her up, I think."

Hare's last few sentences were peculiar. His only act of discretion was to stop his musings on her injury and to go no further. He did not, however, seem to regret expressing a sort of seemingly sincere disbelief that such an elderly woman had an injury at all. If I had known him better, I might have said that he seemed irritated with my great-grandmother for some reason. And he did not appear to be irritated because of the request for a car ride from the train station. Rather, he seemed somehow perturbed by her injury, as if it were indeed a reality but at the same time a trying circumstance—not to him personally, but to some sort of standard that he felt had been disappointed. He seemed not to disqualify the accidental quality of her injury, but at the same time he seemed to intimate that only certain types of people are mortal enough to allow chance to reach them.

Hare busied himself with a difficult parking spot and then got out of the car with our bundles and computer disks. We had parked on a side street in Huntington Village, and I quickly noticed, as I gained the sidewalk, that the gym Hare had spoken of was not far, just around the corner on Main Street. Its bright, aggressive, electric sign could be clearly read even from the side and from a distance. The print shop was right before us, however. Hare and I ran the paper in, and my new Editor-in-Chief handed in the latest issue of *The Pauktaug Press* with little ceremony. Soon, Hare and I were on the sidewalk again, and his spirits did not rise perceptibly, but I would say that he somehow appeared free of something. One might have thought that the evident reason for any display of disburden then from Hare was because that week's paper was done, but I had seen this cycle of chains to liberty and liberty to chains more than once in Hare, and I could not yet say what were the factors that allowed for manumission and what caused his subtle imprisonments—for there were times when I saw him laboring over editorial work or even his own writing and yet the tapping of his foot or the shuffling of his legs made it seem that he had almost two minds, and that he could set the one free whilst the traditional mind labored at traditional cogitations. It was hard to say where this second, this new kind of mind might be within Hare, but it seemed at full liberty then as we made our way to the health club where Lisa Hare worked. Hare's traditional mind was cooling down almost to a resting state—for, indeed, I had to address Hare more than once with a question as we walked along—and it was his second mind that seemed to be intensely active, more than I had yet seen it. But, again, I could not say where this mind was, save that it jounced and flicked and called out its presence through extra though subtle energetic motions in Hare's walking style.

I asked Hare my question a second time: "So we're just going to pick up Lisa and go to dinner around here somewhere?"

"Oh, no, Rex! It's only—what?—about five-thirty or so. Lisa's class isn't over until six-thirty. We're early. You're going to use the gym with me."

"Oh, come on!" I laughed. "I don't even have the right clothes."

"I've got a locker with lots of clean stuff for you to use. And it will be better for you anyway than all that old cotton stuff you run in. I sweat the way you do, and it's about time that someone showed you that some of the new material really is easier to wear than a soaked pair of shorts and a soaked tee shirt when you exercise hard."

Though it should not have surprised me that I had been seen by then as a runner by people who knew me in Pauktaug, it somehow shocked me to think of Hare observing me run by at some point—much as I had observed him (and Pocket) from my own windows on more than one occasion. It was not that I was embarrassed by my own comparatively slow speed. And it was not, as Hare's latest remark indicated, that I was embarrassed to learn that my running attire—especially considering my perspiration tendencies—was amateurish and rather foolish. It was, rather, that I felt that running was slipping away from me as my own, peculiar discovery. I was not quite ready to share it, or to acknowledge that countless others embraced and thought about it and thought as much of it as I did—though I was not sure that many others saw in it the metaphorical gristmill that I felt was still left untapped by the experiences it yielded and the strange, pounding abstractions it seemed somehow, but not yet clearly, to propose. But mainly I felt a strange sort of embarrassment, a feeling of being exposed—especially with the idea of Hare observing me in my running. It was a strange sensation, especially considering that Hare had already looked over my shoulder, in a sense, many times at my work, at my thinking, during my time at the paper—and I had felt no awkwardness in that. But the prospect of having Hare as an unknown observer of my running, this drove a strange and unaccountable strike of malaise into me. And at the core of this strange feeling was the sensation that I had been observed not in a physical activity but in a sort of intellectual or cogitating activity—as if Hare had been much more at my most private shoulder in seeing me running the pavements of Pauktaug than when he saw me laboring before him at my chosen profession.

But as Hare and I reached the entrance to the gym, somehow my own curiosity as to the prospect of exercising with the likes of a Hare—which was just short of having an invitation to observe the still unproven miracle speed of Pocket or Hare up close—controlled my preoccupations. Though I had little chance to see any of Pocket's or Hare's speed in a gym, I felt that a chance to observe what was possibly the second fastest man in the world—and a man who as yet would make no real public allusion to his athletic skill—observe him in any athletic context, would be a singular, peculiar sort of privilege.

Even from the outside the gym seemed to impress me with an aspect of cleanness and brightness. And right at its front door was a notice that one should wipe their feet thoroughly before entering.

After we both observed this command upon the mat in the vestibule, we passed through the second door and then slowed to a near standstill. Hare's second mind seemed to wish to take a pause and smile. And I paused, as well, to look around the large first floor area.

After gazing about for a time, one could tell—even without

reading the historical plaque on the building's outside that confirmed as much—that the building into which this gym was built
was an old firehouse. The first floor—which was divided into sec-
tions by groupings of aerobic machines, groups of cable-styled
weight machines, and a pair of distanced service stations behind
which indolent, bored, gym attendants overlooked the entire
scene—was evidently the main garage of an early twentieth-century fire station. The brick walls on both sides of the enormous
room had been nearly covered and concealed by mirrors, but ves-
tigial marks of an earlier and functional style of architecture left
telltale signs, along with firefighting paraphernalia that was tacked
to the ceilings and along some of the exposed beams. The mirrors,
of course, gave the impression that the large room was even larger
than it was, but I was soon aware that the mirrors had manifold
functions in such a place.

As Hare recovered from his pause upon first entering the gym,
I looked to the opposite far wall, which was free of mirrors. It led
out to the back of the building, and in through its own doorway a
small, wiry, feeble, extremely elderly and cautious man in street
clothes was making his way into the gym. I scanned the rest of the
clientele for a moment—perhaps, at that time, a half-dozen men
and a half-dozen women on the treadmills, stair climbers, and rowing machines (and perhaps an equal number hidden by the knotty
metal maze of the rows of toning machines closer to the back of
the gym)—and thus the old man's intensity and lack of evident
self-consciousness made me smile at the incongruity of his appearance on the scene. I did not feel that I could possibly feel ill at ease
in the company of so many veteran exercisers if this elderly fellow
had no qualms about using such a gym.

Suddenly I felt Hare's arm on my shoulder—as if he were
beckoning me forward to something very definite he had always
wanted to show me. Yet soon it was clear that he was merely guiding me to the main check-in desk a few paces before us. He did

not hear me again as I asked him a question (this while we waited for the young man at the check-in counter to free himself from a phone call).

I tried again: "I guess early evening on Friday is a good time to come. There don't seem to be too many people here."

Hare heard me on my second attempt. He had been looking up at the ceiling, from where one could hear the dull sound of some kind of loud music and what sounded like the thud of many feet and bodies landing on the floor above, they only in an approximate synchronization.

"You're right. This is a good time to come if you want to use the treadmills and other machines on this floor. Downstairs—in the free-weight room—that's probably pretty clear right now, too. But there are some really crowded times—especially in the mid- to late-morning when there are hordes of young mothers here. They leave their babies in the nursery over there."

Hare nodded to a little room to the left, just behind the check-in desk—a little padded room filled with plastic slides and large balls and miniature, mock gym equipment. At that moment there were only a few children in the room, quietly sitting around a little table and playing with plastic cups.

"So the late morning won't be of much use to you here," Hare said in an unusual tone. At first, since I was not looking at him, I took him to mean that the gym at that time would not be of much use to me because it would be too crowded. But because his tone sounded odd, I looked to him and saw that he had made a little, wry expression with his statement. He had made a joke about the unavailability of the women I might meet at that time of the day—in the morning, that is. This was the first time Hare had made any sort of lighthearted allusion to the subject of a possible romantic search for me. Such humor had not appeared to me to be in his style, even in the most elusive, innocent sort of way, so it was curious to me that he should suddenly make such a statement and with such little preparation. I wondered why he had chosen that occasion.

I did not follow up the wry expression with any questions of my own, and Hare let it drop for the time being. He continued: "There are, however, a lot of people here right now for the classes upstairs. There are two going on right now. Hear it? And see all the cars in the back? Some times you can hardly find a parking spot back there and yet this part of the gym and the downstairs can be almost empty."

The elderly man I had seen enter the back entrance of the gym had just about made it to the check-in counter as the worker on the telephone finished his call and looked to us. The elderly man had that peculiar, self-serving skill of some extremely elderly people to truly believe he had arrived first on any scene, and he looked at Hare with feeble, yet unvocalized remonstrance when Hare was acknowledged as next on line.

Hare was obviously a familiar to the young man behind the counter—and to nearly all the regulars at the gym, whether it be from his routine appearances at the gym himself, his marital connection with Lisa Hare of the gym, his familiarity to business citizens as the editor of *The Pauktaug Press,* or known or merely recognized at a distant, somewhat reluctant level, as the man who might either be one of the fastest men in the world or as the man possibly connected with a local race scandal that had pretensions to fool the world. But even though Hare's familiarity with this young gym attendant was characterized by a coolness, a jadedness that was generated by the young man's own personality, I would say that Hare himself projected, if not an evident aloofness, if not an unapproachability, then the look of a man on the verge of a realization and not to be disturbed—and not the look that those would have, or would affect, if they were on the verge of a great abstract realization, but rather the look of a man who is just about to see something realized in the immediate physical vicinity, he seeming to expect something predictable, like finding a lost item where he suspects he left it and he just about to go there to find it. The intensity of sincere distraction that can attend something physically imminent and touchable in the near future is what seemed to float about Hare. I had the feeling from time to time that he half hoped—and this as if there was no one else he could hope this from—I might be the one to march ahead on his subtle signals and find that lost or expected item and show, even without him telling me anything in words, exactly the spot where he himself had expected it to lie all the time, and thus to prove him absolutely correct. I would look about me from time to time with the expectation of finding that physically imminent sign or object, and I would often feel that I would catch just the glimmer of a look from Hare—as I had after we came into the gym—and that look seemed to intimate that I should keep looking about me, that the object in question was much closer and much more evident than I suspected. But I never saw it—not then. And then the look would pass, and I was then never sure that I had seen it at all.

Again, though familiar with Hare, this attendant before us projected a jaded, distant quality that demands description. I had encountered this type of young employee—he perhaps a year or two out of high school, he somewhat pursy if not frankly on the edge of obesity, and he seeming extremely inconvenienced by nearly all activities—had encountered this type of fellow, and came to expect to, in many types of stores and restaurants, but would never have expected, though I had never been inside a health club before, to find one in a gym.

Though the pursy young fellow acknowledged Hare and myself as next on line—we had been the only ones on line, in fact, until the appearance of the elderly man—the elderly man blurted out his six-digit I. D. number to the boy and the young fellow disregarded his own command as to who was next and typed in the irritable, ancient man's number.

This bothered my sense of fairness, but Hare remained stoical for the time being. We moved in closer to the desk as the elderly man hobbled away toward the aerobic machines. Hare gave his I.D. number and then asked that I be signed in as his guest. This last request required the inconvenienced young man to bend over and retrieve a notebook from below the counter. This required great effort from him, and he expressed as much with the start of breathlessness when he reappeared from beneath the counter. He deferred opening the book—perhaps by way of recovering from the stretch of retrieving it—and allowed himself to answer another phone call before signing me in.

Hare still stood in stolid silence. Finally, my sign-in as a guest was accomplished, and I could not fail to comment on it as Hare and I made our way to the back of the gym so as to descend the stairs to the locker room.

"They should fire that kid. Is he always like that?" I protested, not without a little effort to be heard—not only because Hare was still in his somewhat remote state, but because there was a mild throbbing of dance-club-like music coming from various speakers all over the first floor. Mercifully, it was not as loud as one would find in an actual dance club.

As we descended the stairs, I began to fear that I would have no satisfaction from Hare. I tried once more: "This seems like a nice place. Why is there such a rude little punk at the front desk?"

And then what I took for a little concession or agreement, though cryptic, came from Hare: "None of the other kids who work here are like him. I can't stand to hear him breathe. I really can't."

We said no more of it, and as we landed in the basement, I became further absorbed by the clean and presentable look of the place. It was brightly lighted, even in the basement, and we walked through a pleasantly old but remodeled hallway, past an enormous free-weight room—a room filled, as well, with advanced workout machines in great number—then past a room with a clouded glass doorway. At first I believed I saw the image of the Pauktaug Girl emblazoned on the large pane of frosted glass, but as the door opened and revealed a real and shapely young woman in the flesh, I knew this to be no spot of the Pauktaug Girl's. This room was a separate, private area for women.

We then arrived in the men's locker room.

"Here, Rex. Here are some things for you to wear for today. Still feel awkward about the gym?"

"No. It's interesting that you ask. I just noticed that I've forgotten all about my hesitations. I don't know why for sure."

This pleased Hare. He gave a mild, approving nod, as if to say, "Now we can truly get started," as if my hesitations had extended much further back than that afternoon. Yet he did not feel compelled to investigate my new willingness to explore the gym. He just took my new assurance almost as a positive promise from me, it seemed, that I was at the start of an extensive new process. Then he reminded me, obliquely, that he had seen me running on more than one occasion.

"Tell me what you think of those things—the shirt and the shorts—after you start sweating for awhile. Tell me if wearing those doesn't make things easier on you than wearing those old cotton sponges when you run."

Hare and I reentered the noise of the hallways and noted the increasing crowds, and he suggested we go up to the second floor and look in on Lisa's class. But we stopped on the first floor and surveyed the sudden overflow of people. A certain strain of women overwhelmed me—the treadmills and machines had suddenly and unaccountably become filled with many of this type.

These were the women who work toward maintaining the striking forms they had as adolescents. And with an intense, daily application to the treadmill and the other aerobic machines, and with an intense daily routine of just the right amount of toning—

that intensity marked by an equal intensity of will that knows how and when to hold itself back from too much resistance training—and most likely with a rather vigilant regard to what they eat each day, these women achieve, quite often, something rather remarkable. For as opposed to the beauty that their lithe forms suggested without effort when they were adolescents, these highly maintained women now suggest comparable bodily profiles to their adolescent shapes, though granted with less of the bloom and softness; suggest profiles that, whatever the motivation, are molded, maintained, and driven by some one or manifold, overriding, governing idea. They have the same dimensions as when natural adolescents, but now the vigor of maintenance suggests something of far greater interest. And, again—and though the idea may be the same and superficial, as far as ideas go, in most cases—their forms are now driven by some idea, some force of will, and not by metabolism and youth. And surely there must be exceptions to the common ideas—some women driving themselves on beyond the issues of vanity and sexual appeal, driving themselves on to project a physical shape for some abstract purpose. What that might be I could not yet say.

It was mainly this last type of woman that caught my eye when Hare and I turned away once more from the main floor of the gym to take to the stairs again.

Hare gave a visual nudge to me when he saw this same view (behind us on the main floor and on the stairs), as if he had been confirmed in something he had assured me of all along, though we had never discussed it—that something being the variety of possibilities seemingly presented to a young suitor in this environment. Now that I could see that such allusions were not uncommon for Hare, I thought little more about it, and accepted that Hare had his eye out for me.

The women on the stairs were on their way to the second floor classrooms. There were two classes in progress, and three women passed Hare and me during the ascent—two of them carrying their own mats for a class of some kind of yoga or stretching routines.

It might be appropriate at this moment to remark on the appearance of this last type of gym girl in a few further respects. It goes without saying, nearly, that the modern attire of the fit gym girl is like the clothing of many summer runners—it is rather, in some cases, very much like the woman is wearing nearly nothing at all, if it is not like she is wearing nothing altogether, if not less than nothing. And this description is really something more than just a turn of phrase. But how less than nothing? For ages it has been a woman's option to show or conceal that amount of herself that she deemed appropriate or inappropriate enough to attract attention. But when has it been that a style—and presumably a style with claims to function—has ascended to such popularity (though that popularity confined generally to exercisers) that is more often than not just a bit tighter than one's own form? It is more revealing, in a way, than nakedness—these tights, these midriff-exposing-tops that are casually sported now. And these items somehow skipped over the levels that even the wearing of bathing suits or underwear in situations of exercise would have revealed. It is odd that a tightness—that is indeed more revealing than nakedness (for is not a relief map often times more telling than even a more detailed, exposed traditional map?)—that a tightness of such degree should cause less consternation than public nakedness.

Yet—and this with all arch, male humor hopefully at bay—there must be something of greater interest to all this, as well. Perhaps public nakedness is still frowned upon so that there is some regard for traditions being abandoned at a reasonable pace. But this new kind of more intense revealingness, it seems to give a nominal heed to human covering and traditions, and yet it surpasses even the wildest attempts of the nudist to put all concealments aside. Surely there is something of greater abstract interest here.

Few good souls would hesitate to tell the misguided student, the misguided office worker, that her attire might be too revealing. All hurry to aid the woman who finds that the surf has knocked off her bathing suit top. But no one would dream of telling the fit gym girl, the fit summer runner, to conceal themselves. Why this universal acceptance of an exposure profoundly in reality—and in its deeper, more inscrutable implications, profoundly beyond nudity? Is it merely because most concede that such apparel has been developed as well with an optimum exercise use in mind, in addition to the yet only suspected purposes proposed here? Perhaps. I cannot say for sure. But I can say that I never gazed so intently upon the female form in such an exposed and seemingly sexualized state that it also gave forth to ponderings and suspicions beyond the sexual. In fact, these clothes have made it doubly challenging to be furtive in one's study of beautiful women—for the initial deep, short, and common procreative gaze often yields to a very innocent, and intellectually shaken stupor of speculation and wonder that can sometimes last quite beyond the allotted interval of civility and personal safety.

Hare and I jogged up the stairs in the wake of young and youngish women dressed in such a way as I describe above, and we entered a narrow, long hall, the walls of which were lined with cubbies for coats and clothes and broken otherwise by two, distantly spaced, interior doorways that led to the two large classrooms that took up most of the second floor of the health club.

The general nightclub-like music was still rather forward and forceful in the hallway. We tried to take a look through the frosted glass window of the first door—after two of the women who had preceded us on the stair went into that classroom—but we could see very little, save for what appeared to be a full class, spread out all across the large room, each woman appearing to be in the midst of the start of a yoga routine. Even though this could have been the warmup stretch for another class, Hare rather thought that this room hosted Lisa's class, for he could hear no music coming from within—nothing, at least, that could compete with the din that was in the hallway, so he rather thought that it was the yoga class that his wife was to lead at that hour.

But just for fun, we ambled a bit further down the hall to investigate the other classroom.

"I'm not sure who would be leading this class," muttered Hare, but he seemed somehow driven to investigate. The third woman who had passed us on the stairs was still fidgeting in front of a cubby. She had no mat like the other two women who had gone into the first classroom—the mats making Hare even more sure that the first room was his wife's yoga classroom.

Hare suddenly nudged me and told me to ask the woman, the girl, what class was in the room before us then—the second class-room. I did so.

"This is the advanced step class. It's a little late getting started today, but I think the teacher is in there, and they're just about to start," she replied as she buried a few things into the back of her chosen cubby and then vanished through the door in all her trans-nakedness into the back of the classroom.

Hare and I both started at the sound that suddenly exploded from behind the closed door of this second classroom. It seemed so loud that one almost assumed the class within would stop, everyone of mutual accord, and not resume until the stereo equip-ment had been turned down. But to my astonishment, the figures that could be made out in silhouette—through the cloudy glass door that was just like its counterpart down the hall—continued their step exercises with no sign of relenting and no sign that the music must be intolerable, since it was even deafening for those standing on the outside of the classroom.

I looked to Hare, thinking that I would see in him a bit of the same astonishment I felt, perhaps still combined with the vicarious interest he felt for me because of the new and extensive social pool.

But neither of these sentiments appeared on his face. He seemed to project a sudden look of acknowledgement and mild disgust—as if he somehow knew who or what was the cause of this sudden outburst of sound—and what look of vicarious hunter's interest he felt for me I would almost say had been altered into a sort of flight response, a desire to move his charge away from the scene at hand. I could not be sure of my last interpretation of his face, but Hare did, indeed, seem to think that it was best to suddenly dismiss the upstairs area altogether until Lisa should come down to the first floor on her own at the end of her class.

Thus Hare and I went back to the first floor, and I was to have my first introduction to the weight machines of the gym. When Hare and I came out of the stairwell, I was astonished to find the gym population even further increased—a full crowd was there then, but not so much of a crowd that Hare felt he could not show me around and demonstrate things without feeling rushed.

We began with a machine called *the shoulder press*. Of course, as a beginner, I asked Hare what use such exercises might be to him, or to me, as a runner (even though I was pleased he had directed me there to start, for I was vain of improving the upper part of myself). He replied that we would address the machines that aided the legs in good time, but that a general toning of the upper body was often of great use to one's running. Of course, he warned that excessive bulk would naturally not be of any use to me as a runner.

Thus we began our survey of all the machines that addressed the upper body. Hare retrieved one of the card-like sheets that the personal trainers used to outline a newcomer's routine, and he listed the machines I was to use—not so much in a particular order as much as in the order that they became available for him to demonstrate them to me. He told me that I could change the order to suit me—and to give rest to certain muscle groups that might be invoked too much if one particular machine was followed too closely by another—and to change the order for the sake of flexibility when I might find the gym to be crowded.

What was really of note to me once more was that Hare's shape was hardly that of one said to be perhaps one of the fastest men in the world. But as the whole demonstration of Hare's and Pocket's run of the spring was said to be characterized by exceptions and unusual circumstances, I thought that this strong appearance of Hare's should not give me too much pause to think. As I reported of my first meeting with Hare, he was not the frail, emaciated form one almost expects to find in the world's fastest road runners. He was stout, stout of muscle, as if his running had hardened all of him—and as if his upper body weight training was just a cover for the unusual, unique, and comprehensive effect that running had upon his entire form.

Hare and I continued our survey of the gym's weight and toning machines as the hour of his wife's class continued to wear on. The gym continued to fill and crowd with all manner of souls, as well as numbers of fit, trans-naked women who could not be ignored by my eyes—no matter how polite and attentive I wished to be toward my guide. Hare only smiled at this from time to time as he took a breath between his phrases of guidance.

The club-like music of the gym continued to pound on—and seemed to increase with the growing noise that came with the growing population—and still, as well, one could hear the faint thud of the music from the classroom above.

Hare and I moved over then to a line of the machines that dealt exclusively with one's legs.

As with the upper body machines, the lower body machines were more or less self-explanatory after Hare gave me a bit of basic guidance. And there was a little picture, as well, on the side of all of the machines—a little outline of the human form and its basic muscle groups. Each machine's little decal highlighted the muscle group that was focused upon by that given machine. And I must say that—save for that of the lawyer or doctor—perhaps in no other modern arena does one see such a concentration of Latin terms. The little illustrations not only evoke, by their use of Latin terminology, the classical overtones of the study of human anatomy, but also the Greco-Roman fascination with athleticism—with the idea of the total Man, the balanced human being, the individual of equal parts mind and muscle. Thus, even though many of the vainly motivated at the gym will hardly profess that their efforts have anything to do with the ideals of Classical Republics to be realized in this new one, it is quite interesting to hear the common patron of the gym so readily accede to the use of these terms—terms so much in contrast with the words they would use in almost any other given situation. For no one—hardly even the gym zealot himself—would play the body part identification game with a toddler by asking him or her: Where are your abdominals (instead of, Where is your tummy)? And these same dedicatees of the gym would hardly refer in mixed, common company—for they, like most modern men and women, would hardly wish to be cited for affectation under any circumstance—would hardly use such terms themselves when referring to one of their own body parts.

Yet the modern gym has resurrected a separate sanctity for these terms, as if in invoking these titles for these body parts to which we commonly refer by other names in the course of the day, they somehow take on a separate function from their everyday use—as if, indeed, there must be some undiscovered purpose for the *Transversus abdominus* area that the *stomach,* the *belly,* the *tummy,* cannot answer.

These little decals and their illustrations were to meet my attention increasingly, especially in future and regular visits to the gym as I became more and more advanced in my routines on the weight machines, and needed a diversion to ponder when I was in between sets of difficult repetitions. More than anything else, as I became more and more conversant with all of the muscle groups and their proper classical names, I noted that there was a machine (or a free-weight exercise) for nearly every muscle or muscle group that could be pictured on the little illustrated outlines of the human form—that is, save for the extremist of extremities: the feet, the hands, the head (though there are exercises for muscles that probe to the very frontiers of these parts).

Thus when one contemplated the diagrams, one was reminded of the common assertion by science that nearly all human beings go to their graves having used but an inconsiderable, or a shockingly low, fraction of their brain's capacity and potential. And as the brain and head appear small on these decals, their scale seems inconsiderable in comparison with the body—especially again considering that only the merest fraction of the thinking mind pictured on the decal is ever truly engaged to its full potential. In other words, how much of the body goes unused as so much of the brain goes unused, as well? Thus, in looking at the full diagram of the body, it would seem no wonder that a tacit agreement to use terms sacrosanct to the gym seems in order, for on the grand scale of the full grand body, what grave, magnificent percentage of unused power must reside in such vast stretches of muscle and flesh that surely cannot be there for only their ostensible and as yet discovered use? Why else do we reserve these aspiring classical terms for the muscles when we work them in a gym outside of all discernible practical function? Surely there is more than increased health and sexual attractiveness in this effort. Such things I began to ask myself when I pondered the little pictures between sets of repetitions. But if I could be led to dismiss my own suspicions as silly, when I found myself pushing all the harder on a machine when a staggering trans-naked siren wisped past in dewy breathlessness, then how quickly might the mass of humanity say that they merely use their gym terms, when pressed to it, simply to serve yet another of tired old Earth's many, many cliques?

Hare guided me on from machine to machine, carefully noting

on my workout card each machine, the weight I was to use, and the number of sets and repetitions, until we had covered nearly the entire circuit of weight machines on the first floor of the gym. We both noticed when the music thunder ceased to beat in the classroom above. Hare was sure that both classes would end at about the same time—meaning that Lisa Hare would be down soon. But then the thunderous music began again in renewed earnest, and Hare did not know what to make of that, but since his wife's yoga class hardly used music of that sort, he was still sure that she would be down quite soon. It was nearing six-thirty.

Hare made some final note for me on my card as I finished with the leg press machine—executing on that an exercise for the calf muscles. Hare himself took to a duplicate of the same type of machine that was just next to mine, and it was then that I noticed that the feeble, elderly man I had seen enter the gym at the same time as Hare and I was just then taking to a chest press machine and sitting himself down there with great, labored difficulty. The elderly man's action also came under the scrutiny of a lesser-toned, more socially desperate, member of a group of gym fellows who had been at the drink counter sipping a shake some time before.

"I was using this," was the way the younger man marked the machine for his own.

"Huh?" said the feeble, elderly man, with that sibilant sort of staccato ejaculation that denotes a man truly hard of hearing.

"I'm using this machine," repeated the younger man, with a stolid, still, but somehow effeminate impatience that was intolerable. Though everyone in the gym was perspiring, this man's sweat surely was odorous, I thought. He looked profoundly ugly to me, and he looked of a doughy softness then as well.

But though I was certainly not an admirer of the elderly man either, I thrilled to the simple, logical challenge the old man gave to the assertion that he (the younger man) was "using this machine."

He crinkled his eyes and wrinkled his mouth, and gave a hoarse little bark of "When?" I gave an inward cheer to the old man, but the confrontation continued. However, I could not monitor the next few phrases of exchange between the old man and the young man, for I watched as Hare suddenly leaped up from the leg press machine and moved toward the scene of the action just described.

Were it not for the incident between the two men at the chest press machine, I would have given all my attention to Lisa Hare then, who had just appeared from the stairwell. But the scene between the aggressively feeble and the feebly territorial held me rapt a bit longer—especially as Lawrence Hare himself seemed to be making his way to the site of confrontation, as well.

Lisa waved as she caught sight of her husband and me, but Hare held up his forefinger politely to her when she was still not far from the doorway leading from the stairwell—his gesture just asking for a moment in which he had to attend to something. This seemed to please Lisa, as if she had not seen such deference in a long while, and she came to where I was—and we watched the unfolding scene together.

"I've been using this. I'm on this now," continued the young man, who looked all fat to me then and no muscle.

Again the elderly man replied with something in which I could exult: "You're on this now?"

But then Hare entered the exchange: "No, he's not. I'm on this now." This confused the old man, but it was clear that Hare did not care if the old man understood how justice was rendered to him. Hare only cared that the younger man knew that he (Hare) was being arch.

"I've been on this the whole time," reiterated Hare. "That hasn't been clear to you?" he smiled.

The younger man left and rolled his eyes.

Lisa turned around from this scene to greet me with a smile.

But in her smile was not only a warm reception for me, but a relieved approval for her husband, as if she had not seen him assert himself in such a way for some time. But I could not say so for sure. I had only seen her once before and it was her physicality that then, as before, struck me with intensity. As Hare took a moment to take a drink from a water fountain that was right before the chest press machine, I had a moment to look straight upon his wife as she began to speak to me. (I say this as if it were untoward for me to do so. But it seemed so; she was so shockingly magnificent in her physicality that just to look at her seemed an invasion of Lawrence Hare's union.)

She smiled to me and asked me how I liked my first visit to the gym. And did it make me ready for dinner? And did it make me ready for a few social surprises? I hardly recall how I answered these questions.

She wore only the tightest of yoga pants, and the tightest of tops—all in black. And she had delicate, small running shoes, and tiny white socks that dipped below the ivory curve of her ankle bone. Her chestnut, red hair was pulled back in a pony tail, and she undid this in the course of my unremembered conversation. She shook the deep damp from her hair—a damp that darkened it considerably. And she had an even, clean, deep sweat that beaded all about her ribs and the muscled false ribs that were created by the bleating sinew all about her breathless navel. Her sweat deeply imbued her black clothes, leaving no spot dry—so she did not have the unclean appearance of half-permeated attire. The black was blackened altogether. And the comprehensive sweat moved in refractive, animated filigree, in between the equal thousands of tiny, exquisite dots that comprised the latent astronomy of her bodily freckles. This moving water of her own making, and the breathlessness that made her very leanness pant as if there was still a mildly enthralling feminine pursiness to her frame, made her freckles seem the one tangible, two dimensional, touchable mark on her skin, on her deep and watery, animated satin in relief.

But this, still, was not what transfixed the eye above all. She sported, perhaps above all the women I had seen there who had challenged the very definition of nakedness, a trans-nakedness via her yoga pants that defined, I thought, the very reason why women are so commonly held to be the exemplars of sexual beauty in humanity, if not of physical beauty in the physical universe. It was in the very tightness of her gripping shorts—the manner in which legs and torso are spliced, are soldered as if by perfect, painless fire, are linked as if by tender bonds and brought together to form a smooth and unburdened perfection at the genital crossroads of the two legs. She was so smooth and flat at this stupefying angle that it would seem almost that surely there was no external genitalia to the form of Woman at all. And in a way, what man does not recall the shock when he discovers that there is not simply an entrance-way there, surrounded by simple flat skin? What man does not hold, even past his first shock of revealing photographs or challenging textbooks, the impression that slender, perfect women must be free and flat and smooth as the naked doll one finds forever skinny-dipping in abandonment in the toy corner of a baby sister's bathroom?

Whilst I knew, could still tell, that Lisa Hare was by all means constructed after the fashion of the healthy human design for women in that area of confluence, the way she stood before me then challenged all thoughts I held of the sacredness of matrimonial possession. And yet my thoughts were not dishonest, would not lead to any ultimate disaster of personal conduct. I mean only to say, that she presented a primacy of primalness—as if her body breathed before me as a symbol of human form before human history or before the arrival of the sexual accountability that even Nature must enforce for the benefit of survival. She presented a sexual sight beyond the sexual then. And thus, in the midst of her roaring nakedness, she presented almost a lewdness that had become pure and disassociated from any connection with peopling the world with new babies—and disassociated from recreational sexual gratification somehow, as well.

But then her eyes and her personality came to bear, and I broke into traditional shame. The music of the club came back to my ears, and I heard her distinctly ask me if I had finished taking the tour. It was then, too, that I looked away from her sweet and friendly, human platonic smile and to Hare, who was looking at her from behind as he finished drinking at the fountain. My traditional shame, traditional embarrassment, of longing upon another man's wife yielded to another fascination when I could clearly see that Hare's face and demeanor had for some reason returned to its inscrutable mindlessness—and his body seemed to twitch, or rather seemed pitched to twitch, to verily think for itself, once more. And it seemed it was Lisa Hare's magnificent form that was the port-hole symbol to this vague, large inscrutableness. I looked in the far mirror, and could make out the view that Hare had of his freckled, dewy, black-banded wife. Because of the tightness, again, of her shorts, that seemed to squeeze at her like a rubber straightjacket—to control thighs, a groin, gone mad—and because her arms were folded before her so that they could not be seen by Hare where he stood, and because she pulled her hair away from her neck again and restored her pony tail, revealing a spinal column that traveled all the way down from her moistened collar bone (dividing all above her waist in two), she seemed a being made merely of two, enormous, undulating, intermittently dilated, legs. He looked up from his water, as unpossesive and yet as moved by her as I had been, and then he looked about the room in an involuntarily reel, a sweep of the eyes, embracing the multifarious symbol of the gym as a consequence—just as that same multifarious symbol of the gym had not long before been the catalyst itself to his general, mysterious emanations. And then Lisa turned around to him and smiled with the deep, sincere, gleam of her personal, bodiless mind and personality, and this jolted Hare perceptibly—at least to me perceptibly, for Lisa turned to me again with the same gleam as if she had seen nothing unusual in her husband, save perhaps just a bit of the disappointing return of that look that hid the original affableness that she might say defined the man with whom she had fallen in love. She had jolted him with her mind via her smile and eyes, had jolted him with a reminder of some insoluble truth that he had accepted and welcomed but at times exultingly forgot only so long as Lisa was turned away from him—then her back was suggestive to him of that very thing that her front, her personalized person, her face, her thinking, agent, viable and intelligent mind, could not support.

And then the weights fell. In the time that I had been preoccupied by Lawrence Hare's seemingly vacillating source of sentience and by the form and beauty of Lisa Hare, she still standing before me, the elderly man on the chest press machine had set himself to raising an inordinate amount of weight, not only for his level of conditioning and age, but for anyone of his diminutive size.

The old man had raised the great weight with the foot pedal that allows one to get in and out of the machine's hand grips without straining the upper body (and he did this, peculiarly, only using his left foot), and when he released the pedal, not only did the weight come crashing down so as to send the hand and arm grips flying back in such a way to surely injure, sprain, some part of him, the weight bars themselves landed on the singularly peculiar and amateurish and unwise spot in which he had chosen to wedge his right foot. Thus the weights came flying down, catching his feeble foot and tennis shoe—catching these and crunching them, as if the weight machine had been a sort of dull guillotine meant to crush its subjects rather than make clean cuts.

The old man cried out, dryly croaked out, in a peculiar, elderly way. But this is not what was of lasting interest to me in this scene. Hare had returned, seemingly via sight of the physical suggestiveness of his wife's form (even though her own personal projections had seemed to shake his hold for a moment), had returned into his inscrutable, mysterious regnant body. And though it had been the Hare of common human intellect that had marched over, I believe, to the aid of the elderly man when he was besieged by the foolish, covetous, younger weightlifter, it was this unique, still insoluble Hare that turned casually, with little or no regard for physical weakness or infirmity and watched with a stoic indifference as the old man struggled in the vice squeeze of the chest press hand grips and under the crushing force of its weight bars. Men on machines at both sides of the old man were at his side to help virtually at once, and others were on the scene only a few seconds later—including Lisa Hare. Hare quietly drank from the water fountain once more and cooled and fueled his cogitating, mysterious frame, and listened with confident, self-justified indifference, it seemed, as the old man floundered under the thumb of gravity.

Again, Lisa Hare was among those who helped the elderly man from the chest press machine. She scolded him in a soft, motherly sort of way, as others checked to see that the man was unharmed. And Lisa Hare sent him home with a reprimand that no one should do so much so soon—or does so without getting hurt either immediately or later on when they find that their soreness yields to pain and injury.

Hare made his way toward me as his wife finished her ministrations. I said nothing to him about the issue of the old man, for I could not be absolutely certain of what I had seen in Hare. And when Lisa Hare returned and had no reprimand for her husband, no reproach for a peculiarly motivated sin of omission, and no censure for the look in his total physical bearing that I continued to mark so long as Hare was in the gym that day, I knew I had no intimate witnesses with whom to share my speculations about the mysteries in Lawrence Hare's manner.

Appended to the mild breathlessness that Lisa Hare had felt in coming from her yoga class, she added a few affected puffs of fatigue in having had to deal with the old man's recent and self-inflicted battle with gravity.

"So, who is ready for dinner?" she smiled and asked.

Hare and I said that we were both ready to go back downstairs and change, and be ready to go as soon as she was ready, as well.

"Well, I have to shower and change and dress. And there is one more thing—"

At this moment the loud music from the class above suddenly stopped. But despite this augmented quiet, I could not hope to hear what Lisa Hare whispered into her husband's ear behind her cupped hand because of the unceasing thud of the music all about the main gym.

"Sorry to whisper, Rex. But this is about you," she added.

"Oh, all right," I smiled in helplessness.

Hare drew away from his wife and shrugged his shoulders before he answered her. "No, neither of us saw her. But, hey, I don't know the fellow well enough to ultimately speak for him, but I like to think I know just enough about him to say that he's better off on his own."

The Hares continued to be discreet and hushed, but I could make out this last phrase quite clearly. Lisa Hare grimaced affectionately at her husband and dismissed him silently as obtuse and difficult on some subjects.

"Wait here," Lisa suddenly commanded to both of us with a smile, and she jogged back to the stairwell and vanished upstairs. As Lisa had been taking to the stairwell, I noted that the music above had commenced once more in the second classroom.

"I think my wife has matchmaking plans for you. I'm sorry, Rex. I had hoped to just show you the social pool and leave you to your own choices. But my wife can't help herself. She mothers in all directions."

I was quite intrigued, but I disguised this for Hare's sake and said simply, as if I were affecting to suppress embarrassment at the prospect of his wife's idea: "Oh, that's all right. This should be fun. What is the plan?"

"I don't really know yet."

Hare handed over my workout card to me—and yet did so with a slight reluctance that seemed to be a hope and a warning that I make good and proper use of his instructions. I thanked him for all his efforts.

During Lisa Hare's absence the loud music beat from upstairs ceased once more, remained silent for a minute, perhaps two, and then resumed. And then Lisa Hare appeared again on the main floor of the gym.

"Okay, guys. There are going to be four of us for dinner. Okay?"

"Sure," I said, trying to seem as if I did not know where this might be leading.

Hare said nothing and did not react.

"Now, Rex, you've never met Dale. Have you?" Lisa asked. I had suspected that this might be about Dale Pocket. Yet I thought it a little too much wishful thinking to believe that she was the one Lisa had in mind for me in this circumstance. And I was a little fearful of the prospect, as well, since it had seemed to me that Miss Dale Pocket had already engineered an absence from another attempt to pair me with her.

"No, I haven't. But I confess I was supposed to have—"I began. But Lisa was indifferent to my answer. She was more intent on impressing me with the following.

"Well, she just saw you. I had her take a peek from the stairs. And she's excited to meet you, and she's nervous about it. So don't say anything to let her know I told you all this."

I looked to Lawrence Hare. He had taken back my workout card, and was examining what he had written there for me.

"Well, every guy is interested in Dale, Rex," Lisa continued. "So you are a lucky blind dater. Believe me." I think Lisa made up the part about Miss Pocket being nervous in meeting me. But everything else she said was true.

"Now Dale's class is running over for another ten minutes—she started late—so let me get Rex here all officially signed up since you've done everything else it seems, Lawrence."

Lawrence Hare looked up from my workout card and handed it over to his wife. "Lawrence, why don't you shower and start to get ready, and I'll take Rex through the last steps and give him the exam."

Hare complied with this proposal and vanished into the basement. Everyone seemed sure that I was already set on paying for a gym membership, and I did nothing to counter this assumption. Thus Lisa Hare led me to a little room near the first of the check-in counters, this room very close to the nursery area I had noted upon first entering the gym. She paused before the nursery's window and looked in for a long, cloying moment. (I never saw her husband do that, not even once.)

I should remark at this point that I felt a bit awkward already about being off by myself with Mrs. Hare for the gym sign-up-session and minor screening or examination. However, I tried to remain mindful of Lawrence Hare's characterization of his wife—that her warm, almost aggressive graciousness was nothing but the sign of her incipient motherliness.

We entered a bare room, and she closed the door, leaving the sound of the pulsing gym music behind for the first time since my arrival at the gym. The room was clean—and not only of extraneous objects, but also in an antiseptic, almost hospital-like way. Lisa Hare offered me a chair before a small round table, and I affected to catch my breath, fuss with my clothes, and look at the few fitness posters that hung on the clean, white walls.

As much as to protect the interests of the gym as to protect the newcomer to a fitness regimen, a slight, albeit nominal and ultimately silly and inconclusive fitness evaluation was part of the gym's ritual for signing on new members.

After a very cursory toweling of her neck and waist, Lisa Hare began this routine by taking my blood pressure. It was as she fitted my arm with the band for the blood pressure monitor that I became sensible of a peculiar and very telling lack of self-consciousness, not just in Lisa Hare, but quite unusually, in myself. There was no way, considering the way Lisa Hare appeared— what with her perfect form and personal warmth and her trans-naked body poised only a yard away from me (and even less when she struggled with the Velcro of the arm band)—no way for any man not to regard her in a sexual light (and this no matter how coded a man was, no matter how loaded with principles and scruples his conscience might be). And since I could reliably count on my system of moral self-checks, it suddenly struck me as a bit disturbing that I did not feel self-conscious around her. Again, though my running had taken me a long way along the line of bodily self-reform, there was still an evident belly below my chest—and the little table was not quite enough to conceal it. But it was my realization that I had not been thinking of concealing it that disturbed me. Even when I thought about my paunch— pushing its mild and pliable way from behind Lawrence Hare's loaned shirt—as I was beckoned closer to Lisa Hare when she could not easily fit the arm band upon me from her place on the opposite side of the table, I was disturbed that I knew it was not going to disturb me. I suddenly realized that I had made a sort of unusual, threatening leap with Lisa Hare. Now, of course, one might say that mere romantic, recreational sexual posturing would be unnecessary for a woman of Lisa Hare's perfections considering what she was wearing then before me. But I think she leaped to another level of disturbing flirtation, of disturbing intimacy, without bearing any of those seductive powers directly in her mind. I have only sensed this a few times in my life in romance, but Lisa Hare began to touch and handle my arm for the sake of the blood pressure reading, and to pull at my borrowed shirt in a sort of motherly caretaker's sort of way, her motions of a manner that bespeaks a woman who regards her sexual subject not as the object of romance, but as a carefully, intimately selected, quietly regarded potential father figure to her as yet unborn but anticipated children. Only in that way could I receive the sort of sexual intimation I believed Lisa Hare projected without feeling self-conscious about my own still incomplete sexual suitor's physical resurrection.

I mean to say that Lisa Hare, as we jabbered a bit about the gym and the reading that slowly appeared on the blood pressure monitor, seemed to regard me with the calm, almost embracing look of hard-won intimacy that she gave to her husband when she believed she had seen a bit of his old self cutting through the mysterious, nearly impalpable remove I had detected in him at the gym that day.

As Lisa Hare directed me in a delicate, assured, confidently intimate yet not untoward manner from my chair to the scale, I took note that none of her actions in her trans-naked attire ever had the quality—when she was by necessity forced on more than one occasion to bend over right in front of me to retrieve a dropped pencil or paper, or when from an effort to reach over the table toward me she was forced to inadvertently display her chest more than once—never had the overtone of the seductress testing her wares (or trying to double-test them in this case, since in a sense all was there to see already).

Instead, I had the feeling—without there being any dowdiness or uncouth commonness or indiscretion to it—that she walked before me like a newlywed bride, sweet and quiet in her practical whiskings about a bedroom in between the torridity of early marriage. And I, in this scheme, was quite expected to be the fellow in that room with her.

After a silly body-fat analysis (from which process it was hard to believe that anything certain could really be determined about my body-fat state), Lisa Hare led me to a small plastic step in the center of the room for a brief heart rate test. After stepping on and off this step for a few minutes, Mrs. Hare took my pulse several times and bantered for a time about Dale Pocket.

"There is no way you're not going to like this gal. Every man loves Dale. We just can't find the right one for her. But I think you're it!" Lisa Hare confided to me with a wink as she released my wrist to me.

So that what follows is not taken to be an intimation that there was some sort of open marriage between Lisa and Lawrence Hare, I must say that I never had the sense that Lisa Hare was courting me to challenge their relationship or that she had some to-me bizarre hope of maintaining multiple partners in a physical sense. She merely displayed before me a sort of maintained hope for what she seemed somehow to intimate could not be realized any longer in her own union. Yet she did this without intimating that in any way their romance was beyond salvation—or that it was not without its times of perfect realization and happiness. There was instead a hint, I felt, that Lawrence Hare was more and more the man before Lisa Hare that I, as well, cryptically saw him to be that day in the gym. And, in fact, I rarely, if ever, saw him after that day that I did not think he was vacillating with greater and greater intensity toward favoring the inscrutable bodily awareness and intellectual vagueness that he had hinted at that very day. Yet for all Lisa Hare's trans-naked displays, and for all Lawrence Hare's still mysterious bodily centerings, the Hares were still rather proper in their conduct.

I must invite one to remember these qualifications when I report that Hare entered the room at about the time I was completing the stair-stepping test, and that Lisa Hare's sexual openness toward me did not seem to vanish with his presence. In fact, her display seemed to offer him relief, or relief for her sake, to offer him some sort of peace of mind to that piece of his mind that was still functioning in a traditional sense. But with the same oblique moments of vision in which I could catch these views, the Hares also displayed a solid presentation of a couple that would indeed have and hold till death did part them.

"Is Dale coming?" asked Lisa of her husband.

Hare closed the door of the little examination room. He had showered and changed back into his formal working clothes from the business day, but he seemed more interested in my immediate examination for gym membership than in our prospective evening out together as a group. He showed an immediate curiosity as to the precise point I had reached in the little screening. But he did not neglect to answer his wife.

"Dale will be over here in a minute. She's still talking to a few of her class members. Where are you with Rex, Lisa?"

"Just finished taking his resting pulse! Rex is getting himself fit, Lawrence."

I just smiled, along with everyone else (as everyone took relaxed sitting positions around the table) at this bit of kind but very premature praise. Lisa then looked down at the form on which she wrote. She held the clipboard up in a bit of mock-solemnity and friendly mock-formality, in preparation for asking me a few questions. Lawrence Hare's vigilance and curiosity, as to my perceptions of the whole scene, were quietly placed upon me as I readied to answer the interview. Hare seemed pleased that I somehow knew that there seemed to be some mysterious worth to his as yet un-confessed, oblique and inscrutable way of thinking. He gave me a look that seemed to say that he would be listening with interest to what I said. I somehow must have projected back that I would in no way mind this. And the entire scene settled into an uneasy but somehow relaxed state—as one feels when an impermanent repair procedure gives one a sense of relief and time to sigh over something that one knows will need true address at some later point.

"So, Rex," Lisa asked me by reading from the form on her clipboard, "What would you say is your general goal? To keep the weight off? Lose more? To build muscle?"

Hare leaned in a bit, as if I then had a chance to give an oblique, cryptic, but revealing answer to what he seemed to believe was almost a Sphinx-like riddle. I took the opportunity to be both plain and allusive.

"Quite honestly? I guess a little of all three. But it's also something more than that now, as well."

Somehow each of the parties within my hearing heard what they needed. Lisa, I think, jotted down a general note of ambition for me, but she did not seem to hear my latter phrase. Hare, on the other hand, seemed very pleased, almost relieved of some fear that he had misjudged someone he had thought had high potential for unique sympathy with his inscrutable way of thinking. And, of course, Hare seemed indifferent to whether I had said with precision whether I merely wanted to keep my weight off, lose more weight, or build muscle. It was quite something more for him than that. And thus from that moment I felt that Lawrence Hare wanted to think that it was I that he could trust more than any other human being in the world.

When I said, in effect, that my fitness cause was something more than just the common cause, I surprised even myself with my self-cryptic candor.

"Why did you start running, Rex?" Lisa continued.

"To get thin again," I said, thinking that I had returned to giving answers that were only common and had no more content than what they seemed to sound out with their plain words. But Hare was still pleased, even with this, and we were in league—one that I could not define, yet one that did not fill me with fear somehow, though I did not know what its limits or purposes were.

Beside the still unnerving flirtatiousness of Lisa—which had brought an unpredictable and ominous air to Mrs. Hare for me—she seemed suddenly very pedantic and silly in a way. It was almost as if she took pleasure in the mechanical form-filling that one takes when they play, as children, at school or librarian or office worker. This is the air that she took on as she officially filled out my forms for membership in the gym. Hare, as if he had spent some part of his new intellectual self beyond wise pacing, rose from his seat and restfully pondered an anatomical diagram of the human form that was cleanly framed and mounted on the wall.

With nowhere truly comfortable to look about me during this quiet easing of the pace of that odd afternoon, I stood up and looked out of the small window and through the blinds that looked out onto the main floor of the gym. But I looked out at the precise moment that something curious, something unique was happening on the main floor. To my chagrin, I could not see the subject of the event. It was something in the dead center of the blind spot created by the door and the wall of the office—the blind spot augmented also by the reception desk, just outside on the gym's main floor.

I could only see the wake caused by the subject of the event, or the wake of the circumstance that seemed to be steadily closing in on the area where Lisa and Lawrence Hare and I were ensconced behind the door. I think the eyes of the overly-bulked fellows at the drink bar were the first to alert me to the event, to the seemingly stentorian but silent statement that glided along the floor of the gym. Was there something being carried along the aisle? Was there a fight going on? What could possibly be happening in that blind spot that commanded the absolute rapt silence of the fellows at the drink bar? I did not suspect it was even one of the trans-naked beauties of the gym, for there were so many of those girls there that they raised what would be considered great beauty to an average. The bulked fellows did not nudge each other as if one of them did not see the sight—as is often the case when an attractive woman passes a group of men. Yet it was still unclear to me as to by what they were stupefied, reverentially enraptured, even in their seemingly thick-necked obtuseness.

And then it was evident that the mysterious event that I could not see was closer still to where I was behind the door and window of the office. Why do I call it an event? I call it so because as this phenomenon, or event, moved closer and closer to our doorway with even speed, each and every person—including the blasé young fellow behind the check-in counter; including, even, women and some of the young children that were being led out of the nursery—each and every individual stared at this sight, this event, yet not a word was said to this phenomenon that was still unseen by me. Somehow this person or mysterious sight, not only did it not address anyone or elicit address from a single human being, but it did not elicit comment from any of its witnesses to a fellow witness. Whatever the stunning sight was, the unique and possessing physical element that it had to be, it spoke nothing with its physicality through its silence to cause comment from others to others. It commanded viewing; it commanded breathlessness in observation. Yet though I was convinced of its reality, of its sureness as a physical presence that insisted on veneration, amazingly, though it was indeed corporeal, it left no wake that I could see in the faces of those who saw it. They saw it, but there was a silence in its great inimitable beauty that seemed to speak nothing, to say nothing, to think nothing. Though its physicality caught the eyes of all, it made no hails and received none.

Soon this mystery made its way directly to the door, and then the door opened, and then it was clear that the mystery, the woman then before me, was without question the woman I had seen in the photograph in Charles Pocket's office, and thus the same woman I had seen during my first run in Pauktaug. It was clear that this event, the physical power and edifice that was somehow without a wake, was Dale Pocket.

Like Lisa Hare, she wore astonishingly little clothing. My eyes even darted between the two women for a comparison along those lines, and I noted quite a few things at once. To begin with, I noted that Lisa Hare's cryptic maternal emanations somehow transformed at that very moment from a bizarre flirtatiousness toward me into an eager look that I be duly impressed and grateful for a look at the woman with whom she had labored to pair me. Then I looked for an instant over the beautiful frame of Lisa Hare and then back to Dale Pocket.

Dale Pocket was perhaps a year or two younger than Lisa Hare. But the distinction in their appearance by age was subtle and important in its implication. I have mentioned that Lisa Hare achieved a perfection of appearance by holding to a peak her beauty by the most colossal of physical efforts. She was a phenomenon of maintenance, of holding one's self, catching one's self at the top of the hill, but always kept there only by a massive battle, a massive effort not to go over and down.

But Dale Pocket was inches from her summit, and the effort she seemed to need to put herself so high, and so close to the peak, somehow seemed to intimate an effortlessness. She seemed rather to hover at her summit—to hover at a level of peaking from which she had no immediate fear of rolling away. Thus all her blaring interests in physical self-development—the evident workout regimens that were scrawled about her soft, tanned person in the subtle script of tone and feminine sinew—seemed only a kind of benign, sexually appealing overkill, a holding up of several candles, to alter an old phrase, to show the sun. This figurative writing, this figurative evidence that was laid atop her already perfect beauty, subtly flexed when she shifted her weight from one leg to another, and when she rested her one arm against the jamb of the open doorway—and then, too, in beautiful muscles atop her shoulder blades when she closed the door behind her and shut out the din of the gym.

Yet for all her evident exercising and training, I must say that she was not dry or muscled looking. She was simply ideal, if one can say so. Yet try as I might to read what all that extra sinewy writing might be saying atop her already perfect beauty, I could make out nothing definite. At first I thought that maybe the figurative scrawl was simply in a language that I could not yet read. But then for a moment it struck me as an aimless sort of hand, like that of child imitating the cursive of an adult before the child can even read or write in print—and what motivated that imitation in this case I could not say. But I let that pass from my mind on looking once more between the two unequal, trans-naked beauties, before Dale finally spoke.

I noticed then as well, in that instant of looking between the two women, just after Dale made her entrance and closed the doorway, that Dale's skin was a perfectly clear white—that is in the few places where it did not have its perfect, even tan. Lisa Hare, as I have observed, had an array, a galaxy of minute, patterned, latent freckles all over her body. And, again, this gave Lisa an intriguing three dimensional illusion to her skin—as if her stars, her freckles, were slightly above her own perfect skin—and this feature was totally absent from Dale Pocket. Dale's skin, again, was without flaw, thus it seemed flatter than Lisa's.

Lisa's skin was flawed in the sense that it was now being held firm by detectable effort, whilst Dale's was still all perfection by the will of nature's decree. Dale's body was infinitely superior to the perfections of Lisa Hare's, even though there seemed to be some edge of earned credit in what defined the flaws of Lisa Hare's beautiful body and skin.

Lawrence Hare looked toward Dale Pocket as she entered and began to speak—he looked to her as would any human being upon the entrance of another person or upon the entrance of any moving object into a space. And I would not have been surprised had I detected, in any man, a latent sexual reaction to the entrance of Dale into a room. But, rather, I could tell that Lawrence Hare felt little or nothing on seeing her. He did, however, seem compelled by the sight of her to move in a subtly romantic and sexually receptive way toward his wife. And somehow I was certain that this was not a competitive gesture toward me or a means of shunning his old inamorata; it seemed, rather, that the sight of Dale reassured his common intellectual self, or some part of his mysterious and new intellectual self, of a decision he had made in selecting Lisa. There seemed to be a singular dynamic between these three people—despite the fact that Dale Pocket and Lawrence Hare had once been involved romantically. And on seeing Dale, seeing her sexual perfection, I would not have wondered if Lawrence Hare's reluctance to see Dale and myself set up together was based on a little bit of old-fashioned jealousy. But that was not the case, I could somehow detect, when I saw Dale and Lawrence together for the first time.

I could only say that Lawrence felt in league with me for some reason—and he felt my admittance to that league would somehow allow me to see something in Dale at some point that he had already seen. Yet I could tell that he was content to allow me to find this out at my own pace, as if he was so sure of what he saw in me that he had no fears of my being paired off permanently with Dale Pocket.

That sense of league also allowed him to be indifferent to the attentions his wife had given me. But perhaps he affected indifference because he was confident in my sense of traditional honor—a confidence, if he ever felt it, that I can say was not misplaced in me.

And finally, of this unusual dynamic—until I can remark on Dale's contribution to it—I can say that Lisa had a look, as observed above, that seemed to surrender all her former flirtations, her maternal-based flirtations toward a fathering prospect. She looked toward me, then, in a manner of maternal-based matchmaking, as toward a brother-figure, a son-like figure. Now I felt that she was simply pleased that she could offer me, in a motherly-like way, a romantic prospect in which no mother's son could possibly find visual fault.

"Hey, Lisa. Hey, Lawrence," began Dale Pocket.

And then she said, "Hey, Handsome," to me, and my shock was only matched by my pleasure at her humorous allusion to the obvious attempt to pair the two of us together once and for all. Dale was the kind of woman that moved a man of compunctions to pray at the first sight of her, to earnestly pray, that there would be nothing about her that would make it a moral compromise for one to form an almost immediate romantic alliance with her. I should remark again, as well, that like Lisa, Dale stood before me wearing less, in a way, than had she stood before me in utter nakedness. And though she had just led a loud and long class in a dynamic and aggressive step routine for over an hour, she was remarkably dry and kempt in her appearance, save for a wildly appealing pair of watery beads that descended her brow and bypassed her perfectly mascara-marked eyes. Her body shed these two shiny orbs of crocodile tears, for I do not think that even her body was concealing a post-workout fatigue—the tears seemed almost meant for me, a wild, incongruous affectation of demure, vulnerable, and feminine coy tears, squeezed out from an explosive, immodest, and totally revealed womanly form.

I might recall at this point exactly what was said in the office. It would be better for me, instead, to say, that from the very first moments of my personal connection with Dale Pocket, I was sure from her direct signals of affability and interest toward me, that here was a relationship that I might have, keep, and maintain, right from the very start, with little fear that things needed proving, that any trials of courtship needed passing, that any probationary period of unsureness on the woman's part had to be waited out. From the very start, I could tell that Dale Pocket was giving me that sort of experience that some fortunate fellows recall with great, smiling incredulity when they are asked about their seemingly effortless connection with one, singular, unmatchable goddess. This was one of those cases where there was nothing I needed do even from the very start. It is the kind of thing—and I think many people can report similar experiences—where one feels a bit ill at ease at first with the simplicity of so great a gain won with such little effort. And yet, then comes the even greater realization that one cannot really find anything wrong with accepting the gain. One has just found someone—and what a boon to find that someone a goddess—who desires, at first glance, one's company immediately and quickly. There was a sureness that our relationship would continue from that very first meeting. I cannot say why it was that Dale should have approved of me so quickly, but she simply did, and I was not going to challenge her interest.

After a little bit of talking around the table in that examination room, Dale and Lisa repaired to the women's locker room to shower and change from out of their trans-naked clothes. Lawrence Hare showed me the way back to the men's locker room, and I showered myself and changed back into my clothes as an editor of *The Pauktaug Press*.

Soon I found myself on a dinner double-date in Huntington Village—suddenly admitted into this strange trio and augmenting it into a quartet. Dale never commented on the missed appointment of the night before, of her brother's and sister-in-law's attempts to have us meet at the Pocket house back in Pauktaug. She never referred to that, and I never challenged her on it (not even in the spirit of good-natured ribbing).

Though it was not to be clear to me for some time how the Hare's could maintain such a close alliance with Dale Pocket— what with her former romantic connection to Lawrence Hare—it did satisfy me quite quickly that it might be possible in this day and age to advance to the platonic in such a way, and that it did seem clear that Dale might not only be in greater alliance with Lisa and Lawrence because of her peer and vocational associations with them, but also, I thought, because of her dislike of her brother's and sister-in-law's uncouth, invasive gossipy-ness, of which I had had a sample on the night before.

People often decry the fellow who allies himself with the first gal he romantically meets in a new environment. But there could have been no more desirable and seemingly affable woman to find anywhere, I firmly believed, and so I felt all too glad to be free of sifting through prospects, and all too glad to have an almost instant intimate romantic partner virtually fashioned for me—as had been my new position and apartment—by the unusual young couple of Pauktaug, the Hares.

"Have you joined the Pauktaug Running Club?" Dale asked me with perfunctory expectation as the table was being cleared by the busboy. She and Lisa wore wispy, flowered dresses that were captivating. I almost neglected to answer Dale's question at first, for one could look at them in these dresses, it seemed, for long immodest moments—dresses which not long before I would have considered revealing, but after the trans-naked revelations of the gym seemed positively cloisterish.

"No, not yet. You know, I've only run by myself so far."

"You should join the club. It's fun. You'll like it," said Lisa.

Lawrence Hare was sipping his water religiously. He seemed oblivious to his wife's phrases.

"You know, you really should join the club. It's not only fun—made up of a lot of nice, great people—but it's the only way to get faster, really," inserted Dale.

"What is?" I asked.

"Running with other people—running with people that are faster than you are. If you chase rabbits, you are bound to get faster."

This last phrase brought Lawrence Hare out of his physical reverie. He seemed mentally and affably present, but the physical intellectual self, the mysterious self I had noted in him at the gym, had been quite far away. But, again, this last phrase of Dale's seemed to stir a memory in him, but it faded quickly. He looked at Dale for a brief moment—not into her eyes or toward the source of her speech. Rather, he scanned her entire body for a brief, brief instant—not in a sexual way, but in some allegiance to a code of his inscrutable, trans-mental intellectual self. And just as quickly as he was brought to attention by what she said, he seemed to dismiss viability in Dale after he surveyed the length of her flawless frame. I looked myself, then, and could only see a few appealing damp patches in the folds of her dress, near where she crossed her legs—dampness from the quickness with which she had leaped from the shower and into her dress for dinner. I saw nothing odd. I saw nothing to read in this save the obvious for my own physical fascination in her romantically and sexually. But otherwise, I say again I saw nothing in her body to read—and I thought since I saw nothing to read that I must be missing something.

The Hares politely left a bit early that evening, but not before inviting me to the monthly meeting of the Pauktaug Running Club, which was to be held on the very next night, Saturday, at the Pauktaug American Legion Lodge. I accepted heartily, and I told the Hare's, as well, that I was grateful for their help with my great-grandmother. Lisa Hare assured me that either she or Lawrence would pick up my great-grandmother on her arrival back in town late Saturday night, and then the Hares left me alone with my ideal, stunning, new partner.

It is very difficult to remember anything about the rest of the evening in that restaurant. I stared at the scrawl that was the text of her body, her form, for some hours, I think. And it did not matter to me that I could not really make out what all that figurative writing of her body might be speaking. I was too smitten to care; we both left for Pauktaug and ended the night with a long walk through town—a walk that was difficult for us both to bring to an end.

But even for all that focus upon Dale that evening, I look back and remember how I wondered after the distant, roving eyes of Lawrence Hare. He had been present and pleasant and affable in all the traditional ways. But after a time—even after I stopped noting that evening that there was a distant, other self to the man—I could not help but watch as the waiter had to return time and time and time again to our table to refill Hare's water glass. For in the midst of our happy and chatty conversation, Hare constantly downed glass after glass of water, as if he were hydrating not only his body, but that other self that was embodied by his body—as if the present and pleasant diversions of the dinner were but a small, insignificant, and barely tolerable tangent to the writhing and insuppressible expectations of his mysterious and larger physical self.

CHAPTER 10

THE PACK:
THE RUNNING CLUB

It was difficult to part from Dale even that first night. Somehow there was a great sympathy, a silent sympathy that obviated words, which, when added to the extreme physical attraction I felt for her, made a lot of the usual months-long preambles, the difficult getting-to-know-one-another choreographies, seem unnecessary in our case. Somehow she seemed to see something in me that was deeply familiar to her. I only sensed this, or guessed at it—for she said nothing. And as I have observed, I could not read what her inscrutable but fantastic bodily form was saying to me outside of sexual implications. But I felt there must be something written there. And what could be familiar in me to her? I could not say. What might be said to be familiar in her to me? Only that she was a physical ideal—such an ideal that she dashed the long-held truth, inculcated in my mind from even the start of my life by people I admired and trusted, that even when considering the great beauties of the world, subjectivity and the perception of human character would always leave open to debate the standard of human beauty and perfection. It is possible, I think, having met Dale Pocket, to feel convinced that there is human physical perfection.

Dale kissed me aggressively before we parted, and then virtually slinked, stalked away with the very grace of a sated leopard in the velvet and waning witching hour of the new day.

A man could feel the very blood in him whilst watching her unique mixture of firmness and pliability verily glare at one as she showed her back from head to heel—as she vanished from the park and toward her car. She intimated, if I might say a word for what is usually mocked as man's part of Man's tiresome preoccupation with idealized sexuality, that there was something far beyond enticement to mere reproduction in a body as powerfully representative of human perfection as was Miss Dale Pocket's. Her voice was not currency; her body was—her body a coin, a currency of the values of natural laws, summed up not in human spirit, but in the only confirmable, touchable evidence of the universe: physical matter.

I slept late into the next morning, languishing awake in bed for quite some time, as well, with images of Dale Pocket in mind and with the simple lazy luxury of being able to skip an early morning rising for a run—not only because it was a Saturday, but also because I was slated to run with the Pauktaug Running Club for the first time that evening.

Just before lunch I had a long telephone conversation with my mother and father. My mother was irritated that it was not I that was going to pick up her grandmother at the train station that evening. I was not sure how to respond to her save to become short—to intimate that perhaps I should just leap in on a sincere and apparently devoted relationship through my nominal claim by ties of blood. My mother became irritated herself. But I finished the call with a long listening session concerning my father's dissatisfaction with the grass care their club's golf course was receiving at the moment.

I went with the group for the run before the club meeting that night. Though the run was billed as a mild, recreational, one-hour run, a mere preamble to the monthly meeting, the pace of even the main group was such that I did battle with my nausea reaction several times along the way of the hilly Pauktaug Village course. I learned that Hare and Pocket almost never ran with the group. They were back at the Legion Post readying for the monthly meeting. Though Dale had not promised to appear at the run, I was surprised to find her absent, though I did expect to find her at the actual meeting of the club. Lisa Hare, however, flattered and puzzled me by being my only familiar companion on the run.

When the group returned to the parking lot of the Legion Post on Main Street, most of the runners headed straight for the restrooms or to their cars to change for the meeting—some, like Lisa Hare and myself, lived close enough to the Legion Post to jog home for a shower before returning for the meeting.

When I returned to the Legion Post, I descended the stairs just inside of the main entrance. There on that stairway was a lean and very tall fellow—a very runner-like looking fellow. I had not seen him on the run that evening. What was so astonishing about this fellow was that he was descending the winding stairway to the building's basement—where the meeting hall was—backward. He paused a few times and tested himself in taking a step or two forward, but then he paused, seemed to consider something grave, and then resumed his backward descent of the stairs. I took him to be testing the stairway for a moving venture—in other words, he appeared to me to be trying out the pathway for having to carry, say, a couch or other large object down that stairwell. I even asked him, since I overtook him pretty quickly in his fitful, backward descent, if that was what he was up to, and if he and any other fellows needed help.

"No," he laughed in a lightly condescending, tolerant sort of way, "stairs are hard on the knees. It's easier on the knees to take stairs backwards."

I passed him then and asked no more.

I passed through a wide, paneled hallway before the entrance to the meeting room. There, often in a dance-like pairing with framed, aged, prints of the Pauktaug Girl, were aged plaques with carven names—names of the fallen, and prints of battle scenes, mounted and glass-entombed folded flags with red stripes turned an ancient rose pink and blue stripes turned a deceptive and meek baby blue. There were swords. And there were many, many photographs of the entire assembly of that post of the Legion for a given year or a given decade—going back to the age of bunting and Sousa, to the days when Memorial Day was Decoration Day.

I took my seat in the already filling meeting room, and watched as most of the runners left the bar and took their seats as Charles Pocket, President of The Pauktaug Running Club, banged the gavel and prepared to call the meeting to order. To my relief, both Dale and Lisa, stunning and lemony-sweetened by the remnants of showers and dampened new short dresses, took the seats next to me. I did not see them come in, but it was both awkward and a peculiar thrill to have Dale lean in and nudge me an elbowed hello, a physical hello that was marked by millions of years of evolutionary proprietorship—and I seemed claimed and spoken for with a flattering yet slightly disturbing immediacy.

Lisa looked over her shoulder. "Why is Lawrence standing all the way back there by the doorway? I told him to come join us. What is he doing?"

I looked back to see Lawrence Hare. He seemed so fixed on the proceedings ahead of him, over and past the crowd of the seated assembly, that my eyes followed his to the front of the room, and I knew that it was foolish to look back again and try to hail him.

One might ask, before I describe the proceedings of the meeting, that beyond taking care of club business (planning races and future meetings) and covering a little social ground, what use might there be in a non-running running club meeting. One might ask, might joke, what do people at such a meeting with such an interest talk about? Do they just stand around and talk about their times—their race times, that is? Why, yes! In fact, that is indeed what they do. And all during the chatty overture before the last sounding of the president's gavel, one could hear frequent citations of times in innumerable spots all around the room: *Under two hours; over two hours; 3:45; ninety seconds; four hours; forty-two minutes; fifty-nine minutes.* And in there one also hears such things as: *If only a second faster; just shy by a minute; oh, as much as ten minutes slower than last year; oh, six more seconds than before.* All these citations of time came from all directions, as if one were on the edge of a little universe that truly judged itself by temporal issues alone. But then the judge-like gavel sounded that last time from the long and crowded desk at the front of the room (where all the club officers then sat), and the running club meeting came to order. The veritable present Father of the running club, Charles Pocket, began to speak, and all became quiet.

After a brief preamble, and some cursory small club execution of parliamentary procedure—mainly the reading of the minutes of the last meeting (in which it was recalled that a sports physician had lectured on the topic of stretching; and then a resolution was presently passed to send formal thanks to the good Doctor)—Charles Pocket moved onto the more pressing issues of the meeting.

"We've come to the time of year when concerns over the possible and likely second running of the Pauktaug 10K Race have to be discussed. Well, we're pretty certain that the race will be held on any account, but there are certain variables that we're not sure of. To begin with, there was an inordinate amount—according to the company that is offering us the chip timing service—an inordinate amount of unrecorded times in our latest test of the chips, and even some jumbled and likely incorrect times, and we suspect it may have to do with the historic trolley tracks on Main Street near the finish—that the tracks may pose some sort of problem for the equipment."

For those who do not know, I should say here that the chip to which Pocket was referring is simply a little computer chip encased in a plastic shell that one attaches to their running shoe. It gives one a very precise reading of their race times—and for any number of split times along the course of the race. One needs only cross a sensor mat that is placed at given sites along the race course—start, finish, and at chosen split locations—and the chip is read by the mat and sends the information to a computer for an instant tabulation of a racer's progress and their results.

"I'll need a few volunteers for a test that the timing service wants to run on next Wednesday night. I need a few runners willing to meet me at 7:00 PM, here—outside in the Legion parking lot—and we'll run some tests for the fellows from the timing company. They think they know how to stop the quirks related to the old trolley tracks."

Pocket asked for a show of hands from willing volunteers. He raised a group rather easily and noted these names. I looked back at Hare at this point; he did not respond to the call, and he remained motionless and fixed in his study of Pocket and of the council of club officers who sat in a row at the long front table.

"There is another issue concerning the upcoming race that I wish to formally address. This isn't easy for me."

And it was clear, that despite the evident self-confident and slightly paternal condescension of Pocket, he did indeed seem to have some compunctions, or embarrassment, in directly talking about himself in relation to the next topic.

"Again, I feel funny making such a formal announcement of this. But I think it is best—since so many are expecting the opposite of me—that I formally announce my intention to sit out this race. Though my friend—and close second-place finisher—has raised hell with me over this, I even got *him* to agree that maybe both he and I, for the dignity of the race, and for the sake of getting it off to a good, clean, lifespan, should just work the administrative aspects this year. We are, believe it or not, thinking of adding a Pauktaug Marathon, a sort of 'Gold Coast' Marathon next spring, as well. Actually, it looks like that is really going to happen, so I think it is best if we give our full attention to that—Lawrence and I—and take some of the silly controversial pressure off of our new and, I think, very viable races."

A general and sincere murmur went up through the crowd with each mention Pocket made of his intention to sit out the next race.

To his credit, Hank rose from his seat and requested permission to speak. I did not know that he was there, and that he was a runner, until I saw him then. Permission granted, he spoke rather persuasively.

"I think we all know that there would be no 10K race here in town, no possibility of a new marathon for Long Island's north shore, no real core for our village's running community, without Charles Pocket. And, frankly, I don't think that any of us doesn't know that Charles Pocket not only saved this club during several logistical and financial crises, but honestly saved our group from dissolving on more than one occasion—and not only because of his sound business advice, and willingness to assume the presidency when almost no one else was even willing to run for it, but also by numerous gestures that just make him a good, good fellow."

There was a general and benign murmur to all of this—not an affected applause. I looked back at Hare at this juncture, and he had the most peculiar, beaming, animated look on his face. I had never seen a grown man look so animated and proud over a testimonial for another man. There was almost a look of touching solicitude to it—and its sincere fervor was only matched by what I felt was a sort of unique, if not disturbing, intensity. And it was not because the eulogy and defense obliquely touched on matters concerning himself; it was because Pocket was the main concern that Hare seemed so gratified.

Hank continued: "And I don't think there is any question that the two fastest men in the world are in this room." Here a cheer went up through the assembly—sincere and heartfelt, as for a true cause, as much as for familiar and dear figures.

"So, not only in fairness to you, Mr. President, and to Mr. Hare, but for the club, the race, and the village, I think I speak for all when I say that not only do we want you both in the race, I think that both of you must be in the race."

There was another general and earnest cheer.

The club's secretary, sitting a few seats to the side of Pocket, raised his voice over the din: "In lieu of Pocket or Hare, both being club officers and being too much concerned and too modest, I make the motion myself that the club resolves that both Charles Pocket and Lawrence Hare, for the sake of the club, the second running of the race, the Village of Pauktaug, for their sense of honor—and for proof that Man has not yet even come close to his best speeds on this old Earth—must run the Second Annual Pauktaug 10-Kilometer Race. All those in favor?"

A rousing round of *ayes* filled the room. Pocket smiled, and that old look of paternal cockiness came over his face again, but not before—and this was odd, I thought, and unmistakable—he looked to the back of the room and caught Hare's eye.

I looked to Hare myself, and I saw Hare's grave and earnest face seize the right of paternal power for a striking and autocratic moment. He nodded to Pocket without a smile, and then Pocket smiled as I had never seen him smile yet.

"Well, despite my position as president, it is not for me to debate the resolutions of our adamant throng, is it? I'll run this race!" Then came a cheer from the club.

Of course I did not really feel that it was the club's common sway that really influenced Charles Pocket. I think the attorney's and politician's spirit in him had said certain things that he felt he had had to say. I am sure he had been resolved to run the race all along if he could. But I will say that there was something uniquely vulnerable and helpless, peculiarly unresolved and unschooled about him, when he verily seemed to look to Hare for permission. I looked back to study Hare one more time, before Pocket resumed the club proceedings, to see if the unusual and observable dynamic between Hare and Pocket might still be seen in Hare's face. But he was gone.

Pocket proceeded with his address to the club, but with a practical celerity that seemed to be headed for levity and finality: "The only other thing I want to report is that our course will be officially certified this year. I'll be guiding the officials over the course—and putting them up at my home while they are here in town at the end of next week. However, I'm not sure if we will have the same cable coverage as last year. They may have too many options—since there are so many new small town races all over the country, and they may be a little skittish because of last year's problems, but I'll be working on that."

Pocket then beamed with his paternal, political ease: "In addition to the small, usual spread that we have here at the monthly meeting, my wife and I would like to invite you all to a full reception we've set out for you all at our home. The pool is still open—it might be a little cold—but we just wanted to have you all over once more before we close that down. All are welcome, and I'm going to turn the meeting over to my fellow officers and get on home, to get ready to see you all there."

There was mild applause to this, as well as the usual commentary by many fellows that free food and drink would draw them anywhere. Dale and Lisa asked if I would go over to the Pocket's with them, and I, of course, said yes. Dale insisted on driving.

I sat in the back of the car as we three drove to Charles Pocket's house and as the twilight grew over the village.

"You know, Rex, I saw you once before I met you at the gym." Dale looked long into the rear view mirror with the green marble richness of her eyes as she told me this. "You were running in this neighborhood—right near the newer part of the cemetery, and I think you passed me."

"Yes, that was me—" I started. I was going to say more, but Dale continued. She took her eyes off of the mirror as she continued to speak, and focused ahead as the last long stretch before the turn to the Pocket's driveway came into view.

"You know, Rex, that was only a week ago, and I didn't think you were in very good shape then. You've made, somehow, a tremendous leap—in just a week somehow. You even look different."

I just smiled at this; I wasn't sure what to say. Soon we reached the driveway and parked.

It was a pleasure to walk from the car through the cool breezes floating off of the Long Island Sound—what with the two beauties by my side. The wind would occasionally blow in such a way that a perfect outline of their perfect shapes would be revealed through their dresses (especially Dale's flawless form), and then when the breath of God became spent—or He perhaps abashed, even ashamed, at the perfect forms He had created in these women—He seemed to hold his breath an extra bit longer, so that the dresses would loosen again and cover the glory of Mankind in Woman.

The house was already crowded when we entered. Dale's niece squealed at the sight of her young aunt, and she immediately led Dale by the hand up the stairs so as to show something off in her room.

I got separated from Lisa in the crowd, and I accidentally wondered into a room that was just off of the enormous living room. This smaller room was being refurbished, and it was being done in the most painstaking and artful manner—all the work and carpentry, I mean.

I suddenly knew that there was someone behind me. It was Lisa.

"Lawrence is doing this, isn't he?" I asked. It looked so much like the same hand had to be behind what was then before me as had been at work in my apartment.

"Yes, he is. Can you believe with all that he has to do—all that he has been up to—he is still able to help a friend out on this level. He amazes and confounds me at the same time."

"Oh, really? What do you mean?" I inquired frankly and somewhat to my own surprise when she let this little yet telling remark slip out.

"Oh, I don't know. He's just spreading himself thin." She offered that rather curt, meaningless cliché for an answer, and with that she closed the window for inquiries along that line. Yet she did not wish to close off the tone of intimacy that was somehow created by this little unfinished room. Her lingering made me uneasy, and perhaps the source of my uneasiness led me to somehow say the thing that seemed the most awkward thing I could have offered. Yet it slipped out from me, and I could not recall it. But Lisa received it eagerly.

"With this kind of work, with this kind of skill, can you imagine the child's room, the nursery that Lawrence could build for you one day?"

"Yes, I can," she said quietly, and she moved casually closer to me—not increasing the tension, but certainly not relieving it for me. Then quite to my surprise, she asked with sincerity—and without the least trace or hint that she wanted me to answer in the negative, "Rex, do you like Dale? I hope you do. I think she is perfect for you. She likes you, you know."

I think I said a few mumbled affectations of modesty and unsureness. I noted that Lisa somehow combined her motherly qualities toward me with the strange romantic intimations that made me so uncomfortable—thus I was afraid to distance myself from the one part of her and thereby slight the other (the two parts almost seeming unaware of one another, even when they were mutually present). And I must say that somehow the two parts did not seem, and this was strange to me (but somehow true), to conflict with one another. Yet, of course, I was unnerved. And the intimacy that this little side room created, so close to the passing din of the crowd that continued to fill the house, was disturbingly romantic to me in overtone, and I led her out and into the flow of the house—into the running pack that was filing out and into the pool area like a crowd at a race's beginning, shuffling to a course's start.

There was indeed a crowd, a slow moving line through which one had to funnel to get toward the pool area where everyone was assembling. Lisa continued in an oddly intimate manner with me as we slowly made our way to the back of the house.

"You know, if it wasn't that Dale doesn't want to have any children, I'd never have been able to be with Lawrence. I think they would still be together."

"Ah, no!" I said, trying to sound casual yet at the same time grave. "I'm sure there were other reasons."

"Well, yes. I think there were. But I'm not perceptive enough to tell you what they are." This remark was curious, I thought, and it interested me. But I did not feel it was any of my business—nor did I wish to find that I had won the intimacy with Lisa to ask after such a thing.

"How about you, Rex? Do you want children?"

"I'm not sure. I think I do."

"Well, that may be a problem for you and Dale. But she seems to like you like I've never seen her like anyone so suddenly. I'll bet she'll change some things for you—"

I tried to interrupt her here—so that I could remind Lisa that Dale and I had met for the first time only the day before. But she continued.

"Again, if I was sure that Lawrence and I were brought together by anything, it was because I was sure that he wanted a baby."

For some reason I did not feel that it was out of order to pursue her last point a bit. We were entering the patio area, and as Dale was before us then with her niece still by her side, I felt that nothing untoward or overly personal could emerge on any account.

So I said, "Well, I'll bet he still does. You're both young. I'm sure that if he was really resolved along those lines that he still feels that way deep inside."

"That's it!" she said in mild exclamation, even as we came into Dale's orbit. "That's just it. I don't think he feels the same way deep inside. He will say it and mean it. I think he even thinks it and means it, but there is some other part that is thinking now for him, as well—and it thinks something else."

This was another curious remark, but I had to let it go—for not only was it not in me to fuel and entertain another person's inclinations toward what I felt was a strong hint at infidelity, but I was, as well, even less inclined to pursue such a thing, even in the most abstract recesses of my own mind, with the wife of my generous new employer and developing friend. But, again, I had to let it all go, for Dale was there with her niece. Then Lisa said, she somehow carrying our privacy a bit further than it could last, "But you want to have children, Rex. That's good. That's nice."

Dale, to my relief did not hear this last remark, and I took the opportunity to introduce myself to her niece. The child was a little forward and obnoxious to me, so I was relieved when Charles Pocket suddenly stood up and called for everyone's attention.

As the crowd quieted, I whispered to both Dale and Lisa that I wondered where Lawrence was.

"He's supposed to be here—" began Lisa.

"Yes, he's here. I saw him," Dale added.

Lisa finished: "He had to leave the meeting early to help Charles and his wife with this."

Then Charles Pocket attempted to address the crowd. As he started to speak, and as I looked around at all the extensive arrangements that had been made for this ostensibly impromptu post-meeting reception, all of Pocket's statements about balking at the notion of running in the Pauktaug race, and even his acceptance to run by the supposed force of the club's will, seemed doubly staged to me—doubly, because there was always that paternal, somehow fraudulent, patronizing air about him. But then again there was that look of requested permission he had seemed to put to Hare—that was the only part of the whole thing I could not quite fit into my character study of Charles Pocket.

Pocket stood up on the firm end of the pool's diving board, so that he had a little podium from which to speak. He moved out onto its end while he made his last—and effective—effort to silence his guests. Of course, many joked that he should take care not to fall into the pool.

"My wife, Lynn, and I really want to thank all of you for being able to come to this little extra reception. Please help yourself to drinks and food in the dining room, and the pool is open, too. I won't say too much. But I did want to make one last announcement. Last year, last fall, we had a dollar from each race entry go to the Special Olympics. No slight meant to that charity, but because there are some local causes I think a lot of us would like to see given help, I'd like to divide the donated dollar in half this year—subject to everyone's approval—one half still going to the Special Olympics, the other half going to Long Island Sound recovery efforts."

Pocket seemed to be looking intently at one face in the crowd when he entered upon the subject of the charities. I followed his eyes, and I found Lawrence Hare. He was standing alone in the crowd near the sliding doors leading to the dining room. When Pocket mentioned the subject of the charity toward the Special Olympics, Hare only gave a passionately indifferent expression of aggressive blankness, and when the issue of the Long Island Sound environmental charity was raised, somehow this allowed Hare to double this look of indifference, this expression of angry disdain toward what he felt somehow, I believe, was a foolish tangent, a red herring concern—inexplicably (to me) he seemed to indicate that Pocket's public falseness or skewed interests were at their most false at this moment.

And then Pocket became brave; he seemed to wrangle for the paternal initiative, or for whatever mysterious contested ground existed between Hare and himself (mysterious, for I do not think it was based on competitive athletic instinct). He addressed Hare particularly.

"So, with the issue of the second running of the Pauktaug 10K, I'd like to nominate my good friend and club officer, Lawrence Hare, to the administration of the charity department of the race."

Polite and somewhat presumptuously expectant and intimate looks filled many of the faces as all looked to see how Lawrence Hare would receive this offer. Thinking he feigned a sort of mock-disgust at the prospect of having more work piled on him, most of the assembly just lightly laughed when Hare was seen to flash a dismissive and angry wave at Pocket. Then he disappeared into the house. Pocket thanked the entire group once more, insisted that they enjoy themselves, and then he began to make his way to the house himself.

I stood with Dale, her niece, and Lisa for a time in silence, and I watched as the throng continued to gather around the pool—everyone looking rather like members of a penguin colony on the edge of the water, or even more like a seal colony, especially when those already in bathing suits decided to simply slide into the pool from their reclining positions on deck chairs.

Dale asked if I would get something to drink for her niece and her from the house. I assented to this readily.

It took me awhile to make my way through the seal colony and into the back of the house. I was just about to fulfill my duty of finding something like a lemonade or juice that I could bring to both Dale and her niece, when it occurred to me that I might find, or at least see, Hare and Pocket. I looked through the hordes around the tables of food and in and around the adjacent rooms. And then I thought to try a look in the room that was being refurbished—the little library.

And there I did spy Hare and Pocket, and I almost walked in on their conversation—that is, until I could hear that it was somewhat near the finale of a curt and cool exchange. They spoke in tense whispers, and what with all their whispering and hushed tones, it made the room that had put nurseries into my mind seem all the more like a nursery to me.

I slipped away and retrieved some lemonade for Dale and her niece.

The evening wore on, and I conversed with my three female companions—Dale, Lisa, and Dale's niece, Angela—until I could tell that Dale was interested in going, and that she wanted me to leave with her. I was eager for this, of course, and while Dale vanished to say her goodbyes and to see her niece off to bed, I sat with Mrs. Lawrence Hare in the brilliant starry blackness, under the black-cat-velvet stage curtain of the Long Island autumn night.

Lisa suddenly volunteered a stunningly pertinent comment—right in the middle of our aimless watching of late bathers in the pool.

"You know why Lawrence is disgusted with Charles?"

"No, I don't," I said, and by saying as much, I confessed what I had thought I alone had secretly noticed that evening.

"Well, I think he's disgusted with Charles since Charles nominated him for this extra club duty."

"Lawrence doesn't want the extra work?"

"No, I don't think that's it. It is just that Charles is a little bit too much of a tit-for-tat person. And he'll take anything you offer by way of a return if you claim you don't mind giving it. Frankly, I don't know why Lawrence thinks he has to do all that work remodeling Charles' library. You'd think he really was building a nursery or something for us—but in their house!"

Lisa's image of the nursery struck me, simply because it had struck me more than once myself now.

"So you think Lawrence is disgusted that Charles asked for this running club administrative favor because he is already doing extra work here, the remodeling, on the house?"

"No, there's something else. Last night, Lawrence and Charles went out onto the Sound together. I guess Charles ultimately thinks *he* was doing Lawrence a favor. But I know Lawrence is always hoping that things will be done for just the sake of blood-brother generosity. I told him that most people aren't like the way he is—especially Charles."

"What did Lawrence want Charles' help with out on the water?"

"Oh, Lawrence wanted to get some pictures of the man or men who are stealing from all the traps. Charles has a good camera, and always seems to get good pictures, so he said he would help Lawrence to get some shots of the guys out there doing all the stealing. The police, the harbor police, the coast guard—whoever is supposed to control all that—haven't really satisfied Lawrence's complaints, so he thought he would get some pictures himself and start to use the power of the little old *Pauktaug Press.*"

"Did they get any pictures?"

"No. Well, yes, but then Charles dropped his really good camera into the water and lost it—right after getting some pictures of the guy that bothers Lawrence so much, since he is always into our traps. It was the same guy that he said you and he ran into. And he said that this man was crazy mad, crazy furious. And he must think, this guy, that they got the pictures—because he didn't see the camera fall. Anyway, I told Lawrence to leave all this to the proper people, because this guy sounds scary to me."

Dale appeared at the back door and waved me in.

"Anyway," Lisa added as we got up from the seal pool and stretched, "I think Charles, even with all that Lawrence has done, wants something for his time and for that camera. He really is a disgusting little brat sometimes. Don't tell anyone I said that."

I just laughed.

"And I'm worried about Lawrence. You know, I rarely see him sleep. He doesn't seem to suffer for it—not at all. But it still concerns me."

We were directed into the living room by Dale, Charles, and the amorphous, mildly aimless, sad and desperate ghost, Lynn Pocket, where we were asked to watch a little last-minute recital that Charles Pocket insisted Angela give on the piano.

"There's a guy—used to be in big piano competitions—who works over at the funeral home with his uncle and aunt. He teaches the kids around here sometimes," whispered Charles Pocket into my ear as his daughter began to play. The child looked terrified and reluctant, but she also seemed perversely driven to perform her little number for the dwindled crowd.

"I'm glad Lawrence isn't here to see this. He just hates to watch it when the Pockets make their children perform something," Lisa whispered into my other ear.

Lawrence Hare was indeed gone, for Dale gave Lisa a ride back into town when the evening was done, and then Dale had me follow her back to her apartment on Main Street. It was getting very late, and though Dale showed no signs that I needed to wander off, I felt that some sort of remembrance of the old Victorian mating game had to be remembered by someone. But I mean no slight to Dale Pocket with that last remark. I have made mention that there was a mysterious part to Dale—something physically transcendent in her of which she was aware but of which she was not consciously in control or could intellectually manage. Thus she hovered over this inscrutable beauty-power of hers—which was almost a state of mind it was so strong—hovered over it in a defeated state that could not seize what was hers because she could not comprehend what its use was for. And thus, because of this strong awareness of, but impotent command over, her almost revolutionary physicality, the common steps of sexual romance and friendship seemed a bit unnecessarily complex and tedious to her. This is not to imply that she was not selective, and, in fact, I never had evidence that she had ever had any significant intimate contacts with men other than Hare or myself. I only mean to say, that in lieu of making the leap to this level she knew she possessed but could not comprehend or control, she must, at the same time, have found the other levels childish and easy to control and master. So if one can understand that I am somehow trying to describe what might sound like a combination of specialized, evolved, ascetic intellectual *and* loose liberalized woman, but really mean something quite other than that, for she was unique—for she was in the center of those two extremes without being formed by their average—then perhaps I have done some small justice to the curved physical magnificence (which was somehow at once the intellectually incipient magnificence) of Dale Pocket.

I intimated that I really had to return to my apartment, so rather than become too enmeshed in a difficult extrication from within her home, we sat in a delightfully tentative pose for a wonderful vacillating hour on the fire escape-like stairway that led to her high third floor apartment. She had changed from her summery dress into a perfect fitting pair of shorts and tank top—the latter with the most tenuous, most delicate, almost brittle looking pair of white straps over her shoulders. She sat one step below me on the old wooden stairs, and she looked ahead as we talked and would look back at me from time to time—we both studying the night mostly, and checking each other's smiling faces intermittently.

Thus I could study her beautiful back and shoulders quite intimately and without pause. The muscle and bone of her lovely and defined shoulder blades would flex ever so delicately but clearly in the cooling blue autumn midnight light, and that entire area of her body began to look like axe heads pointed to the perfectly exposed, knotted, lean, taut, rope-like coil of her spine, which vanished up into her dark hair. It would seem that her body would cut its connection from her brain if it could—and let this perfect feminine form reign free of all doubts and flaws of mind—but the lovely axe blades of shoulder blades seemed forever poised before that figurative rope in doubtful, profound, hesitation and unstoppable compunction.

So with the tame union of awkward early kisses—tame in light of the fact that engaging this singular woman at the orifice of speech seemed somehow the most tempered and conservative of actions, no matter how rich the contact—with this quiet and traditional beginning to what was our solid affair, I parted myself from her at 2:00 in the morning and insisted that I get back to my own apartment.

When I arrived home, two messages impatiently flashed their waiting status on my machine. The first was from Lisa Hare.

"Rex, I'm sorry to bother you. I can't reach Dale. Her ringer is off, I think. It's about ten past two, and Lawrence is either off on the water or somewhere else with Reginald—doing something with the traps or who knows what! Anyway, I don't have the car, and Nancy just called, and she's at the station. I don't know why she picked this hour, but that is when she did tell us she'd be here, and Lawrence said he would get her. He doesn't forget things—ever. So I'm worried about him. Please call me if you get this soon."

I started to call her as I began to listen to the second message, and then I paused as I listened to the recording. It was a firm voice, an elderly but somehow unaged voice that came through.

"Rex? This is your great-grandmother. Hello. I'm in a funny

little fix here. Lawrence Hare was supposed to be here to get me, and there are no cabs here at the moment. Hope I didn't wake the new working boy in town with this, but I could sure use a rescue if you know where the station is—the East Northport station. I can't reach Lisa. I just got their machine, so I'd sure appreciate a rescue if you could manage it."

I called Lisa Hare, and I assured her that I would go to the station right away. She wanted to go with me, but I said it would be easier for me to meet my great-grandmother on my own. I made up that latter condition, for I felt uncomfortable riding around alone with Lisa late at night—even for a short time, and even with an elderly chaperone waiting for us quite imminently at the station. I told her I would call when I got Nancy Whisker safely inside, and that I would check to see if Lawrence and Reginald were accounted for and all right.

I found the station pretty easily; it was only about a ten minute drive to the southwest from Pauktaug Village. And there, all alone, but astonishingly confident and matter of fact about everything, was my great-grandmother, sitting on a bench near the pay phones and with just a pair of light travel bags at her side. I got out of the car and went to her. She greeted me very warmly, and I saw her to the car and put her things in the back. I called Lisa Hare from one of the pay phones, and she sounded relieved—saying that Lawrence had returned. He extended his thanks and his apologies to me, and he said that he could not account for his not making it there—that he, too, confessed he almost never forgot a plan in his life. Lisa Hare sounded relieved, and I could hear her giving kisses to Reginald as she cheerily said goodbye and thanked me once more. Then she quickly asked before hanging up whether I wanted them to wait up and help me see Nancy into her apartment. I replied that all would be well, and that I thought we could manage on our own.

Now, just as had been reported, my great-grandmother—who

insisted that I call her Nancy (which was somehow not as difficult for me to do as I thought it might be)—did have a limp from
her injured foot. But I would have to say that she was the most
astonishingly fit woman for her age I had otherwise ever seen. She
did seem as if this little injury had humbled her permanently in
some physical way, yet if the vacillation between mental feebleness
and physical feebleness that Hare attributed to her could be given
any credit, then I would have to say that this slight wound and her
slight signs of brittle motion (from her extreme elderliness) left
her in the strongest of mental states. She was not only very
friendly and alert, but she was eager to talk with me, even then at
that hour. And I could tell that she was relieved to find that my
writing and my mind and character in person were one and the
same.

"Do you feel wakeful, Rex? Do you feel tired right now, I
mean?"

"No, not at all really. I'm actually quite excited to finally have
a chance to meet you. I wish it weren't so late. Then we might stop
and talk for a bit."

"Well, why don't we do that?"

I could see no reason not to. The diner on Main Street in
Pauktaug Village was open for twenty-four hours on weekend
nights, so we quietly made our way there. Thus, after spending
time with a young woman, Dale, of nebulous mental inclinations
or orientations—such that she seemed to wish her powerful body
would take over for her thinking—I switched to the company of
my great-grandmother: a woman of weakening, though still surprisingly strong physicality, who was quite clear of mind, who had
faith, I could see, in the worth of what the human intellect and
senses could tell the human heart. She had a faith that the human
mind was no cheat and was not a cheat's gift of an inadequate
Creation—she broadcast the total adequacy of the humans soul
(adequate to meet all adversities, adequate to meet all joys). And

she was generous in her forthcoming qualities, and did not seem averse to sharing on any level—including that most chambered level (that of the currency by which we reveal our true minds, our true levels of education): the grist reserve of analogy, the metaphor source from which we project our deepest beliefs. Hers were wide-ranging, humble at times and arcane at others, and I could not imagine a better meeting with my hitherto mysterious great-grandmother, or a better way to pass the time of my idle wakefulness brought on by my growing physical and romantic fascination with Dale Pocket.

For the most part it was clear to me why the Hares—especially Lawrence—found such interest in Nancy Whisker. She seemed to point, for brief moments, to the type of companion, or the type of ideal, that a Lawrence Hare at times somehow hinted to me he was calling for from the human family. Yet, again, she was now incurably humbled by age and by her injury—but there was still a remarkable power to this woman who would become my best friend in Pauktaug.

We talked a little of my parents and of my past. Then she puzzled over Lawrence's failed appearance that night.

"He's never, ever, been late for an appointment or forgotten anything. I hope he is all right."

Then we talked over tea for as much as an hour or so. And I listened with silent fervor—this came after I told her of my interest in Pauktaug's past and of passing the Sunken Cemetery during that evening's run—listened with fascination as she told me of her love for her home village.

"You know, Rex, the house you passed right next to the Sunken Cemetery was my girlhood home. I was born there. And my husband and I lived there—and in the city apartment which I still have—for all our married lives. Here, on Long Island, I just have the apartment in Pauktaug now. But when I was a little girl we used to play in the part of the cemetery that is sunken, eaten up by the water now. And there was an old road, a path, that ran on the outer edge of it, just behind where the beach's edge used to start—but even that road was covered by water at times. You could walk that into town at low tide, however, and climb the ladder of the dock, and pretend that you had come in from a long voyage at sea. That is what my brothers and sisters used to do. We'd take that path into town for errands for my mother and father—or to get candy or to go to the movies in the summer—and we'd meet people in town and pretend that we had either come from a boat or had emerged ourselves out of the sea, like some kind of new creature, a little bit advanced beyond mermaids and mermen. And then we would go back the same way, and it was fun to watch the surprised people on the dock, who might not see the path from where they were standing, as my brothers and sisters and I descended back down the ladder with our parcels or bags and seemed to be disappearing down back into the water.

"And then one late summer night a wonderful storm came, a hurricane. And there had been wonderful thunder and lightning storms on the nights before this, too. Do you like storms, Rex? You're not afraid of them?"

I confessed that I liked them very much, which was true, and that I was not the least bit afraid of them.

"Good. So, on the last night before the hurricane, I remember the sound, after the rain and the thunder and lighting had passed, of the crickets in the old cemetery across from our yard—just where my brothers and sisters and summer and school friends had been playing tag late into the lightning-bug-evening earlier that night. And I remember first loving the smell of autumn here in town on those nights.

"And then the hurricane came the next night, and I remember we woke up and there was a crowd formed in our yard and on the road above, looking down at the old part of the cemetery. My mother and father would not let us look, because the storm had taken the cemetery—had washed it through with sea water—but had left, somehow, most of the headstones still standing. (They always build—I think they are due for a new one soon—some kind of protective barrier of soil and rock from time to time to try to keep what's left of the Sunken Cemetery, but the water will probably take it all eventually.)

"But somehow some of the graves had come open in the soft and sandy soil. It looks like a beach there, with headstones, now. Have you seen it?"

Yes, I had seen it. It is magnificent, I told her.

"Yes, it is magnificent," she beamed and smiled back to me.

"So my mother and father did not want us to see that several graves had been opened by the storm, and when the tide and the water flowed out and left the old cemetery a Sunken Cemetery, several skeletons could be seen lying out in the open, some still held together in bodily forms by old, old, tattered clothes from centuries past.

"And that night, my father—who was a wonderful man—had my brothers and my sisters and my friends on the porch, and he still would not let us look at the cemetery, for the Town Fathers were already working to clean up the graveyard and re-inter the bodies. And already everyone in town thought that there was a sort of wonderful novelty to what had happened. But no one would speak it yet. They all had to pretend it was a loss, an historical loss—and a shame to the dead who were exposed.

"But my father, he kept us up late (even though he would not let us look) and he told us what he saw. He saw three skeletons of what he thought were young men, he said. And the sea had come and let them out of their graves. And these were the bodies of young men who loved life so much that they did not want to be spirits or ghosts or angels—they just wanted to run again in old Pauktaug like boys once more. And it was the sand that got them. There they all lay, so close to freedom, he said. Each was in a still somewhat intact set of trousers and jacket, and their bodies lay stretched on the ground, in the soft sand, they seeming to reach for the freedom of the road that had been washed away. And then the sun caught them in the morning, the powerful and unfair time-keeping eye of God, and He dried them out as they struggled to make it out of the sand to the freedom of the road—where perhaps the lovely Pauktaug Girl might still be waiting for them."

My great-grandmother took a brief pause.

"Do you know what it is like to run in the sand, Rex?"

"Yes, I think I do."

"Then you know what happened to those boys who refused to be angels or devils or ideas or memories. They tried to run again and got caught in the sand."

I thanked my new friend for my night of quiet surprise, quiet talk, quiet and welcome and wonderful sleeplessness, and for her ghost story.

"Well, it's not supposed to be a ghost story. It's supposed to be a last-chance-of-the-body story, or something like that," laughed Nancy Whisker.

After a moment, my great-grandmother settled into a mild graveness: "Again, I only hope Lawrence isn't angry with me."

"Why would he be angry with you?"

"Oh, it's silly! I should not even mention this. But Lawrence's parents both became ill at the same time—both with cancer at around the same time, and they both died within days of one another. No one loved his parents more than Lawrence Hare, I think. (I knew them all my life; and they only got sick when Lawrence was finishing college. His father was the Methodist minister here. His mother was such a good, quiet woman. She let herself get heavy, but I think she could have been quite athletic at one time.) Anyway, when they fell ill, however, Lawrence seemed just the opposite of a son who loves his parents. The sicker they became, the more irritable, disgusted, he became with them. He really seemed to resent their physical fallibility. But I'm sure that was just his way of feeling what he was feeling then. But I'm almost afraid I'll lose my friend because I hurt my foot."

"Oh, don't be silly!" I insisted as I paid the diner check.

I escorted my great-grandmother up to her apartment in the dark and sleeping Hare apartment building, and then I went home and slept a sound sleep myself into the lateness of Sunday morning.

With so much I wanted to set down on paper that next day, I went into the office on Sunday afternoon to retrieve some of my notebooks, and there I found Lawrence Hare brooding over some writing of his own.

He thanked me sincerely for retrieving Nancy Whisker from the train station, and said that he regretted that I had to go out there to pick her up. I replied that it really was no trouble—that I was just glad that he was all right.

"Oh, I'm fine. Again, sorry, Rex." Then he looked at me in a telling way—though, as in the case of many of his cryptic expressions of body and face, I could not say precisely what he meant— looked at me and volunteered a phrase as a matter of form. But he said it in a way that was meant to tell me a great deal, and in such a way that the empty phrase was sure to be received by me as untrue and as a cover for some other more significant truth that I could not yet make out—but of which he seemed certain I would soon understand on my own.

"Sorry, Rex," he said. "It just entirely slipped my mind."

And, again, I knew this was not the truth—or not entirely the truth. We said no more that day but parted pleasantly, and I went for a run by myself later that afternoon.

CHAPTER 11

RACE: 10K

My first week in Pauktaug shadowed what many suc-
ceeding months were to be like for me in my new
home. I continued to run. I worked at the paper and
settled into a routine there. And I began to have my little series on
the history and influences of Pauktaug presented in the paper. I
continued to spend time with Nancy Whisker. I marveled at the
mysterious but consistent inexplicabilities of Lawrence Hare. I
went to the gym regularly.

And I became more and more fit. I spent days and days in
complete wonder at my fortune in my alliance with Dale Pocket.
It was all I could do to keep myself at work and somewhat disci-
plined—for otherwise all thought would have crumbled in deference to my worshipful preoccupation with this quiet and flawlessly
built woman. It was all I could do, as well, to keep us from virtually cohabitating after a just a few months. I tried to preserve some
memory of forms—but it was very difficult when one looked upon
her, for all else seemed to collapse, all intangible ideas and abstractions, in the presence of her tangible and irrefutable and vocifer-
ous argument of body.

There were social outings—double dates—with the Hares, and, for the most part, I felt free of the awkwardness I had felt earlier in the presence of Lisa Hare, and she seemed settled and pleased by my flowering romance with Dale Pocket. Lawrence Hare, however, seemed to regard my alliance with Dale with a sort of just perceptible, mildly indifferent disgust—as if I were going through a stage that was inevitable, but for which I would eventually lose interest. I had no intention of losing interest in Dale, but I must say that I was confident that Hare's subtle disapproval of my romance with Dale had nothing to do with old connections or revived jealousies. There was something more significant to it, yet I could tell he intended to say nothing about it—and I did not wish to bring any such things up on my own, on the remote chance that I merely had read too much into the peculiar silences and bodily mannerisms of Lawrence Hare. Perhaps he had meant nothing by his gestures, I thought—and, as well, I really did not know him (or any of them) very well at all.

There were even evenings of triple dates—just two instances I can remember, I should really say—with the Hares and with Mr. and Mrs. Charles Pocket (once at their home, and another time a sort of impromptu dinner date in the adjacent village of Northport). Of the first triple date, I was disappointed to find little to observe of the mysterious connection I had thought existed between Pocket and Hare. At that meeting I remember mainly the sad image of Mrs. Pocket, who, though surrounded by affluence, and putting forth no more effort than any other dinner party hostess, had the strange and melancholy and desperate quality of seeming like a servant to her guests when she entertained. She had little to say and offer on her own in a peculiar sort of way—outside of upper middleclass citations of all the places she had been and was planning to go within the year. Everyone was polite and grateful to her, but paying her any mind was a difficult affair. The second triple date was brief, and the restaurant was noisy—and I can only recall Dale's escalating intimacy with me as the most significant factor of the time following that meeting, which seemed to come on the heels of her gathering that her brother approved of me in a quiet and business-like sort of way, as if I fulfilled a certain basic checklist and there was no need to say any more on the subject.

He seemed to say to her: "He's fine. Churn out the babies with him, and let's hear no more of you," even though Dale still seemed indifferent to the topic of children. Maybe Charles Pocket thought that once the approval came from him, her compunctions on that topic would also vanish. I did not really care either way. Dale was not a mere object to me, but someone of her physical magnitude was, at the same time, a sort of commodity from which I could not turn away—and so long as I did not betray certain basic principles of good citizenship and honesty, I did not think that any old, half-hearted but righteously professed requirements and standards I had set in the past could tear me away from this woman.

My only break from these routines came when I flew down to Arizona to see my parents at Christmastime. And then I returned and a blur of routine began again. Though my life took on that embarrassed intensity of privacy and aloofness that one in a new and passionate pairing can experience, I did wander over to the running club monthly meetings on occasion. And at the April meeting just before the second running of the Pauktaug 10K, I volunteered for a number of duties for the race. At the elementary school cafeteria, three nights before the race, I could be found—along with Lynn and Charles Pocket, Lisa Hare and Dale Pocket—attaching little identification stickers to the race bibs for the thousand or so runners who had registered. I do not know where Lawrence Hare was that evening for sure. But I think that later that night Charles Pocket said that he was going to join Hare for a second attempt to capture some photographs of the lobster trap bandit or bandits.

More than a hundred of the club's members were there at that volunteer evening—many, most I should say, I had never seen before. Many of the members who no longer seemed to run much but who still fancied themselves as runners or as part of the running culture were there—potbellies and all.

And it was at that late evening volunteer work session, that my little adoptive Pauktaug circle insisted that I try a race for myself. Thus I registered that very night for the second running of the Pauktaug 10-Kilometer Race—and so I walked away that night with my very own number for my first foot race. And two nights later, on the night before the race itself, I assisted at the elementary school once more, where registered runners could pick up their numbers and packets for the race (the packet containing the obligatory tee shirt and numerous silly sample amenities that are generally found in race goodie bags).

But it was that morning of the race (and that day of the race) in which so many of the principal questions I had had, concerning certain particular Pauktaugians, would return to me with telling force—questions posed to me again with such an impact that I would experience an inner revulsion of embarrassment and self-doubt that I could have ever put my first wonderings aside for so long a time.

Though I had been warned many times over by dozens of advisors to go to bed early, I stayed up late with Dale that night before—or rather, stayed up moderately late with her, and then lay awake in fascination with her so near me. And in inserting this I do not mean to keep a lascivious tone always at hand—rather I mean to say that the sexual sight of Dale, its suggestiveness beyond sexuality, always kept me pondering some other intimation that her body seemed almost ready but never quite able to speak.

Thus when we rose for the race, we were both perhaps a bit more spent than one should be—especially myself. But there was a unique power to Dale's appearance even in a weakened state—as say when an actor or actress with a notable, stentorian speaking voice, falls ill, and their hoarseness only adds yet another creditable dimension to their power of articulation. Thus the figurative voice that was Dale's body, because of the few hours of sleep we had had, and because of the extra-early hour in which we had to rise, was hoarse. Her body had that look that beautifully-complexioned, suntanned women can have when fatigue has dimmed their radiance. She did not have that pale, ivory-like pallor as of Celtic Romantic heroines who waste away as ghosts in their suitor's memory or before the suitor's eyes in living consumptive whiteness. She had a pallor beauty, a slight touch of fatigued gray that was very seductive for its meekness against the raging power of her health and tanned beaming. Much as one can watch a slight bit of condensation evaporate from a table top, after one lifts the hand away from that surface on a humid, hot day, one could watch Dale's indefatigable and stentorian but still mysteriously silent health of body virtually evaporate this pallor as we dressed for the race.

Dale took a bit of extra time to ready herself that morning. She was doing a bit of stretching in the shower, I think, so I called out that I would wait for her outside. The street was already bustling with dozens of volunteers—especially in that zone of the 10-kilometer course, for the finish line was only a few hundred yards away from my apartment building. As one looked to the finish line banner, one also looked along Main Street toward the water.

I was not there long when Dale appeared. It was a rather warm morning already, and so neither of us wore anything in the way of warmup clothes. What Dale wore was so striking, so extreme, that had she been anyone else, I might have suggested she be a little more modest. But not only was I hesitant to sound like an increasingly possessive or dictatorial partner, there was something mysteriously striving to be spoken by her body, some odd universal idea, even through the blaringly loud running attire she wore that morning.

She wore the tightest of two-piece running outfits. But as I had seen her in such things before, I must say that that is not what made this outfit so striking. It was its color. She had on the brightest of yellow—a sort of taxicab-yellow with touches of white as stripes running down the brief covered stretch of her thighs. It was almost a sort of very modern comic book heroine's superhero outfit—Dale a sort of Sunwoman. Yet Dale did not seem to invoke the powers of the sun as her own; somehow Dale intimated with her sun-yellow a new foe against the long held notion that the heliocentric planetary system had forever displaced Earth or Man as the center of things. She did not so much as invoke brightness in invoking a star; she invoked centrality.

Some might put in a word for modesty at this point. Was Dale immodest? Did not most men, in a way, see her body, more or less, no less intimately on the street than when I saw her in the midst of private passion? Somehow, I say no. Ultimately, I could never cite Dale for any violations of physical discretion. Thus I must say that there were two points of view one had to assume in seeing virtually all of Dale Pocket. And that mysterious, almost speech-like role her body assumed, seemed revealed to all Man, in a way, and not just to men (though I can say that the sight of her was often merely ogled by the shortsighted). She seemed to know that her body said something, and she looked earnestly for someone to tell her what it meant. Perhaps because I came so close to suspecting this second nature of her body was the reason I was granted access to its first nature. So, again, as to the first nature of her body, Dale was rigidly selective; as to the second nature, she was a loose woman looking frantically about for self-explanation. And, again, since I at least seemed to ponder the need for an explanation, she would rest in my embrace when her human will was too tired to put forth its otherwise constant and nagging insistence for knowledge of the basic truth.

The starting line for the race was very near the parking lot of the elementary school, and Dale and I parted ways upon reaching there. She went off to find Lisa Hare, with whom she was going to run the race, and I was left with a mild, silly, volunteer task—guarding the baggage bus (a school bus into which runners could leave marked bags of belongings that would be transported to the finish line for pick up after the race).

I had hoped for a glimpse of Lawrence Hare or of Charles Pocket before the race began, but I was not to have it. In the months leading up to the race, Charles Pocket had allowed himself to grow into a public running figure. Though he kept his training more or less private—I still caught glimpses of him in the earliest of morning hours—he did grant occasional interviews for local cable television and radio. However, to his credit, a lot of these efforts were not so much a yielding to the curiosity of others on the issue of his imminent attempt to prove that he was without question the fastest man in the world at 10-kilometers (if not the fastest man in the world altogether), but more as an effort to promote Pauktaug's local race and the charities it served. And to his credit, as well, Pocket nearly vanished altogether from the race planning scene—delegating many of his powers to other willing volunteers for the last weeks right before the race—so that he could both remove his more controversial self from the scene and so that he could finish his training in privacy.

Hare, however, who was never the celebrity that Pocket was—though his rumored time in the last race could make him as fantastic a figure as Pocket—seemed as busy to me as ever. And I know that Hare took on many of Pocket's duties near the end of the last weeks of the race's preparation.

Hare seemed even more removed into his mysterious, silent, yet somehow voluble frame of body. But, of course, I often dismissed this ostensible quietness, abstractedness, and aloofness, to the distracted and scattered attentions of a too-busy man. During these pre-race months, Hare also entrusted more and more duties to me at the paper—while still logging more than full days there himself—and that silent trust was generally enough to satisfy me on the plane in which I wished to be recognized by Hare. And with each piece I turned in (not only editorially but also in the cases of my own writing) Hare seemed silently pleased, still confirmed as if in some impression he had formed of me even before we met.

Thus on the morning of my first race I was all on my own. Though I did catch sight of Dale and Lisa one more time at the start, I had this first race experience very much to myself indeed. Not knowing precisely what to do, really, I milled about after my baggage bus duties had ended and marveled at the pre-race sights. I watched in bemusement as Kee-Poh, who was running a race for the first time that day, as well, tried to fulfill the arduous task (given to him by the running club) of guarding the pair of portable toilets that had been set aside for elite runners.

Though I did not know the names, I had been told that Charles Pocket had succeeded in gathering a respectable field of elite, fast, professional runners for this race—which had, despite its slightly scandalized and humble beginning the year before, already succeeded in considerably enlarging its total number of entrants.

I looked up at the helicopter that hovered high above the starting area, several hundred yards into the course. Charles Pocket had been pleased that he had succeeded in getting local cable stations to carry the event, but he had not been as successful as the year before in getting more substantial coverage for his building of a small-town foot race.

As the starting corrals filled up and became more dense, I gave up on my stretching affectations (I still did not stretch too much before or after running, but the sight of so many stretchers set me to thinking I should at least pretend to that virtue). Then I caught a glimpse of Randy and Kee-Poh (both drafted into running this new race), but I could not reach them because of the press of the crowd. And I could see in the immense pack that so many wore little paper wristbands that noted a runner's intentions for their split times. These wristbands looked very much like those that are worn by newborns for identification in maternity wards. And I recall making a comment to myself: "That doesn't look so odd, for isn't a baby's first word not really a word, but really the kick the mother feels from baby in the womb? A baby kicks, tries to run, before it tries its voice."

I suspected for a time that some sort of opening ceremony was taking place, for there seemed to be someone speaking over a public address system at the front of the packed corral, but I could not hear anything definite, what with the sound of the crowd and the helicopter. But I must have been hearing the last steps before the firing of the starting pistol, for soon I heard the distant crack of the gun itself and there was an amusing impulse of the packed crowd I stood within to move forward, but it could not. Yet eventually one began to move, and soon I was at a full trot and crossing the starting line and first sensor mat that read the little chip one wears on their shoe. These mats, or the equipment adjacent to them, sing out with a little whistle-like squeal when one passes over the mat itself with one's chip. The squeals are so frequent, so numerous at the start, that they virtually form an incessant squeal that eerily and excitedly sends one off into a race—sends one off officially through a little wall of sound that sanctifies and confirms one's registered presence in the event.

As well, one can hear the numerous beeps from runners starting their watches as they reach the start—those beeps sounding like crickets spread out across a grassy field, each chirping its own claim as to when the measure of life and summer precisely begins.

I remember a great deal about that first race. In addition to having noted Dale's clothing, I was forced to admit there were many beautiful and almost exposed women in the event—so many virtually dressed in a sort of comic book costume of bright color and superhuman implications. There were hosts of healthy people of all genders and ages, in fact. And there were some, too, that approached the race with total levity, appearing in true costumes. There was one fellow, in particular, who was dressed in full clown regalia; I smiled as I passed him (he bent on waving to all who cheered for him). Then I was shocked as he passed me with ease somewhere after the third mile-marker.

By this time in my running career I had given in to having my own official running clothes, finally discarding my cotton shorts and tee shirts from my wardrobe for all time.

But not much of what I can say about my first (and very slow) running contest will differ in a marked way from most any other fellow's or gal's experience of a first race. Perhaps I would have dwelled on its subtle little details, implications, aesthetics, and suggested analogies, had what happened to the leaders at mile five not happened. What I give below I give after sifting through many accounts. I retain what does not conflict between testimonies; without exception, I discard the things that were peculiar to any one account.

When I reached mile five myself, there were police cars and ambulances blocking half of the road. I merely assumed (with a sort of new-found athletic pride) that I was witnessing what was part of the almost pseudo-military challenge and toughness of my newly selected sport—that toughness reducing someone to heat prostration or comprehensive cramping (someone who had not prepared, I felt via my comic arrogance, with the same toughness that I had).

Then I reached the mid-section between mile five and the finish line. Not far from the Hares' apartment building, and on their side of Main Street, another group of police cars and ambulances was gathered around an unseen, fallen victim.

After I finished the race myself, I began to learn the story.

Hare and Pocket had followed the elite, the leaders (there were three fellows from out of town who formed this vanguard), and Hare and Pocket seemed to follow without trouble. Though the early pace was very fast by any runner's standard, and hardly a shame to the most seasoned professional, no one noted that it was in any way particularly threatening to the world record pace or world record finishing time for the 10-Kilometer distance. However, the entire time that Hare and Pocket followed the front three runners, they seemed, said some, to almost be coasting—to be saving something, even something spectacular for the end of the race. Of course, among those who knew Hare and Pocket, this display brought on the wildest of cheers, and almost angry encouragement that they should prove what they could really do and not wait too long. But other, quieter people, like Hank of *The Pauktaug Press*, noted something much more interesting about Hare and Pocket as they sped along with ease behind the three leaders.

They seemed to be having words. Hare seemed to be admonishing, cajoling, angrily insisting on something from Pocket—and while he did this he seemed able to virtually circle Pocket and maintain an almost casual, seemingly stationary, set of mannerisms (like one who was hardly in any way under aerobic stress). Pocket stayed slightly ahead of Hare and listened, after a time, in silence to these commands, these criticisms—only answering with a raising of his hand, as if in attempt to silence Hare.

This peculiar circumstance was corroborated by many on the sidelines, and it was also confirmed by the lead three runners, who thought it astonishing, that while they (the leaders) were doing all they could to hold the lead with breathless effort, two older fellows could shadow them and be seemingly in the midst of a philosophical debate, and yet refuse to hold their tongues for a bit and pass the leaders with ease. One of the leaders said that passing and making a move was the source of the debate, however. He reported, as well, that Pocket was adamant in his conservative approach, and would not be prodded. This fellow then reported that he could not understand why Hare himself did not simply leave his companion and take the lead.

Then they approached the water stop near mile five. Of course, it is now an age-old rule amongst road racers that one should not generally accept any sort of refreshment along the course except from official race volunteers. However, people often eschew this rule, and they are generally safe in doing so. And it was doubly hard to determine on that day who was working for the race in any sort of official capacity, since while the tee shirts for the registered runners had arrived, the distinguishing tee shirts for the sideline and water stop volunteers had not made it through the mail in time.

Thus, there was some surprise, but not too much shock, when a man in a baseball cap, sunglasses, and what looked to be a phony beard (sported, some thought, just for the sake of race day good cheer and silliness) came running out onto the course, as if an early representative of the final water stop. He attempted to thrust a cup of liquid into Hare's hands—this fellow not having an easy time of this because of the incredible pace of the nearly even front five runners. Hare did not even seem to note the fellow's presence as all five blazed through the water stop and refused drinks of any kind.

But then, as if the stasis of the pace offended him, Hare suddenly took the cup from the silly looking man and thrust it at Pocket. The silly, phony-bearded man dropped away and disappeared. Pocket refused the drink. Hare shouted something in anger, and gesticulated forward like a raging officer on a battlefield. Some then said that Hare looked as if he were about to throw the cup away—this as he drifted slightly ahead of Pocket and came even with the three parallel leaders (none of whom played anymore at games of drafting). But then, as if in residual disgust for Pocket, Hare offered the cup to one of the lead fellows now at his right. Surprisingly, this fellow accepted, and he took an amazingly long draught of the drink, especially considering the closeness of the race, the pace, the nearness of the finish, and the tense and even threatening way with which Hare had offered it to his fellow runner.

Pocket came almost parallel with the leaders. They ran in this remarkable formation, five abreast for a half mile at truly great, truly remarkable human speed. Then the order of what happened next is debated.

With the finish line in sight, the fellow who had drunk from the cup suddenly came to a halt, crumpled the cup in his hands, clasped his stomach and clenched his forehead, and then fell to his knees. He collapsed completely unconscious in the middle of the road.

At virtually the same time that this fellow left the group of five abreast, Pocket began to sprint at an almost trans-human rate, but then after ten seconds of that pace, he broke his stride and clenched his chest. He pulled out of this last surge for the finish line and collapsed himself, as well—with a precipitous crash, and he fell straight into the sidelines.

The two visiting elite runners who remained went on to finish the race. Hare, on seeing Pocket in the midst of his oblique collision course with the sidelines, stopped running and returned to the scene. Emergency medical workers and police were soon all over the sites of the two falls—and also quickly on the scene of the dubious water stop.

When I finally finished the race, I could not find anyone that I knew well enough with whom to speak. And I did not find out anything about the crises near the race's end until I returned to my apartment and the phone rang.

"Rex, this is Nancy. Lisa just called me. She's with Dale Pocket over at the hospital in Huntington. Charles Pocket was taken there along with that other runner who was poisoned."

"Charles Pocket was poisoned?"

"No, they don't know what happened to him yet. But Lisa would like you to go and get Dale; Lisa thinks she should stay with Mrs. Pocket. But I think Lisa should be back here in town with Lawrence. Do you know that they have him over at the police station? They have him there for questioning. Can you believe that?"

I assured Nancy Whisker that I would drive over to the hospital.

Getting my car out of the lot was not an easy task because, though the race was over, there was still an atmosphere of minor festival going on in Pauktaug—and yet it seemed to be conducted by it overseers with a frantic hope that this second of Pauktaug's foot races would not also be credited as bringing a strange sort of misfortune to the town.

I drove over to Huntington Hospital and found Lisa Hare and Lynn Pocket.

"No more running for him. Do you hear? No more running!" sobbed Lynn Pocket when she saw me in the emergency room, and she shook her finger at me in a scolding style, as if reprimanding me in the gravest way would insure her husband's retirement from any and all strenuous activity.

"Thank you so much for coming over, Rex," Lisa smiled. I grimaced that thanks on that account were silly. And then she asked, "Rex, you haven't seen Lawrence yet? Have you? He wasn't back from the police station before you left? Was he?"

Before I could answer, we started to shuffle instinctively toward Charles Pocket's room, or rather his screened-off area, and Lynn Pocket took time to mop her blurred makeup and to insert, "Well that is the crazy part. That's crazy—the police not only asking Lawrence questions, but holding him for questioning."

I had not heard that Lawrence was in any way really being "held" in the legal sense, and the mere fact that Mrs. Pocket would insert this did not seem so much a coming to his defense as it seemed her attempt to flail out, to plant via wild intimation any possible idea that might bring further protection to her seemingly tenuous future with a living, healthy, husband.

Lisa Hare just silently shook her head in an assuring negative when Lynn Pocket got slightly ahead of us—that shake of her head to assure me that there was nothing quite that grave facing Lawrence at the moment, though I could tell, as well, that her assurance was one that was looking for a reinforcing assurance from me. At that point, I did not know any of the story of the race's ending, so I could give no assurances—I could give no intimation that I even knew what was going on precisely—so Lisa just faintly smiled and took my arm as we all went to see Charles Pocket.

"Hey, Rex!" exclaimed Charles as we entered his little curtain-formed room. "Can you believe this fuss over a side stitch at the end of a race?"

"Charles," interrupted Lynn, "you collapsed; you were unconscious. You were at a professional's pace—and beyond it—at the end. And it made you faint, collapse. You're not going to run like that anymore."

"Ah!" he groaned, and he waved a loving dismissal to his wife.

Dale was there with her brother. She stood there in her astonishing tan skin and yellow tightness of clothes. She looked confused by her concern for Charles, and by the nature of the cryptic assurance—the cryptic reinforcement, even—she could not resist suddenly offering to him at this point.

"I fainted once on the track, Lynn, a couple of summers back. It can happen sometimes," said Dale.

"You see!" smiled Charles to his wife.

"Dale!" hissed Lynn. "Dale!" she exclaimed, and Lynn Pocket controlled the feminine part of the room with the authority of her anger—this the only time I ever saw her do this. Her belief in her own point of view was infallible for this one time. And for all the motherly instincts of Lisa Hare, she did not seem interested in showing that instinct towards Charles Pocket; her maternal dream was set on the untouched future, so she said nothing to aid Lynn. Dale, however, had offered a cryptic violation of a feminine code, a code to protect and preserve health at all costs—even above the instinct to human striving and experiment. Lynn would not have this point of view on any account on that day, and since Lisa Hare was silent, Lynn Pocket reigned over the room.

I soon heard the story I give above as to what happened at the race's end. Lisa and Dale whispered it to me in hushed bits and pieces when we left Pocket's little area while a doctor spoke to Lynn and her husband. Then Lynn came out and asked the doctor to repeat to Lisa and Dale what he had just told her. Lynn told me that Charles wanted someone to talk to for a bit that was other than an overly-worried wife.

"Hey, Rex. You know I know that Lawrence isn't responsible for what happened," began Charles Pocket.

"What about the other runner? What about the guy who drank from the cup?" I asked.

"Well, they won't tell me too much, but he's going to be okay. But he was poisoned all right. I'm sure they know Lawrence didn't do it. It was just that some people on the sidelines saw Lawrence forcefully offering this guy that drinking cup. You know that I know who it was that gave Lawrence that cup. It didn't occur to me until I thought about it for a little bit—but it's that guy we've been trying to get a picture of out on the Sound. He's a real nut—more of a nut than we even expected it seems. I wish we had a picture to offer the police—something more concrete."

"Did Lawrence know who he was?"

"Apparently not, or I know he wouldn't have taken the cup. But I bet he'll know after he thinks about it. I hope he knows that I didn't say he's responsible for any of this."

"I'm sure he knows that," I said.

"Well, I'm responsible for almost getting someone killed in a race that I organized. I should have gone out and bought tee shirts—any kind of uniforms—for our volunteers, when the volunteer tee shirts didn't make it in on time."

"Hey, Charles, this wasn't your fault. Believe me. This crazy guy could have worked his way in somehow if he wanted to badly enough. Anyway, he seems to have been gunning for Lawrence specifically."

"Yeah, I thought of that. Lawrence *or* me—the fellows that have been trying to get his picture and 'Expose the Crisis Out on Sound and Bay.'"

"Again, Charles, this wasn't your fault."

"Well, I hope not. I still wanted to do that fall marathon for the town."

"You still can."

"Yeah, I bet we can," he smiled, in a childlike but still sincere and resolute way, and I knew he meant to do it.

"Hey, but what happened to you, Charles? Was it the old problem from high school that you talked about?"

Pocket became almost angrily earnest, like a child hiding some never-to-be-relented-from secret project. He hissed that I should be silent—intimating that my casual mentioning of that history was a violation of a sort of pact between him and me (and perhaps Lawrence Hare). I did not realize until then that such a pact existed to such an extreme extent, but it was clear to me then that it did.

"Lynn still doesn't know about that. Even the doctors couldn't find anything wrong with me today. They're just telling her out there now—again!—that there doesn't seem to be anything truly wrong with me. I just pushed myself into a crisis today—a crisis that didn't have any help from a problem with my body or sickness. But I fully intend to run again, Rex. It's just that I have to be quiet about such things for Lynn's sake for awhile. She doesn't know about the high school track incident. It isn't something that is going to ruin our marriage if it comes out, but I take the mild risk of keeping it from her so that I can start running again after all this blows off—without her having too much evidence that she can cite against my training again. She doesn't really believe in this sort of thing, the running, all that much—what it's all about. Do you know what I mean?"

I was not sure that Charles Pocket himself had a firm conviction as to what it was all about. I evaded his question by asking one of him.

"Some say you and Lawrence were arguing about something. What was it?"

"Oh, yeah. He's crazy. Yeah, sure, I was thrilled that we were practically coasting along with these unbelievably fast guys. But at the same time, I have a family to think about—and I wasn't feeling all that well near the end, just wasn't feeling quite right. But Lawrence starts hollering and flailing—you'd think he wasn't running at top speed at all to look at him—yelling that I had a responsibility to run as fast as possible, that it was my duty to Man or something like that. But that's just Lawrence. He's a nut. A nice nut—but a nut."

"Does he talk about things like that a lot?" I asked.

"He'd be after me with his philosophies for Man via the human form and its perfections, as he calls them, all the time—if I hadn't realized some time ago that I had to stop entertaining those conversations. He eventually eased up on that, though, but I know he thinks about it all the time."

"Why did it suddenly come up in the race again?"

"Because it was officially timed; it was a public forum for display. And he thinks for sure that I am the faster runner. He even lingers behind so as to push me. I yelled back that I'd try and chase *him* if he wanted to really see me run fast—and then we could see what he was really capable of, too. But he insisted on staying back there, like he was going to push me into my best possible speed."

"Are you faster than Hare?"

Pocket paused and was thoughtful for a moment; then he was doubly quiet with his answer because Lynn, Lisa, Dale, and a nurse made their way back into his area.

"I don't know," he whispered. "I may. I might just be faster. I don't know."

And then he raised his voice: "Well, what I really hate about what happened is that it is going to make things doubly difficult for the autumn race. How are we going to attract more runners when we have people getting poisoned on our course?" He laughed a bit at the absurdity of the situation. I laughed a bit, too, and then patted him on the shoulder and wished him well.

Dale seemed ready to go home. Lisa whispered that she would linger there a bit longer (and volunteered once more to take Lynn and Charles Pocket home when he was discharged), but would soon leave on any account if she could not satisfy herself as to what had happened to Lawrence with the Pauktaug Police. I assured her that Lawrence and the police were most likely already done with one another—and that they both probably had a good laugh over any confusion (and that the only grave issue was resolving any threat that this peculiar lobster fisherman might continue to pose to either Lawrence or Charles or to both).

I escorted the only slightly stunned Dale Pocket out of the hospital and to my car. Since she wore so little and seemed so revealed in her trans-nakedness there were looks of puzzled astonishment from many passers-by—even from the wounded in the emergency room—and as I led her out of the hospital with my hand around her bare, tanned waist, it must have looked like I led a new kind of newborn out into the sun for the first time. From out of the maternity ward of Venus, perhaps, I led this yellow-banded goddess child—her bottle and formula a green container of sports drink that she clutched with her free hand.

Dale went home with me that afternoon. After we both changed and recovered from the race, I offered to go out and bring things back to the apartment for dinner. And when I left my building, I finally ran into Lawrence Hare. He had spent the afternoon describing the mystery assailant with the poison drink cup to the village and county police, the harbor authorities, and the coast guard officers from Eatons Neck. He had himself connected this man, as had Pocket, with the fellow that they both had tried to photograph on more than one occasion while he stole from Hare's and other lobstermen's traps.

"They were angry with me—after we straightened out the confusion about the race incidents—that I tried to take on the situation out on the water with this guy myself. I told all these people all about this guy several times before! Did they think I felt like waiting for them to do something about it?"

"Lawrence, did you talk to Lisa? She's worried about you."

"Yeah, I reached her at Charles' a few minutes ago—she was in the shower there, and Lynn said she would tell her I was okay. She knows I'm all right."

"Well, I mean she seemed really, really worried about you," I added, with an intrusiveness with which I even surprised myself. Yet Hare did not take the slightest offense. He heard, registered, what I said, but some part of him was fully focused on something else.

"Oh, yeah, yeah," he replied politely, and with a gruff, traditional, masculine appreciation of my intent. "She'll be fine. She'll get the news. I'll see her in a few minutes anyway, I'm sure."

"Well, I don't mean to pry—" I started once more, again on the subject of his wife.

"Rex, how did Charles look to you?" he suddenly asked with great concern. He was really asking me what I thought, and not asking for a reassuring generality. "You see, I haven't seen him since he fell. The emergency medical people wouldn't let anyone but next of kin even near him. It really was insulting. And I haven't spoken to him yet."

"Well, I think he looks okay. The doctors can't find anything wrong with him. And Charles still wants to keep his little secret from his high school days between you and me and him and the lamppost—or maybe the mile-markers, I should say." I let this slip out on purpose—as a kind of test for Hare, though I was not sure of what I was testing.

"Good. Good. He told you about that day for him on the track in high school?"

"Yes, he did, way back when I—"

"Good, very good. Reginald, come! Reginald?"

Just then I saw Reginald come running with great speed from behind Hare's building. And then I noticed that Hare was still in or had put on a new set of running clothes.

I joked, "Going running?" I hardly expected the answer he gave.

"Yes, Reginald and I are going to hit the road for a little. This morning's race didn't do much for me really."

I laughed. But I could soon see that he meant what he said, for without looking too stern at the same time, he failed to laugh back.

"So, besides the whole crazy man and poison cups issue, Lawrence, what happened out there this morning? I mean, how did, how would, the race have gone for you?"

Curiously he said nothing about his own performance. Instead he remained curiously focused, curiously involved and proprietary about Pocket.

"Nothing happened really, he just didn't come close—not close at all—to giving what he could. He threw today away, actually—actually he—"

"How did he throw it away?" I asked.

"He stood on the edge of seizing so much, but he just lingered with the rest of them, no matter what I said. He didn't just throw today away, he threw it all away today—threw everything away for everyone. But we're going to seize the chance back in the end—next time. I'm sure of it."

I did not know what to make of such talk. Perhaps he was just trying to be silly and light or affectedly tough and sports-preoccupied in speaking in such a cryptic manner. At least I found it cryptic. Perhaps he just meant that Pocket had missed a chance to win a race—and perhaps the *all* he referred to was just the thrill and notoriety such a win would have brought to the village of Pauktaug, and perhaps the *everyone* was just the village familiars and the little circle of runners I had come to know in my time on Long Island. Maybe that is all his words meant. But then Hare began to run in place as I took my leave of him, and he suddenly jogged and then dashed off into the fading light of spring. And his body seemed to say something to the contrary—that the *all* he had referred to referred to some great All and the *everyone* he had referred to referred to some great Everyone. I could not say for sure, but Hare's running body, his running form seemed to say something like that with sureness. Some part of my own sore body could say: Yes, that was indeed what his body had said. But my mind was unsure, and I could only smile as I saw Hare and Reginald vanish in a northerly direction along Main Street.

There is a common turn of phrase that one hears people use to mean that someone has taken advantage of or abused another in a heartless, selfish, nearly cruel and dismissive way—*to walk all over someone.* Though Hare's stride, his running form, was flawless, and it implied a lightness that would make one say that his virtually speaking body strode upon the Earth, spoke upon the Earth, with levity, there was also something pummeling about its strikes upon the ground, upon the Earth itself. He did not just run or walk upon it, he walked all over it. And there was something grand in this, even though it bespoke an arrogance, a sense of command, on and of a level of refinement that I do not think I have ever encountered before and will not likely ever encounter again.

Hare faded around a corner with Reginald, and soon I returned to my apartment and forgot all in the comprehensive representation and history of all matter that was the beauty of Dale's embrace, in the wrapping of her body, her arms, her legs.

I mentioned sometime back, that Lisa Hare's stomach muscles suggested a beautiful pattern, as if they were their own sort of brail. But though I have said that it was Dale's body that seemed closer to speaking, saying something, because of its perfections, for all our caution in the midst of intimacies, I feared fathering not a new sentient being through her, but a baby made of stone—for Dale's washboard hardness suggested that she had a belly full of polished rock. Thus, even with all practical cautions duly observed, I was very careful with her.

CHAPTER 12

HARE'S FIRST ARTICLE

The rest of that spring and summer passed rather uneventfully. Though the authorities could not track down the man who brought attempted murder and poison to the second running of the Pauktaug 10-Kilometer Race, lobster fishermen—including Lawrence Hare—continued to suffer from theft. And later on in the summer, after Hare had a glimpse of someone at one of his traps (that someone escaping into the darkness at Hare's approach by boat), Hare began to carry a camera himself in the hopes of photographing not only a thief, but the man he was sure was also the more serious criminal from the spring race.

Despite the bizarre turn of events at the last race, the official timing methods and greater vigilance at the race seemed to legitimize Hare and Pocket as local heroic figures. Though there was no official finish time for them, of course, it was agreed upon by most that had they finished, their times would have proved—if not record-breaking or near record-breaking—then at least on their way to proving that something miraculous had also happened in the first race the year before, and that with a little more work, something even more astonishing might happen later on.

Because of half-hearted pledges to his family that he would refrain from running, Pocket gave no more promises to appear in any future races, even though his enthusiasm for planning the autumn marathon seemed unabated, and that race seemed sure to go on, and it would. However—and I mentioned this to no one, not even to Pocket himself—on sleepless nights, hours past midnight, or sometimes an hour or so before dawn, I caught glimpses of both Hare and Pocket running together on Main Street, at a severe and serious training pace.

My romance with Dale Pocket continued, and we lapsed into a routine that had us nearly living together.

But now, most telling in my memory, it was after that spring race that Lawrence Hare seemed to impute an even higher trust in me. Though he continued to work like a madman at all his duties—including his editorial work at the paper—his actual editorial article writing dwindled to nothing with the end of his series on the return of seals to the local waters. He gave over that space to me, and I was flattered and proud to accept. He said he was working on a new series, but that he wanted to compose all the pieces first as a set, before releasing any one article. I consented to this idea—not that I could have countered him had I wanted to—for I was too pleased with the venue he offered me to care much about his reasons for holding his own writing back for such a long time.

But Hare's trust in me seemed to grow in another way, as well. He sought out my company more and more, and I was stunned when he began to invite me along as an occasional running partner, and as a rather steady gym partner. When we ran together, he would make up for the difference in our abilities by doubling back, cutting across open spaces to create longer distances for himself, or by racing ahead and back to me—all the while keeping me intermittent company and never himself seeming fatigued at all, no matter what dashing he had to do to create an illusion of evenness between us.

And it was then that he began to let little things slip out from deep within him—little details about running and exercise, little perceptions, analogies, faiths, beliefs. Yet as I look back I can hardly remember him saying a thing, and yet he must have, for I have memories of a great deal. But I think it best to give Hare's own account of his unusual ideas.

Much later on, when the autumn came, when the start of my second year in Pauktaug was under way, Hare came to me on the night before the marathon and gave me a pair of articles. He reported that they were still unfinished and rough, but that he wanted me to have them—that I was to go over them and print them in *The Pauktaug Press.* I am still mulling over them, and I have yet to run them in the paper, but I give them here. He gave me the articles perhaps because the thrill of the imminent race moved him to do so, or perhaps it was because of his reading of my last piece on Pauktaug and the Pauktaug Girl (he seemed to like that article of mine a great deal, and he gave me his own two articles immediately after reading my latest little work, I think). I cannot say for sure.

I have reported that I became a steady partner of Hare at the gym. I will start by giving his article on the gym (or what seems to start with ideas from the gym). It was never clear to me in what order I should place his articles, but I will give the gym piece first, since it was at the gym that I logged the most hours with Lawrence Hare. All of his writing was in his own hand.

THE BODY-THINKING
By Lawrence Hare

At the gym today I wore a cotton tee shirt. Using mainly the upper body machines—which fold the torso at times, in a way (as in the case of the abdominal/crunch machines)—I noticed that sweat marked my tee shirt in a series of horizontal rings or stripes around the front of my body (and likely around my back, as well). The marks began at, or just below, my chest line. When I wear a cotton tee shirt in running, the sweat permeates the shirt—the wetting, after a spotted start, perhaps, grows to be even and complete. The contrast of these two types of perspiration pattern is striking. In keeping in mind that the gym mainly suggests a subliminal attempt on Man's part to return, or reach back to and salute, his distant, distant quadruped ancestor's past (by building up his figurative front legs), I felt that the horizontal sweat lines suggest stratification, like rock or soil-layer stratification, in a fossil dig.

Unless such things, such ideas, such intimations of truth, are noticed, no one's workout will do anything but come up short. One can strain to erase a pot-belly—raise that bulk and mass to the chest—but, again, unless one registers these ideas, one never goes quite high enough. He that is working hardest at the gym should be uttering anything but grunts. Yet there is always more to it than just avoiding the grunting. There is also the false hope to be avoided, that false aspiration of reaching back to the quadruped past. Strengthen the arms, the chest, the stomach, we may, but we shall never walk on all fours again—never run as one of the swift forebears and still be Men. With such efforts we are but meek imitators—that still must stand on twos—and have shortchanged ourselves of so many repetitions to the brain, and we are less Man than when we first had hopes of being Man. But I have no disdain for the grunters, and I have no common, hackneyed reverence for Man's brain. Should Man at the gym grunt for what I take to be the true brain, then he will turn out all right.

As one uses the weight machines—raises a given number of the weights, silver blocks, layers—it is as if the hardened, silverized, sediments are being lifted again and again in the search, the dig, for the quadruped, the upper-arm-strong forebear. The fossil is not found below or between the layers, but rather it is hoped that its ghost will come to life again (re-evolve) via the repetitions, come to life again in the adaptations of the person in the weight machine's seat. It is almost as if the man or woman in the seat hopes to resurrect that arm-strong self by the very labor that they use to search for the ghost-bones, the ghost-blueprints. In a way the grunting weightlifter is over the scholar in this manner—he combines both mental scholarship and the dig into one thing. But, again, the weightlifter wishes to become the thing he digs for, or take part of its properties unto himself, unto his body. The very cables—on the gym machines—suggest to me the cables from elevators in mines—they going up and down to remove the coverings (the weights) from the past.

Just as the human being is said to suggest, if not definitely reflect, many of the former stages of evolutionary development of Man and his forebears, whilst he is developing in the womb, the gym suggests much the same thing for its user. Each weight machine seems to lock Man into a violent remembrance of some former permanent shape of which his present form is but the ghost—locks Man into positions that his limbs once favored, and makes him violently pine over options not taken or preserved. And at the same time it forces him to hold onto this present form, to probe its every last possibility (forces him to revere the evolution within self, the evolution of acquired characteristics above all other modes of change), forces him to search—via micro-tear after micro-tear of muscle—in the fibers of the present muscles for some resource to prove that the Mind is not ultimately attached to a body that cannot serve its (the body's) ever advancing discoveries via exercise and conditioning. In the gym Man labors to prove the Body an adequate and a greater match than the external evolutions of the Mind.

The whole Man Against Nature theory is most importantly invoked not in Man now attempting to preserve his environment so that it and he can survive—nor is it so much how Man eats and takes care of himself for his body's sake and his own personal longevity—it is really mindful, rather, of a long, long-standing error. When the first hominid picked up the first tool, Man started down a path of increasing presumption that his great glory was his Mind, his tool use, his ability to augment his personal and intellectual power via tools and technology—his extra-bodily advances. But lying in neglect—despite millennia of misdirected, unfocused, un-interpreted athletics—for thousands upon hundreds of thousands, even millions, of years has been this body waiting. Since the first tool was taken up, the greatest tool was made into but a holder—a mere vehicle of realizations for the Mind.

Not for nothing this resentment of the hands and frame to carry anything during a run or a race. Usually Man is content to say that each should carry his burden, but then behold the willingness of volunteers to tote and distribute water and other items along the route of a foot race. They will even permit the dumping of cups (and clean these up, too) rather than see Man carry something, anything suggestive of a tool, during that time (of the race)—that time of latent, unrecognizable but instinctive hope for Man to reclaim his body turned holder, for a tool, a Mind, unto itself. Race volunteers are like time-traveling anthropologists going back millennia, begging the first hominids to take the first right step and never take up the tool at all. "Hold nothing! Take nothing in thy hand. Run with no cups, no tools in thy hand. Thy Body is the tool; *it* is thy Mind." The heart, the Body-Thinking, has writhed within man since that first fateful mistake of tool-bearing—but at last his heart and body will think for him at last, and dismiss the head for all time. No more of this Mind! The Body-Thinking is the thing!

Teachers often chide the active bursting child of a morning, who has left some important paper or assignment behind, "Did you leave your brain at home?"—or better still, "Did you leave your head at home?"—or that reprehensible phrase, "Are you sitting on your brains?" Foolish certified teacher, these questions will be met with a *Yes*, almost a literal *yes,* one day, by some Man truly full of heart, his body a Body-Thinking.

Have you noticed despite its musical noise, its grunters and groaners, its occasional pausing gabbers, that the gym is generally a hushed place, where few approach one another? What accounts for this? When I was younger and in school, I was heavy, even obese. In gym classes I felt alienated from the laconic and oftentimes corpulent teachers who gave seemingly judgmental silences to the inept and unfit and who at the same time gave seemingly silent approval to the wieldy. These old, corpulent teachers—their Minds seemed to be gone to me. But perhaps their bodies, however beaten their own, knew of the Body-Thinking future for Man, but could not quite realize it, preach it, for the young.

But, again, there is something to the silence, the more or less private code of the gym. It says as much as "Quiet! I am thinking." And it is the Body-Thinking, not the Mind, that says this.

Man is a runner, a biped, at last. Thus we work toward the treadmill in this visit to the gym. But one must look about a bit longer at the setting before attending to the highest business at hand. Weights, weights, everywhere—

Each machine in the gym is designed, it seems, to augment the resistance, the frustration, the clutching invisible glue of our Mother source, to glue us to positions that we have all assumed in frustration in daily life. Extra gravity is here added to the gestures, the motions, necessary to perform some of the most casual, innocuous, seemingly easy but quite often most frustrating tasks. We augment in the gym the challenge of so many tasks that are ultimately made trying to our hearts and bodies by the demands of gravity. Surely there is a theme of ultimate escape in this—hope of escape from the very Mother herself, the Earth.

Man, the Body-Thinking, will escape via his own speed, not via tools, not via the products of Mind, from this Earth. The Father, God, left us with part of himself in our Minds.

But we are still feeble and mortal and helpless—and stuck in the solid forms that He does not need to share. And we are not like our Mother, the Earth, what with this shard of the Father's ghost in our brains. Thus, perfect the body and escape the Mother; perfect the body and forget the sliver of legacy left us by the absentee Father. Forget the thinking mind. Render thyself a Body-Thinking.

Leave the gym and its machines behind now. Leave the treadmills, as well. Let us take to the local track and pursue this further—

When one is lapped—as on a track—the sense is that one has someone both behind and in front who is faster. And as the lapping gets faster and faster, the lapper, that Body-Thinking, forms a sort of solid, fills the loop. And, as well, if then the center of the track, the core, becomes not only ultimately negligible, but non-existent in its role as a distance, a space, to be circled, then does it not, too, become as if an infinitely compacted solid itself? The football field, the core, the gridiron at the center of the track, is crushed as into a ball. Man, the Body-Thinking, expands this ball with his lapping, his Body-Thinking forming an ever accreting solid from its infinitely fast lapping. And, thus, Man will fill the Universe, space, with his own controlled solid, his Body-Thinking.

Man, the highest representative, the highest form, of matter, will wage war, then, a war of control, against the nebulosities—spirit, space, vacuums, ghosts, gods, God—that claim superiority because of their untouchable states, and Man will make this Universe one that is all-outside and no insides. Hence heretofore struggling Man's deep chill at the notion of ghosts and spirits. The Body-Thinking will squeeze out these formless, cowardly, things from the Universe. We will form true hard bodies, and with the tension-plagued blood pressures of Man, squeeze out the last bits of God's hold within.

The Body-Thinking does not fear death on account of

losing consciousness. The Body-Thinking fears a possible personal immortality founded on God's ghostly, disembodied, promise. The Body-Thinking will be no ghost. It will not haunt here; it will live here. What personal immortality the Body-Thinking will have will arise from its efforts to perpetuate its animate carbon self—and to pitch that against the steams and puffs, the spaces and the voids. Materialism can be raised as to a cause—raised to Matter gaining ground on emptiness, filling the voids with its confirmable, tangible, honesty.

The Body-Thinking would never ask, as so many speculators commonly do with a hackneyed smile of humbleness: Whence matter? It would ask, Whence space, emptiness—and any meek, nebulous Being who would choose to rule an invisible Kingdom?

If God cast me in His own image, then why cannot I assail him, land a punch, pass him in a race? He only wishes He were cast in my own image. He fears me and what I have come to know. Why else hide in vast, fractious, voids of space? Why else drive men mad with fragment-slivers of God in mind, in the mind of Man? He fears and admires, covets my body.

Shadows! Solids throw them! Shadows do not cast, throw, solids. I have you there, Ghost Father, Deadbeat Father of them all. You are my shadow. I turn on the high noon vision of Matter's imminent ascendancy and dismiss you, my shadow, for all time.

For you are a foe, something to fear. For does not even a single tiny bubble, injected into my system, kill me? I expel even the more vacuous bubbles of Mind. I reject Mind. Matter is over Mind. Beauty is deeper than the skin.

CHAPTER 13

HARE'S SECOND ARTICLE

As the autumn approached, I continued to spend more and more time in the company of Lawrence Hare and Reginald. Once, sometimes twice, a week we would go in the lateness, lighted only by the moon or the stars, to the battered cinder track behind Pauktaug's old elementary school building—that building just to the southwest of the village's downtown, on Main Street.

Here, again, as in our times on the road, Lawrence Hare seemed to tell me great sermons of his thoughts on running, and of what he hoped to gain for himself and for Man via running. Yet now that I look back on those nights on the track, I do not definitely recall that he spoke much at all. There must be some reason that my memory should always begin with this sort of false yet somehow true recollection, but I cannot say why.

Sometimes Dale and Lisa would join us at the end of these workouts, if they were not too tired from their work days at the gym. After the four of us were done, we would all go to a diner or all-night restaurant and talk of the imminent, new, marathon for Pauktaug.

But on the nights when Hare wished to make the workout long, and it was implied that I should stay and observe if not continue with him for the full session, and when Lisa and Dale did not have the energy to appear or the energy to wait through a long stay at the track, and just when I thought Hare could linger no more, he would stay. For oftentimes, even in the very dead of the latest darkness, Charles Pocket would come at midnight or later and join us for intervals on the track. He would smile to me and nod—in such a way that he did not ask that I deny his having been there, but it was clear that I was to comply in the secret as to the effort that was being put forth at these workouts.

I worked harder at my running at those witching hour interval sessions than I have ever worked at something physical. Many times, Reginald and I would lie down in the late summer blackness, in the center of the track, on the old football field, and watch as Hare and Pocket—virtually a perfect match for one another in terms of speed—would course around that cinder band. They appeared to go so fast at times that it seemed the track must be contracting. And many times I would imagine that I comforted Reginald when it seemed that the rate of the runners circling us was so great that soon the track would certainly strangle us.

I never timed them. They never timed themselves. But surely something astonishing took place on the track on those silent nights in late summer and early autumn. They would press on with their overzealous workouts—designed by Hare—until Pocket would finally insist that he was spent, and even hurting a bit, not only in his legs, but even in the very core of his torso, of his trunk.

Hare would dismiss Pocket with reluctance, and not to my surprise but still to my astonishment, Lawrence Hare would often leave the track and take to the streets with Reginald for a road run—or Reginald and Hare would take to the Sound in the lobster boat and check the traps, or check the black water for thieves or for signs of returning seals.

It was also at these track workouts that I began to detect the first signs of a running injury for myself. It was a mild problem with my calves at first, and I ignored it. But by the time the race was near—and I had trained hard (I was tremendously fit, and slimmer than I had ever been since high school)—I could not train or run at all. Thus I was condemned to volunteering on the sidelines for Pauktaug's first marathon.

Perhaps I ignored the growth of my injury on the track because I was so distracted by what I thought I had heard Hare tell me about the track. But, again, as I look back, I do not think that Hare and I spoke much at all during those workouts in the darkness, and I cannot account for my confused memory. And nor can I account for the fact that when I read Hare's two strange pieces on running, like this final one, I felt that I had heard Hare discuss this material with me at length before. Yet I knew that he had not.

FINISH BEFORE YOU START
By Lawrence Hare

A race's starting gun seems tied to the very origins of running—to remembrances of running as means of flight or as hunter's pursuit. The starting gun is a ceremonial remembrance of the old running, of its primitive origins and source. Interestingly, in a race there is no rabbit or pursuer, but we create figurative versions of these things in the incipient practices of the Body-Thinking. A rabbit is a sort of pacer. He can hold one back or he can push one on—implying that the mind of the person using the rabbit is present, even acute, but not able to trust what he thinks is his untrustworthy, mindless body. But an independent Body-Thinking must be somewhere in this world—one that drives its person on in ever-increasing mile splits.

The rabbit holds one in place or pulls him on. But where is the pursuer for the fastest runner? Where is the figurative threat from behind in the modern race? What comes up behind the potentially world's fastest runner to hunt him, to push him on? What is that character called? Surely he is called something more formidable than *rabbit*? For an actual four-legged rabbit's speed is not aspiring, bent on achieving anything other than flight. Their flight is for mere survival.

There is a flight, however, that escapes from more subtle places than mere annihilation. This flight pursues something—but it does not wish to eat, to hunt via its speed. It is somewhere outside of hunter and hunted—a pure place somehow beyond that chain, and that pure place is at the heart of that which I am trying to express and to report.

There is something to all our efforts at pacing, our regard for time in running—especially split times. How do I regard split times? They are something that should be a smaller sliver with each passing mile—not to be balanced according to difficulty of mile or position in the race, or the place on the course. It should be split, this split time, split over and over, made a cause, a vehement quest of hair splitting till the distance between two points is as naught. It should be split until—even on a flat plain in a course of the Universe—the far point, the finish, is somehow even on the same spot as the start, or even behind the start. Might not the Body-Thinking go back to the start of all, to the start of all time, and set things right in all ways if Man starts things over again and reigns himself over this Universe otherwise born of a careless pilot?

The official at a track meet fires his gun to start the race—as God fired his gun at the start of the race of time. But Man at last emerges from the matter that spins about the track of the Cosmos and begins to lap it and God. The starting gun can have been the Big Bang, perhaps. And God is also the rabbit, the mystery that draws the run on—but alas even this mystery will be lapped and Mystery will not always be some importunate rabbit always ahead. We will challenge mystery once and for all and not praise it since we have simply till now not mustered the energy and effort to challenge and pass it.

Man will lead and puff new laws into the Universe—from the breathlessness of his greatest sprint yet.

Why does the rabbit run after the gun is fired?—as much as to lead Man and matter on and along the track as to hopefully placate him. But Man also has the mysteries, the rabbit, on the run. They only remain mysterious so long as Man is not in his best shape, form, Body-Thinking condition. And he will get to that point at last. He will get so fast that he will end his run before he began—and go back so far as to vanquish the careless and airy God and Father of this scoffed, material Universe.

Does not the common man know that Earth's demise at the hand of Man, even his most aggressive pollution, will drive him on—drive Man—on to better things? There are moments when pollution, the thrusts of rough, gruff, advancing Man, reminds one of the boy defying the Mother; jumping from a ledge just a bit too high; leaving a coat or hat behind in winter; defying curfews for the exploration of bold, valuable things. But the whole range of pollution, the whole collective distress of the Earth at the hand of Man, seems at perverse glorious times like the victorious incipient moments when the son turns to the mother and hurls his insults, casts his horded criticisms. They pain the Earth, the Mother, that has gotten him this far, but these words make him fly. The redness of the sunset in these modern days—scoffed at by unsentimental men who point out (with a hackneyed attempt at dry humor) the real cause of the redness (pollution), or sighed at with despair by sentimental men who think they should miss the old sun or are sad to know why the red sun is really so pretty—the redness should be thought a glory. It is not an angry, red sun. It is the sign, the first real sign of the growing power of the angry, just Son, Man.

God, careless father, dropping Man here in a causeless libidinous creative fling—having his presumed seven day affair with the blue-eyed beauty Mother Earth—has left his son, Man, a bastard, a child with no father. (All he left behind from this affair was the scent of his cologne—the gravity that reeks so and keeps us glued to the Mother's side.) Aye, the pretty fallen woman, the single parent, Earth, has done her best, but is the son to stay here for all time with her, minister to her in her feeble dotage because she cannot take, handle, the growing collective power of the angry fatherless Son? I, a Son, shall at last break the cycle of a careless, libertine Universe. I, the first real, present, powerful father with influence, will send my son out not to meet his Grandfather, but to displace and dethrone the old, nebulous deadbeat Father of them all.

The men of God today, they are almost as a tired, sickened, representative voice of the fallen Mother—even, yes, of the single young Mother grown old and misty and weak and romantic about some past seven day romance that was more like an epic case of rape than anything else. They croak and chide, the holy men, the ministers, as if in Her voice: "But love your Father; I am sure he is out there loving you. And love thy Mother; do not wound her with thy remorse and petty power."

This mother was but a careless whore that allowed a God to use her and leave her nothing but a cold circle to spin—in some mad remembering fantasy of her one night of dancing romantically with God—and left her a cheap lamp of sun that is fated to burn out, or to consume her, as fire consumes the beaten old career of many an aged flower that falls asleep in bed, cigarette in hand, and burns in her own fire.

And the environmentalist, he is but like a foolish, misguided, misremembering sentimentalist child of the falling and failing Whore Mother—as if one could ever bring back the full strength of the early, young Mother. And they to pretend that she was ever really kind to her sons, her bastard children—to fantasize about a perfect Mother that never was! All she ever did was spin about her sun, her sad lamp or jewel souvenir of the God, from the mystic John—He never to come calling again. And she always waiting in place. And she let her children grow up in neglect. And now we are to care for her!—to fantasize she has been some noble Mother and now a dear old Granny!

This feeble Mother is not able to see that her son has grown strong and too big for his house! She is not proud at all—but only asks that now that he himself is strong, to spare her. Well, too late, Mother! The man of God can speak as if for the Mother Earth and say, "Love your Father." And the environmentalist can bemoan and sentimentalize for the Whore. But for true Man, if his Mother is not proud of him, then he is proud for himself. It is not her house to protest for any longer. It is his, and he is Man of the House. And he will reign in the Universe as the first responsible Father. It—the Universe—is not his Father's house—he, Man, is Man of the house. Bastard boy grown strong, too strong, I say, and too just to need temper his growth, his collective advances that crush the Earth.

Ultimately, Mother Earth does not care for her old body, but cares that the bastard boy, in displacing the nebulous, never-to-be-seen Deadbeat Father, will then lose any last shred of love for his Mother—for then, in taking the place of God with ease, Man will see that she mated with a bum of the stars. But, alas, one would think her proud then of her child's strength. But, no, she threatens to crumble as Man is nearly ready to step away. She is more afraid of the loss of her last secret illusion (that Man, the bastard Son, may have thought she once had a romance with a worthy beau) than she is proud of her miracle of an unexpected pregnancy unto the Universe. Vain old call girl!

But some Body-Thinking shall be the first real father.

And my son shall see me. I shall not leave him, hide from him. And I will launch him to something—not leave him with a wet-nurse of rock in the depths of red-light space. I shall truly wish him better than me. Any real God will be born of someone, some little god, some Body-Thinking, who wishes more for his son. The new God will spring from a father that wanted him to be the Father—spring from one not forced to take false praise from children he has never acknowledged. The new God will not have children; but he himself will spring of elders, of a Body-Thinking. He will be childless and not make the errors of the first mute God.

So much of religion, faith, presses that there is always to be and always has been a great mystery, great mysteries, for Man to ponder—to feel humbled by. But it *is* in Man's power to know, to reveal, to uncover. What hasn't Man solved, dissected, learned to know which he has been allowed to get close to? What tiniest of things, even, does he not now stand on the edge of seeing and solving? What aspects of disease, the microscopic, the immediate, has Man not brought himself nearly into a state of comprehensible mastery because of his ability to command propinquity? Thus, only distance remains. Hence the appeal of the Marathon. Its greatest figurative appeal is not its metaphorical application to mere feats of common human will, but as a symbol of a once classically monstrous human distance that has and will continue to be found narrower and narrower with the great gains of the fleet and un-superstitious modern man of running, of a Body-Thinking. Soon there will be a man, not only who will make this course seem to take a negligible amount of time, but a man who will leap instantaneously from line to line, and then a man who will finish before he started. (Should this not be an inevitability if Man's times keep getting better and better?) And then the Deadbeat Father, the Deadbeat God and course master who fired the starting gun will be caught as he slinks away from the family reunion areas at the finish line—or at least, man himself will be there at both ends to encourage himself as he sets out to run, encourage himself as a father to himself if there was never any Father there to begin with.

Man's external means—his external evolutions—are as a course-cutting if he does not run on this course via his own two feet.

Perhaps the God that fired the starting gun did not know what his firecracker of unsentient dust would come to, and he abandoned his gunpowder and paper mess in an unkempt, rainy July 5th of a yard—abandoned his mess like a crate of kittens at a shelter, as an importunity of his carelessness upon the three-dimensions. But those kittens were to return to the seat of fire as kings of beasts, then kings— and beyond man-eating, they are onto the fire-eating, God-eating. And via the Body-Thinking, which will finish its race before it starts, the Milky Way to shake like mane, the comet's tail to flick upon command, the solar storms, the solar tongues of flame, to lick clean the bones of the careless Father!

CHAPTER 14

TAPERING

O ctober of my second year in Pauktaug came. After a little more than a year of seeing Dale Pocket, I was seriously thinking of asking her to marry me. And though I cannot think of why I thought it so necessary, for I certainly was going ahead with my plan no matter what their reaction, I still thought I should ask my parents up to New York to meet her first. To my relief, my mother declined my offer of the marathon weekend; they were too busy with activities and engagements in their retirement community to make it up to Long Island at that time, she said. Pleased at this turn of events—for the thought of fulfilling this ritual of introduction, and leaving any intimation to my mother that she had any sway over my inclinations, fatigued me a great deal—I chatted a bit longer with my mother than usual. And in letting my guard down for a bit, I made a critical error. I had forgotten, just for the moment, that there was an area of conversation that I did not wish to entertain with her.

"Rex, how is my grandmother doing?"

I could not be evasive about the news I had of Nancy Whisker at that point.

"She's very ill. She's critically ill, actually."

"Then I think your father and I had better come up, Rex."

I tried to argue against my mother's sudden change of plan. I veiled my indignation at her evident dreams of legacy as much as I could, though my mother's sudden eagerness to be in Pauktaug for a mercenary death-watch made me almost physically ill. But since I was not brave enough to tell my mother exactly why I thought she was coming to New York—even though my tone was curt and exasperated enough to be fairly clear even though I did not speak it—my mother escaped my counterattack by beginning to affect to explain to my father, who was by then by the phone as well, what she felt needed to be done. And just as quickly as she affected to enter him into the middle of this supposed three-way conversation, she insisted that she had to get off the line to discuss the necessary plans with my father, and then to call the airline so that they could be up for the marathon weekend, which was just under two weeks away.

My great-grandmother had indeed declined seriously over that summer. She was declared terminally ill by September, and though she had but weeks to live, save for the limp she had had since I met her, she remained surprisingly strong, especially for a woman said to be as ill as she was, and also for a woman as old as she was. She was strong in her spirits, as well, for even when something pained her in her spirit, she seemed able to dust the pang away with sincere fortitude. However, the inexplicable social distancing of Lawrence Hare from her since my arrival gave her fits of puzzled sadness that I could not explain away for her.

"I'm not sure what it could have been, Rex. Do you know? Did I hurt his feelings somehow?"

"No, I'm sure you didn't. It's probably because they think (Lawrence and Lisa) that they should defer to me because I'm a sort of relative of yours. Maybe they think they're staying out of my way or something like that."

"Well, did they say anything like that?"

"Actually, no."

"You, see, Rex, I know it's not that. Of course Lisa is still good to me, but there is something about Lawrence that I don't understand. And yet I feel like I would understand—that's why I don't feel angry at him. He hasn't done or said anything unkind. But that is just it—he hasn't done or said anything. I enjoyed their help and all, but I enjoyed their friendship more. You see, Lawrence is a lot like you, I think. You two get along pretty well, don't you?"

"Actually, we do. You know, I think Lisa would spend her usual time with you if she wasn't a little embarrassed, didn't feel a little awkward, about the distance Lawrence has put between himself and you."

"I know that, Rex. I know," and I could tell that she knew. And I could tell, as well, that she knew that Lawrence Hare had reasons beyond the merely petty, beyond the merely social for his decisions. It was then that I knew that Nancy Whisker had some of the inklings I had had about Lawrence Hare. But she was ultimately no wiser about the ultimate characterization of the man than I. She had merely brought me to Pauktaug on a sort of suspicion that Hare and I would be sympathetic on a literary level. She knew somehow, at the same time, I think, that Hare's sympathy with spoken and written language was fading, and that she would no longer be able to study him if he began to communicate his curious beliefs solely by physical expression. She knew that a younger person—but one of her ilk—was necessary, if anyone might have a hope of following the man who seemed the most worth watching in the Village Of Pauktaug.

Thus, my great-grandmother had appointed me as a sort of proxy student of Hare for herself, and at the same time had provided Hare with the writer and friend he seemed to have required at a specific time.

"You know, Rex, I'm sure that up until now I never really

needed too much physical help with anything. I've been lucky about such things. But I let the Hares think they were more help than they were. But I think they knew that we were all pretending at that, just so that things could remain coded and comfortable. At least I knew Lawrence knew that that was the way things were. Lisa has more simple wants, though. She took pleasure in pretending to help me. I feel most badly about her. But Lawrence, he wanted a witness, a secret witness. I could not be that so much after a time—at least I knew I could not last forever for that. That's when I had the idea of calling on you. Does all this sound strange? Have you felt that that was what he has really asked of you? To be a sort of witness to him?"

Astonished at Nancy Whisker's knowledge, more or less, of my entire role for a year in Pauktaug, though I had hinted at many things to her, I could only say, "Yes."

I would have shown her Lawrence Hare's two unpublished columns then, had he given them to me at that point. But that was still just a little bit further in the future.

We had this conversation on the porch of her childhood home, in view of the Sunken Cemetery. She had wanted to see it one last time, and she was friendly with the family that had bought her old house—thus they did not mind if we both sat on the edge of the empty, early autumn porch, and listened to the last of the lingering, solo crickets.

Nancy Whisker said absolutely nothing about the intentions she had for her property or her money. She said nothing about wills, and this was a great relief to me. Thus I could sincerely report to my mother—who, for all our disparity in personality, could always tell when I was fibbing or omitting information—that I knew nothing of the family's only chance at a rumored minor fortune.

As odd as this may sound to some, though I wished to keep my unique and different friend in Nancy Whisker as long as I could, I preferred that she not live so long that my mother could get to her. That would embarrass me intensely, even though I knew that Nancy did not connect me with my mother at all any longer.

I remember walking Nancy back to my car when the light was low and the hour was late. The limp that she had had since we met was exaggerated now, and I could tell that her unique physical strength was growing dim—and the sounds of the last stand crickets seemed an appropriate and brittle music to accompany our last walk to the car. I studied her intently as she seated herself. I noted that I had only noticed slight bits of the intermittent mental frailty in her that Hare had remarked upon when he and I first met. That had never seemed to bother him. But somehow, that limp had annoyed him, I think, for he was never as intimate with Nancy Whisker after hearing that she was no longer the free walker that she had always been. And somehow to my shame, I felt, after I closed her door and made my way around to the driver's side of the car, that her limp had irritated me, as well. It was a petty, small, cruel little annoyance to feel—but, incredibly, some deep part of me felt that there was a justification, a rightness, in my reaction. And somehow Nancy Whisker seemed aware of this strange symbol that her limp projected, and she seemed, at times, sincerely ashamed of it on a level as inexplicable as the disdain that Hare felt—and I latently developed—for it from the point of view of healthy, young, strong men.

Somehow, this wound and its concomitant suggestiveness, made her mind sharper, and thus I only saw a woman—save, as I have said, for some minor lapses and forgetfulness—who was as vibrant intellectually as any young woman on the edge of keen, sharp, metaphoric yet still concrete discoveries. There was nothing quaint to her sharpness of mind; her limp seemed to keep a renewable viability to her brain. Thus one did not merely credit her as being sharp for her age; she made one forget her age when she spoke. But then when she walked and limped, a sudden pall crept over some unseen but surely touchable part of myself, and I could not shake a sense of apprehension I had for the surge of rightness I felt clanging through some new judgmental sinew flexing within me.

I drove Nancy Whisker home, and I had tea with her one last time in the quiet spaciousness of the living room of her apartment.

She passed on a few days later. And with the help of Lisa Hare and Nancy Whisker's attorney, a funeral—that my great-grand-mother had long ago arranged—was quietly carried out just a few days before the marathon.

To my relief, each and every item in Nancy's Pauktaug and Manhattan homes went, by decree of her will, to relief societies, and I was glad that I could tell my mother that there was nothing, not a single object, left behind. As to any money that Nancy Whisker had to bequeath, it was not for me to know, and the attorney said nothing to me about that subject—also to my intense relief.

Rather than attempt to lie about the situation, I opted to commit the sin of omission as far as my parents and the funeral were concerned. So I did not call them about the death of Nancy Whisker—and just decided to allow myself this deception, for I simply could not bear to have my mother present at the funeral. They were still slated to arrive on the day before the race, and I let that plan stick. Of course, I cannot say how much difficulty and painful undercurrents I created for myself in affecting to forget to call them. But I could survive the pull of that kind of undertow.

Of course, Lawrence Hare did not appear at the funeral—an anomaly that seemed quite predictable and part of some larger basic sense to me, since I had known Hare then for more than a year. But slightly to my astonishment, he appeared at the restaurant to which Charles Pocket insisted on taking Dale, Lisa, his wife, and myself after the Thursday afternoon funeral in North-

port. (For some reason, Nancy Whisker was interred in Northport
—a village just slightly to the west of Pauktaug.)

Lisa Hare was not surprised by the appearance of her husband
as he sat down to the late lunch. I, of course, was not offended, and
Dale was indifferent. But Charles and Lynn Pocket looked slightly
perturbed by the whole affair—if not because of Hare's absence at
the funeral itself (and then his casual appearance at the restaurant
after) then because he brought Hank, our sports columnist from
The Pauktaug Press, along, unannounced.

But the Pockets were a gracious sort, generally, and they had
our reserved table changed to a larger one to admit all seven of us
for lunch. I was relieved that Hank was there, for after saying a few
obligatory condolences, and being introduced to Lynn Pocket, he
launched into some genuinely good-natured talk about the forthcoming marathon.

"Are you running in the race, Rex? I know that Randy and
Kee-Poh are."

"No, I'm afraid I can't. I trained for it. I really did. Only it
seems that I trained too much. I can't believe how my one leg is
hurting me—but only when I run. I don't feel it when I walk. I
don't understand it. I'm not just balking at a little soreness. I really
can't run it."

I looked instinctively to Hare at that moment. His face did not
move; his body did not move, and of course he did not say a word.
But as I look back I could have sworn that he shrugged his shoulders and raised his eyebrows in disdain, as if to say as much as
"What can I do? I am virtually alone." But I know that in actual-
ity he said nothing, and did not move at all in his chair.

Hank continued: "Well, how about you Lisa? Are you running
in the race?"

"Actually—" she paused then as if she were close to sharing
something very intimate with the entire table. She looked at her
husband, and then she seemed clearly decided to hold back her

longer explanation for a time. She simply said then, "I haven't been feeling well."

She looked at Hare and frowned with her mystery—a mystery to him, as well. He looked back. His look was not unkind, but it was neutral. As I remember things, he was very still otherwise. He may even have said something to his wife, but I cannot recall what it was.

I leaped in on what may have been the silence then and asked, "What is it, Lisa? Are you all right? Are you okay?"

Lisa smiled to me with an intensity of gratitude that made me uneasy. She was seated next to me, and she put her hand on mine for a moment to thank me with a sort of public and private statement of intimacy.

"Yes, I'm okay, Rex. But thank you. Thank you."

I looked then to Dale—uncomfortable to find that she may have seen something in this gesture. But she saw nothing to disturb her. She could read nothing in her own body; thus she could not see, read, hear that I also saw nothing in Hare's speaking body that was meant to comfort his wife. And neither was Dale a woman of traditional words; thus she sat there oblivious to the romantic advances upon me which she could have been confident I was trustworthy to thwart—had she not been trapped somewhere between abandoned, traditional language and the language of what would have been her fluent body (had she known how to make it speak). Instead, after catching her eyes for a moment, she smiled sincerely to me, and then began to contemplate one of the tendons in her forearm.

"But how about you, Dale?" Hank had turned his questions to my possibly imminent fiancé.

"I'm sorry. What was that?"

"Are you running the marathon?"

"I'm going to do the half. Just the half marathon."

"Oh, okay. Well at least we have the men of the hour—of the

forthcoming hour—running the race!"

Lynn Pocket suddenly tested her forceful but frail voice in this nebulous domain of old and new languages: "Well, Charles is certainly not running it."

"Oh," winced Hank, "that's too bad. What a waste!"

"A waste that he won't risk his health to prove that he might break some silly record?" asked Lynn Pocket.

"No, a waste that he put all that training in—all the way up until now—and isn't going to even run the race."

"What is your name again?" asked Lynn of Hank, to hint at her anger.

"Hank."

"Well, Charles may have jogged a bit with Lawrence when Lawrence trains at the track. But that's it." She looked at her husband. Everyone looked at her husband. Everyone looked then at Lawrence Hare.

I saw him lean back in his chair with pride. Even for those who had never seen the human body speak, it was impossible not to see a veritable language floating out from the silence of Lawrence Hare's body. There was a faint but still perceptible answer of absolute compliance and dependence wafting back to Hare from Charles Pocket in this same language. Everyone could see it, could hear it.

But Lynn Pocket carried on bravely. Yet I know she saw what everyone saw. Even Dale saw this exchange between Hare and her brother, and she began to smooth her arms vigorously, and to study them—as if they would tell her what to do, which side to choose.

Lynn Pocket challenged Hank again. And now traditional language would confirm her fears, and she could soon have no doubts.

She said, "No, Charles has done a lot for this community and for the race. And I don't even mind him jogging a bit. But he knows that we decided, very seriously, that he would not race anymore."

"Well, that's a good idea, probably," added Hank as he looked at Charles Pocket. "Especially since you've had a sort of a little, mysterious—and I guess similar-to-now—problem ever since high school. I saw that one mock track meet you ran in high school, Charles. You probably can't remember who was there. But I was still teaching at the high school then. I know that Lawrence here was in the stands that day, too."

Mrs. Pocket insisted that Hank clarify what he meant—that he elaborate on this story. He did.

There was a moment of silence at the table, of silence on all accounts possible. (I felt like I was a guest at a custody battle hearing, privy to a tension to which I wished to have no privileged view.) Then Mrs. Pocket surveyed each member of the table. She could read the truth in her husband and Hare. She had it confirmed in standard language from Hank—that Pocket was going to race that weekend, that he had trained for it, and that he had had a life-long intimation that his body was both gifted and yet physically threatened by its own gift. This standard language confirmation, again, came from Hank. She could know where *he* stood.

Lynn Pocket looked to Lisa Hare. She saw innocence in her. Then she looked to me, and I do not know how, but she knew I knew. And though I had never made a pact, never signed to a conspiracy, I had known all along that I was privy to something that was worth protecting from those who might try to stop it with petty, traditional, demands. She saw this, and she looked away from me with a betrayed hostess' electric scorn, and she could be relied upon to speak what she thought quite plainly, quite traditionally: "Thanks, Rex. Thanks a lot. Thanks a million!"

Then she looked to Dale Pocket. Dale looked down to her arms at first—as much as to defer encountering the challenge and question of Lynn's gaze as to beg of her perfect, tanned body to tell her what to do, what place was hers in the Universe. I had had a vision of Dale, for quite some time, walking a sort of figurative tightrope. Now she was falling from this sudden gust of wind. But even Dale's toes—her lovely, perfect toes, resplendent in red polish and made sweet and inoffensive by their perfect smallness and tan—were strong enough to hold to the rope if she fell. But she looked to her body—after looking once more to see the language flowing between Lawrence Hare and her brother—and her body said nothing to her. Thus she let go of the rope, and fell back down to the Earth, and she landed in the net of millions of years of Mind, of spoken language, of predictability.

"I didn't know anything about this, Lynn." Her traditional mind had not. That was true. She did not lie. Dale knew, however, that she had just let go of some part of herself that could have been part of the conspiracy; thus she still felt a bit exposed, a bit caught. But she had a right, in a way, to claim full innocence. And she did. "I really didn't know, Lynn, that he was doing anything but jogging a bit."

Dale looked at her brother then and attacked him with traditional force—with a ferocity and lingual sincerity I had never known her to use.

"That's really kind of sick, Charles. It really is. You have children and everything, you know. Come on, Lynn. Let's go somewhere else. This is all making me a little sick."

To my amazement, this resolution was entirely accepted by Lynn Pocket. She looked to her husband in disgust and with a new sense of untested control.

Mrs. Pocket commanded: "Come on, Charles. We haven't ordered anything yet. Let's go. I think we should just go home. I don't feel like sitting around a table and chatting with this particular mix of people. It isn't right—something about it isn't right."

Her husband did not move. Lawrence Hare leaned back in his chair—or maybe he did not (maybe I just think this happened)—with a deep breath of total triumph.

"This is ridiculous. All this over, stupid, ugly, smelly old running!" hissed Lynn Pocket as she left the table.

Dale followed her, but not before leaning over and hissing something herself just for me in my ear.

"He's my big brother. And I'm the aunt to his children, you know."

I was fascinated not only by the intensity of her sudden anger, but also by the untried quality of her language. She sounded almost new to verbalized passion. She had made a choice between two potential and (for her) yet untried languages, and she stumbled in her very traditional choice as she tested it for the first time on me. I could not help but smile, very, very faintly.

She saw this. She blazed, but not for the smile. She blazed because I knew that she could have known the truth had she been able to read something in her perfect skin, her unbroken voices of rippled calves and thighs, her sinewy arms, her chest, in her unbroken voice of body and form. She blazed red with anger because she knew that she could have known—and could have been a part of that truth. And she could see that I had always suspected something of this. And she hated that I could translate between the two languages, even though I was not really fluent in either one as a speaker myself. I could only listen in and eavesdrop. She blazed a beautiful red, even through her tan, and for at least that moment, her body spoke indeed.

Dale Pocket followed Lynn Pocket out the door of the restaurant, but not before Lisa Hare called out, "Wait, I'll come with you!"

Lisa pushed away from the table. She did not look to her husband or to Charles Pocket. She did, however, say goodbye to Hank and to me, and she added to me, as well, "I'm sorry, Rex. We'll talk later." And then her lovely, delicately freckled galaxy carried and swayed itself away and left us remaining four in the darkening restaurant.

I looked to Hare with a look of disbelief and embarrassment. Perhaps I literally said (I cannot recall now for sure) or only projected with my face or body somehow, "She'll talk to *me* later! Why?"

Though my disbelief may have been in order, my embarrassment was not necessary, for Hare simply looked back and said, or said as much in silence somehow (again, I cannot recall for sure), "It doesn't make a difference. Pay it no mind."

But then there was another look to me from Hare. He seemed to banish the entire table conversation to oblivion, and to concentrate on me in such a way that I knew (I cannot say how precisely) what it was he wanted me to address.

"I won't be able to run the race, Lawrence," I said. "I really won't be able to. If I were to run this marathon, I think something serious and permanent would happen to my legs."

Then Pocket spoke up, perhaps to break the silence.

"So, Rex. What do you think of all this? Do you think I am a terrible fellow?"

Without hesitation, and with a completely unrehearsed sincerity with which I surprised myself, I said, "Not at all. I don't think there is any question that you should run this race. This race should be run, and you should run it as fast as you can."

Though one might think that this was a moment over which *The Pauktaug Press'* sports columnist would have lingered, Hank at this juncture decided to excuse himself—just as the waiter came (the waiter sure that he could safely take a drink order from our quieting table at this point). Perhaps Hank just did not wish to commit to paying for a lunch, or perhaps he felt embarrassed by the whole odd exchange at the table, or perhaps he somehow felt aware of an understanding that now existed between the three that would remain at the table—a sports understanding of sorts to which he did not feel inclined or privileged to be welcomed. I cannot say for sure.

Yet after Hank left, it was clear to me that Hare had been extremely pleased by what I had just said to Pocket. All hints of Hare's displeasure of my withdrawal from the marathon seemed completely removed. He exuded an approval of me that was unique and specialized, coming from him—he had an approval for me that was customized for me alone, it seemed. I alone was to be his reporter. No one else. Thus, he spoke up.

"Rex, Charles and I are going to talk over our strategy, our intentions, for the race now. Are you going to be up later? Can I call you later? There are a few last things I'd like to get straight with you about the race—your volunteer duties and such. And more importantly, there are some things about the paper I want to get done tonight if we can."

I assented to all of this, and left the restaurant on instinct at that point. I returned to Pauktaug and fell into a deep sleep in my apartment. The phone rang well after midnight, and I thought for sure it was Dale, calling to pretend that her sudden surge of the evening was meant to be forgotten. But it was Hare. He asked me to come over to the office.

I remember that as I made the brief walk over to *The Pauktaug Press,* I thought to myself, "Since Dale did not call tonight, I probably will never speak to her again." This was probably overly sober and pessimistic thinking—so that I could be surprised later on if there was a call, or at least already inured to silence if she never called. But I will report right here that, indeed, we never did speak again. Our romance ended with much the same swiftness that had characterized its start. But I was too absorbed to feel much emotional loss at that time—save for brief pangs that flitted across my mind, which were most likely mere sexual regrets in elaborate masquerade.

I found Hare sitting at his desk. The sole light in the entire office came from his own little room, and I did not turn on any other lights when I entered. That one light seemed a followspot that had found its final target of maximum import, and I took a seat opposite Hare in the darkness of his office, and watched his shadowy figure as he spoke to me from behind his desk. It was hard to see the details of his face, for the lamp was aimed in such a way so that he could read the papers on his desk. Thus only his torso was clearly illuminated.

"Did you take some pictures?" I asked him, for he was unloading a roll of film from one of our office cameras.

"No. But Charles went out on the Sound tonight in one of my boats, just to rest himself for a bit before going home after today, and he thinks he got some photos of the fellow who has been giving us all this trouble all this time. In fact, would you take care of these for me? I'd like to run one of these pictures if they're any good—for next week's paper."

Hare had never asked me to take care of photographs before, but I agreed to have the photos developed and to select any that looked presentable. I was going to ask more about these duties when Hare moved forward with a list of items he seemed to have before him in his mind.

"I hope you don't mind, Rex. But I found your latest, and I suppose last, piece in the Pauktaug History series. It was sitting right on top of your desk. I hope you don't mind; I've been reading it."

I was a little surprised that Hare had removed the paperwork from my desk, but I did not mind, for the piece was almost done. I was too curious about what he thought of the article to wonder how little privacy I had in my part of the office.

"Rex, you've been holding up too much of the paper on your own. I have been working on some things to follow your series. I haven't—not since I finished the group of articles on the seals in the Sound and the bays—included anything of mine in the paper for a long time. But I've been waiting for something that would link the last of my seal essays with what I have now. Hopefully someone out there knows that our entire paper—or at least parts of it—are part of a great sequence. You know this, at least, don't you, Rex?"

I only smiled at this. I was not quite sure what he meant, or what he could mean.

"Well, I have been working on a new series of pieces. Now I'm ready to use them, because your piece—I want to send it out with this issue tomorrow, if you don't mind—is exactly what I have been waiting for. It is clear that you've understood what I've been needing all along. You've written my link between the seals and what I have now. Your piece on the Pauktaug Girl is perfect."

"Well, thanks, Lawrence, you can certainly use the Pauktaug Girl piece now."

He did not even hear my assent, my statement of permission. Instead, he read the following aloud with great, gratified intensity (an epigram I had found for my article in George Meridith's *The Egoist*)—as if I would certainly know what it was in the passage that had fulfilled his unstated requests so precisely.

"She was fleet; she ran as though a hundred little feet were bearing her onward smooth as water over the lawn and the sweeps of grass of the park, so swiftly did the hidden pair multiply one another to speed her. So sweet was she in her flowing pace, that the boy, as became his age, translated admiration into a dogged frenzy of pursuit, and continued pounding along, when far outstripped, determined to run her down or die."

And then he read aloud the very start of my own material in the article.

"And the modern, the living Pauktaug Girl, has parted her skirts to the world—much as glamorous lady hitchhikers of yore might show a leg and bring a potential ride to a screeching halt. In shorts and short skirts, the modern, living, healthy and beautiful women of Pauktaug seemingly bring technology to a hushed and reverent standstill with the sight of the untapped and evident promise of their beautiful, sculpted, running legs."

"Well, I'm glad you like that, Lawrence, for that was one of the things that I was worried about. I even thought about getting rid of that."

"Oh, no, Rex. That part we're keeping. The whole article goes out tomorrow with this week's issue. Therefore! I want you to take these two pieces of mine. Issue them, order them, as you choose. Do what editing you think is necessary. Alter the presentation, if you feel you need to, but not the content. No, let the material run as it is. But this material has been too much with me for too long. But I need it to run in the paper. And I need you to take care of these for me. Present them as you see fit. I can't go through them anymore. I can't really think clearly as I used to anymore."

I had never been entrusted before, at least not with raw material of this kind, with Hare's own work. He had given me things to proofread for basic mechanical errors. But he had edited his own material for style and length—virtually on all literary levels—exclusively on his own in the past. I have given earlier the two pieces he handed over to me that night. How was I to handle them? How was I to introduce them? I could only take them then, when he handed them across to me in the darkness, and promise that I would do all I could. To that promise I have been true. Mercifully I never promised to print them in the paper. If there was a silent, an understood promise that I would, then I must say that I have only been able to keep it by issuing them here in the privacy of this narrative.

"Thanks, Rex. You'll do a good job with them, I know." Hare began to work through some large boxes that he had stacked behind and around his desk. As he worked one of the boxes open, I noted that my eyes had adjusted somewhat to the darkness, and my vision alighted on the little gallery Hare had on his darkly paneled wall. First my eyes fell on the photo of Lawrence and Lisa that I had first noticed a year before—the one in which I had been fooled as to Hare's identity because of his former weight trouble. But then I looked once more, and very carefully, at the framed and mounted piece of animation art that Lisa had given Hare as a wedding gift.

I was about to ask Hare precisely what the image in the animation cell depicted, even though it was still strikingly familiar to me. And I would have guessed what it was had I been able to study it on my own in private, but Hare suddenly began to speak again, and I was distracted from that image for a few moments more. But I resolved to ask him about it.

Hare held up a long aluminum pole. It was in plastic wrapping, and one could see that the pole had a sharp, javelin-pointed end for the sake of inserting it in the ground. Hare removed the plastic wrap and attached a large plastic placard that attached to the top of the pole via a slot.

"Mile six!" Hare exclaimed. "The end of that is almost at the 10K mark. Anyway, these are the mile-markers we're going to use for the race." Hare examined the pole in the dark light until the coldness of the metal must have faded in the grip of his warm human hands.

"Anyway, Charles would like these to be put out by 5:00 AM on the day of the race. The volunteers are all set, but we wondered if you would put these out for us in their respective places. And there is one mile-captain vacancy that we would like you to cover for. We lost one of them. Would you do it?"

I was happy to volunteer.

"Good. You'll be at—I have it written here. You'll be at—oh, mile six. So here! Here is the marker for your station. The volunteers at that mile will know their duties. But as mile-captain, you're just there to make sure those duties are done at the right time."

Hare then handed over a large file of paperwork that enumerated all the duties that I was to oversee for mile six. It had lists of volunteers, the times that their tasks were to be executed, and it had various designations for the locales of police, radio operators, and emergency medical workers.

As Hare spoke, he continued to remain more or less a talking torso for me in the darkness. He almost seemed to have no head, if one squinted a bit in order to clearly see what was lighted and most easily seen. I happily assented to all his requests for mile six, and then during a lull in the enumeration of my duties I suddenly asked him about the framed animation cell.

"You don't know what that is?" Hare rejoined with quiet surprise.

"No, I don't. But I feel like I should. It is very, very familiar to me."

"That's a picture of Jor-El's lab."

"Jor-El?"

"Superman's father—his Krypton father."

"Oh! Oh, of course!" I said, perhaps a bit too loudly for the smallness of the space and the intimacy of the darkness and the hour. But I was sincere in my surprise, for I did indeed know precisely what the image was. There were no figures in the picture, however.

"There's the ship, of course, in which the infant Superman will escape from Krypton," Hare mused. "Are you familiar with the lore of Superman, Rex? Have you considered some of its finer, its best intimations?"

"Of course, I love that sort of thing," I said. "Who works at an American paper and doesn't think of Clark Kent from time to time?"

This did not move Hare to react or to move at all. He was silent and still.

"Of course I think I know what you really mean," I continued. I was pleased at what I could remember. "There is, of course, the Christ-like symbolism of the Father sending a savior to Earth, and there is—oh, this I like very much—there is the idea of the crystallization of the entire immigrant experience—that Clark Kent stands for both the assimilated and the ethnic contributor to America. And there is all the heartland mythology in all of that, too, and—"

"No, Rex, that's not it at all." Hare rose then and turned out the single light. He placed the opened mile marker back into its box, and then straightened himself upright once more and stretched. The star and moonlight of a rich northern October flooded in through the sweet-odored trees that had grown increasingly leafless with the season.

My eyes adjusted, and I could see Hare risen before me in full bodily profile before his window. Did I hear what he then said to me? Or did his body speak it? I cannot recall. It does not matter now. He said it to me, one way or the other. But before he spoke, I noted that the moon was hidden from view, even though its light brought an icy glare into the deathly old house that cradled our offices. I could just see Hare standing, standing on the sickly blue glow of Earth, standing against a backdrop of stars that seemed as finish line banners—seemingly not so far away that if one ran toward them with real heart for a time, looked down at one's steady feet then for a bit, and then looked up again, that they would be a bit closer surely, even reachable, if one had the will to keep running just a bit more.

"No, Rex, that's not it at all about the Superman story."

He paused one last time. He shifted on his feet. Perhaps he flexed his legs a bit, and rolled then just a little on the able balls of his feet.

"People take the fable all wrong. This, Rex." He pointed down, as if to the ground, to the soil outside. "The Earth, Rex. This, here—*this* is Krypton."

He may have said, spoken, a few words in parting to me at the end of that night. I cannot now remember what they were. I walked home in the silent lateness, a bit more conscious of the pain in my leg than I had been ever before, and then I slept.

CHAPTER 15

MARATHON

My mother and father arrived at the airport on Saturday, and, of course, I spent most of the drive back from the airport enduring phrases my mother had picked up over a lifetime for such occasions. They arrived to find the funeral and burial over—thus I had to hear that she felt deeply hurt, betrayed, that she did not have a chance to say goodbye. I had to hear each and every one of all the phrases that are well-rehearsed by all the millions of the world's false mourners. But then my parents saw my large apartment and some of the pretty parts of Pauktaug Village, and they turned some of their passion onto to the new prospect of legacy that I seemed to present myself and to intimate via my new living and working arrangements. Father was rather passive about most of these points; however, I did not see him put a stop to my mother's more obvious attempts to case the scene for chances at grave robbing or to inquire after my new earning potential.

Since these were the points that meant the most to my mother—and since, then, she would be most able to determine my truthfulness in answering questions about these things—I was able to report with simple brevity and honesty that there was nothing left to be expected or taken care of in the way of Nancy Whisker's estate and that my apartment's size could be credited only to my luck that my employer was my landlord, and willing to rent it out for considerably less than even half its worth, and that my earning potential had already, most likely, fully matured and seen its heyday.

That Saturday became deeply dark and rainy and cold. As the evening approached, my mother pretended to noble suppressions and insisted that we all go out to a nice place to eat—and that I should invite my girlfriend.

Thus I spent the entire dinner in a pleasantly empty and cozy restaurant with my mother and father by the harbor, explaining to them—and an eavesdropping, idle hostess—why it was that the girl I had thought I was going to marry was so quickly and so pain- lessly removed from my life altogether.

My mother reported that she felt foolish for making the trip up at all—that I should have had the thoughtfulness to keep them updated so that they could have decided for themselves whether they might have wanted to move their trip to another time. I replied that the airline would indeed have changed their tickets, but that there would have been a fine, a fee for making the change—because they had chosen to fly on this trip on a carrier other than the company for which my father had worked, and they were as the regular flying public in this case.

My mother looked grave and earnest and subtle at this sug- gestion, as if I had made a vast, complex, oblique and grand moral intimation worthy of the climax of an English novel.

"Is that true, what Rex just said about the airline tickets?" she asked my father.

My father paused over his plate and nodded a bit of grave credit to me: "Yes, it is."

I mean no attempt at a mild-yet-devastating dismissal of my

parents with the relation above. I am sure that one had this impression of my mother and father from the start, but I give this little aside at this point so as to say that all during dinner only an automatic part of myself was present so as to handle the queries of my mother and father and to address the process of their visit. All during the evening, all I could wonder about was whether the heavy rain would continue—and if it were to go on, would it greatly influence the times of the runners for the race in the morning.

My parents decided to sleep in on the morning of the race. My mother had told me she was not interested in going, before she had gone to bed the night before. My father agreed that he, too, was not interested in the race.

"After all," my mother said with an insider's smile and confidence, pretending with this that we had been through an ordeal and that we were now on better and more intimate terms than ever, "if you're not in it, if our own son is not in it, what interest could it have for us? But have a good time helping out."

I left in the early, early morning and in the darkness and in the thick, cold rain, and attended to my mile-marker duties. I opened each mile-marker from its packaging and put them firmly in place, and then I went to my own mile position. I placed the mile-marker for mile six in its appointed place with speed and ease—since Hare had already opened it from the packaging.

I found only a few of my volunteers in place. However, the radio operator for my mile was in the right spot. I looked at my paperwork and asked him, by name, if he was the fellow that was assigned to my mile.

He hesitated for just a second when I presented his name to him. "I'm sorry, did I say your name incorrectly? Do you prefer to be called something else?"

"Oh, no," he smiled as he finished setting up a little tarpaulin tent around his radio and table and seat. "You got it right. I'm just struggling with this gear before it gets rained on too much. There!

Let's try things out and see how things are going at the starting line."

My capable but quiet companion had conversations with several other radio operators along the course—these volunteers coming from various amateur radio clubs from the area, and they spent as much time getting to know one another via their medium as in talking about the race.

Finally, my sole companion reported that even though the registration had turned out an appallingly low number for the full field, the rain and other factors (such as the troubles from the earlier races), had seemed to cut down even that number by a third, if not closer to a half. We were to expect less than a few hundred runners to pass our point during the course of the race.

The rain continued to pelt the trees and the course, but soon the hour of the starting gun approached, and one could hear the crack of the pistol over my companion's radio, and then one could hear the same crack over the open, actual air, though faintly, several seconds later.

I walked along part of my territory for a little while. A few more of my volunteers had appeared, but it was hard to spot them at first. The rain was so strong that the volunteer tee shirts had long vanished under raincoats and jackets. But because the rain was so hard and the hour early, and because Pocket had cleverly guided the course through some of the remotest, looping parts of the village's back areas to the west and east of Main Street, I had no trouble with any angry motorists who wished to cross the course as the estimated arrival time of the leaders or the main pack drew near. In fact, save for a few groups of curious, wiry little boys on bicycles, I had no trouble at all with my mile—even with a skeleton force of volunteers.

Though it would not have been particularly astonishing as a finishing time for a 10K race, the leaders were said to be approaching my six-mile- and subsequent 10K-marker with what seemed impossible speed for a marathon split pace. My radio man reported this to me with an admiring and gratified calm when I walked back to my main post, which I had relocated to about two hundred yards from the mile marker—so that I could share the little tent with the radio fellow.

"Really?" I said between my mild panting (I could not believe how much conditioning I had lost since my leg injury began to hold me back). "Really? Who are the leaders?"

"They say it's this Charles Pocket and this Lawrence Hare guy—that they're together—that the one is right behind the other."

"I have to go and see this," I smiled, as I began to make my way from the protection of the tarpaulin and toward the mile-marker.

"Wait!" called out my radio man. "I'll just take a little break here. It can't hurt. I want to see this, too."

Since the whole perfect race arrangement as set up by Pocket had rather fallen to pieces, I did not think that the radio man's abandonment of his post by no more than a hundred or two hundred yards or so could hurt too much. As well, the fellow seemed to want to feel the excitement of the race and the rawness of the rain. He brought his thermos along into the heavy, cold, sweet autumn shower—as if to equip himself for the one little adventure and bit of roughing it he might have for himself that weekend.

We came to within a hundred yards of the six-mile-marker. I stopped there, even though I preferred the view offered by the site where the mile-marker stood—for I did not want to draw the radio fellow too far from our tent, just so that we could not be accused of a complete dereliction of duty should some extreme and unexpected emergency arise.

We were positioned on a stretch of Sunken Cemetery Road that ran nearly parallel to the relatively near shore line of the Sound, and both sides of the route were pleasantly surrounded by thick woods. When the leaders would appear, nothing could distract one from an accurate sighting of them—for there was nothing else of color or motion to be seen for a mile in either direction (save for the blowing autumn leaves).

And then, emerging from under a dip and around a corner, Pocket and Hare seemed to grow from out of the ground. And as they drew nearer, not only did they seem to grow taller and larger, but the bottoms of their legs and their feet came into view, and as they approached the mile-marker, their feet could be seen clearly as separate from the Earth. But what was more astonishing than their speed, and their defiant spectacle of human heat and muscle against the autumn cold and autumn weight of drenching water, was that they seemed to be in the midst of an intense—no, a raging—argument. And despite their great speed, and their perfect form, in the midst of their shouting at one another, I could clearly make out that Hare had fallen behind Pocket and shoved him forcefully in two, quick, successive instances.

The two runners came to a halt in the center of the road, just parallel then to the six-mile marker. They stopped because Pocket threw up his arms and then leaned over with his hands resting on his thighs as he gasped for air. Hare continued to jog, or to virtually shudder in place, and he shouted at Pocket with a hoarse, desperate, commanding and proprietary stridency.

Pocket waved Hare away. Hare continued to circle Pocket. Then Charles Pocket righted himself and shouted back at Hare— and at the same time clutched at his chest and winced with pain.

Something about the mile-marker caught Hare's eye at this moment, and as he continued to shout at Charles Pocket—shouting things like, "There's no question! There's no question, no pausing! You must. You have no choice! This you must do"—Hare ran to the mile-marker pole, tossed aside the card with the mile number on it, and seized the pole itself from the ground and brandished it like a spear. He wielded it like an officer does his sword when he must force reluctant soldiers out of trenches and into battle.

I began to make my way with a silent, cautious, speedy walk toward the scene.

Pocket continued to clutch his chest. Hare, still shouting, stood behind Pocket and then began to push at Pocket with the mile-marker spear. Pocket flailed back, even swung two punches that did not land, and then, still in some sort of debilitating pain, all mixed with breathlessness from the great pace he had just abandoned, he was forced to run from Hare—who was pointing forward along the course with his free left hand as he shouted and commanded and threatened with the prod. Pocket was forced to run as if for his safety.

Pocket suddenly made a dash off of the course and sprinted north along a private drive that mildly ascended to the short escarpment that overlooked the Long Island Sound in that part of the village. Hare gave pursuit, and I realized that I was giving all myself to pursue the both of them.

I looked behind to find that I, as well, had a pursuer. My radio man had flung aside his coat and hat, revealing a younger, fitter and potentially more threatening image than I had yet imagined for my sole companion along that lonely stretch of road. But he still clutched to his silly thermos, giving him at the same time, a harmless, schoolboy sort of appearance.

Because I had eased up on my training, but had not eased up so long that I had lost all of my fitness—the breathlessness from my earlier walking along my mile must have served as a sort of warm-up—I felt surprisingly fast in an aerobic sense, and I simply looked past the pain in my calf as I sprinted after Hare and Pocket.

I reached them both where they had come to a halt on the edge of the little cliff before the Sound, where the woods give way to a view of the water and the small beach below. Hare had mortally wounded Pocket with the sharp end of the pole. He had impaled him—as if in driving Pocket on, his will to direct the fastest man of Pauktaug to some new greatness had caused him to push too hard, to drive the spurs too deep into the hide of a reluctant but unique courser.

It took me a few moments to catch my breath as I slowed to a stop behind Hare and behind the failing body of Pocket (who lay face down on the ground, the long pole sticking out from his back). I did not say a word. Even more than at the shock of this scene, I marveled at the rate of speed with which the two runners had reached this spot, for there was already a sense of quiet to the moment, and a considerable pool of blood collecting from a modest flow.

Then my radio man came up behind me. Hare and this fellow looked to one another.

"Perfect! Perfect!" cried the winded man who had followed me. "Perfect! You don't need me at all! You've gone and done it all! I should have known that the world doesn't need my help! Perfect! Perfect!" He laughed that one word, *perfect,* in a mad way—in an almost theatrical, stage-like way.

Hare looked to this man again. I could tell that Hare knew the face, but I could also tell that Hare dismissed the recognition, and then with a glance at Pocket's expiring body, Hare dismissed the entire scene—as can a man who sees an entire dream, an entire investment of total commitment vanish before him, an entire legacy disintegrate that he had worked to foster and perpetuate, but he still able to reset entirely, to recover with a deep breath and begin again, start to run again.

Hare looked at his watch, and with the same speed with which he had pursued Pocket to the edge of the Sound, Hare raced away from it to rejoin the marathon course. I paused for a moment, not knowing what to do. I left Pocket in the care of the strange radio man—the latter ministering to the dying runner with swigs from the silver thermos—for something told me to return to the course with my best possible speed. I fought the great pain of my leg and made it to the site of the mile-marker with all the sprint I had in me.

The main pack had not reached that stage of the course yet. But some of my volunteers had wandered up to the abandoned site of the radio tent. There they stood over Hare's lifeless body. Just parallel to the tent he had paused, after running at a pace no one had seen before (in fact they said he moved so quickly that it was difficult to recognize his features). And he had clutched his chest, in much the same way Pocket had been reported to do on like occasions, and then fell to the ground on the edge of the course. The volunteers and emergency medical workers formed a tight, kneeling cordon around his body, so that when the main pack went by, no one even knew that there was any trouble, and the rest of the race went smoothly.

Hare is said to have muttered a few words before he passed on altogether, before his body went silent. Some say he muttered those few words—but they cannot recall what they were. Others say he was completely silent, yet they still recall Hare speaking something notwithstanding that silence.

The police found the body of what I had thought was my radio man slumped over Pocket's dead body. He rested in a sort of sitting position—his left arm supported by the pole, as if he were still engaged himself in the act of impaling Pocket with the sharp-pointed mile-marker. Pocket had lasted long enough to take an offered drink from this man, and in addition to the mortal wound from the spike, lethal amounts of traditional poisons as well as a mix of industrial-grade fertilizers were found in his stomach. The spurious radio man was also dead, and in his right arm he still clasped the empty thermos, from which he had also refreshed himself, perhaps inadvertently, after completing his perverse mission of duty to the silent and ubiquitous Mother onto which Pocket and Hare and he had ultimately come to rest.

In the woods later on, the police found the body of the real volunteer radio man whom had been assigned to me. It had not been easy to spot him from the course, for the bright yellow and orange autumn leaves that the heavy rain had brought down had covered and camouflaged his marathon volunteer shirt. Later, the police came to wonder why Hare's fingerprints were on the mile-marker. I told them I had seen him handle the pole on the night before the race.

Someone on the police force thought it best to stop Dale Pocket and pull her out of the race. I never saw her that day. Of those I knew who had run the first and only Pauktaug Marathon, only Kee-Poh, from our office, finished the entire race. He finished in a respectable time of four hours, ten minutes—pretty good for a first marathon. But Randy, also of *The Pauktaug Press*, decided to pass on the full marathon. She went in the gate at the halfway point and was heard to say and laugh that she would never go through that again. It was not worth it, she said.

CHAPTER 16

MORE POWERFUL THAN A LOCOMOTIVE

My mother and father left Pauktaug quite possessed with an opposite drive to that which had brought them to Long Island. They left with the desire, after the scandal of the race, to carry away as little as possible from New York. I still see them at their Arizona condominium on holidays, and they are then more or less the same as I have always known them to be. But when they left not long after the race, I was only too glad to be unattached, to be free of the charade of kin and clan.

After meetings with the police, I repeated my story twice without the slightest discrepancy arising between my two tellings. Since I was so completely alone in the world for the first time, I had only my own comprehensive conscience to answer to, and thus I allowed myself access to a trove of noble lies. Thus Charles Pocket was reported to have been impaled and poisoned by the same suicidal madman who had wrested peace and smoothness and safety from the running of the Pauktaug 10K in the spring.

On the Tuesday after the race, Lisa Hare called me in the morning. She was crying, and she sobbed that she had no one, no one at all, to help her with any kind of a funeral. Though her innocence had absolved her to the Pockets at the luncheon before the race, it was clear that she was now no longer to be connected to the Pockets by the Pockets. They associated her with too many other things at this point. Somehow, after only a year, I had become Lisa Hare's sole old friend. I consented to see to the details of a service for Hare, though I was rather sure that anything traditional would have irked him.

Only having had the experience of Nancy Whisker's funeral in Northport—yet thinking it strange to call any funeral parlor outside of Pauktaug for Hare's case—I wondered for a few minutes where to begin. But then I recalled the night of the reception at Charles Pocket's house, and the mention of the young man who gave Pocket's daughter piano lessons—the man part of a family funeral home business in Pauktaug. I was able to recall the name and to reach him by phone.

I talked to this young man for a time, and then he referred me to his aunt. She informed me, after consulting a file, that dispensation for a small service and Hare's interment in the family crypt at the Pauktaug Rural Cemetery had been arranged long, long ago by his now deceased family.

I was uneasy for awhile about my lies to the police, and much to my sense of further uneasiness, no one appeared at Hare's late afternoon funeral and burial on Thursday afternoon.

As to no one coming to the funeral—maybe Hare's body had shouted something along the course that race morning, yet no one could quite trust their senses to speak to anyone else of what they believed they had heard. Thus maybe hundreds stayed away in mutual uneasiness, each knowing a secret truth, conveyed by means they could not credit, yet not a one suspecting that anyone else could have heard, as well, the same shoutings from the sprinting form of the editor of *The Pauktaug Press*.

Or perhaps the village was just tired of scandal and tired of running. But as the minister (from the same church over which

Hare's father had once presided) finished the service before Hare's coffin, I noted that Kee-Poh was standing by me in the bright autumn sun. He muttered in his curious accent that he had liked working for Hare, and that he was glad that Hare had suggested he try a marathon. He had enjoyed the race very much, and I watched him, after he gave Lisa a little hug, limp away back to his car—Kee-Poh still sore from his Sunday run of 26 miles, 385 yards.

Lisa Hare cried a little then, but she stopped herself so as to insist that I come back to her apartment and have dinner with her.

"I can't watch them put the coffin away for good, Rex," she said. I told her to go back to the village, and that I would be happy to join her for dinner in a little while.

I stayed on for a little bit and watched as they placed Hare's body in the crypt. He had been a bit too strong to have been clasped again by the Mother into an embrace of six feet deep. But he was not so strong that he could jump away, leap off, run away altogether, and so I watched with confidence as they sealed his family tomb of stone and old lead—with confidence that Hare would forever rest not entirely returned to dust, but always in calling distance of his origins.

I thanked the minister and the men from the Gourd Funeral Home who had taken the ride with the coffin over to the Pauktaug Rural Cemetery, and I went over to Lisa's apartment.

I approached my dinner appointment with Lisa in a curious moral state. My sense of final weaning from my parents, the enormity of the liberty I had taken with truth and immediate justice in recent events, and my likely freedom from my connections with Dale (of which Lisa already seemed certain)—all of these things seemed to leave my conscience very isolated, and answerable only to the complex doctrines that comprehensive individuality had constructed for me out of my inherent spirit and the peculiar turn of events through which I had just passed.

I went in Lisa's apartment thinking that if things headed in her direction, I could not think of any inner checks that might arise to stop me from attaching myself to Lisa Hare. She was beautiful, and she had always seemed to harbor a romantic affinity for me. And though she was not flawless like Dale Pocket, she was a physical sight unlike most any other.

The latter point was still true. When I entered the Hares' dining room, Lisa was still dressed in her black dress, and despite her skin's timbres of sympathy for reds and browns and touches of orange in her clothing, she ascended over the clash of black with her supreme terracotta richness of skin and hair and delicate freckles.

We had dinner together, and Lisa cried more than half of the time. After we ate we sat on her couch, and she told me she was expecting a child. She asked me to hold her, as she cried with even more force, and I sat there, stunned and a little repulsed, and even more shocked at my innermost reactions—which dismissed what had been perhaps my dishonorable first thoughts on entertaining a romance with Lisa Hare. And then I contemplated my perhaps even more discreditable gut reaction to her most recent revelation. Perhaps I merely had the reaction of a selfish, proprietary, hunting bachelor. But I had had a special and new kind of training in ideas of the fostered and their fathers, and I did not want to have any part of such things for the time being.

So with a desire to protect myself from much more than falling in love with a woman who already has a child by another man, I sat silent for awhile, absorbed Lisa's tears, and then gently pushed her back and asked her, "What are you going to do, Lisa? Where does your mother live?"

She seemed to take that last question as a sort of order. Or perhaps, from pride, she just pretended that going to live with her mother had been her plan as soon as she learned of Lawrence's death. Lisa's mother lived in Florida, and she thought it best, she said, if her little boy or little girl grew up with as many loving people around as possible.

I saw Lisa Hare on a number of occasions before she moved some months later, but there was never an intimation of a sympathy between us again, and we never discussed her late husband—save for when she told me later that she had to hurry herself to Florida for her forthcoming baby's and her own sake, for she learned that the lobster business that Lawrence Hare had taken over from her father had been living on capital for some time, and that there was nothing left to keep that concern running. And just before the final race, Hare had sold off the two buildings he had owned, as well. Lisa Hare had no income as a pregnant personal trainer—and the paper had certainly brought in little if anything at any given time—so she vanished from Pauktaug altogether before the coming of the new year.

I catch glimpses of Dale Pocket from time to time at the gym. We do not speak, and nor do I learn much about her as I watch her take to the treadmill for unremitting, often long and taxing workouts. She remains very much as I first saw her, perfectly statuesque—a body of matter that exalts in itself even above mind, but that matter still not quite able to walk from its pedestal and live on its own.

I worked with Kee-Poh, Randy, and Hank to get the paper out for the weekend following the race. I assumed full, permanent, editorial duties the following Monday morning, and before I even had a moment to delve into the books to discover that *The Pauktaug Press,* just like Hare's lobstering business, was surviving only on a nearly depleted reserve of capital from the coffers of Lawrence Hare himself, Nancy Whisker's lawyer contacted me to report that *The Pauktaug Press* was to be the immediate recipient of my great-grandmother's enormous monetary estate. Her legacy was endowed "so as to allow the Editor-in-Chief of *The Pauktaug Press* to sustain the periodical's unique character and literary tone in light of increasing modern pressures to alter its format to a more commercial presentation." The sum of the paper's inheritance was enough to keep *The Pauktaug Press* going for at least five years, and thus I consider it my duty to remain so long as I can keep the paper running as I had found it.

As I work in Hare's office, I often look up at his gallery and wonder how many little boys, bedecked in red towel or sheet for a cape, since the creation of Kal-El, have played at Superman. And how many equal thousands of little girls, playing at mother games, have inadvertently played the role of Lara-El, mother to the last son of Krypton? But how many boys have ever played, and how few men have ever taken on the role, or ever will, of the father, of Jor-El?

My leg still bothers me a little, but I still keep up my running. However, I have lapsed a bit in some of my initial zeal for high mileage and for almost quixotic visits to the gym. Thus I have gained back a little of the weight that I had lost from all my running over that first year in Pauktaug. But I trust I will lose it when I get back at some point to some real training. For now, I hope all my work on the paper will allow my injury a chance to subside.

I have also lapsed back into my habit of drinking sweet tea— a habit doubly hard to resist since Fred and Rita, my old friends from Georgia, have come to stay for awhile this winter. They keep me in sweet tea and pie, trips to restaurants, and in the role of tour guide for their wondering eyes during their first-time trips to New York City via the railroad.

They will leave in a few days, but I should remark that I will not be left quite entirely alone. Though I am left temporarily gun-shy of fathering and of adoption in terms of the great race of the human race, I can look to my side, even as I write this and close this little record book, this runner's log, and see Reginald Hare sitting dutifully and dotingly on my sofa a few yards away. I am now his permanent guardian; he is now my permanent ward.

And again, I continue with my running. But no matter how much effort I put forth, no matter how much the early morning shock of winter wind drives me forward along the powder and salt of the empty beaches of the Long Island Sound, or through the quiet crowd of stones in the Sunken Cemetery, Reginald is always a faster runner than I am.